A GOOD LIAR

PART I
OF THE TRILOGY
BETWEEN THE MOUNTAINS
AND THE SEA

A GOOD LIAR

BETWEEN THE MOUNTAINS
AND THE SEA

RUTH SUTTON

HOAD
PRESS

First published in United Kingdom
by **Hoad Press** in 2012
Reprinted 2013
2 Lowther Street, Waberthwaite, Millom, Cumbria LA19 5YN
www.ruthsutton.co.uk   ruth@ruthsutton.co.uk

ISBN-13: 978-0-9523871-7-6

A CIP catalogue record for this book is available from the British Library.

Prepared for publication by Aldridge Press
enquiries@aldridgepress.co.uk

Cover illustrations: schoolchildren in 1930s © Pam Moore; young woman, 1900s,
courtesy of Doris Dean and gallery.hd.org; Wast Water, Cumbria © Mike Franklin
(http://mikefranklinphotography.wordpress.com)

Editorial: Charlotte Rolfe
Design: John Aldridge
Cover design: Kevin Ancient
Text illustrations: Heather Dickinson
Typeset in Bulmer 11.5/14.5pt

Printed and bound in UK by TJ International, Padstow

ACKNOWLEDGEMENTS

I would like to thank many people who have in various ways helped with the writing of this book.

The staff and facilities at the local history libraries in Barrow-in-Furness and Whitehaven, and at the Dock Museum in Barrow, have been invaluable sources for historical background. Dave King at the Eskdale Mill provided much of the information about its history. Above all, many of my neighbours and friends have shared their memories of our community that have helped me to create a context for this story. I am very grateful to all of them.

Others have supported me through the long and difficult business of drafting and re-drafting, encouraging me to keep going and set my sights high. Special thanks for this must go to Judy Coghill, Charlotte Rolfe and Mick Shaw. Along the way I've also had the great good fortune to work more briefly with Louise Doughty, Tobias Hill, Gillian Slovo, Sarah Dunant and Sarah Bower.

Finally, as the book finally came together Heather Dickinson's illustrations, Charlotte Rolfe's editing and John Aldridge's book design and production skills have all been invaluable.

Many thanks to you all.

RS, Waberthwaite, March 2012

CHAPTER 1

Barrow-in-Furness, Lancashire: October 1916

JESSIE THOMPSON HAD been lying to her mother all her life. Even as a very young child, standing on a stool to reach the kitchen table, she'd pretended to wash her face in the big bowl, splashing the water, wiping her hands on the towel, for the sheer joy of defying her mother's expectations. As a girl growing up, she'd clung to lies to define her independence. She'd lied about Clive too, and all the secret meetings, but now she knew the lying had to stop. All week in college, and this morning on the noisy train to Barrow, she'd known what had to happen, and she was dreading it.

The walk from the station to the terraced house in Harter Street reminded Jessie how glad she was to be away at college. It was the smell that struck her as soon as she got down from the train, a smell of smoke and soot, and salt carried on the wind from the Irish Sea. Today the wind was gusty, with a sprinkle of rain that passed as she struggled down the hill. Catching sight of herself in

1

a glass shop front Jessie saw her neat shape, crowned with a tangle of dark curls, a white blouse tucked into her long navy skirt. Her favourite hat, worn to boost her courage, had already fallen victim to the snapping breeze. After retrieving it from the gutter outside the station, she had tucked it away in her bag, abandoning her hair to its fate.

It was Saturday morning and the wide streets were crammed with vehicles and people. Despite the rattling of passing trams Jessie recognised incomers' accents from far away, Scotland and Ireland. She'd heard there were folk from Belgium too, refugees from the German invasion, who lived in squalor in the Scotch flats, the tenements on the other side of town. Rising above them all, the town hall spire and the tall chimneys of the ironworks vied for dominance. Everyone in Barrow was there for work, on ships or steel, guns or shells. Smuts from hundreds of chimneys stained the flapping washing and the shipyard hooter summoned shift after shift to an endless production line. Vickers shipyard governed the town, making the rules, building the houses, different standards for different grades of the workforce. Clive's house in Mikasa Street in Vickerstown, across the bridge on Walney Island, had a bathroom and a small garden, one up from the fitters but not as posh as the foremen's houses on the promenade

Jessie pushed open the door of 23 Harter Street as quietly as she could and put her bag down in the passage. Sounds from the kitchen told her Cora Thompson was at home, but the words Jessie needed would not come. Before she could compose herself, the kitchen door opened.

'Oh it's you,' Cora said to her daughter. 'I didn't remember you were coming home this weekend.'

'I didn't tell you,' said Jessie.

'Well, you're here now. I'm just on my way out to Aunty Barbara's, and then the shopping. Want to come?'

'No, no thanks. Feeling a bit tired actually.'

'You stay here then, pet,' said Cora. 'Stella's asleep upstairs, in the back bedroom, so don't wake her. She's at work later. Worn out, poor thing.'

'Stella?'

'The lodger, from Preston, didn't I tell you? Now I'm on my own and with your sister on the other side of the world, I'm renting out the back room to help make ends meet.'

'What about Dad?'

'Your father's dead to me, dear. We won't see him again. Good riddance, Barbara says. Well I'm away. Back about five. Help yourself to whatever's in the pantry, but not the ham. That's for tomorrow.'

And she was gone.

Jessie made herself a cup of tea and thought about how easily her father had been cut out of the family, pecked and scorned by his disappointed wife until he could bear it no longer. 'Going to visit me old mam,' he'd said as he headed for the Irish ferry. That had been nearly a year before and his name had hardly been mentioned since. At least he was out there somewhere, she thought, not dead and buried like Clive in the cold ground, lost to her forever. She sat at the well-scrubbed kitchen table and sipped her tea, still trying to decide what to say when her mother eventually returned. She would have to say something. Two months gone already and soon it would start to show.

With Cora not there to forbid, Jessie took her tea into the front parlour and put her feet up on the hard couch under the lace-curtained window. Even there, in the room reserved for company, a thin film of soot covered everything. She put a cushion behind her head and lay as comfortably as she could, her hands together on her stomach. The child was in there, growing. It was only a few days since she'd seen the news of Clive's death but she remembered the short notice word for word. Cora sent the *Barrow News* every week and on that sunny Sunday afternoon Jessie had taken the newspaper to the seat under the birch tree in the long back garden of the college hostel in Ambleside. The front pages were always about the war. Clive had told her how reading the names of boys he knew among the listed dead made him made him feel sad and guilty. No one from Vickers could be conscripted. People called it 'the funk hole', the place where cowards worked to avoid the war. Jessie had been thinking about that and the life ahead of them when she reached page five, the local news. A headline caught her eye:

SHIPYARD TRAGEDY: YOUNG MAN KILLED IN FALL

On Thursday afternoon Clive Whelan (21), unmarried and residing at 11 Mikasa Street, Vickerstown fell off high staging in the new airship hangar at Devonshire Dock. He struck his head on the side of the dock before falling into the water, and was pulled out of the water by others at the scene. Dr Ware's services were summoned but he could only pronounce life extinct. The body was subsequently conveyed to the mortuary.

She'd tried to get up but her knees had given way. When they found her she was still lying where she had fallen. Golden leaves from the birch tree had settled on her dark hair, shining in the autumn sun.

'He was my fiancé,' she said to Sister Bailey after they helped her into the house. 'We were going to marry. It was just the once.'

'Just the once what, dear?' said the sister kindly. Then she'd said they would ask Jessie's mother to come and Jessie had used all her strength to say no.

Now she lay on the couch in the front room, thinking about Clive and the quiet room in Mikasa Street, where they'd made love as the rain hammered on the window and thunder echoed round the inland fells. Just that one time. They'd never meant it to happen, but when they got caught in the storm and splashed breathless into the empty house, it just did. The thought of it burned in her mind. The cool white of his body, the sounds he made, the feeling of being possessed by him. She'd wanted him so badly then and she wanted him still, even while his child grew inside her and she would never see him again.

They'd been so happy that day, on the beach on the southern end of Walney Island, away from the weekend crowds at Biggar Bank, just the two of them. Cora believed that her precious elder daughter, the clever one, the one with a future, was out with her friend Clarice: that was the lie Jessie had provided and her mother had accepted, because it suited her to do so.

'Do your folks know about me?' Jessie asked Clive.

'They know there's someone, but they don't know who,' he said. 'I'll tell them when we're ready.'

And then Clive told her about his new job, about the special tiny rivets on the airships and the skill it took to handle them, and that he'd been specially chosen and would probably have to move south. She'd prepared herself for losing him, and then he asked her – no, he told her – that when she finished at college they would be married and start a life together, away from the dirty noisy town, away from her mother and his family. That was what she knew that day, and that was what she wanted. But now he was gone, and Cora still knew nothing.

Jessie woke with a start when Cora came back into the house. For a moment she wondered where she was. She would have to tell: it couldn't wait any longer.

She got up and walked through into the kitchen where Cora was standing by the range, waiting for the kettle to boil.

'Tea?' said Cora, half turning to look at her daughter. 'You don't look well, pet. Maybe you should see Dr Doggett, he's always so understanding, isn't he?'

'Can you sit down a minute, Mam?' said Jessie, leaning on a chair to steady herself. 'I do need to tell you something.'

'I'm all ears,' said her mother, sitting down as she was bid. 'What is it? Something good, I hope.'

'Not really,' said Jessie. She didn't know how to say it. 'Mam, I think I'm pregnant.'

'Nonsense, dear, that's impossible,' said Cora, brightly. 'You don't even have a young man. You must be late because you're not well. I told you, you need to see Dr Doggett. Now I'll make that cup of tea and we'll go –'

'No, Mam,' said Jessie. 'I'm not going to see the doctor. I talked to the sister at college. She thinks I'm nine weeks gone. The baby's due in May.'

'What baby? You can't be. Who …?'

'His name was Clive Whelan. He worked at Vickers.' She hesitated, watching the colour drain from her mother's face. 'He's dead. He was killed at work, last week.'

'You're having a baby, and the father is dead?'

Jessie nodded.

Cora got up from her chair. First she stood quite still, then leaned forward, pushing her anxious face close to Jessie's.

'You're hiding something from me. This is nonsense. Who is it really? Whoever it is, you have to marry. Nine weeks, that's not too late. We can say it was premature. These quick weddings are happening all the time …'

'No, Mam!' Jessie shouted at her mother. 'Listen to me. Clive and I were engaged but we didn't want to say anything just yet, not till later. We were going to marry when I finished at college. He's a good man. Good family. Mikasa Street. They've got a bathroom.'

'A bathroom!' Cora shouted back. 'What good's a bathroom

6

to us now? He's dead. You can't marry him, he's dead. And now what will we do?'

'I can have the baby. We were engaged.'

'No you were not engaged, you stupid girl. I didn't know about it. Do his people know?'

'What?'

'About the baby, do they know?'

'No.'

'Thank God. You can get rid of it.'

Jessie stared at her mother.

'Get rid of it,' Cora spat the words again. 'You have to. No wedding? You can't just stay round here getting big. What'll people say? You have to get rid of it.' She stumbled to the sideboard and reached for a jar off the top shelf. 'Look here,' she said, pulling notes and coins out of the jar. 'I've got money. There's that woman, down near the docks, everyone knows about her, she'll do it. Here, take the money.'

Cora threw the money onto the table. Coins clattered on the floor.

Jessie could not speak. Cora talked on, as if to herself, bending to pick up the coins. 'That's it. You can get it done, and then go back to college. No one any the wiser. Don't tell me about him, I don't want to know. Then we can pretend it never happened. What were you thinking of? All that money I spent on you, and you go and get knocked up by the first boy who looks at you. Typical, head in a book all the time, no idea what's going on. Off with the fairies, like your dad.'

'I don't want your money.'

'Well you won't get it from anyone else.'

'I won't kill the baby.'

'Oh yes you will, my girl. No daughter of mine, parading round the streets like a common tart for all to see. You'll do it, or you'll

7

leave this house.'

Jessie looked at her mother who was pacing up and down the small kitchen. Spittle flecked the corners of Cora's mouth.

'Stop shouting, Mam. That girl upstairs ...'

Cora closed the kitchen door and leaned against it. 'How could you?' she whispered, staring at Jessie but still not seeing her. 'Did he seduce you? Did he hurt you?'

'No, it wasn't like that.'

'So you gave it up, like a useless common girl. After all I've done for you.'

'I won't get rid of the baby,' said Jessie. 'You can't make me.'

'Well, you're not having it here. And you can't keep it. They won't let you.'

'Who won't?'

'That precious college of yours. Respectable girls that's what they want, not common whores.'

Jessie sobbed suddenly, covering her mouth, but Cora kept on talking. 'Barbara, she'll know. She'll know what to do. She's family. You have to talk to her.'

'No, I don't.'

'Well I will then. Someone has to do something. What a mess. Stay here.'

Cora opened the back door, then turned.

'You haven't told anyone, have you? Do they know?'

'Who?'

'His folks, whoever they are.'

'No. I told you that. They're good people, Mam.'

'I don't care how good they are. So long as they don't know, we can get away with it. Don't want them interfering, thinking they're better than us. Mikasa Street! You stay here. Don't talk to anyone. I'm going to Barbara's.'

* * *

Seven months later, in a tall brick house in Carnforth, three young women lay in beds lined against the walls in a top floor room. There was a fourth bed in the room but it was empty, a grey blanket tucked in at the corners with fierce precision. A late spring wind from the east was roaring in the empty fireplace, but the young women did not hear it. They were listening instead to their friend who was crying in the brightly lit delivery room at the other end of a long corridor. The sobs rose to a scream that made two of them cover their ears while the third shut her eyes tightly. The sound faded for a while and one of the young women spoke softly into the silence.

'She must be done soon, surely to God.'

'Three o'clock, she started,' said another. 'What time is it now, Jess?'

There was a pause before a third voice answered.

'Gone midnight,' said Jessie. 'It could be a while yet. Try not to listen, Molly. Get down under the blanket.'

'I've tried, it's no good. I can't bear it. What are we going to do?'

A bed creaked as Jessie got up. 'I'll put the light on. No, wait. Can you close the door, Ann, so they can't see the light?'

Dim light seeped across the draughty room. Jessie got back into bed quickly, pulling a shawl around her.

'Let's talk,' she said. 'That might cover the noise when she starts again.'

'How long will it take?' whispered Ann. 'They didn't tell me it would take this long. I thought once the water broke the baby would come straight away. I won't be able to do it, I know I won't.'

'Try not to think about it, Ann.' Jessie reached for her hand. 'Some babies do come quickly but not the first one usually.

Remember Eunice? She said she couldn't remember a thing about it and you know what a racket she made when she was having hers.'

'When did she say that?'

'Before she left.' Jessie went on, as calmly as she could, 'I told her we could hear her making a noise and she said she couldn't remember. She laughed.'

'Can't imagine Jean laughing after this,' said Ann. 'Does it hurt that much, Jess?'

'How should I know?'

'You're clever. Schooling and that. You know more than me and Molly put together.'

'Not about this, I don't.'

There was silence in the room for a few minutes, save for the whine of the wind.

Ann spoke again, 'What will you call the baby, Jess?'

'Don't know,' said Jessie. 'If I can't keep it, I don't want to give it a name. That's their job.'

'Who?'

'Whoever takes it. They have to name it. It's theirs then, not mine.'

Molly pushed herself up a little, holding one hand under her belly. 'I want to keep mine. Only for a little while, but it has to have a name. Harriet for a girl and David for a boy, after me dad.'

A brief silence, then Jessie spoke again.

'I don't want this baby. Never did. It was Clive I wanted. This should never have happened.'

Molly stared across the room at her. 'Oh Jess, you can't – it's Clive's baby. Could look like him, be like him. You can't say that.'

'Maybe I did want it, at the beginning,' Jessie went on, as if she hadn't heard, 'but now I know I don't. If I keep it we'll just be poor and miserable together. This way at least it gets a life, a proper life, more than I could give it. And I can live too, with no one to worry about, no one who can go off and leave me. Independent. That's the only way for me now.'

'Where will you go, if your mam won't have you back?' asked Molly, unable to envisage a life so alone.

'Anywhere,' said Jessie. 'While the war's on there'll be work. In a factory, making wings or engines or something. I'll get a job.'

'My cousin's in Chorley, making planes,' said Ann.

'That's what I'll do,' said Jessie. 'Give the baby away and get out of here and start again. No ties. No looking back.'

The other two were silent, shocked. Jessie had never spoken like this before. Not long afterwards they heard more screams from down the corridor, then a man's voice raised in anger. As grey light dawned, the three young women heard the new baby cry.

Jessie's child was born in the early hours of a cool damp morning. She had strained in silence throughout the night, gripping the midwife's hand as tears ran down her rigid face. They let her see him for a few minutes, to glimpse the dark eyes and the wisp of dark hair, before he was wrapped tight and taken from her. Four days later, still unnamed, he was carried away by Enid and Arthur Pharaoh. No papers, just an agreement to give the boy a respectable home and them the child they had always wanted, while his real mother turned her face to the wall.

Jessie's body punished her. Milk leaked from her breasts, the tear in her vagina burned and itched as it healed. She wept in the night, ashamed and bereft. Lying sleepless, haunted by a baby crying in the next room, Jessie planned a future without Clive, without her baby, and without her family. She was twenty years old, she could earn a living and support herself and she knew that she would survive. If there was no one she cared for, no one could hurt or betray her, or die and leave her. Self-reliance was her only

11

choice and she embraced it. She was no longer Jessie Thompson. She would take Clive's name, the only thing he could leave with her. She would be Jessie Whelan, whose birth certificate had been lost in the chaos of the war.

Cora wrote to Jessie, cutting her out of her life just as she had done with the husband who'd disappointed her and had been driven away.

'It's over now,' Jessie read. *'No one must know. You can't come home for a while. I'll tell people you've found a teaching job already. Go somewhere, anywhere you won't be seen. For pity's sake don't tell anyone. I couldn't bear it.'*

The war dragged on. Jessie's job in Chorley paid well, and sharing a tiny house with four other girls was tolerable. Jessie lied about her family, rubbed Vaseline into her stinging hands, counted her money at the end of the week, spent little and saved as much as she could. Just before the war ended she found the address of the teachers' college at Edge Hill, just outside Liverpool, and wrote to the principal. She told them that she had been in teacher training for two years, but had been forced into war work to support her widowed mother. Now she wanted to complete her studies and follow her vocation.

'Surely, Miss Whelan,' said the plum-faced man sitting at the centre of a long polished table, 'with such a long interruption of your studies, er, that will be a problem for you, will it not?'

Jessie thought for a moment. She'd expected this question.

'You might think so, of course,' she said, smiling at the younger woman sitting at the edge of the table. The lies came so easily now. 'My mother was anxious about that too, I know.'

The woman smiled back and Jessie went on, shifting her eyes to the plum-faced man who seemed to be in charge.

'I have kept up with my reading when I could, in the local library, you know. And being at work has helped me to understand more about the lives of our children, and what they need from their schooling. I feel I'm a better person now, better able to do the job that will need doing. I just the need the chance to complete my training, now that my mother has married again and no longer needs me.'

Jessie looked down at her gloved hands and the panel murmured.

Outside the room, Jessie watched the light play through the stained glass in the window and smiled. She'd planned for this chance, and knew that they could not resist her. When they offered her a place at the college, she was modestly grateful. Jessie Whelan would be a fine teacher.

Chapter 2

Ulverston, Lancashire: May 1937

In the front bedroom of a tidy terraced house in Ulverston, just ten miles from Barrow near the northern shore of Morecambe Bay, Enid Pharaoh lay dying. Inside her thin skull, veins had furred and narrowed. Recent memories had disappeared into a void: those of long ago were sharp as pins. On the other side of the room, a young man with dark hair and dark eyes stretched his long back against the wall and looked across at his mother. He knew she was close to the end. Part of him was willing it to come, soon. She looked already dead, flat in the narrow bed, hair scraped away from her forehead and toes turned up under the grey blanket, like an effigy on a marble slab.

A blue curtain turned slowly in the breeze at the half-opened window. Light and sound filtered through, as if from the bottom of a deep sea. Muffled drumbeats from the market square, on the other side of the small town. There, and down the neighbouring streets, children waved and cheered as the coronation parade passed by. The nailed boots of the Boys' Brigade band sparked on cobbles as they marched, tiny flags, red, white and blue fluttering over their heads.

The dying woman heard nothing but the buzz of a desperate wasp on the windowsill. Her fingers stroked the sheet and her mouth moved.

'Arthur,' she called, and again, louder, 'Arthur.'

The young man stepped to the head of the bed and lowered his face to speak into his mother's ear.

'It's John, Mam, John.'

Enid opened her eyes and peered at him. 'Don't be silly,' she said, impatiently. 'You can't be John. He'll be home from school soon, ready for his tea.'

John sat down miserably on the end of the bed and looked again at the open window. He yearned to be outside, in clear air, far from the stale misery of sickness. He wanted to shout into his mother's face, to drive out the chaos in her brain. It had been weeks since she'd seemed to understand anything, except perhaps a reality beyond his memory. For as long as he could, before his father's death and his mother's decline into madness, he'd been able to escape after work in the brewery office was done on Saturday afternoon, up to the great granite slabs of Wallerbarrow Crag or the challenge of Pillar. When John was climbing in the mountains all the lonely shyness of his schooldays was forgotten. He could relax in conversation about rocks and pitches, not personal things that left him silent and self-conscious. He was happy there, but not here.

For a few weeks at the back end of the previous year Enid had known that her mind was coming apart. That had been the worst time. In her lucid moments she would seize his hand and whisper fiercely into his face. 'I'm going mad, I know I am. Can you finish me off? Please, John, please.' The doctor had told him, 'As it gets worse, it'll get better. Quite soon she'll lose the reality, and then she'll calm down.' And it was so. The panic had faded into innocent childishness, and all John had to do was accept the lunacy without question. But it irked him almost beyond bearing. Today of all days, when the brewery was closed for the coronation, he could be out, on a rock face, not here in this stifling house. He picked up a magazine from the floor and killed the wasp on the windowsill with a single blow.

The effigy on the bed stirred, but he turned away and escaped downstairs. He made tea and brought her some, propping her up on two pillows, helping her to drink with a spout that he held to her mouth. Enid sipped for a while and then lay back. After some minutes she opened her eyes again and began to talk. He listened, sitting once more on the end of the bed.

'John was such a good baby.'

He strained to hear the words that fell into the azure quiet of the room. Enid's mouth made a winding motion before she spoke again.

'We got him quite early, he was just a tot, just a few days old, and he took his bottle straight away. Do you remember, Arthur, how he sucked so hard on the empty bottle, how he got the hiccups?' She laughed, a hissing sound. 'They told us his mother was a very respectable girl who'd made a mistake, not at all what you'd expect in that place in Carnforth. We brought him home on the train. The people in the carriage smiled at us. You were nervous holding his head, it was too small and floppy.' She laughed again. 'We were so happy. Remember?' The voice faded, and in a second or two she slept again, the left side of her face betraying the slight droop of mouth and eye.

John stared at the sleeping woman. He put his head in his hands and sat very still. Minutes passed. Enid was quiet again. He jerked suddenly upright. He had to move, to get away, down the stairs and out into the air. He crossed the deserted street and opened the front door of a house on the other side. 'Mrs Barker,' he called down the dark hallway. 'I'm going out. I won't be long.' A woman, older than Enid, with tightly permed grey hair and vermilion cheeks, emerged from the kitchen at the back of the house, wiping floury hands on a flowery apron. 'That's fine, dear,' she said, looking at him carefully in the dim light. 'I'll go back over and sit with her. You go out and enjoy yourself.' She stretched to pat his shoulder. He flinched slightly.

He turned down the street, taking the familiar route to his aunt's house in Church Walk while his mind churned. Late spring sun warmed his face and an early swift darted above the trees but he didn't notice either of them. Some things made sense to him now, but others made no sense at all. Mam and Dad had always been kind and he'd lacked nothing they could give him, but something had never been right. He didn't look like their son, different shape, different features, different everything. They seemed older than other people's parents, more like grandparents. But he was their son, everyone said so. Could he believe what he'd just heard? His mother had been crazy for weeks. He broke into a run up the last few streets, towards the monument like a marooned lighthouse that stood on Hoad Hill beyond the town.

The varnished front door of the Church Walk house was open and John went straight in without knocking. Everything was quiet, save for a soft sound from the front room. There in an easy chair, short legs stretched in front of him, lay a man, fast asleep and snoring gently. Beside his stockinged feet on the floor was an empty glass. John stood for a moment, looking down at him. Uncle George had always been good to him, with none of the edge of his wife and her sister Enid. Did he know? Had he been lying all these years? John trawled his memory desperately for signs, issues avoided, conversations left unfinished. Nothing.

'Uncle George.' John's voice sounded loud in the small room.

The figure in the chair stirred. George Youle grunted and opened his eyes, then sat up suddenly.

'What the ...? Oh, it's you, John. Frightened the life out of me, standing there like that.'

'The front door was open. I didn't want to wake you, but …'

'I must've nodded off. Anne's out somewhere, doing good works probably, like she does. How's your mam today?'

'Rambling again, but she said something, just now. I want to ask you about it.'

The empty glass at George's feet fell over and he bent to pick it up.

'I'll have another beer while she's out. Want one?'

'No thanks, but can you wait a minute? I must ask you this. '

'Out with it then, lad, if it's that important. But sit down, making me tired just watching you.'

John sat on the sofa, leaning forward to watch George closely.

'It's something Mam said, just now. She called me Arthur, though she's done that before. I told her it was me, but she just carried on. Talked about the day they brought John – me – home from Carnforth on the train, just a few days old. That's what she said, "Brought him home." They always told me I was born in Barrow, before they moved here. Sounds as if they got me from someone else, as if I wasn't their baby at all.'

George listened in silence. He leaned back in the chair.

'Oh, God,' he said, rubbing his face with his hand. 'I knew this would happen sooner or later. I told her, both of them, but they wouldn't have it. It's not right lying to a kid like that. It's going to come out sometime, and then what?'

'What's going to come out?' John leaned further forward suddenly. 'Tell me.' His voice was louder, demanding. 'Tell me Uncle George, please. Where did I come from?'

George got slowly out of the chair and put a hand on John's arm. Then he raised the young man's face and looked at him, waiting for the look to be returned.

'Now then, lad,' said the older man at last. 'We don't need your Aunty Anne for this. Just you and me, it's time we talked. Long overdue. Let me tell you what I know. This might be a shock.'

George sat down again. He took out a large white handkerchief from his pocket and blew his nose, giving himself a moment to think before looking up again and taking a deep breath.

'Your mam,' said George, 'Enid, she didn't give birth to you, John. Her and Arthur adopted you, just after you were born. Your real mam couldn't keep you and they must've found out somehow. Enid were desperate for a kiddie, and they adopted you, loved you like their own. That's all I know. All these years they kept it from you. I told Anne. It'll come out, I said. The lad needs to know. But Enid wouldn't hear of it, and Anne said that was that. Even Arthur couldn't change her mind, and God knows he tried. And since he's gone, well …'

John sat upright on sofa. George looked up at him, unsure what to do. Silence hung in the room. Through the open front door the sound of the coronation parade crept in, whispering around them like smoke.

CHAPTER 3

Newton, Cumberland: May 1937

JESSIE WHELAN, HEADMISTRESS of Newton School, woke to the sound of rain on her window and started to worry about all the plans for the day ahead. She felt her pulse quickening and sat up suddenly. 'For heaven's sake, woman,' she said to herself. 'You can't control the weather, and you're not responsible if it rains.'

It was early, but the gleam of light encouraged Jessie to abandon the pretence of sleep. She'd tried so hard to keep coronation fervour under control at school, but the effort to do so was more exhausting than giving in to it. It would have been much easier to let the children spend all their time making flags and costumes at the expense of their normal routines, but if she'd done so Mr Crompton in the other class would have done the same and the place would have been in uproar. So Jessie had insisted on business as usual until the last minute, and now suffered the consequence of a night disturbed by anxieties about not being ready.

She lay on her back on top of the covers to settle her mind a little more. She had nothing to prove in the village, not after all these years, and had never regretted coming to Newton and staying so long. Teaching in Liverpool after she qualified had been fine for a while, usefully absorbing all her energy and time. But slowly, quietly, the dust had settled and she'd recognised what she wanted for herself. She had seen the job at Newton and applied for it even before she found the village on a map, at the mouth of the River Esk in Cumberland, between the mountains and the sea. The only place they could find her to stay overnight had been at Applegarth, with Agnes Plane. Stylish, generous Agnes and the glorious view up the valley both persuaded Jessie to overlook the overbearing Reverend Leadbetter, who told her that she'd got the job 'because we couldn't find a suitable man'. Agnes had rolled her eyes when she heard about that, and the two women laughed about it still.

The little clock on the table by her bed showed five-thirty. Too early. The coronation parade wasn't due to assemble until after lunch, hours away. There were still some flags and bunting to put up in the village hall, and she wanted to make sure that the school rooms were swept and tidy. None of that would take very long. Some of the children were probably awake already, pestering grumpy parents about their costumes for the parade. Everything had been too rushed.

The band from Ganthwaite had been a last-minute thing too. Everyone wanted a band for coronation day, and a village as isolated as Newton wasn't very attractive to the best of them. If she'd been headmistress of a school in Whitehaven or Millom the band would be no problem. She'd chosen to stay in Newton all these years because she loved its distance from the world, and its timelessness. Farming was still much the same as it had been in the last century. No tractors yet, everything pulled by horses: a slower, softer pace, the sound of hooves, not engines. There were motorbikes around, and the occasional car, but mostly the silence was broken only by the insistent cawing of rooks, the mew of a buzzard or the chatter of geese on the wing above the estuary.

She took off her nightdress and washed herself in cold water in the basin, easier than bothering with a kettle and washing downstairs. As she dried herself she caught her reflection in the mirror on the other side of the room. Once she'd had a waist, a real waist. Not enough light to see the stretch marks but she knew they were there, and her breasts were flatter and heavier than they'd been twenty years earlier. Clive had loved her body: would he still? She wished she could get through a day without thinking of him. Being busy helped: maybe that was why she made herself do so much.

A few new clothes wouldn't come amiss, she thought, looking through the uninspiring wardrobe. Maybe that navy and white two-piece she'd seen in the *Whitehaven News* the other week. 'For the fuller figure' the advertisement said. Agnes always looked so smart, but most of her clothes came from London. They'd been there once together, to stay with Aunt Elvira in Pimlico, and Jessie had tried to enjoy it but she'd felt awkward in such sophisticated company and had been glad to get away.

She looked at herself in the mirror again, turning her head from one side to another. What about the hair? It wasn't fashionable to wear it long, but it had helped Jessie look older when she needed to, and the routine of controlling its dark thickness with pins and combs pleased her. The hair stays as it is, she resolved, no matter what. She chose a pale blue blouse and navy skirt, sensible but just bright enough for what was supposed to be a jolly day, despite the grey morning and threat of rain. And flat shoes. Too much walking around for anything else, thought Jessie, though she expected that Agnes would wear a little heel, and Caroline Leadbetter too, keeping up appearances as the vicar's lady.

The long list of things to do was downstairs, but most of it was fixed in her brain. The parade was arranged, starting at the school and down to the church. Lionel Leadbetter would do a brief service ... at least I hope he does, she thought. The children were too excited to sit for long and he hated it when they fidgeted.

Caroline had warned her he was threatening to say something about the sanctity of marriage. Surely not in the circumstances, but you never knew with Lionel. Personally, Jessie didn't care whom the last king had chosen to marry, so long as no one had to call that American woman 'Queen'. And now he'd abdicated and his brother had stepped in. What a farce it all was, but she would have to keep those views to herself on coronation day.

Back to the list. Children organised, band booked, Mrs Braithwaite and the Women's Institute ladies in charge of teas, thank heavens. The bonfire and fireworks were someone else's problem too. Probably Andrew Leadbetter. He hadn't been back from Scotland for long but he seemed to be an asset to the village. Good-looking young man, too.

* * *

Several hours later, the procession wound up the lane from the church between hedges that had been growing for a thousand years, whitened with blossom, with pink campions and bluebells among their roots. On the fells cloud shadows swept fast across the land but in the shelter of the lane it was warm and almost windless. Jessie dropped back to encourage some straggling children and fell in beside Caroline who was clearly having trouble with her shoes.

'Knew I shouldn't have worn these today,' said the vicar's wife as she accepted Jessie's proffered arm. 'Never wear new shoes for more than a few minutes the first time, my dear.'

'Not far now,' said Jessie. 'It's gone well so far, don't you think?'

'For a moment back there I thought we'd have some trouble. Lionel does hate it when the children rustle sweet wrappers, but he didn't need to stare at them for quite so long.'

'No mention of the sanctity of marriage, though.' Jessie knew that Caroline had urged her husband to keep it short.

'No, thank heaven.'

'And the tea will be good.'

'Oh we can count on that,' said Caroline. 'Mrs Braithwaite's got it down to a fine art, which is just as well, as I didn't get any lunch.'

'Nor me, and I was awake so early I really needed some.'

'I had trouble sleeping, too. Not just today's events, either. Did you notice anything, just now, at the church?'

'No,' said Jessie, 'apart from one or two children I need a quiet word with. Why?'

'What about Andrew? He's my eldest child and he's twenty-five years old, but sometimes I despair. Did you notice he wouldn't go into the church? Sat outside on one of the gravestones through the whole thing, smoking those nasty cigarettes of his. They seem to smell even worse than the normal kind.'

'Maybe he just doesn't believe any more,' said Jessie. 'If he doesn't, then he's better off not pretending, surely.'

'I think it's more about him and his father. It was bad enough before he went off to Scotland, but it's much worse now. If they hadn't given him that house at the quarry when he got the manager's job, well I think they'd have come to blows, really. What is it with men and their sons? Why can't just accept their differences and have some respect for each other? Why does it have to be about who's in charge?'

'Is that what it is?' Jessie was surprised to hear Caroline talk like this. 'I was just thinking how useful Andrew will be to the village.'

'Do you think so? Maybe he just needs to settle down. Shouldn't have any trouble finding someone. Good job, good prospects, healthy, quite handsome in his own way. Agnes says he looks like, what's that man's name, on the films?'

'Stan Laurel?' Jessie squeezed her arm as they laughed.

'No, no. In *Mr Deeds* … Gary Cooper.'

Jessie pictured Gary Cooper and thought about Andrew. 'Well he's tall, that's a good start. I'll have to sneak another look at him and let you know. Come on, we're getting further behind.'

'Wait a minute, dear,' said Caroline, standing still. 'Before we catch up with the others, did you hear about Alice Kitchin?'

Jessie said nothing for a moment, remembering.

'No,' she said, as brightly as she could muster. 'What's Alice been up to?'

'That's just it,' said Caroline, 'Nobody knows. No one's seen her for a few days apparently. One of her friends at the Hall sent a message to Alice's mother, and Bill Kitchin went storming up to the Hall claiming that they'd sent her away somewhere, demanding to see Sir John. He made quite a scene apparently. Sir John mentioned it to Lionel.'

'Oh dear,' said Jessie. 'Have they sent her away?'

'No, that's just it, they haven't. So we're wondering whether she's just taken herself off, with a young man maybe, or to find a better job. She's a bit of a madam, I understand.'

Jessie was determined to give nothing away. 'I'd say she knows how to look after herself,' she said. 'Let's not worry about it yet.' They walked on, and Jessie struggled with her feelings about the girl and her future.

In the village hall the coronation celebrations drew to a close. The prize for the best costume was awarded to ten-year-old Mary Capp dressed as Britannia. Caroline gave each of the children a commemorative mug engraved with the date and a picture of the new king and queen. After that, mercifully, the noise level dropped as most of the children were taken home to change out of their costumes or their Sunday best clothes, ready for the bonfire and fireworks at the Hall. A small gang of the most boisterous escaped to the river to play more games of their own.

Jessie went back to the schoolhouse, glad of a break from

conversation and supervision. The freshening breeze from the sea carried the sound of a train crossing the viaduct. As she put down her basket to open the front door a young man emerged from the village hall carrying a stack of chairs. He put them down by the side of the road and smiled at her.

'Glad that's over,' he said. 'Hopefully this new king doesn't run off with another woman and we won't have to do it all again for a while.'

Jessie laughed. 'Not much chance of that I think, Mr Leadbetter. They look like the soul of respectability to me. Thanks for your help today by the way. And you're looking after the bonfire as well, I hear.'

'All we have to do now is light it and stand back. I love a good fire.'

'Me too.'

'You going to the dance on Friday, at Ganthwaite?' he asked. 'Band's coming from Whitehaven.' He lowered his voice and his face towards hers. 'Better than that crowd today, I hope.'

'They did very well,' she said, 'Scotland was more lively for you, I'm sure, but living here brings its own pleasures.'

'Aye, it does,' he said, looking at her. 'Well, I'll get these chairs back to the Farriers.'

Jessie watched him as he turned the corner towards the pub.

A child's voice, shrill, rang out behind her.

'Miss! Miss!'

She turned. Down the hill a small gang of children was running, not in the usual carefree way of children but anxiously, straining, crying out to each other, wild and tense. The boy who was shouting was ahead of them.

'What is it, Peter?' said Jessie, in her calmest teacher voice. The boy stood in front of her, gasping for breath. She held his thin shoulders and bent down to look into his face.

'It's alright, Peter. I'm here. Just take a breath and tell me.'

'I can tell you, miss,' said a smaller boy who had caught up to them.

'That's alright, thank you Frank,' said Jessie. 'I'm sure Peter can manage now.'

Peter settled himself, planting his feet squarely on the ground.

'It's Alice, miss, we saw her.'

'Alice Kitchin?'

'Yes miss, she's down there.'

'Down where, Peter? Start at the beginning, pet, and tell me the story.'

'It's not a story, miss,' Frank piped up quickly. 'It's true, honest.'

Peter took a deep breath. 'We went down to t'river, miss, after us tea.'

'Yes, and?'

'Tide were coming in, miss, under t'bridge, running fast like. We saw something in t'river, miss.'

'That was me, I saw it first,' said Frank.

'No, I did,' said one of the girls.

'That's enough thank you, children. Carry on, Peter, you're doing very well.'

'We saw this thing in the river, miss, like an old sack or summat. So I went in, to see what it was, like. And the tide turned it over, miss. And the face was there. It were Alice, miss. In the water. She's drownded.'

Chapter 4

Eight days later a report appeared on page four of the *White-haven News*, with details of the coroner's findings:

The Whitehaven coroner Mr Samuel Armstrong recorded a verdict of accidental death in the case of Miss Alice Kitchin, aged seventeen, who was found drowned in the River Esk near Newton Church on May 12th, after the Coronation Day celebrations. She had been last seen leaving Ganthwaite village hall late on Saturday May 8th. Police Sergeant Arthur Partridge reported that he had consulted the coastguard and the local tide tables before concluding that Miss Kitchin had fallen or slipped into the river on her way home from Ganthwaite and that the body had been washed to the other side of the river by the unusual wind and tides of the following days. Evidence was also heard from Miss Phyllis Monck, a friend of the deceased, that Miss Kitchin had insisted on walking home alone on the night in question. There was no moon and it had been very dark. Miss Kitchin had said that she had walked that path many times before and was sure she could find her way.

Evidence was heard from Miss Jessie Whelan to whom a local child had reported his discovery of a body in the river. Dr Michael Harding had examined the body at Whitehaven Hospital. This examination indicated that the girl had unfortunately drowned, possibly impeded by the long dress that she had been wearing for the dance. Sergeant Partridge had checked the path where it runs close to the river, and had spoken to all the parties involved. He was of the view that Miss Kitchin's death had been an accident and had occurred shortly after her departure from Ganthwaite. The jury accepted the medical and police evidence and recommended a verdict of accidental death by drowning. The coroner extended the condolences of the court to the girl's family. He warned that paths close to the river could be treacherous after rain and in profound darkness.

Jessie Whelan put down the newspaper and closed her eyes for a few minutes. They didn't know. She'd thought that the autopsy would have revealed Alice's pregnancy but they must have been looking only for the cause of death, nothing more. She made herself another cup of tea and tried to think.

It was nearly a month since Alice had turned up on her doorstep that Sunday afternoon. Why couldn't she have talked to someone her own age, or the doctor, or even her own mother? Now Jessie was burdened with knowledge she had not wanted then and certainly didn't want now. The wretched girl seemed to be bent on unsettling her, even from her grave. Jessie put down her cup as the shame of her selfishness washed over her. She'd been surprised to see Alice at her door that day but she couldn't just send her away. Years before she'd tried hard to get Alice's parents to agree to send her to the grammar school in Whitehaven, but to no avail. Mr Kitchin had been downright rude to her in the shop when she'd tried to talk to him about it. He'd raised his voice, just to make sure that everyone knew that the off-comer schoolteacher was poking her nose in where it didn't belong.

'Stay at school?' he sneered at Jessie. 'Waste o' time, waste o' money. She'll be married soon enough. Needs to 'elp her mam with the little 'uns instead of filling 'er 'ead with books.'

Alice had left school at the first opportunity and gone to work at the Hall. The Skeffingtons were well pleased with her by all accounts. It would have been the 'downstairs' people who might have tired of Alice's prattle. As a child, Alice's pose as the star of her own drama had been forgivable, given the chaos at home, but as she grew it became so tedious that Jessie had been quite relieved when she left school. The emotional temperature dropped perceptibly in her absence. And then there she was, sitting at Jessie's table, tears welling in her eyes, whispering that she thought she was pregnant. 'At first I thought I'd just missed one, by accident, like,' she'd said, 'but then the next one didn't come either and I didn't know what to do. Now I've missed three, miss, but I dursen't go to t' doctor or tell me mam.'

'Do you know who the father is?' asked Jessie, dreading the questions that were yet to come.

'I think so, miss,' the child replied.

Jessie looked at her. 'You think so?' Her voice sounded louder than she expected. 'Are you saying that you've, you know, been … intimate with more than one person?'

'Intimate?' The girl hung her head. 'Cannut say, miss, honest. I just want you to help me.'

Jessie felt sick. She got up and fussed with the fire to give herself time to think.

'You'll have to tell your mother, Alice. It's no good telling me. I

30

can't help you, not with this.'

'But, miss,' wailed the child, 'I cannut. She'll tell me dad, and he'll kill me.'

Alice sniffed and sipped her tea. 'I could get him to marry me, I suppose. I bet me dad would make him.'

'Who?'

'Mr Alexander, up at th' Hall.'

'Alexander Skeffington?'

'Yes, miss. He's powerful fond of me. We could be married and I could keep the baby.'

'Mr Skeffington is the father?'

'Well, he could be, miss,' said Alice, smiling shyly. 'I don't know what Sir John would say, though. Don't think he'd want his precious son marrying the kitchen maid.' And she laughed. 'Have you got a biscuit or a bit of bread, miss? I'm starving.'

Jessie wanted so badly to hit her that she stood up too quickly and the chair fell backwards onto the flagged floor with a crash. Memories of her own shame and loss clashed and collided in her mind, making her hold onto the table for a moment to steady herself. Alice looked up.

'You alreet, miss?'

Jessie took a deep breath. 'Just felt a bit dizzy,' she said after a moment's pause. 'I'll be fine. A biscuit, you said? I've only got scones, I'm afraid.'

'That'd be grand, miss. Anything, really. Must be the baby making me so 'ungry.' Alice smiled brightly again and Jessie turned away towards the cupboard to fetch the child her food. Alice ate as if she hadn't eaten for a week.

Watching Alice loading a second scone with butter and jam was too much for Jessie. She had to speak, to break the silence.

'I've told you I can't help, Alice. Would you like to me to come with you and you can tell your mother what you've told me?'

'Oh, nay, miss, that'd just make it worse. Mam wouldn't want anyone else to know. She mustn't know I've talked to you about it. She'd be shamed.'

In another gust of memory Jessie heard her own mother's voice, loud with anger and fear. 'I'm afraid you'll have to go anyway,' she said to Alice, turning away from her again. 'I really can't help until you've told your family.' Jessie almost pushed the girl towards the door and out into the lane. As she turned back into the kitchen a sob bubbled up from her stomach, and she held her hand over her mouth to stifle the sound.

It was early in the evening, but she drew the heavy curtains in her bedroom against the light and lay face down on her bed. For so long she had managed to block it out, but now the memory of being pregnant and alone descended on her like fog, unavoidable, rancid. Her strong rational self knew, still, that she had done the right thing, for herself and for the child, but her strong rational self was not strong enough. She pressed her hands to her head and lay still. When she woke a little later, pain was pounding behind her eyes. She drew back one of the curtains and looked at herself in the dressing-table mirror. Even in the half light she could see that her eyes were puffy. She looked so old, more like her mother. She touched her mouth and neck, looking for signs of age and decay.

The following morning at school she felt wretched, but who would notice? The children couldn't guess at the nagging pain that shredded her peace of mind. She had made her choice all those years ago and she had lived with it ever since. She had built a wall around herself, brick by brick, to protect herself from further hurt, and now this scheming child had torn it down.

At Alice's funeral, Jessie prayed with more than usual intensity, for forgiveness, and for peace. She remembered the pale green of the walls in the hot room where her son had been born and the sweet smell of his tiny body. Tears squeezed through the fingers she held tightly over her eyes. She hoped anyone who noticed would assume that her grief was for Alice, not for a different child lost twenty years before.

Sitting next to her in the pew, Agnes Plane surmised that her friend had something more on her mind than the tragic death of a former pupil. She wanted to put her arm around Jessie, but stopped herself. When the congregation followed the small coffin out into the churchyard, the wind was raw from the east, and Jessie shivered as they watched the coffin being lowered into the ground. From where they stood, at the outer edge of the group clustered at the graveside, Reverend Leadbetter's voice was snatched away by the wind and scattered onto the incoming tide behind him. Just out of sight, behind the church, was the muddy tidal pool where Alice's body had been found only a few days before.

Agnes expected that Jessie would say something to the family, or to the vicar, or suggest they went back to the Farriers, but instead she went back inside the porch and sat on the bench while people drifted down the churchyard to the gate. Agnes sat beside her. 'Let's go back to my house for tea, and not bother with the Farriers,' she said quietly, and Jessie nodded. 'I'm so cold,' was all she said.

'My car's just up the lane,' said Agnes, as they got up. 'We'll be home in no time, and out of this wind.'

They climbed into Agnes's car, a shiny new Morris 14 bought with cash at Mr Bell's in Whitehaven only two months previously. On the way up the hill they passed Mr Kitchin's horse and trap that he'd brought down to carry those who would struggle with the walk.

'I'm afraid I could never warm to Mr Kitchin,' said Agnes to her subdued friend. 'I'm told he had much to say to Mrs Eilbeck about this car, where the money came from, you can imagine.'

Still Jessie didn't comment, staring out at the hedges whitened with blossom. 'Apparently,' Agnes went on, 'Mrs Eilbeck announced that no man would ever marry a woman who drove her own car. Must say I haven't lost any sleep over that!'

It was mid-May, but the fire in the living room was laid, and Agnes lit it as soon as they arrived back. Jessie kept her coat on and watched the fire take hold, as Agnes made tea in the kitchen and took the cake from the tin.

Agnes carried the tray through into the living room, where Jessie sat with her coat pulled tightly round her. She poured their tea and placed Jessie's beside her without speaking further. 'Cake?' was the only word spoken for a while, with a shake of the head the only response.

'She was just a child,' said Jessie after some minutes of silence had passed.

'Alice? Indeed she was, dear,' replied Agnes, 'although she had the look of a grown woman the past few months, don't you think? Maybe working at the Hall, being around new people was making her grow up faster.'

Jessie seemed not to have heard her, and continued in the same quiet tone.

'She enjoyed being at the Hall. Said it made her realise there's a big world out there, and she wanted to get away.'

'When did you see her last?' said Agnes, leaning a little closer, trying to break through into the space that Jessie had created round herself.

'Only a week or two ago,' Jessie said, after a pause. 'She came to see me at home. I was surprised. I hadn't talked to her properly since she left school, and that was three or four years ago. She was such a bright child then.'

'What made her come to see you?' asked Agnes. She was

surprised that Jessie had never mentioned this visit.

'She wanted to talk.'

'Yes, but why, what about?'

Jessie was silent again for some time before she spoke. 'She said she was pregnant. She wanted help. I couldn't help her.'

She lowered her head, and Agnes saw that Jessie was crying again, tears running unchecked down her face as she held the cup in her lap with both hands. Agnes leaned forward, took the cup and saucer and placed them on the table, offering Jessie a handkerchief. Jessie took it, wiped her eyes, blew her nose and then held the damp hankie, twisting it between her fingers.

Agnes took a minute to think about this news. 'Did she say who the father is, or was?' she asked.

Jessie shook her head. 'She said she wasn't sure.'

'Oh Lord,' Agnes picked up her tea and took a sip. 'What have we come to? How old was she, seventeen, and she doesn't know who the father is? How many men could there have been, for heaven's sake?'

'She thought it might be Alexander.'

'Skeffington?' Agnes was incredulous. 'Surely not. He's engaged, isn't he, to that Ramsden girl from Cockermouth? What was he thinking of? And Alice, too. What was she thinking of?'

'She thought Alexander would have to marry her, and take her away.'

'Oh Lord,' said Agnes, again. 'What a mess. Do the Skeffingtons know?'

'I don't know,' said Jessie. 'I tried to persuade Alice to tell her mother, but she said her father would kill her, and the father, whoever he is. I don't know whether she told anyone else, or whether she'd seen the doctor. Probably not. I did wonder about Sir John coming to the funeral, but that doesn't signify anything really. Alice did work for them after all.'

'What are you going to do?' Agnes asked after a pause. Jessie shrugged slightly. 'What can I do? First I thought the post mortem would show it, but it didn't, at least as far as we know. Now I don't know what to do.'

'No wonder you were so upset at the funeral,' said Agnes, getting up to add some more water to the pot. Jessie hesitated. She could tell Agnes now. After all, it was twenty years ago, and she trusted her.

Agnes returned with the teapot. 'More tea?' she said.

But the moment had passed. 'Yes, please,' said Jessie, looking up. 'I'm feeling better already.'

Later that evening, in the blessed privacy of her own room, Jessie opened the bottom drawer of the little bureau and took out an envelope that was silky and frail. She opened it carefully and pulled out a piece of paper and a small photograph. The sepia image was of a young man wearing a white shirt, dark trousers and a waistcoat. A large hat shaded his face, but the strong nose and chin were still visible. He stood confident and casual, his hands in his pockets. Clive, just weeks before his death. Jessie unfolded the note. The writing was small and precise.

Mikasa Street
'Darling Jessie, I miss you so. The air in this house tastes of you. We will be together, I know it. In the meantime we have to work hard and love each other in secret. All my love, C.'

Jessie put the note down and sat on the bed, remembering the smell of tobacco on his clothes and the curve of muscle at the top of his arm. Did she still love him, after twenty years, or just the memory of him? There'd never been another, and now the chance was gone. She lay down, curled into a ball and wept.

CHAPTER 5

AUGUST. A HAZY SUNDAY. Breeze from the south, hardly stirring the heavy trees. The land breathed slowly, imperceptibly, as if asleep under the sun. Tides crept up and down shingle and sand, silent save for a creamy whisper at the edge. On the beach the air shimmered over warmed stones. Fields and valleys smelled of grass. Sheep crowded into shade, panting.

Jessie woke as the twittering of the house martins nesting under the eaves filtered through her open window. The previous evening, as usual in the summer months, she had waited until the pale light began to fade before closing her eyes, and slept deeply until first light. Now she lay quiet, naked under a sheet. There was nowhere else she wanted to be: Agnes's offer of a few days at Whitby had been politely declined. Instead she relished the solitude, and responsibility for no one except herself.

For a while she slept again, then woke with a start. Sunlight scented with hay spilled into the room. The little clock beside Jessie's bed said it was not yet seven. The usual dream had disturbed her: walking alone in a vast house from room to crowded room, half dressed but apparently invisible, unaware and unashamed. Suddenly, a memory of Clive hit her: his face, his voice, the white skin of his belly. She longed to forget, but she could not. She knew it was useless to regret. His death was an accident, a circumstance of war. If he hadn't worked at Vickers he would have been at the front. He didn't mean to leave her, and he never knew about the baby. So many times Jessie wanted to share the story, to put the memories to rest, but she never had. Agnes was her closest friend, and revelled in her singleness: 'No husband, no children, no debts.' Jessie had never found the courage to admit, not to Agnes, not to anyone, that she had stolen Clive's name and turned her face to the wall while Clive's child was stolen from her. It was so long ago. She had served her sentence and waited like a prisoner for release from the guilt.

As the first glance of sunlight hit the back windows of the house, Jessie took her second cup of tea into the garden. Runner beans had lengthened overnight, hiding deep in foliage. Plums on the old tree were beginning to blush. She found a ripe fruit at the centre of a cluster, teased it into her fingers and then into her mouth. Juice ran down her chin and dripped onto her clean blouse. It didn't matter. Nothing mattered today.

She read her book of poems by Emily Dickinson, sitting by the back door, feeling the sun on her arms. Voices passed in the lane but she didn't look up. For lunch she picked some lettuce from the garden, and some dried ham from the pantry and made herself a sandwich. In the middle of the afternoon, as the sun began to dip and a slight wind heralded the incoming tide, she thought about her new bicycle, still unused, standing in the dry heat of the shed behind the house. Brought into the brightness of the yard, the bicycle gleamed and glittered as Jessie wiped it down. It looks too big for me, she thought, too clumsy. But she was determined to ride, to shake the torpor of the day.

As she pulled on her cycling trousers in the warm glow of the curtained bedroom, she remembered Clive again, that day on Walney, when they had their lives ahead of them. He'd borrowed a bicycle for her and she'd worn an awkward skirt. This time, the unfamiliar seams of the trousers rubbed against her thighs.

The day had cooled, but it was still warm. From the house to the top of the brow, the road was steep and after a few strenuous yards she gave up the attempt and walked, pushing the bicycle beside her. At the top she stopped for a moment to regain breath and think about how to deal with the descent. Behind her to the west lay the sea, winking in the afternoon sun. Ahead of her the narrow road sloped away down the hill and round towards the river. She pushed off and then sat up on the saddle, enjoying the draught through her hair, hoping the brakes would be enough to avoid catastrophes. As the road flattened out she smiled and gripped the handlebars a little less tightly.

She turned down the rutted lane that followed the river towards the hills at the top of the valley. The physical effort distracted her. She felt different somehow, not herself. Trees met over her head and the ground underneath was damp and slippery. She alighted from the bike and picked her way along the side of the track, where small stones gave her shoes some purchase. It was humid and airless under the trees. Jessie's thin blouse clung to her back. Close by, the river slid quietly along, cool and inviting. She leaned the bicycle into the hedge, opened the top buttons of her blouse and climbed over a stile thinking of kicking off her shoes, letting cold water trickle over her feet.

Something snagged the edge of her vision: a bird, maybe, or an otter. She stepped gingerly down from the stile, hoping to see whatever it was, and crept along the bank to where a hedge of reeds stood motionless. A splash. She waited. Another. She used both hands to part the reeds, and caught her breath. Just a few yards away, on a patch of muddy grass beside the tidal stream, a man sat on a box, casting a line into the water. His naked back was turned towards her. There was something familiar about the shape of the head, the dark hair. The man propped his fishing rod on the far side of the box and stood up slowly, stretching both arms above his head. The muscles of his shoulders flexed under the skin.

Jessie held her breath, lowering her hands. The reeds swung back again to block her view. He hadn't seen her but her heart was beating hard. She stepped back, away from the reeds, ducking her head to avoid detection. Before she climbed the stile back into the lane she waited, motionless, to make sure that he wouldn't see her as she slipped over the wall and out of sight on the other side. Her mouth was dry. She felt furtive, ashamed, and unbearably excited, holding in her mind the man's shape, the angle of his shoulders, the broad leather belt low on his hips. When she felt able to move again, she eased the bicycle out of the hedge, turned it carefully round and pushed it back along the track, into the darker shade of the trees and then out into the light, round the bend following the river, the sun full in her face, burning her cheeks. She hung her head, breathing slowly.

Back at the schoolhouse she parked the bicycle by the back door and went in, closing the door behind her, quietly, as if she were still afraid of revealing herself. She ran cold water over her hands, then splashed her face, pushing back strands of dark wet hair as she stood straight again. The cold water was refreshing, but still she felt exhausted. She climbed the stairs, pulling herself up each one, took off the damp trousers and lay on her bed, watching the slow movement of the curtains.

Later, as a horse and wagon crunched passed the house heading homewards from warm fields, Jessie woke with a start and lay still, the image of the man etched behind her eyes. Suddenly she knew who it was. Andrew, Lionel and Caroline Leadbetter's son. It was him she had seen by the river, Jessie was certain now, something about his quietness, the length of his back, his neck.

She got up and went downstairs, poured cold water from the

tap into a glass and drank it down. The image of Andrew stayed in her mind. She hoped she would see him again, talk with him about the wider world.

'For God's sake, Jessie,' she said to herself, suddenly. 'It's because he looks like Clive, and that was twenty years ago. You were young then, and so was he, not much younger than Andrew is now. Why do you do this to yourself? You're a middle-aged woman. Do other women think about such things?'

The southern sky had been flickering with light, unseen by Jessie, and it was a shock when the first thunder crashed over the house, followed almost at once by the roar of rain on the front windows, opened earlier to catch the air. She rushed to close them against the torrent, flinching as white light and deafening noise bounced off walls and the road. The small house was surrounded by water and sound, and she cowered for a moment, hands over her ears, breathing hard. When it eased she sat upright in a low chair, and realised that she was crying, overwhelmed by an utter loneliness that had descended on her as suddenly as the storm. It was so long since she'd loved or been loved, truly loved, just for herself. If she disappeared, vanished in the storm, whose life would be pierced with the wrenching grief she had felt for Clive? No one. There was no one.

CHAPTER 6

ENID PHARAOH WAS dead and buried, taking with her to the grave all that John had so badly wanted to know. Aunty Anne was still determined to keep her promise to her dead sister and tell him nothing. John convinced himself that it didn't matter: nothing mattered apart from getting out of the dismal Ulverston house as soon as he could, and leaving the past behind him. But in the night he dreamed of finding her, that other woman whose face was always in darkness.

In Enid's spotless kitchen Mrs Barker stuffed the damp towels into a large basket, along with some cups and saucers she had brought with her across the road for the obligatory funeral tea.

'I'll be off now, John,' she said. 'You'll want to be alone to grieve properly I'm sure, after such a difficult day.' John looked across at her, unsure what to say. 'I think it went well, today,' she went on, 'As far as these things can ever go well, if you see what I mean.'

'Mam would have approved of it,' he volunteered, 'and the vicar did a good job, I thought.'

The vicar had indeed done a good job. Having known the deceased for several years, and understanding full well how rigid and cheerless she could be, he had managed to make her sound both friendly and forgiving. The church had not been full, but all the right people were there to pay their respects. The choir had turned out in force, even on a weekday, in recognition of Enid's commitment. It was all as it should have been.

John wondered if Mrs Barker knew. He turned away and leaned against the sink as she passed through the kitchen door into the hall, then raised his voice a little so that she would hear him, and stop, and take him seriously.

'Did you know?' he asked.

'Know what, dear?' She turned around, but he kept his back to her, still looking out at the small backyard where red geraniums in a bright blue pot caught the late afternoon sun.

'Did you know that Enid and Arthur were not my real mam and dad, that I was adopted?'

Mrs Barker hesitated for more than a moment and then pulled out a chair and sat down, putting the basket on the floor at her feet. 'Who ...?' she began, but the rest of the question did not come.

She looked at his long back against the light.

'I was never sure, but I did wonder,' she said. 'It was something your mam said when I was making her bed, a few weeks ago. She said something about catching a train from Carnforth, just after you were born, and about how long they'd waited for you. When I asked her something about it, she said that they'd "got" you, and then I began to wonder. I never asked her outright, of course, and I was fairly sure you didn't know anything. Did she tell you herself, before she died? Sit down a minute. Tell me what she said.'

John made a noise between a laugh and a snort, a bitter sound, as he pulled out a chair from the table and sat down.

'She didn't mean to tell me,' he said. 'She thought I was Dad, that last afternoon, and talked about bringing me home on the train after they'd "got" me. That same word she used with you. I went up to ask Aunty Anne about it, but she was out doing coronation teas and Uncle George just told me. He said it was high time and he wished someone had told me earlier.'

He still could not look at Mrs Barker. She placed her hand on his arm, but he turned away from her.

'Uncle George couldn't tell me much,' he said, 'and there's lots more I need to know. All he told me was that the home in Carnforth where they got me was for unmarried mothers and that it closed down after the war. He didn't know who my real mother is, or my father ... I still don't know who I am.' He felt a block in his throat and dropped his head.

Vera Barker stretched out, grasped his chin with surprising energy and pulled his face around towards her own.

'Now look here, young man,' she said as John blinked at her. 'It's not my place to say this, and not the right time I'm sure, but I'm going to say it anyway. Enid and Arthur were good people. They only ever wanted the best for you and they decided not to tell you about your real parents. They loved you, in their own way. I know it's been hard for you, them being more like grandparents I suppose, and you being the only one. But you have been loved. You are who you are. You're a bright lad, with a good job and prospects. You haven't found a nice lass yet but there's plenty of time for that. Now you have this house and everything in it and people might say you're sitting pretty, however sad the circumstances. Some people have to wait half their lives for what you've got already.'

She sat back, flushed, defiant. John looked down again. He could feel his heart in his chest. No one had spoken to him like this before and he didn't like it. He pushed back the chair and stood up.

'Thanks for helping today,' he said, desperate to get out of the small kitchen and away from her. 'Now I have to get on with things.'

Mrs Barker pursed her lips, picked up her basket and left the house.

At last John had the place to himself. Upstairs the smell of urine and disinfectant was beginning to fade. His mother was gone, buried in the earth beside her patient husband. He was free to do whatever he chose. He began by walking into the front room where he was rarely allowed. Bright white antimacassars adorned the hard chairs, and the glass-fronted china cabinet in the corner bounced light into the room. There was so much stuff.

He looked around the tidy, soulless room where the first thin layer of dust had begun to form after days of neglect. There on the mantelpiece was the photo he'd known all his life. Taken in a studio somewhere, in Barrow probably, with a big potted plant behind the chair where Enid Pharaoh sat with a baby on her knee. Arthur stood behind her, one hand on her shoulder.

They looked quite old, even then, but pleased with them-selves. Arthur's hair was slicked down on each side of his small head from a straight centre parting: small round glasses made his face look even rounder than normal. Enid sat erect, her hair pulled back and her knees together, legs crossed at the ankle. You couldn't really call it a smile on her face, but she looked a lifetime younger than the last time he had seen her just a few days before, when he'd got home to find the doctor upstairs and Mrs Barker drawing the curtains in this very room.

John looked hard at the photograph. Now he knew it was a sham. They had taken him from someone else. He was not theirs. He turned the photo on its face.

Another photo stared back at him from the top of the bookcase. He was always surprised that his mother should have given this picture pride of place in the front room. It had been taken by one of the boys he went climbing with, on a mountain summit just a year or so ago. John remembered looking down at the camera and beyond it down into Mosedale, and then up again to the pyramid of Great Gable. He picked up the photograph and looked carefully at himself.

The angle of the camera made him look even longer and thinner than he actually was. Dark hair flared away from his head in the wind. He was smiling because he was happy, feeling strong and confident as he often did in the mountains. They had climbed all morning, and now were about to run down the scree just for the fun of it. John remembered the tension in his knees as he hurtled down, feet planted sideways to stop him falling, loose rock sliding away. The boys had cheered his last few strides. Then they walked down the valley to the hotel at Wasdale Head, where beer had never tasted so clear and sharp.

* * *

There were few secrets in the small town. John was dreading going back to work, facing the pretence of sympathy from people he hardly knew. At the end of his first day back at the brewery he escaped with relief. Safe in the privacy of the quiet house he sat at the table in the kitchen, leafing idly through the *Evening Mail*. In the 'Situations Vacant' section something caught his eye. It was a job in the office of a quarry up in Eskdale on the west coast, close to the narrow gauge railway that John had always been interested in. They wanted someone for the accounts. He could do it.

The pay might not be as good as at the brewery, but after the day he'd had, he reckoned it was worth it. He had money, as Mrs Barker had so clearly pointed out to him, and now he could make choices for himself. He found some paper, wrote a letter there and then, and posted it when he went out again to get pie and chips for his tea.

Waiting for a response made him even more fed up with the brewery than he'd been before. The longer he waited the more the sickly smell of hops and the predictability of the work irritated him. He didn't want to talk to people, and when he tried to do so nothing came out right. He thought about his mother, his real mother, the one who'd given him away. Why did she get pregnant if she didn't want to keep him? And who made her pregnant? He might never know his own father, and that was her fault, too. Everyone had lied to him. Even Anne and George had let him down. They'd lied to him for years. How could they?

By the time the letter arrived early in September he'd almost forgotten about the job. The letter was officially from the manager of the quarry, but seemed to have been written by someone else. Whoever it was apologised for the delay in responding – 'circumstances beyond our control' – and asked John to make himself available for a chat the following week when the writer, a Mr Timmins, would be in Ulverston on other business. The meeting, when it came about, was positive. Mr Timmins was satisfied. John was delighted.

There were some matters to deal with before he could leave the Ulverston house for good. The house was his by right, but Mr Southward, the agent, looked at him strangely when John announced he wanted it sold as quickly as possible.

'Your parents?' said the elderly man, looking at John over his glasses.

'Both dead,' said John cutting off the enquiry. 'The house is mine and I want it sold.'

'Perhaps you could rent the house,' said Mr Southward, trying to curb the impatience of the angry young man in front of him.

'No,' said John with finality, 'I want it sold.'

And so the sale of the house and everything in it was set in motion. John had one last thing to do. All his previous attempts to find any clues about his birth or his parentage had failed, but now he tackled the search with a frantic urgency. In vain he hoisted himself up into the dusty loft, searched every cupboard in the house, pulled open every drawer.

Upstairs in Enid's old room, the room where she had revealed her secret before she died, he looked again through the old chest of drawers next to the window. Bending down to pull open the stuck drawer at the bottom, he yanked so hard that it came right out. At the very back of it, John noticed a scrap of paper, its corner caught between the base of the drawer and the side.

Carefully, he pulled it out, placed it on top of the dresser, and smoothed out the creases. It seemed to be the first page of a letter, but the ink had faded. He pushed it closer to the light. The writing was large and flowery.

Furness Road

Wednesday

Dear Mrs Pharaoh

Forgive me. If you don't want to consider this we need never speak of it again. You told me once how much you and Arthur have longed for a child.

There's a lady in the choir at church whose niece has got herself into trouble. Respectable family, the Thompsons, not what you might expect. This war is turning everything upside down. Anyway, the girl is in The Oaks, in Carn-forth. Baby due in a few weeks. She's prepared to let it go, according to the person I've spoken to – a respectable person but I can't tell you –

That was all. The back of the page was blank. John read it again, trying to take it in. Who wrote it, and when? It must his real mother they were talking about, and he was the baby about to be born.

He felt his heart thumping in his chest and leaned against the wall for a moment. He re-read the paper a dozen times over the next few hours, and finally folded it into an envelope to keep with his other treasures, the only things he would take with him. Enid's old chest of drawers had reluctantly yielded its secret, and when the house clearance man took it away, John was glad to see it go.

Chapter 7

Early in October, John took the train heading west to Barrow and then north up the Cumberland coast, to a new job and a new life. Bad weather was forecast, and by the time the train left Barrow, rain was running down the carriage window and a westerly gale screamed through the tiny gap at the top. At a place where the line skirted the beach and sea spray salted the rain, John was not surprised when the train slowed and then stopped, with no station in sight. The conductor walked down to tell the few passengers that the track was washed out ahead of them and they could go no further. John picked up his bag, dropped down onto the track, turned up his collar against the wind and rain and started to walk the mile or so north into Newton.

On reaching the village, he struggled into the Farriers Arms, red from the wind and soaked by the westerly storm that shrieked in the trees across the road. The place seemed deserted, but in the back bar and the 'snug' fires were blazing in the hearth. He called 'hello' and a large woman emerged from the kitchen at the back. She wore a scarf around her head, from which wayward strands of grey hair escaped and defied recapture. The woman's face was flushed, and she wiped large red hands on a large blue pinafore as she came through into the bar where he stood dripping, his bag at his feet.

'The train stopped,' he offered as explanation of his presence. She looked at him blankly. 'The line's flooded. We have to wait. I'll have to, you know, find another way, or maybe stay here a night?' His voice rose to turn the statement into a request, but the only response from the landlady was, 'What can I get you?' It was as if his explanation was either unheard or unnecessary.

'I'll have a pint, please,' he said, eying the various taps along the bar, 'of the Hartleys.'

The landlady pulled half the pint, holding it up to the light before finishing it off. He handed over coins and took a first sip before risking another attempt at conversation. 'Where is everybody?' he asked.

'Haven't you heard?' said the landlady. 'There's a ship run aground on the beach. They've all gone down to watch.' So that was why the place was empty.

'I have to stay here,' she added. 'If they can get the folk off the ship they'll bring them up here to dry out. I've built the fires up. You could dry out yourself if you want to. It'll be a while yet before anyone gets here.'

John took off his coat and sat down with the pint. It was quiet and warm, and his trousers began to steam in the heat from the fire. He could stay there, waiting with the landlady for people to return from the beach with stories of storms and rescue. That would be easy. That would be what he'd spent his life so far doing, apart from the climbing. He did what was expected, the safe thing, the thing that kept him away from awkward encoun-

51

ters, not knowing what to say to people. 'Stay where you are, John,' his mother would have said. The person who called herself his mother, that is.

John drank the rest of his pint of beer with unaccustomed speed and got up from his seat by the fire. 'I want to go and see,' he said. ' Can't get much wetter, but have you got a coat or a jacket I could borrow? I'll bring it back.'

The landlady looked him up and down. 'I've got some stuff might do for you,' she said, 'not been worn for a while, but it would save your clothes. My man was nearly as tall as you. He won't be needing them any more.'

She disappeared upstairs and returned with a huge pair of waders, and an old coat. 'This lot'll keep the wet off you,' she said, handing them over. 'Leave your bag in the snug. I've got things to do.'

The landlady retreated into the kitchen, leaving John to work out how to put the waders on without lying on the floor to do so. In the end he did lie on the floor, wormed his way into the waders, struggled to his feet, pulled the braces tight to keep the waders up to his waist and buttoned the jacket over the top. It was short in the arm and long in the body, and the buttons were stiff in the heavy fabric, but it would do the job. He left his bag in the snug and clumped heavily out of the pub, over the deserted road now strewn with branches, and down the path to the beach.

Five minutes later he struggled up the final rise in the dunes. The gale hit him full in the face and pushed him backwards. Wiping the rain from his eyes, he could see people lined up along the crown of the beach, and a larger crowd at the far end. They were all looking out to sea, where a steamer had its stern towards them, engines full running and smoke swirling into the wind. A man standing next to him shouted, 'They can't 'ang on much longer. The anchors can't hold 'er.' Even as he spoke there was an audible crack and the ship began to swing broadside to the gale, bucking as the incoming surf buffeted along its length. 'That's it,' shouted the man, 'they're in real trouble now.' At the other end of the beach, where the narrow road from the village ended, there was a commotion. 'Ehyup,' said the man. 'Here's the Rocket Brigade.'

As they peered through the brown foam blowing up the beach, a large vehicle bounced into view. It had huge wheels and a flat bed, on which half a dozen men in oilskins and hats were trying to keep their balance. As it stopped they jumped down and began hauling equipment off the back, setting up a solid tripod on a flat grassy patch at the top. Orders were shouted and well-rehearsed activity produced a rocket launcher, pointing into the wind towards the steamer.

'What are they doing?' asked John of the man who seemed to know what was going on.

'They're going to fire a line to the ship. They fix the line to the mast, and use the buoy to carry folk off. It usually works, but it's slow.'

By now the first rocket was ready to be fired. It snaked away, its tail shredded by the wind, but fell well short and the crowd groaned as it disappeared into the sea. 'The wind's blowing it back,' said the man. 'They'll 'ave to try again.' The second rocket got closer, but also fell short, and the crowd groaned again. Four small boys pushed past them to get nearer to the action. The third rocket arced higher, urged on by the roaring of the crowd. They cheered as it skittered onto the sloping deck. 'That's the first line across,' shouted the man to John. 'Now they pull the heavy line over. There it goes.' They could see activity on the deck as crew scrambled for the line and a figure climbed a little way up the mast to tie it fast. Then the breeches buoy was winched across. 'Watch this now,' said the man. 'They shove someone in them trouser

53

things and then they pull at this end to get them across. Good job the line's good 'n high, or they get a right soaking on the way in.'

'I'm going over there!' yelled John, pointing towards the Rocket Brigade truck, and he set off, slipping on the wet stones. Head down, watching his feet, he bumped into the first of the onlookers, who looked at him and pointed out towards the ship. On the deck of the steamer, they could just see a small boat being lowered from the sheltered side into the water. Six or seven men, and a boy, or a small woman, struggled down into it. John pushed on through the crowd towards the truck. A young man, as tall as John, and broad with curly hair plastered to his head by the rain, leaned back on the bonnet of the truck with binoculars trained on the steamer. 'Bloody idiots,' he muttered, 'They'll never make it in that thing. Surf will pound it, or the rocks will get them. Why can't they just wait? We know what we're doing.'

He lowered the binoculars, and handed them to John without a glance. 'Amos!' he shouted to one of the men hauling on the line that was inching the buoy towards safety. 'Tell the others we have to speed this up. When that bugger's out of the buoy get it back fast. They must be panicking out there.' The breeches buoy with the man's legs kicking underneath it was getting close to the beach and two of the crew went down to pull it through the surf. Holding a bundle tight to his chest, the rescued man struggled up the beach, cheered on by the crowd. Somebody slapped him on the back. Another shook his hand. The buoy began its jerky passage back to the vessel, which still slewed and lurched beyond the surf like an elongated horse pulling wildly at its tether.

Meanwhile the small boat, propelled by oars at either side, caught the full blast of the storm as it pulled away from the shadow of the ship. For a few seconds it disappeared altogether. John strained to see any sign of it. The crowd groaned and people shouted useless instructions into the screaming gale. There was the little boat again now, cresting a wave and surfing in at an angle. The oars flailed uselessly. 'They don't know where the rocks are,' shouted the young man. 'Wait, wait,' he yelled into the wind, and snapped his fingers for the binoculars.

'They're going to catch those rocks,' he said, 'They won't make it!' He turned to John looking at him fully for the first time. 'Who are you?' he asked.

'John Pharaoh,' said John immediately, compelled by the authority in the man's voice.

'Well, John, I'm Andy Leadbetter. I'm in charge of this lot. You and I are going to get those people off, before they drown right here in front of us.' He took John firmly by the arm and pulled another man along with them, shouting into his ear as they stumbled down the steep bank of pebbles towards the waves.

Down they went, into the surf, towards the boat that seemed larger now, tossing in the chop where the rocks were just below the surface of the rising water. 'It'll be deep and then get shallower,' Andrew shouted into John's ear. 'We'll go out, you stay here and pull them through when we get them out of the boat.' John stood his ground, knowing that he dare not go much further. Even standing was hard enough, as the backwash on each wave swept past his feet and scoured the pebbles out from under him.

The boat had stopped its forward rush, caught on the rocks as Andrew had predicted. The men on board had given up trying to row and were struggling out into the water, unsure of the depth, knowing that others were wading out to help them. Andrew had almost reached them. John saw the incoming high surge too late to stagger back out of its reach. The wave, higher than any he'd seen before, rose around him, its crest breaking in his face, filling his eyes and nostrils with salt water. It pushed him backwards and he fell heavily onto his side. It took him a while to get up, but the rush of the ebbing wave helped and he was upright again before the second big wave hit him. He spluttered as the wave broke in his face. He was too deep in the water to keep his balance, and tried to move his feet back higher up the slope. But he couldn't move one of his legs. On his right side, the leg of his waders had filled with water and the weight was holding him fast.

There must be a way to get my leg out, he thought, as he wiped the water from his face and coughed to clear his throat of salt. The braces, undo the braces. Before he could start to get his hands inside the coat to loosen the braces, another wave caught him and he fell back again. Again he let the water wash over him and used the impetus of its ebb to get to his feet. He pulled at the coat, and struggled to pull it up, trying to reach the top of the waders. He tore at the buttons with his numb fingers but they wouldn't move, locked into the buttonholes. The water was rising and he began to panic. Andrew and the other man were further out, standing clear of the water on the submerged rocks, appearing to walk on the surface. He shouted but his voice whipped away towards the beach on the wind that was now shrieking round his head. He began to tear at the buttons, then gave up and tried again to heave the coat up but still he could not reach in far enough to dislodge the braces and free himself.

The next wave hit him full in the face. He bent with it but could not move his right foot, overbalancing again and wrenching his left knee as he pulled his leg round to support himself against the force of the tide. Using his arms to keep his balance, he shouted but his throat was dry and raw with coughing and salt. They couldn't hear him. He was stuck. The tide was rising. He would drown here soon.

He wiped his eyes and saw that Andrew was coming back, arms around another man, pushing back through the surf towards him. John waved his arms and shouted. 'Help, please, I'm stuck, please,' but Andrew just shouted, 'Hang on!' and strode past a few yards away without a glance. As John turned helplessly to watch Andrew's disappearing back, he fell again, still pinned by his right leg in the waders. This time he couldn't get up so easily. He struggled for breath. The water washed over his chest and head. Small stones scoured his face. At last, the wave retreated. John forced himself to kneel, and then to stand. Cold. Cold. He lifted his face towards the racing sky. Rain and tears washed sand from his cheeks.

A strong hand gripped his shoulder from behind and a knife swung before his face. 'I'm going to cut the coat,' said the voice behind him into his ear. The knife was strong and very sharp. Andrew hacked through the coat just far enough to pull it clear of the braces. He slashed at one of the braces, and then down into the waders to allow John to pull his left leg clear. 'Now the other side,' he yelled as John clung to his bent back. Andrew cut wildly at the braces on the other side and scratched John's stomach with the knife. 'Sorry! Now pull, pull!' Andrew cut again at the side of the waders as John clung to him, pulling his other leg clear. 'Hold on to me,' screamed Andrew as a wave knocked them both off balance. Coughing and blinded by salt and water, John was hauled to his feet and up the slope, the torn waders flapping around his legs. As the two men reached the smaller pebbles out of reach of the tide they fell to their knees and crawled out of the water. John felt the burning of salt in his wound. Andrew struggled to his feet, grasped John's torn coat at the back of his neck and hauled him up the beach. Other hands were helping now. John was pushed and pulled, still coughing, to the bank. He fell to his knees again, retching, feeling the fire in his side, then rolled onto his back and lay still.

CHAPTER 8

THEY CARRIED JOHN into the Farriers, and straight into the back bar where the fire was still burning bright and hot. Others from the stricken ship were there. One of the men held a monkey in his arms, but John was too exhausted to notice. Andrew helped John with his trousers and sweater and wrapped a blanket around his shoulders and over his shaking legs. He poured a glass of whisky for himself, downed it in one, and then re-filled the glass and handed it to John. John sniffed it, and sipped cautiously. Despite these precautions, he choked as the whisky burned into his throat.

'You were nearly a goner there,' said Andrew cheerfully. 'Good job I'd that knife handy. Never wear a coat over waders.'

John stared at him. 'Thought I was going to die,' he croaked, as the whisky lingered on his larynx.

'You and a few others, I reckon,' said Andrew. 'But we got them all off. Had to send the mate back to tell them not to try another boat, and we managed to get them all, even the monkey.'

As if responding to this acknowledgement, the monkey began to chatter, holding its teeth in a fixed grin. 'The captain sent some whisky over, too,' Andrew continued. 'You've just had some.'

John nodded but he wasn't really taking anything in. The place was filling up with wet bodies, smoke and steam.

Someone entered the room. Andrew looked up, saw who it was

and rolled his eyes. 'Oh, God,' he murmured to John. 'Here we go. Trust him to turn up when the action's over.'

The newcomer stepped into the centre of the room. He was tall, well over six feet, with a large head crowned by white hair dishevelled by the wind and standing proud in a halo round the long pale face. Bright eyes contrasted with the damp exhaustion in the crowded room. The newcomer wore an expensive coat trimmed with sheepskin, which he removed to reveal a black suit and clerical collar. The landlady put her head round the door to ask if he wanted a drink, which was accepted with a nod. The man held out his coat to her without a word. She took it from him, also without a word, and hurried away.

Looking slowly round the room, the Reverend Lionel Leadbetter, raised his arms. 'Let us give thanks,' he boomed, 'for the deliverance of these good people from the storm.' One or two of the men bowed their heads, while the rest stared at him. Andrew lowered his eyes.

'Dear Lord,' continued the vicar, his face raised and eyes closed. 'We thank you for your mercy, and for the courage of all those who helped to save these men from a terrible fate this day. May we remember always that it is by your will that we live or perish. Thanks be to God. Amen.'

John repeated 'Amen' in a mumbled response, bred of years of churchgoing.

Lionel took a long stride across the room and rested a hand on Andrew's shoulder. 'Fine work, my boy,' he proclaimed in a slightly quieter tone. Andrew flinched under his father's hand. 'All over by the time the lifeboat turned up, thanks to you and the Brigade. And this poor fellow owes his life to you I'm told.' He leaned down to shake John's hand. The grip was firm and uncomfortably sustained. There was a commotion behind him as the monkey gleefully urinated into the fire. The laughter made

Lionel break his hold and turn around, before making his way across the room and off to find his drink.

'Who was that?' asked John, shaking the feeling back into his crushed hand.

'That,' said Andrew, resignedly, 'was my father.'

John did not know what to say, and so said nothing.

'What were you doing on the beach, anyway?' asked Andrew, holding out his socks to the heat of the fire. By now the room smelled strongly of wet wool and sweat.

'I was on the train,' John said, finding his voice at last through the fire in his throat. 'The through train from Lancaster to Carlisle … it got stuck just south of here and the driver said we'd have to wait till tomorrow, so they could clear the line. There was a tree down, or rocks blown off the walls, or something, not sure what. So I walked up here. Then the landlady –'

'Mrs Eilbeck,' Andrew interrupted him.

'Yes, her. She said everyone was down at the beach and offered me someone's waders and a coat to wear.'

'Oh, lord,' said Andrew, 'They were probably Willie's waders, her man,' he laughed, 'and he was a big man alright. He died last year. Why were you on that train anyway? Where're you going?'

'Here,' said John. 'Newton. I'm starting a new job, at the quarry.'

Andrew turned away from checking his socks to look at John more carefully.

'Doing what at the quarry?'

'Accounts.'

Andrew put back his head and laughed. 'Well I'll be damned. Thought the name was familiar when you told me on the beach, but I didn't put it together. John Pharaoh. We've been expecting you.'

'Who's "we"?' John put down his whisky.

'All of us at the quarry. I'm the manager – well sort of.' He leaned across to shake John's hand. 'They wrote to you about the job while I was in Keswick last month.'

'So that's why you helped me out of the sea,' said John, 'to save the trouble of finding someone else.' This time they both laughed. Andrew found another glass on the mantelshelf, poured two glasses of the whisky and they clinked and drank.

Two more tots of whisky later, Andrew left him for a while, to talk to the men from the ship about plans for their accommodation. John sat alone by the fire. The whiskey and the heat made his brain revolve inside his head. Why? Why did he follow a man he'd never met into a raging sea? He should have stayed in Ulverston. It was safe there. He could have moved out of the house but why come all this way? Maybe he was just different now. Different parents, different person. Maybe this person, the person he had become, took risks. And look what had happened. He'd nearly died. And the man who'd saved him was his boss. John didn't like that. Did he owe this man? How was he supposed to behave towards him?

He looked across the room. Andrew was strong, and everybody knew him, respected him. John shrank further into his blanket as the whiskey continued to boil in his head. When he looked up Andrew was standing in front of him.

'Where are you going to stay?' he said, looking down at John.

'What?' John's mind was fuddled.

'Where are you going to stay?'

'Here, maybe?' Actually John had no idea.

'Here? The Farriers?'

'Yes.'

Andrew laughed so loudly that people looked around. John shrank away from him again.

'Are you going to walk to work, then?' said Andrew.

'I don't know. Maybe.'

'Come on, man. You've must have had a better idea than that. It's five miles from here up the valley, and you're in no fit state to walk tonight, or tomorrow come to that.'

John felt like a child. He wanted to have an answer, but nothing happened. He wanted to sleep.

'I'll have a word,' said Andrew finally. 'Stay here tonight. Sleep it off. Tomorrow I'll bring the bike down and we'll head up to the quarry. There's a spare room at my house, you can have that while you find somewhere.'

He stood up, stretched, finished the drink in his hand and went into the back bar to sort things out, while John stared into the fire and tried to collect himself. At least he had a place to stay. That would do for now. He could think about the rest tomorrow. All he really wanted to do was sleep. The whisky, he shouldn't have had the whisky.

CHAPTER 9

IT WAS THE DAY after the storm. Andrew Leadbetter lay in his bed at the manager's house beside the quarry, staring at the ceiling above him and listening to the wind. The storm had worked its way into every gap in the slates and the house smelled of mould. The ceiling was marked with stains from the snow that had blown into the roof space at New Year and then melted, not enough to drip through but enough to leave a brown stain behind as it dried. Not worth trying to repaint the ceiling until he'd tackled the gaps in the roof, to stop the snow blowing in again. And how long would he be here? Was it worth it? He'd have to get up soon. The yard was a shambles.

For the second time in his life, Andrew thought about getting away. Going to the mining college in Glasgow had been his first chance: coming back had been a bad mistake. If anything it was worse than before, as if his father thought of him as a competitor, to be quashed. Maybe that was the problem. But he wouldn't have got a job like this, or the money, if he'd stayed in Scotland. His dad knew the Skeffingtons who owned the quarry, and the job was there for the taking. But he still shouldn't have taken it. The quarry was in a mess, the paperwork wasn't what Andrew either enjoyed or was good at, and he was tired of his father's bullying. It galled him that most Newton people saw his father as the well-meaning vicar who'd pushed Sir John to put running water into all his tenants' houses. They never saw him at home bossing everyone around. Andrew wasn't the only one who'd had to get out: Alan had escaped to London, Mary to Newcastle. Even Julia, so quiet and compliant, she'd gone too. Mother had been distraught but the old man didn't care: too busy with his 'good works'. Even when the old bugger's motives were good, he was so pompous about it.

There was only one good reason to stay a while in Newton. Jessie Whelan, the teacher. He'd noticed her on coronation day in May. Talked to her, just for a few minutes but he remembered every word. Then there was that funeral, but she was too upset to talk and he left her alone. For weeks he hadn't seen her, until last weekend. He'd been in the shop, Saturday morning. It was busy and she was in the queue ahead of him. He'd moved a little to get a better look at her. Good shape, rounded. Dark hair curled at the nape of her neck. He thought about her back, her skin. Behind his eyes he saw her long hair loosed from the pins that held it, falling onto pale shoulders. As she passed he'd caught the scent of her. Lemons.

He'd had a few women over the years. He knew how to catch what he wanted. It was like hunting, you got a feel for the prey and went after it, planning ahead, thinking about the next move. She might be curious about him, might hear stories about the business on the beach. He'd played it well so far, polite, interested. Maybe she was interested in him too. Can't tell with older women. She seemed to spend a lot of time with that Plane woman. That might be a problem. She was a snob, that one. Didn't like him, and it was mutual. Have to think about that.

Andrew knew what he wanted. No more silly girls, had enough of them. He wanted a woman with some life behind her. There was something about Jessie. She was different from the others in the valley. He could sense the passion in her, see it in the way she looked, heard it in her voice. He had to bide his time, but he would track her down: at the end she would know, breathless, that he had come for her.

He forced himself out of the scant warmth of his bed and into cold clothes that he'd dropped in a heap on the floor. Downstairs there was little comfort in the dark kitchen, still strewn with the remains of the previous night's supper. He left the house, fired up his motorbike and roared off down the valley, stopping as he went to clear more debris and branches off the road. At the Farriers, John was sitting in the snug in front of a plate of bacon and sausage, looking as sick as he felt.

'Eat up, lad. Put hairs on your chest,' said Andrew as he passed by towards the kitchen. John heard laughter and a minute later Andrew emerged with his own plate piled high. A mug of tea was delivered to the table and Andrew drank it in silence as John watched him. Andrew eyed John's plate.

'Are you going to eat that?'

John shook his head.

'Give it 'ere then.'

Without waiting for a response Andrew leaned over, scooped most of John's untouched breakfast onto his own plate and continued to eat. Finally he pushed the empty plate away, wiped his mouth with the back of his hand and smiled. 'I'll enjoy having you around,' he said, 'but I'll probably get fat.' He looked at John's pale face. 'Yesterday shook you up a bit. It would anybody, no shame in that. You can rest up at my place for a day or two while we're clearing up the mess in the yard and then we'll get you started on the mess in the office. I've let things slide a bit. A few days dealing with that'll take your mind off yesterday.'

'Don't feel too good,' said John. 'Awful headache, and can't get the taste of salt out of my throat. It burns. Maybe it was the drink.

I'm not used to it.'

'Soon change that,' said Andrew smiling again. 'Not much else to do round 'ere.'

They got up and John fetched his bag. 'Leave it,' said Andrew, realising it wouldn't fit on the bike with John as well. 'The wagon'll bring it on. Take whatever you want for now and leave the rest.'

As they drove up the branch-strewn valley Andrew wondered why they'd given a man's job to this boy.

* * *

After the necessary clearing up, the rest of the week at the quarry passed without incident. There was no blasting to organise, just the routine of getting stone onto the train for transport to the crusher further down the line. There was also a load to be taken down to the main line at Newton, where the railway trucks were emptied directly down a chute onto lorries waiting on the road below. The chute had needed repair and Andrew wanted to check that all was well before the process could continue.

He travelled down to Newton on the train, sitting up in front with the driver. It was a windy day and the ash and cinders from the boiler flew away from them into the woods, rather than straight into their eyes as happened sometimes. Andrew always loved this trip. Of course it was slower than the bike, but the sound and smell of the steam engine delighted him as it had always done since the first time he encountered it as a child. The line had been in the doldrums during much of his boyhood, but now it was back running successfully again, and attracting visitors too, during the summer. The busy season was over, but the line was in daily use and the quarry would have struggled without it. The roads down the valley were simply not good enough to carry the weight.

The little train rattled through woods and over bridges, at the base of the steep hillside. The bracken was fading to brown and it took Andrew a moment to spot the dappled head of a solitary deer watching from the shadow of birches. As the smoke swirled between them the animal turned and disappeared. To the west the valley flattened into the estuary and the wind brought a tang of salt from the incoming tide.

The chute on the bridge was checked and Andrew was walking down towards the shop when he saw Jessie outside the school. Just like the last time he'd seen her, he felt the shock. She was carrying some boxes into the building, and he quickened his pace to catch up to her before she disappeared.

'Let me help you with those,' he called, just in time: following her into the school would have looked too deliberate. He was determined to talk to her, to check his instinct about her, and this was his chance. She turned, saw him coming and propped the boxes against the wall, leaning against them to keep them steady while he hurried towards her. She smiled at him, thankful for his help. Her hair fell in long curls round her face, caught by the wind. They struggled awkwardly for a few moments while he took the boxes from her.

'Where do you want these?' he asked, looking down at her as she retreated down the steps to give him room.

'I'll show you,' she said, squeezing past him into the narrow hallway of the schoolhouse. He caught the faint smell of her and breathed it in. She opened a door at the far end of the hallway, and he followed her through towards the opposite side of the room, where cupboard doors stood open.

'I had to make space for this stuff before I could bring it in,' she said. 'If you put the boxes down on the floor, I'll get some of the children to help me unpack them later this afternoon. That's very kind of you, Andrew. There are two more like this just outside where the carter dropped them. Do you think you could manage those as well? "Get a man in, dear," my friend Agnes always says when there's a tricky job to do, and in this case, I think she's right!'

'Then I'm your man,' replied Andrew, 'show me the rest and we'll have this done in no time.'

The rest of the boxes were carried into the back room, Jessie holding doors where necessary. When the job was done they sat on the boxes for a minute and Jessie began to pin back the hair that the wind had loosed from its combs and slides.

'It's strange isn't it,' she said. 'We haven't had a conversation for so long and then in just a few days …'

Jessie could see his eyes now. Pale blue.

'You were at poor Alice's funeral, weren't you?' she continued. 'That was a bad day. It was good of you to be there. I was too upset for conversation, I'm afraid. She was just a child, and there's no justice in a child's death.'

Andrew didn't respond, and turned away from her.

'Will you be at the harvest supper on Saturday?' he asked, thinking of when he might see her again.

'I hope so,' she answered, making up her mind about it on the spot.

He could find no excuse for staying longer and went on his way down to the shop. He smiled as he walked: she was coming closer, he could sense it.

Chapter 10

Jessie sat in the hairdresser's chair in Whitehaven and looked at herself in the mirror. The unforgiving mirror was always the hardest part of having her hair cut, and the reason why she didn't do so very often. Long hair had been useful when she first started at the school and wanted to look older than she was. Then she wore it up and pinned to control its thickness and curl, or pulled into the nape of her neck, and she didn't need a hairdresser very often. Now she wasn't sure how she wanted to look and had been putting this visit off for a while. Connie the hairdresser stood behind her, pushing one hand abstractedly through the thick hair and looking at Jessie in the mirror.

'Why don't we do something different this time, Miss Whelan? More 1937.'

'You mean less 1837,' said Jessie. 'Sometimes I catch sight of myself and I look like my grandmother. I know I need to do something but it's just easier to have a trim and avoid the decision till next time.'

'Well, here we are at "next time",' said Connie. 'You had your hair like this when I was at school, and that must be twelve years ago nearly. It's such lovely hair, needs setting off, like, to make the most of it. I don't mean one of those short glossy styles like the Duchess of Windsor, I mean something fuller, to make the most of the curl.' Connie held her hands at either side of Jessie's face, cupping the hair to show how it might look.

'Look at that,' she said. 'See how much younger you are.'

Jessie looked. It was true. She looked more like when she was a girl, in Barrow, all those years ago.

'Tell you what,' said Connie. 'If you're not in a hurry, why don't I get on with Mrs Whittaker and leave you to have a think about it. I'll bring you the book of styles and you can tell me if anything appeals to you. You can sit over there until we're ready.'

Jessie checked the watch on her wrist. She didn't have to meet Agnes until eleven: plenty of time for once. She tried to look at the book Connie had given her but the images in her head were more powerful. For the second time in a few days, she was thinking of Clive and the intensity of his pale body.

Two hours later Jessie walked down to the end of Lowther Street and found Agnes's car, where her friend was sitting reading the newspaper. Jessie knocked on the window.

'Oh my word,' said Agnes, looking up. 'Wait a minute.'

Agnes got out of the car and looked across at Jessie to get the full effect. She smiled.

'My dear, what a transformation. Takes years off you! Turn your head, let me see the back. Lovely. All you need now is something to set it off. What time is it? Eleven? Plenty of time. Come on. We're going to the Beehive.'

Jessie protested, but only a little. She felt good. Shopping for clothes hadn't been planned that day, and she didn't have enough money with her, but Agnes would hear no objections. Before the Beehive closed at noon, Agnes had picked out a sea green jacket, and a dark brown skirt that showed off Jessie's waist. They even found a light silky scarf that picked up the green in the jacket and in Jessie's eyes. Agnes dealt with the sales assistant with enviable confidence and paid for everything from a roll of banknotes worthy of a Chicago gangster. Jessie's routine Saturday morning in Whitehaven had turned into something else entirely. She hardly recognised herself.

As she put on a touch of lipstick before heading for the harvest supper at six-thirty that evening, Jessie allowed herself to wonder if Andrew would be there, and then stopped herself. She was his mother's generation. His mother was her friend. 'You can look good for your own sake, Jessie,' she said to her image in the dressing-table mirror, 'not just to please someone else, let alone a young man.' She picked up the new jacket, went downstairs and walked over to the village hall. Despite herself, she looked for Andrew's motorbike, and was relieved to see that it wasn't there. Now she could relax and enjoy herself without the anxiety of meeting him again.

The weather had come good just in time and the harvest was indeed 'safely gathered in'. Some years it was so late that the men were still working in the fields as the old harvest hymns were being sung in the little church by the river. Jessie hadn't fully understood what harvest time was really about until she moved to Newton. Here it was the busiest time of the year in the fields, and in the orchards where plums and apples weighed down the branches, waiting for a small army of children to shake and pick the branches bare. Newton kitchens smelled of fruit for days, and in lofts and attics apples were laid carefully side by side but not touching, to keep through the winter months. Hay was cut and dried, and lanes were clogged with carts and horses taking it back to the barns. There was talk of a tractor doing the work of several horses and many men in farms further south, but not here, not yet.

The harvest supper followed a familiar pattern each year. Large shepherd's pies were prepared in kitchens around the village and brought to the hall wrapped in cloths to keep them warm. Trestle tables and benches were laid out in rows the length of the hall, with cutlery and pickles. Agnes and Jessie had helped to arrange everything in the afternoon, with Caroline Leadbetter and Mrs Scattergood. Even Kath Eilbeck had turned up for an hour, and they'd been pleased to accept help. Moving tables and benches was heavy work. 'Get a man in, dear,' they chorused when Agnes complained about moving the furniture. Tables were covered with bright tablecloths and the hall was lit with oil lamps.

Jessie sat with Caroline Leadbetter, leaving a space for Lionel to join them. The benches filled up as families arrived together. She and Caroline talked about the storm as they waited for Lionel to say grace and the meal to begin. For the first time Jessie heard the details of the rescue on the beach, and Andrew's part in saving the life of a young man in the surf. Both women noticed when Nelly Kitchin came in with her children. No sign of their father.

'Poor Nelly,' Jessie whispered to her friend. 'She must feel the loss at times like this. Last year Alice was here with us, looking so fresh and alive.'

'I've always wondered about that,' said Caroline, leaning in close to Jessie to hide their conversation. 'The police and the coroner seemed to accept that she'd just slipped and fallen, but I wonder. She was a strong girl, impetuous. Maybe that was the problem, taking a risk, not being careful. Just like her. It can be treacherous down near the bridge, and it was very dark that night, but I still can't bear to think of her calling for help or struggling to get out.'

She stopped, and the two women moved their heads away from each other. Two things caught Jessie's attention. At one end of the hall, Lionel Leadbetter's chair scraped noisily as he stood to say grace. At the other, Andrew pushed open the door and stood just inside it, waiting until grace had been spoken before finding a place to sit.

When they raised their heads again, Caroline spotted her son. 'Well, look who's here. First harvest supper in years. Late of course. Over here, dear,' she cried above the noise and movement as the first plates began to be handed round. 'Move up closer to me, Jessie. Lionel's gone to sit with the Pilkingtons, so Andrew can sit on your other side.'

'Good evening, mother,' said Andrew with mock deference as he took off his jacket and sat down next to Jessie. 'And good evening to you too, Miss Whelan. Twice in one week, we'll have to stop meeting like this.'

'Good evening, Andrew,' she responded. He was too close for her to turn and look at him. He reached for the bread and looked at Jessie as he did so. 'Whatever you've done with your hair,' he said quietly, 'it looks grand.'

'Why, thank you,' she said, involuntarily running her hand over the soft waves that now framed her face. She was relieved that the flush she could feel on her neck would probably be hidden. Mercifully, Caroline engaged her attention and she could face away from Andrew for a while. Even so, she was aware of him. Only half listening to Caroline's account of a WI meeting in Broughton, she told herself yet again that young men like Andrew didn't notice women like herself. He was being polite, that was all. He was talking to a man on his other side now. Good.

Large platefuls of shepherd's pie were consumed, and plates gradually cleared away. The vicar rose to his feet again. 'And now everyone, my favourite part of the harvest supper. I'm told the desserts are all ready, so –'

Whatever he'd planned to say next was lost in the immediate noise as benches were pushed back from the tables and a general stampede began. The children were the most agile and reached the loaded tables first, closely followed by the young men, many of whom had been working in the fields only an hour or so before and had been looking forward to this for days, if not weeks. There was some boisterous jostling as lines formed and snaked around the hall. Jessie and Caroline stayed where they were. It was the same every year, and there was always plenty for everyone. They both knew that some of the cakes and pies were hidden away in the back room, waiting until there was space for them. Andrew had lined up, loaded his plate with cake and trifle and sat down again before his companions stirred. They smiled at his eagerness. 'Just a boy,' said his mother to Jessie.

When Jessie had finished a portion of exquisite pear tart and cream, she turned to Andrew, now well into his second helping. 'Your mother's being been telling more about what happened at the shipwreck. You didn't tell me you saved that boy from drowning.'

Andrew shrugged, not looking up. 'He was alright. These things happen.'

'But what did happen?' Jessie wanted the details.

'Well,' he said, putting down his spoon and turning towards her. 'We were pulling people out of one of the ship's boats that had overturned and this lad got water in his waders and got stuck in the waves. He'd put his jacket on over the top of the waders and I had to cut them off. Always carry a sharp knife, so it didn't take a minute.' He smiled, holding her for an instant with pale blue eyes.

An arm stretched between them to pick up empty plates. Jessie looked down at her hands, unsure what to do or say. Her uncertainty was masked as someone banged on the table at the other end of the room. It was Alan Lancaster, the blacksmith, calling for order.

'Well, everyone,' he roared, and the hubbub of voices tailed away under the onslaught. 'I'm sure you'd all like me to thank the ladies for another grand supper.'

Cheers and banging on tables. Caroline and Jessie clapped

74

politely as women's faces appeared at the kitchen door, and hands were wiped on aprons.

'And now for some entertainment!' Mr Lancaster's voice boomed round the room. More cheers, and the sound of scraping wood as people began to move tables and chairs back towards the walls of the narrow hall.

'I 'appen to know,' the voice continued, 'there's someone 'ere tonight that's got a story to tell us. A very sad story, I understand.' Mr Lancaster lowered his voice for this pronouncement, while people nudged each other and looked around for the storyteller.

Caroline whispered in Jessie's ear. 'Thought this might happen. I'll have to take Lionel away. You know how he gets when other people are performing. You stay though, dear – keep Andrew company. He could do with a night out that's not in some pub or other.' She squeezed Jessie's arm, signalled to Lionel who was heading towards the kitchen door, and moved as quickly towards him as the rearrangement of furniture would allow.

Andrew came around the table to sit beside Jessie with his back to the wall.

'Your father had to leave apparently,' she said. 'You go too, if you want. I probably won't be long myself, although it's hard to get away sometimes when things start to warm up.'

'The old man can't bear not being the centre of attention,' said Andrew quietly. 'Doesn't really approve of storytelling. Some-times it gets a bit close to the bone, you know. I'll walk you home now if you want to go.'

'Not far to walk,' she said, smiling. 'Must be all of ten yards to my front door. But I'll stay a while. I love these stories and there might be some music, too. I think Vince Glaister has his fiddle with him, and it's always a treat to hear him play.'

Andrew smiled. 'Aye, he makes a grand noise on that fiddle. I'll stay a while, if you are.'

The storyteller's tale was long and ludicrous, and the crowd punctuated its various chapters with comments and contributions, and cheers when the long-drawn-out conclusion was finally reached. Jessie laughed with the rest, aware of Andrew's presence beside her without looking at him.

'And now, we've got another treat,' said Mr Lancaster. 'Vince has got 'is fiddle.'

'I 'ave that,' said the fiddle player, taking the instrument out of its battered case. 'And I know what I want to play, but I need some 'elp wi' it. I were playing a tune t'other night and someone joined in singing. He'd 'ad one too many mebbe, but that lad can sing, and he's 'ere tonight and this time he's sober, so it'll be even better.'

Some clapped, some cheered, others looked round the room to find the singer. Jessie noticed the faces turned in her direction.

'Come on, Andy, lad,' said Mr Lancaster. 'We all know who Vince's talking about. You must've learned some good songs when you were away, so give us one.'

By this time everyone had turned to look. Jessie lowered her head to hide her face.

'Vince, you old bugger,' Andrew called across to the fiddle player who stood beaming with the fiddle under his chin. 'You got me again! Danny Boy, alright?'

He leaned down. 'Wait here,' he said to Jessie. 'Won't be long.'

Andrew pushed back his chair, touched her arm fleetingly as he got to his feet, and stepped over the bench to make his way across towards Vince, who was checking and tuning the fiddle. They stood side by side: Andrew was a foot taller than his older companion. Vince played the first few notes of the familiar tune and Andrew's voice followed, soft and clear, filling the hushed space. Jessie listened too, surprised and moved. She couldn't take her eyes off him, even when for a long moment he looked directly at her. Before the song was finished she felt a tear on her cheek and wiped it away.

After the final notes died there was a tense silence: then the hall erupted, boots stamping on the wooden floor and hands slapping the wooden tables. Andrew bowed ironically to the corners of the hall, resisted the calls for 'more, more', shook Vince's hand and pushed back to his seat next to Jessie, his face shining. She turned to him.

'Thank you,' she said, patting him on the shoulder. 'That was wonderful. I had no idea ...'

'Mam always says this village loves to sing,' he said. ' Must've caught it meself, here and at school, even before I went up north. Men sing there when they're drunk. Not that I was ever drunk, of course.'

'Of course not,' said Jessie. 'The very idea.'

The evening was drawing to a close. 'G' neet everybody,' cried Mr Lancaster, and people began to gather their things. Andrew was the star of the show for a while, as some thanked him, slapped him on the back. Jessie stood aside, waiting.

'And now for the long walk to the schoolhouse,' said Andrew, taking her arm. 'Allow me to escort you, Miss Whelan.'

Jessie did let him escort her round the corner to her dark house. 'Thank you again,' she said, looking up at his head silhouetted against the sky and the stars. She held out her hand, and he took it, put it to his lips, then turned and walked away. Jessie watched his tall shape move down the lane before she went in to the house. She shut the door behind her and leaned against it.

CHAPTER 11

AFTER A BREAK in the weather, just long enough for the remaining fields to be harvested, the autumn gales returned with a vengeance as October moved towards November. High wind always excited and disturbed the children, and they kept Jessie and Mr Crompton fully stretched. Rain and wind often made some of the children late for school, or not arrive at all if they had no shoes fit for the weather. This time of the year caused absences for a different reason too. November was pig-killing month in the village and as the butcher did his rounds from farm to farm children stayed at home to watch and to help. Young Percy Hewer told her how he had to stir a bucket full of pig's blood while he was eating his supper, and Jessie had never been able to get the image out of her mind.

One afternoon, under the general heading of 'Nature Study' Jessie and her class were talking about the wind. They remembered the day of the shipwreck, and the strength of a wind that could drive a big ship onto the beach. Jessie had her opportunity to teach them how such winds happen. First she wanted to hear what they already knew and thought.

'Where do you think the wind comes from?' she asked, as the children sat in front of her. They usually worked in two rooms, one on each side of the narrow hallway, but she'd brought all the pupils together to talk. The room was crowded, but there was enough space for each child to sit reasonably comfortably, and she loved encouraging them all to speak and to listen to each other. Suggestions about the wind came thick and fast: 'My Dad says it's from God whistling, miss,' offered Paul, who was small for his age, and sometimes arrived at school bruised and tearful on Mondays, making Jessie wonder what happened over the weekend.

'It's the trees, miss,' said another child. 'When the branches blow around, that makes a wind.'

'And what makes the branches blow around, Susan?' Jessie asked.

Gradually, patiently, asking questions that guided them rather them left them floundering, Jessie teased an explanation out of the children that they would remember as their conclusions rather than hers.

The slamming of a car door, followed by a rush of air as the front door opened, gave Jessie a few moments' notice of an impending visitor.

'It's the vicar, miss,' said Nora who was closest to the window. 'I can see 'is big car.' Jessie braced herself. Two long strides in the hall brought her visitor into the room. The children struggled to their feet.

'Good afternoon, everyone,' cried Lionel Leadbetter, his voice bouncing off the walls of the small classroom. 'My, we're crowded in here today Miss Whelan, are we not? Is there a problem in the other room?'

'No, no, vicar,' said Jessie, gesturing the children to sit down again and smiling at her employer, despite her annoyance at his habit of just bursting in. 'We've been talking about the wind, and I asked Mr Crompton to bring his class in here so that we could discuss it all together.'

'Ah, Crompton,' said the vicar, spotting the young man standing in the corner behind him. 'There you are. Everything alright with you? No problems at home?'

Alan Crompton looked alarmed and slightly pink.

'The storm and so forth,' added the vicar. 'No damage, slates off, that kind of thing?'

'Oh no, vicar, thank you for asking. Our cottage faces north and we missed the worst of it.'

'Splendid,' said Lionel, turning his attention back to Jessie. 'You're busy now, Miss Whelan, but I would like to talk to you on a matter of some urgency. Maybe next Wednesday?'

'I'll be here,' she said. 'Will it take long, do you think?'

'Do you have to be somewhere else?' he said, as if she had refused to meet with him altogether. She said nothing. 'I'm asking Andrew to come, too,' said Lionel. 'We may need his expertise.'

Jessie was curious now but determined not to appear so. 'I'll be here,' she said again, trying not to provoke any more discussion in front of the children who were listening to this exchange like spectators at a tennis match, turning their heads from one speaker to another. Jessie was reminded of the hens in the yard of her previous school, who flapped up to sit on the window sill of her room, following the sound, turning their heads in the same way from one side to another as she raised her voice slightly to reprimand a child. She smiled at the memory as she picked her way between the children to usher the vicar back to the front door. He managed to pat a few heads on his way out. Jessie held the door and watched as he climbed into the gleaming blue Armstrong Siddeley parked confidently in the middle of the road outside. He waved as the car purred into life and swept away up the hill. Jessie closed the door and returned to her crowded classroom. 'He means well,' she told herself, not for the first time.

Later in the day, as the children played in the field behind the schoolhouse, Jessie sat on the bench watching them and wondered about the meeting. She thought she was quite well attuned to local affairs, but she really had no idea what Lionel might want to talk about. Agnes didn't miss much and would surely have told her if anything was brewing. They'd seen something in the *Whitehaven News* about women teachers threatened with the sack: some school boards were unhappy about employing women teachers when there were so many men out of work. Surely someone would have hinted if she were going to be faced with that. The teachers' union had won re-instatement for two women further up the coast. Maybe she should join the union. If it wasn't that, what else could it be? There'd been no complaints about her work, as far as she knew. The school was running well; although she had some doubts about Alan Crompton and the behaviour of some of his pupils, it was nothing that would cause the vicar any concern. And he was going to bring Andrew with him, which was even more of a mystery.

In the few days since the harvest supper Jessie had managed to convince herself that Andrew thought of her only as his mother's friend, and his father's employee, an older woman with whom he could flirt in the most chivalrous of ways, meaning nothing. She liked him. She found him attractive, handsome even. His singing had charmed her. That was all, she was sure now. But still she anticipated their next meeting with a kind of trepidation she hadn't felt for twenty years. Maybe it was 'the change', she said to herself. Hormones all over the place, like an adolescent girl. Silly.

The following Wednesday, the day appointed for Lionel's meeting, Jessie and Alan made themselves a cup of tea after the children had gone home, and waited for their visitors. Alan didn't want to be there, but Jessie had persuaded him to stay. She felt she might need someone on her side. Just after four, the front door of the schoolhouse opened again, and Lionel and Andrew Leadbetter made the small classroom look even smaller. Alan had brought in some full-sized chairs from the village hall, but even so the four of them struggled to find space round Jessie's desk in the corner of her classroom. In the end they gave up, moved the children's chairs to one side and sat awkwardly facing each other.

Andrew sat next to Jessie, unable to see her properly unless he turned around. 'You know Miss Whelan I'm sure, Andrew,' Lionel had said as they sat down.

'Of course,' said Andrew, 'How are you, Miss Whelan?'

'I'm well, thank you, Mr Leadbetter,' she replied, thankful that he understood the protocols of formal address while she was at work. She felt nervous. She wanted to believe she was nervous about Lionel and the meeting, but she knew this wasn't true. It was Andrew. He was the problem. She could not look at him.

Lionel sat up in his chair as though bringing the meeting to order, leaned forward and spoke in an uncharacteristically quiet tone. 'Now I haven't mentioned this yet to anyone else,' he said, looking around him as he spoke as if expecting eavesdroppers, 'so we must keep this between ourselves.' He paused for dramatic effect. 'I want to build a new school. This one is far too small and the village deserves something better. I've been thinking about it a long time, and seeing you all crowded in here last week convinced me that we have to do this.' He sat back and crossed one leg over the other, as if the matter was already a certainty.

Andrew looked aghast at his father. 'A new school? I thought you wanted me here to talk about some of the repairs. How could we build a new school? Where'd the money come from?'

'Ah,' said his father, leaning forward again. 'That's where you come in, Andrew. Now you're in charge at the quarry we can get all the stone we need, and there are plenty of people in this village with the skills to do the job. Think how they built the cathedrals in times past. Good men with the right skills and fierce commitment. That's what we need. Who wouldn't be proud to have our

82

children properly housed in a school built for the purpose, not crowded together, falling over each other?'

Jessie looked down, feeling Andrew's growing annoyance.

'I can't just give you the stone,' said Andrew finally. 'The quarry is a business, not a charity. We work hard for that stone, to sell it, not give it away. The church would need to buy it at a proper rate.'

'Don't you worry about that,' said his father, with a wave of his hand, batting away Andrew's objections like a troublesome fly. 'We know who owns the quarry, and we're all in this together. If Skeffington gives his word, which he will, the deal is done. All we have to do then is decide how big the school should be, how much stone we need, and when to start.'

A brief silence fell. Jessie glanced at Andrew and saw him bite his lip. She stirred in her seat, searching for something to say, to lower the tension if she could.

'Of course we would all be happy to have a new school for our children. They deserve the best we can offer them. But I have to share Mr Leadbetter's concern about the practicalities. Parents of our pupils would be willing to help, I'm sure, but there are many people in Newton who don't have children at the school, and who might not want to be involved.'

'Come now, Miss Whelan,' said Lionel, 'this is about a Christian community, not about who will benefit directly. This will be a school for our grandchildren, for the children who are the future of this village, whoever their parents happen to be. I would expect you to understand that, you of all people.'

Jessie did not respond. She heard Andrew draw a breath between his teeth and wondered how long it would be before his anger with his father boiled over. She wanted to touch him, to calm him, but she did not dare. She dropped her head for an instant, and then raised it again to speak, with the same deliberation as before.

'I hope I understand something about our neighbours and friends, Mr Leadbetter, although not as much as you, of course. There is no urgency, it seems to me. We can manage very well for now in this building, and there is time to make a detailed plan, and then talk to the board and the parish council about the proposal.' She hesitated for a moment before deciding to say more. 'I'm sure no one in Newton would like to think that they'd been pushed into something before they've had enough time to consider it.'

Lionel Leadbetter leaned forward again, and his voice was louder now. 'And I'm sure you're not implying that I could push anyone around, in this village or anywhere else. I've worked for this community for twenty years, long and hard. Who got running water piped into this very building? Who will get electricity into this village? I know what's needed, Miss Whelan, and we need a bigger school. I've got a few years left before I can rest, but I'm not finished yet.'

The old man leaned back again as if the last word had been spoken, but Andrew would not be intimidated.

'Just a minute,' he said, in a tone more measured than Jessie had feared. 'Miss Whelan has to think of the children, the children who are in school now, as well as those in the future. No one doubts your ability to get things done, but you've just sprung this idea on us and we have to think about it.'

'We?' shouted his father, pushing his chair further back. 'Who are "we" may I ask? I've brought you here to sort out the details, not to gang up against me.'

Jessie raised her hand, aware that Andrew was getting up from his chair in anger. 'Of course, no one is ganging up, vicar. We all appreciate your wonderful work in the village. It's just such a big idea – to build a new school – and all of us are trying to consider the details, that's why we're hesitating.'

Lionel looked hard at her, then at Andrew who had now

turned towards Jessie, and then at Alan Crompton, who lowered his eyes under the force of the stare. He pushed back his chair and rose to his feet. 'Very well,' he said quietly. 'You will have to "consider", while the rest of us do something more productive. I have arranged to go up to the Hall this evening to see Skeffington. I had hoped that you would come with me, to support my plan and help with the first decisions, but I can see that you are not ready for that yet. I shall go alone. In the meantime, I think it would be wise for both of you to remember who pays your wages.' He stepped back, moved the chair to give himself space and left the room, leaving door open behind him.

For a moment the only sound in the room was the tiny puff of Alan's breath, breath he'd been holding during the last exchanges. 'Well,' he said brightly. 'That was interesting, wasn't it? I'm already late, so I'm off, if that's alright. Jessie?'

'Yes, of course Alan, you go. We'll talk more tomorrow. Good night.'

Jessie and Andrew remained sitting where they had been, saying nothing more. Jessie began to look around her, thinking about the things she needed to take home with her, but Andrew remained in the same position, and she did not get up. The room seemed oppressively quiet. After a few moments, and still not looking at her, Andrew leaned back on the wooden chair and rubbed his large hands down his face. Then he put his hands back on his knees and sat still with his eyes closed. Jessie didn't know what to say to him. She got up, put her hand on his shoulder and squeezed. She could feel the bones and muscle under the rough tweed of his jacket. Andrew said nothing, and his eyes remained closed. Jessie turned away, towards her desk in the corner of the room.

'Well, we may have to brace ourselves, Andrew,' she said, taking a big canvas bag from her desk. 'Once your father gets hold of an idea, things tend to happen.'

Andrew coughed and struggled to his feet, catching the back of his leg on the chair as he did so. 'Sorry,' he mumbled, bending to pick up the chair.

'Oh, don't worry about the chairs,' said Jessie. 'We have to use the village hall chairs for visitors, and they're on their last legs ...' She laughed at her own pun. Andrew stood with his hand on the door handle, watching her as she placed some books into her bag. 'I'll be off, then,' he said. Jessie noticed that he seemed upset.

'All we can do for now is wait and see,' she said, following him out of the room into the narrow hallway which led to the front door. 'If your father gets the go-ahead from Sir John, we'll both have to jump to it.' She looked up at him as she opened the door. 'Don't worry about it. We'll work something out. We can always have a chat at my house if we need to work out a plan of action.'

He said nothing more, looking at her as he stepped out into the lane. Jessie closed the door behind him. Each of them stood for a moment, the door between them, before they turned away. Jessie didn't see the young man feel his shoulder. Nor did she know how she occupied his thoughts that night.

On Friday evening, two days after the meeting with the vicar, Jessie heard a knock on the back door of the schoolhouse. She opened it and saw Andrew standing there.

'I've come for the chat you suggested the other day,' he said, a line he had rehearsed before leaving home. Confusion swept over her. She stepped back to let him in, anxious to shut the door before the rain blew into the house, and before anyone saw him.

'Have a seat,' she said, pulling a chair from the table for him to sit down. 'Looks pretty bad out there.' Andrew watched as she filled the kettle and set it on the range. Jessie began to chat brightly about what she guessed he was there to talk about, the school, the space they needed, the reactions of the parents. His continued silence disconcerted her. Did he know what she'd been thinking? Was it too obvious that she liked him? She couldn't tell him, or even hint at it. What if he laughed at her, or was repulsed? She turned away from him.

'I need to talk to you, Jessie,' he said. She picked up something different in his tone, but she was unaware of the expression on his face.

'Shall I get the notes I've been making?' She hesitated now, seeing him looking at her.

'No, no,' he said. 'Nothing like that.'

She put the pot and cups on the table and retreated into the pantry to find some biscuits and give herself time to think. There was a slight sound behind her, and she felt his hands on her shoulders. She didn't move.

'Jessie,' he said her name, so softly, and she turned towards him. He was very close to her, his face in darkness.

'Andrew ... but, no –' she said, stepping back, away from him.

He looked down, but stayed where he was, very close to her.

'You must know,' he said.

'Know what?'

'How I feel about you.'

'How ... no, I don't know.' She was struggling to deal with the closeness.

'I thought it must be obvious.'

'I like you Andrew, and I thought, I think, you like me ...'

He smiled at her. 'It's more than that.'

'But I'm old, old enough –'

'You're not old, you're beautiful.'

'Oh no,' she said, looking down, confused, wordless. She could hear her heart.

'You're beautiful,' he said again, taking a step towards her.

She did not move away, and looked up into his face.

'You've noticed me too,' he said, 'I know you have. You touched me, the other day. You squeezed my shoulder. I knew then.'

'Knew what?'

'That you want me, too. I want you, badly.'

'Stop, stop!' She needed time to think. She had squeezed his shoulder, because she felt sorry for him, wanted to reassure him – or was he right? He was so much younger. She looked down. 'I don't know what to say.'

'Don't say anything. Just let me hold you.'

'No, I can't.'

'Why not?'

She said nothing.

Andrew was relentless. 'What's wrong with us being together? We're both single, we like each other. It's a small village and people talk, but we know how to be careful.'

'I don't know. You'll have to give me time to think. I can't..'

He stretched out his hands to her, to take her shoulders and pull her to him, but she stepped away from him again.

He sighed.

'Alright,' he said. 'You know how I feel. Take your time. I could make you happy Jessie, I know it.'

'But I'm too old …'

'No,' he raised his voice a little. 'You're not too old. I've known the young ones, they're silly and shallow and I don't want them. I want a real woman, Jess, like you. Warm and clever and funny like you. I can wait, for a while. But don't make me wait too long. I can't stand it. Drives me crazy every time I see you.'

'I didn't know.'

'Well, now you do. When shall I come back? How long do you want, to think?'

Jessie's mind raced. 'A week,' she said. 'Give me a week. I'll send you a note or something. Don't just come round.'

'Alright,' he said, stepping back in to the kitchen. ' I'll wait. You contact me. You know where?'

'Yes, I know. Your mother –' she stopped, remembering that this man's mother was her friend. 'Caroline told me.'

'Be kind to me, Jess,' he said, stretching his hand to stroke her face. 'I know how I feel.'

She walked towards the back door and hesitated before opening it.

'No one saw me,' he anticipated her question. 'It's sluicing down. No one's about.'

She opened the door and looked down the empty lane. The night was black and wet.

He passed her, stood on the doorstep, turned up the collar of his coat, took his cap out of his pocket and pulled it well down on his head.

'I'll wait,' he said again, and was gone, through the rain.

Jessie shut the door and leaned against it, her hands behind her. She could hear the rain and the thud of her heart. He was right. She did want him, with an urgency that she'd thought was dead and done. What to do? It was dangerous, too dangerous, surely. The gossip, her job, Caroline. Her mind raced on. Maybe it was time to leave Newton. Maybe this was the chance she needed, to start again, with someone who loved her. But did he love her? How could he, but he said he did. But no, he didn't say that. He said he wanted her, that was different. But so exciting. To be wanted, in that way, by a beautiful young man, strong, passionate. She hung her head. What to do? Nothing. Do nothing for a day or two, put it out of mind and see what happens. No decision. Not yet.

A few days passed. Jessie made her decision. She wrote a few words on a piece of paper, sealed it into an envelope and sent it to him at the quarry.

'*Come on Friday, late,*' she had written. '*On foot. Make sure no one sees you.*'

The days passed so slowly.

On Friday, after dark, Jessie left the back door of the school-house open. When Andrew arrived, she did not hesitate. The chase was over. She gave herself to him with an abandon that surprised them both.

CHAPTER 12

A FEW DAYS OF STAYING in Andrew's cold house at the quarry were enough for John. The rough blanket on his bed smelled of damp, and when he tried to air it round the fire downstairs it smelled of smoke. All Andrew wanted to talk about was the chaos in the office, and how he expected John to sort it out. John spent a few hours each day that week in the office, making a start on the paperwork, but dealing with Andrew's bad temper there as well as in the house made him all the more certain that he needed a different place to stay, and soon.

On Saturday morning, he set off early to look for somewhere else to stay. One of the men at the quarry had suggested Hill House, further up the valley, and he headed in that direction as soon as the early morning rain had cleared. Hill House was one of the tallest houses for miles around: John could see the roof-line for quite a way before he came close to it. The three-storey house faced south, a tall, symmetrical building with a Georgian

91

look about it. John approached the front door, but then decided to go round the back where his muddy boots might be more acceptable. The back door stood slightly open, and he knocked on it, peeping into the big kitchen beyond. No one was there, but the door at the far end was open and he could hear the sound of voices faintly elsewhere in the house. He knocked again. 'Wait a minute,' called someone, and in a moment the far door opened further, and a young woman came through into the kitchen. She wore an apron, and the drab clothes beneath it were outshone by the mass of red hair piled ineffectually on her head.

'Well?' she said, and John took a step back as she pulled the door open. He was on the bottom step, but his eyes were still level with hers. He knew what he wanted to say, but the words dried in his mouth. 'I, er,' he managed, but then stopped again, furious with himself. Why did this always happen? Just for once, he longed to speak like a normal person, easily, with the words forming in his head and then coming out of his mouth. The young woman folded her arms across her chest and waited. He tried again. 'I'm looking for a room,' he said, too quickly, but at least he managed to finish the sentence.

'What kind of a room?' she asked, unhelpfully.

'For … myself. To live in.'

'Oh, aye,' she said, waiting for him to say more.

John steeled himself, checking the words he wanted. 'I work at the quarry, er, accounts, and I've just started …' He ran out of words, although the planned sentence was not complete.

'Oh, you want a room,'

'Yes,' he said, as she turned away from the door.

'Mam,' she called, in a remarkably loud voice. 'There's a man 'ere looking for a room.' Half closing the back door, and leaving John on the doorstep, she disappeared.

John didn't know what to do. Should he go in? If he did,

should he take off his boots? As he struggled with the choice, the door opened again, to reveal another woman, older and shorter, looking up at him this time. John was determined to give a better impression. He held out his hand.

'Good afternoon. My name's John Pharaoh. I've just started work at the quarry – in the accounts office,' he added, aware of the status and respectability that this information might induce.

'I'm gae glad for you, Mr Pharaoh,' said the woman without smiling, 'but we dinnut 'ave any rooms. We've family living with us, and the two spare rooms we 'ad are both taken.'

John's disappointment must have been obvious in his face.

'It's lang way from t'quarry,' she said. 'Couldn't you find summat closer? Mrs Robinson in Newton has a room spare, or at least that's the crack.'

'I'd like to be at this end of the valley,' said John, looking down at his feet. 'I like to climb.'

'Climb what?'

'The rocks, you know,' said John, waving vaguely towards the high fells behind him.

'Oh, you're a climber. I thought you said you worked at quarry.'

'I do, but I climb in my spare time.'

'Spare time,' snorted the woman. 'Dinnut get much o' that.'

'Is there anyone else in Boot who might have a room, do you think?'

'Nay, lad,' she started to say, and then hesitated. 'What about Hannah?'

'Who?'

'Hannah Tyson, as was,' said the woman. 'Lives up at mill. She might have space. Only 'er and her man up there. It's worth a try, now you've come up this way.'

From behind the open door John heard a loud laugh, quickly stifled.

'Oh, Mam,' said the unseen person, whom he guessed was the red-headed girl. 'Tha's wicked. Tell 'im to knock real loud before 'e goes in.'

At this the older woman herself laughed out loud, turning away from John and shutting the door as she did so.

Outside, staring at the door that was now just inches from his face, John heard the two women still shrieking with laughter and turned away angrily. Women. Was it him they were laughing at? What was so funny about this Hannah person? Why are women so difficult? Why can't they just talk straight? He'd be better off with Andrew. At least Andrew didn't laugh at him. He turned back towards the lane and leaned against the wall, trying to decide what to do. He'd worked it out, and this was where he wanted to be, near the fells. Andrew didn't want him there, he was sure about that, and the house was so dismal, he couldn't bear to stay there anyway. Every time he looked at those pale eyes he remembered the day in the storm.

Having his own place would be more expensive, but he wasn't much bothered about that. He had a good job, and he had money in the bank from the sale of the Ulverston house. He could afford a place, if he could find one. Hill House would have been fine, but that was out, and anyway did he want to live with women who laughed at him? He remembered the young woman's red hair and kicked a stone that scuttered down the path and bounced off the wall on the other side. He headed up the lane towards the bridge.

At the top of the bridge he looked up and saw the cottage door open and a woman step out carrying something draped over her arm. She hung it on a fence on top of the steep bank that dropped down to the stream below. He squinted into the low sun to see her face more clearly, and she squinted back. One eye was almost completely shut, and the other wide open. The lopsided face creased quickly into a smile.

94

'Now then, young fella,' said the woman. 'What's ta do?'

'Are you Hannah?' John asked. The woman was standing watching him, hands on her hips.

'I am that, and who are you?'

'John, John Pharaoh. I'm looking for a place to live, digs like, and I went to Hill House,' John turned and pointed back down the lane, 'and they said –'.

'Oh I can imagine what they said,' she laughed. 'Summat aboot knocking, was it?'

'Yes,' said John. 'How did you know?'

'Lang story, lad. Are you coming in or shall us stand out 'ere? Better still, you can beat that rug for me if you like.' Hannah pointed to the rug hanging over the fence.

John hesitated. Was she serious?

'Away, lad,' said Hannah. 'Just my fun, tek no mind. Are you coming in then?'

John looked down at his muddy boots, then bent down to take them off before stepping into the house.

'Aye, that's grand. Just blacked range and mopped floor, and it'll be mucky again fast enough without your mucky boots all over it too.'

John was relieved that at least he'd done that right.

'Cup o' tea?' she said. 'Our Fred'll be back soon, and he'll want tea, so we might as well.'

'Thanks. It's colder than it looks today. Wind's come around I reckon, more east than south now.'

Hannah filled a large kettle from a tap by the door and placed it on the range.

'It'll be a while,' she said. 'Sit thi'sen down. How far have you come?'

'Just from the quarry. I've been stopping there with Andy Leadbetter for a few days,' John said, uncertain how much to tell her.

'But you're looking for a place?' Hannah said. 'What's wrong with stopping doon there? They say Andy can be a bit, you know, moody like. Is that it?'

John was caught by this. 'Nay,' he said quickly. 'Andy's fine, it's just that, like, I need somewhere more settled, more permanent. Got a job at the quarry, you see ...'

'A job, 'ave you?' Hannah looked at him hard with her one good eye. 'And what's that, lad? You dinnat look like a quarryman.'

'No, no,' John said quickly. 'Not in the quarry itself. In the office, the books, all that side of things.'

'So, a clever bugger,' said Hannah smiling. 'Well, good for you, lad. Me and Fred never 'ad much schooling, but we're pretty clever too, I reckon. Tha'll stop for supper? Fred'll want a chat, Don't see many folk, and we like to 'ear all aboot 'em, where they're from, all that, tha knows.'

Hannah got up to rinse out the big teapot. As she opened the back door, light seeped into the dark room and John noticed splashes of colour on the slate floor. The dark flagstones were covered in rugs, square and oblong, each with a different colour, and in bold designs. Greens and reds, golds and browns, circles and flowing lines as well as more geometric shapes.

'These are grand,' he said. 'Did you make them?'

'Oh, the rugs. Nay, that's Fred. The Rug Man they used to call 'im, when 'e stopped at Broughton. Been making rugs for years, since he was a lad home from t'war. He'll be home soon. You can ask 'im.'

'It's the colours,' said John. 'I've seen hookie rugs before, but not like this.'

'Folk seem to like 'em,' said Hannah. 'They show 'im a picture, or tell 'im certain colours, and 'e meks one for them. Have to wait a while sometimes, but no one seems to mind.'

'I'm not surprised,' said John. 'They're so beautiful.'

' 'Appen we all have a talent for summat,' said Hannah as she filled the teapot and set it to mash on the range. 'What're you good at?'

John hesitated.

'What am I good at? No one's ever asked me that before.'

'You must be good at numbers, like, to get a job like yours.'

'I suppose so. I wouldn't call that talent, though, that's just a job.'

'So what you do when you're not working?' asked Hannah, leaning against the range, her arms folded.

He hesitated, wondering again how much to tell this woman he'd only just met. 'Well,' he started, 'I do climbing, you know rock climbing, not much good, but ... and I love trains, too, so when I saw the job, you know, at the quarry ...' He waited for a reaction, but there was nothing. None of this seemed to be making sense

Hannah looked at him closely.

'Not from round 'ere then?'

'No, from Ulverston,' he replied. 'Only came up here last week. Got caught in the storm on my way up on the train.'

'Aye, that storm was a bad 'un,' she said. 'Came whistling up this valley straight off the sea. We 'ad a few slates off, but I fixed 'em. That much rain came down the beck, flooded right over t'channel down t'big wheel. Thought for a while it would wash th' whole thing out. It floods fast, that beck.'

Hannah picked up a large tin from the shelf and prised off the lid.

'This is what I'm good at,' she said, 'though I says it meself. I can bake a reet grand cake. Want a bit?'

John didn't bother answering as she cut a large slice of the dark brown cake and handed it over. 'Table's clean,' she said. 'Scrubbed this morning.'

She walked over to look out of the front door, towards the bridge.

'Tea'll keep a minute,' she said. 'I 'ope you like it strong. Think I can 'ear Fred coming.'

John stopped eating for a moment to listen. Sure enough he could hear a faint tapping.

'That's 'is stick,' said Hannah. 'Needs it on account of 'is one leg. Fred lost a leg in t'war in France. Came back without it.'

'Oh,' said John, as the tapping got steadily louder. 'I'm sorry.'

She laughed. 'Oh dinna fret,' she said. 'It were a long time ago. And anyway, that's what brought us together, 'im and me. And we're 'appy enough. Keeps neighbours amused, any road, the one-eyed woman and the one-legged man.'

'Oh,' said John again, struggling to keep up with the information. 'Is that why those women, at Hill House, were laughing?'

'Laughing, were they?' Hannah looked at John. 'Well I'll guess why that was. We 'ad a man come 'ere once, selling summat. And he came to t'door and found me and Fred, you know, on t'floor like. Well we 'adn't been wed long, and ye know how it is.'

'No,' murmured John.

'Well, there we were,' said Hannah. 'And 'e ran away to t'King Billy and told everyone all about it and they've been laughing ever since. So now you know. And 'ere's the man 'imself,' she said triumphantly as the tapping approached the door and stopped, 'My Fred.'

John saw the outline of the man silhouetted against the light in the door frame, the right leg missing below the knee. The stick in the man's hand moved forward confidently and the man hopped on the good leg onto the flags, stepping carefully over one of the rugs that John had admired. Hannah walked round, took his arm and kissed him on the mouth.

'John, this 'ere's Fred Porter, the man o' the 'ouse.'

She helped the one-legged man onto a chair, and the stick was parked alongside while Fred's eyes adjusted to the darkness and he spied John sitting on the other side of the table.

'John who?' said Fred, extending his hand to shake John's.

'Pharaoh,' said John. 'John Pharaoh.'

'One of Whitehaven Pharaohs?' asked Fred, unwinding a scarf from round his neck.

'No, we came from Ulverston, or Barrow, that way, south,' said John, pointing again in what he thought was the direction. 'My dad, well, he came from Barrow, but we lived in Ulverston.'

Hannah brought Fred a mug of tea and another huge slab of cake.

'Look at that,' said Fred to John. 'Naybody bakes a cake like my Hannah. Champion.'

His wife leaned over and kissed him again. John looked away.

Fred smiled. 'Well, John Pharaoh,' he said. 'From Ulverston or Barrow or wherever it is, what's tha doing in my 'ouse drinking tea with my missus?'

Hannah laughed. 'Don't tease th' lad, Fred – 'e's looking for a room. Went to Hill House, and they sent 'im 'ere.'

'Bet they 'ad a good laugh about that an 'all,' said Fred, winking at John.

John stared at them both. He thought he might be blushing and hoped that they couldn't see it.

'Yes,' he said, determined not to get drawn into this private joke between them. 'They said you might have a room you could let me have, for rent of course. I can pay.'

'Long way from t'quarry, lad,' said Hannah. 'He works there, in t'office,' she said to Fred as she sat down at the table with them.

'Aye,' said John, 'but I wanted to be up this end of the valley, closer to the big hills. Just a few miles over the top and I'm in Wasdale.'

'Good pub there reet enough,' said Fred.

'Not for the pub,' said John, 'for the climbing. All the climbers go there. I'm a climber, in my spare – when I'm not working.'

'There's another thing tha's good at then, lad,' said Hannah. 'Numbers and such, and climbing.' She turned to Fred. 'We were talking afore, about what we're good at. Reet talented is John, and 'e tried to tell me 'e isn't good at owt.' She turned back to John, moving her shoulders to use her good eye.

Hannah continued, 'And tha were staying with Andy Leadbetter, t'vicar's lad, at the quarry, tha said.'

'Aye,' said John. 'He offered after, well, after I had a bit of trouble on the way up 'ere.'

'Hang on a minute,' said Fred suddenly. 'This bit o' trouble. Did Andy pull you out of t'sea? When that ship ran aground, last week, in t'storm?'

'Yes, he did,' John was astonished. 'How …?'

Fred leaned over towards Hannah. 'That's what auld Ely were talking aboot, in t'Farriers last neet, and Tom Hanley were there and 'e told me just now. There were someone on t'beach that day, stranger like, and Andy 'ad to pull him out. 'Ad 'is coat over 'is waders. Nearly drowned. That were you, lad. Well, would tha credit it, and 'ere you are, in our 'ouse.'

John hung his head. Everyone knew. He'd always be the stranger that was pulled out of the sea.

'More tea, Hannah,' said Fred. 'We got summat to celebrate. Here's a chap back from a watery grave wanting a room, and here's us in this 'ouse with a room to spare. Couldn't 'ave worked out better.'

Hannah patted her husband's hand and turned to John.

'Gi' us a chance to talk it ower, John. It's all a bit sudden, like. 'Ave a walk up path behind us, that's the quick way to Wasdale, up by tarn.'

John walked up the rocky path behind the cottage, far enough to reassure himself how quickly he could get across to Wasdale. After a while, he retraced his steps to the house, and knocked on the front door. He heard the two of them laughing inside and Hannah was still doing so when she opened the door.

'Come away in, lad, and dinnut bother knocking every time. We learned our lesson, eh Fred? Anyway, we're an old married couple now, most of the time.'

John looked at them both. 'Will it be alright then?' he asked. The previous conversation had made him want to stay, and the walk in the evening light had convinced him. In just a few minutes he'd walked up to the high plateau between Eskdale and Wasdale feeling as happy as he'd been in a long time.

Fred stretched out a hand to grasp his wife's.

'This lass and me share everything in this 'ouse, John, so we 'ad to check that both of us are sure about teking someone in. If you can put up wi' us, tek us as you find us, then we'll be 'appy to offer you t'room upstairs, at a fair rent. If tha wants meals and such you can work that out with gaffer 'ere,' said Fred, jerking a thumb at Hannah. 'And there's one other thing tha might like, too. Shall I tell 'im love, or will you?'

Hannah stirred the pot on the stove before she responded. 'Well there'll be a wait for t'scran, so you can 'ave th' whole story. Get lad some beer Fred, and I'll 'ave one, too.'

Beer to hand, Hannah began the story.

'Well John, it used to be me and me dad 'ere at mill. He ran t'mill and I did everything else. He were a good miller, don't get me wrong, but he were a miserable old bugger at best o' times. Worked too 'ard, and it showed. Any road, he died, sudden like, which were a shock, reet enough, but the good thing was that then me and Fred could get wed. Me dad 'adn't wanted it. Said Fred could never manage at mill, and he were reet. You couldn't, could you, love, not with only one leg.' She turned to John. 'Have you been in t'mill? Well it's all up and down, stairs and trap doors and cogs and God knows what. I 'ad trouble with all those different levels and Fred would have been dead afore dinner, falling down summat. That's reet, love? So Dad tried to stop us. We'd 'ave wed in the end, waited long enough, but him dying, well it brought it on a bit quicker, like. It were Dad who started all that stuff about one-eyed woman and one-legged man. Made a reet meal of it. Grumpy bugger 'e could be.'

'Come on, lass,' said Fred. 'Get to the point or t'scran'll be dry and we all go 'ungry.'

'Right,' Hannah went on, having stirred the pot again and put something else on to boil. 'Well 'e died, and we got mill. Couldn't 'andle it, closed it up. Farmers weren't too pleased, but they just took their stuff bit further down to t'other mill down Birkby and that were that. Then we got to thinking. There's all that water running that gert big wheel, all that energy just going to waste. I found a book in t'library in Whitehaven and Fred asked a few folk and, well, look at this.'

She stepped across to a large lamp standing on the sideboard and turned a switch on its neck. The lamp lit up, brighter than any oil lamp.

'Electric,' said Hannah. 'We run it off that big wheel. First house in t'valley to get electric, and 'ere we are.'

'Might charge a bit extra, lad,' said Fred, 'for t'privilege, but only a bit. We're glad to share it, aren't we, love.'

John beamed at them both.

"Well, you've got a new lodger,' he said, shaking hands with each of them in turn. 'I earn good money, or I will do soon, and we can share that, too.'

Chapter 13

THROUGH THE WEEK before he shifted up to Mill Cottage, John struggled with the aftermath of his experience in the sea. The burning in his throat from the salt water lingered and developed into a running cold and then a cough. Staying in bed in Andrew's damp house was less attractive than going to work, and this was his first week in the job. He already carried the stigma of being an off-comer and a townie, and he couldn't miss his first few days with just a cough. He forced himself to get up and go to work. By the end of the week he was tired but felt he was getting better. The prospect of a new home and new friends buoyed his spirits and his body, masking the insidious whisper of infection.

Just a week after his first encounter with Hannah and Fred at Mill Cottage, John returned there with his few possessions in a rucksack, and set about making a home for himself in the upstairs room over the kitchen. The shelves they'd made for him housed his climbing books, the drawers held his clothes, and what wouldn't fit in there hung on the rail that Fred had wedged across the corner. In this one room John felt more at home than he'd ever felt in the Ulverston house. He sat on the bed and gazed out of the window, across the valley to the brown, green and grey of the fell-side lit by autumn sunlight. The burbling of the beck beside the house filtered into the room. He lay back, relishing the soothing sound at the edge of his hearing, and further away still, only just discernible, the mew of a buzzard. Then his cough returned and he had to sit up to make it stop.

He went downstairs. Hannah was clearing away the lunch from the table.

'That cough sounds nasty,' she said, putting the pots in the sink.

'Just back end of a cold,' he replied. 'Won't last much longer.'

'Room all right for ye? Fred was right proud o' them shelves. Rail across corner felt strong enough when we put it up but I weren't sure it would tek th' weight.'

'It's grand,' he said. 'I feel right at home here. Lucky to have found it.'

'Well, 'appen it were meant,' she said, smiling at him now. 'Tha's 'ad a bad time, lad. It's time you 'ad some rest and a place to call your own, even if it is just a room in our 'ouse.'

'Can't rest today, Hannah,' he said, looking out of the window. 'Have to be out on such a great day. I feel much better, really, and a walk'd set me up. I'll head over to Wasdale and see some mates over there. There's always room in the bunkhouse and I'll be back tomorrow for supper, if that's alright with you?'

'A bunkhouse? Sounds like 'ell on earth to me, lad. All those sweaty men, snoring. I'd rather sleep in t'byre with the beasts!' She shuddered at the thought, and they laughed.

'You and Fred like the house to yourself, don't you? That's what you said.'

'That's just our fun, lad. We do like our quiet times together, just two of us. We've both waited a long time. Dad wouldn't have Fred in t'house, said he were a waste of space. He tried so 'ard to finish us. Wanted me for 'isself I reckon, to wash and clean for 'im. Never forgave me for me mam passing when I was born.'

'I'm sorry,' John mumbled, taken aback by her revelation.

'Dad going so quick was a blessing. 'E couldn't have borne being an invalid, and I'd 'ave gone mad, being stuck with 'im and away from Fred. Now 'ere we are, with a lot of catching up to do. Can't keep our 'ands off each other.' She laughed again. 'And 'aven't you ever been in love like that?'

John thought for a moment. 'No,' he said. 'Not been around girls much, and they don't like me.'

'Don't like you? That's daft. Look at you, tall, dark and handsome. I'd be after you meself if I wasn't old enough to be your mam, and if Fred wasn't around. Tha needs to go dancing, lad. 'Ave a look around. Plenty of fine lasses up and down t'valley. Tha'll see whether they like you. Tha'll find someone who makes you go weak when they smile at you. It's like being ill, that feeling in your stomach, that buzzing in your 'ead. Love, sex, makes th'world go round, Fred says. So we do our bit to keep it going round. Too much mebbe, but why not?'

John stared at her. She talked about sex, just like anything else, like doing the washing or going to church. What would Enid have thought? Hannah caught his expression.

'Sorry, lad. I shouldn't talk so free. Fred says folk don't like it. Mebbe 'e's right. No wonder them at Hill House hardly look at us. Dinnut let it bother you.'

'No, no,' he stuttered again, not knowing what to say. He stepped crab-like towards the door, away from the sharp light that seemed to come from her. 'I have to go, get there before dark. I'll get my bag.'

'Tea afore ye go?'

'No, thanks. I'll get going.'

'Right-ho. We'll expect you back tomorrow afternoon shall we? Supper's at five on a Sunday. Eat with us. Tell us what you've been up to.'

'I will, yes. Just climbing talk. Boring.'

'Nowt's boring, lad when you live quiet like us. Fred and me love to 'ear what's going on in th' world, even if it is just next valley. That's why we wanted you to stay with us a while, keep us joined up to th' world, like. Otherwise it's just the two of us, happy though we are. We don't know owt about climbing, so you're our chance to learn.'

'I'll be back for supper then,' he said, relieved that she'd stopped talking about girls and sex.

It was nearly two when he pulled the garden gate shut behind him and set off up the path that wound over the shoulder of the fell, past a stand of larches and onto the flat, treeless plateau that lay hidden between the two valleys. Shadows of clouds raced ahead of him, chivvied by a north-westerly wind that sharpened the air and made him cough again. The path was stony but dry and John strode out, aware of a tightness in his chest but still elated by a sense of release. The path grew steeper. He was sweating now. Push yourself, he told himself. Get that air in your lungs, breath deep, start living again.

By the time the path flattened and began a gentle descent toward the tarn he was breathing hard and coughing, still sweating, but cold. The sky was brighter up here, picking up the long light of the afternoon sun. He sat for a while on a rock by the dark water, drank out of his cupped hand and splashed his face. The coughing started again, and it was a few minutes before he picked up his rucksack and walked on.

As he breasted the ridge on the east side of the lake and began the steep descent to the Wasdale valley floor, he knew that things weren't right. His head throbbed and felt hot although the rest of him was cold. Dizzy, he stumbled and fell into a wall, picked himself and went on, although the ground seemed to rise and fall unexpectedly under his boots. He thought there was a farm ahead, further down into the valley, but he didn't know why he thought that. He couldn't see it, behind the trees ahead of him, but he knew that it was there. He needed a drink, something hot. Maybe he could stop at the farm. Not far now. He stumbled again. Seemed to be having trouble keeping his balance. Something had given way. Throbbing head. Dizzy. Dark. Have to keep walking.

* * *

Daniel Asby, standing at the door of his farmhouse, had been watching the man stumbling down the path for some time. The dark blue eyes squinted to catch the detail, and he held up a scarred hand to his face to get a better look. At first he assumed the man he could see was drunk, although it was early in the day for that. Drunk or not, the man was lurching unevenly, slipping and having trouble keeping his balance by the look of it. Maybe the pack was too heavy for him. As the stranger came closer, onto the cobbles of the farmyard, Daniel stepped forward and looked hard at him. He was just a lad and there was certainly something wrong with him. The boy looked up, stopped and tried to speak but then bent forward, coughing. The bag spilled over his shoulder onto the ground. He slumped to one knee.

Daniel covered the space between them in a few long strides. He moved the bag out of his way and knelt down in front of the stranger. There was no smell of drink.

'Tha's not reet, lad,' he said.

'I just need to rest a bit,' said John, raising his head and trying to stand. 'I'm cold. Need a drink.'

'Where's tha headed?' said Daniel. He picked up John's bag with one hand and swung it over his shoulder. Then he stretched his hand to John, took hold of his jacket and pulled him up. 'Come away in for a bit. Let's 'ave a look at ye.'

He steered John towards the door, and pushed it open. 'Get kettle on, Edna!' he called into the house. 'Lad here needs summat

107

hot. Sit the'sen down,' he said to John, pulling out a chair and pushing John down into it.

John rested his head on the table. Daniel felt the back of his neck. 'Tha's burning up, lad. Get that scaif off.' He unwound the scarf and John leaned back, his head lolling like a baby's, until Daniel leaned him forward to rest on the table again.

'Edna!' Daniel shouted again. The back door opened and his wife entered. She was a short, round person, a grey shawl round her head. She pulled off the shawl as she came in, revealing short white hair. She looked up, adjusting to the gloom in the house.

'What's up? What's t'yammering?' She stepped closer. 'Who's 'ere? Has 'e 'ad a drop?

'He just came danderin down the path from Boot,' said Daniel. ' Looked pissed to me too, but 'e's not. Reckon 'e's badly.'

'Gi's a look,' she said, pushing her husband out of the way. She bent down and peered into John's face, and felt his forehead. 'By God, 'e's hot,' she said. 'Help me up with 'im, Dan.'

Between them they half carried, half pushed him into the big chair near the range.

'Just lean back for me, lad,' she whispered to him. 'Let's get this jacket off.'

John began to stir, as if waking from sleep. Edna brought some water in a cup and put it into his hand, guiding it to his mouth. That roused him further, and he drank, greedily. 'More please,' he said, giving the cup back to her. She filled it again from the enamel jug by the door and he drained it, wiping his mouth with the back of his hand. He looked around him.

'Sorry,' he said. 'Got really dizzy. Had to sit down. Feeling better now, thanks.' He rubbed his face and scratched his head. 'Don't know what happened there. Saw you in the farmyard and then my legs just gave up.' He smiled weakly at them both as they stood side by side, looking down at him.

'Don't look too good, lad,' she said, putting the cup down on the table. 'How far 'ave ye come?'

'Just from Boot,' he said, pointing vaguely behind him. 'Going down Wasdale. Not far.'

'It's not a walk ye need, lad,' said Daniel, 'It's a doctor. We can get you down to t'pub, that's easy enough. They'll get word to Doc Mackie.'

'Mackie?' said his wife. 'It'll be morning before 'e's sober enough to get up 'ere. Tha'd be better off getting that Baker lass, the one that went nursing, to Newcastle. Tha knows, big lass, what's her name? Helen is it?'

'Nay, not Helen. Nora. Helen's th' older one, married, gone to Seascale. It's Nora that went to nursing. Nora the Nurse, the kids call 'er.'

'That's the one. Nora. What's tha name, son? Are ye from round 'ere?'

'John, John Pharaoh,' replied John weakly. 'Mill Cottage.'

'Mill Cottage, he says,' Edna called out to her husband.

'Wi' Hannah and Fred?' she said to John.

'Yes, Hannah and Fred,' he repeated.

'Well, I 'adn't heard about that,' she said. 'Fancy them two tekin' a lodger.'

Daniel took a cap from the peg by the door and put it on. He handed Edna her shawl.

'We'll take lad in t'cart,' she said, wrapping the shawl round herself. 'You get 'im into t'pub and I'll fetch Nora. Tell Sam to get 'im a proper bed.'

John sat in front of them as they talked, like a child awaiting punishment.

Daniel was away for a few minutes, hitching up one of the horses to the cart. They clattered across the yard and he came back into the kitchen. John was lying back in the big chair.

'Can ye stand?' he said to John.

John leaned forward and struggled to his feet, but one leg buckled under him and he fell back. Daniel knelt down and looked at him. Then he stood up, leaned down to push one arm under John's knees and hauled him up into his arms, taking small steps to steady himself on the floor's uneven flags.

'Get 'is bag, love,' he said to his wife, and she followed him out of the dark kitchen to the cart standing outside.

'You get up, Edna,' said Daniel, ' I'll sit 'im on th'edge. You pull 'im back and then we can lie 'im doon.'

'Fetch us a blanket, then,' she said, as she held John's head and lowered it to the floor of the cart. 'Can't have 'im rolling about.'

By the time the Asbys reached the floor of the valley and the broad track towards the pub, John was mumbling, asking for water. He lay on his side, the blanket over him and tucked around, his knees drawn up like a baby as fits of coughing came and went. Edna knelt beside him, wiping his face with her shawl. Another track appeared to the left, as splashes of rain began to leave dark spots on the floor of the cart.

'Drop me 'ere, love,' she said, 'I'll go down to Baker's. Wi' any luck they'll be back. You carry on and I'll see you up there. Go slow. 'E looks reet done in.' She wiped John's face one more time and grasped his hand. 'Dan'll take you to t'pub,' she said. 'I'll find someone who'll know 'ow to 'elp you. Won't be long.'

She jumped down and set off down the track, holding her shawl with one hand against the wind as the thin rain blew steadily into her face. Daniel clicked his tongue and the patient horse pulled the cart up the valley towards the pub. John lay motionless on the floor. Daniel wondered what was wrong with him, and what would happen. He'd seen people like this before and knew it was serious. The rain fell quietly on them both, the strong and the sick.

CHAPTER 14

THERE'D BEEN A PUB at Wasdale Head for as long as anyone could remember. Certainly Daniel Asby remembered it from his childhood, before he left the valley for the pit at Egremont. All those years underground he carried with him the image of the familiar end wall, visible from the final bend in the road. Dwarfed by steep fellsides to the north and west, and the bulk of Scafell on the other side of the flat valley floor, the pub was the centre of the climbers' universe. From its shelter and companionship the paths ran to Pillar, Gable, and over Scarth Gap to Borrowdale and Eskdale. Many a tired walker, lost in cloud, thanked God when he dropped down below the cloud line and saw the litter of buildings, the gleam of Wastwater and the distant sea.

Sam Phizakerlea, who ran the pub, reigned over this end of the valley like an enlightened despot. He was a climber himself, and gave the climbing community what it travelled so far to enjoy: easy access to the best climbs in England, good ale and congenial company. There were always climbers here, year round. The pile of boots in the porch filled the air with the smell of Dubbin polish. Night after night, year after year, the back bar absorbed stories of slabs and holds and overhangs. New-fangled ideas, like pitons and rubber shoes, were despised and rejected. Real men, – and they were all men – reinforced each other's conviction that they were the true disciples, untainted by the effete modernism of Europe. To prove their credentials, they cheered as one of them would occasionally circle the back bar without touching the floor, finding foot and hand holds on the ancient walls.

It was almost dark when Daniel Asby's cart clattered across the cobbled yard of the pub. The landlord was filling log boxes. Daniel jumped down from the cart. 'This lad's sick, Phiz. Real bad. 'E were ganging down t'path from Boot, thought he was drunk, but 'e's sick. Gi's a hand. Need to get 'im inside.'

Phiz climbed up onto the cart and lifted John's shoulders to slide him down to where Daniel was waiting to steady the lolling body. Then between them they carried John through the low front door of the pub.

'Not the bar,' said Phiz. 'To the left. There's a fire lit in there and we can put him on the settle.'

Phiz took off his jacket, rolled it and put it under John's head while Daniel stood upright, holding his back that had pained him since his accident and would until he died.

'We're trying to find Baker's lass, if she's around,' said Daniel. 'Looks like pneumonia to me. Needs some proper 'elp, I reckon. All we can do is keep 'im warm, let 'im sweat it out. That's what they told us when our Alan was bad that time. Mind you, he died. 'Appen this one could, too.'

'Who is he?'

'Told us 'is name's John Pharaoh.'

'One of the Whitehaven mob?'

'Nay. From away. Ulverston. Lives at Boot he says.'

'Where's his folks? We might need to find them.'

'God knows. He's nobbut a lad. The Porters might know.'

'Fred Porter you mean, the rug man?'

'Aye, 'im and 'is missus, Mick Tyson's lass. He's stopping with them.'

'I'll fetch a blanket,' said Phiz. 'Let's hope we're doing the right thing.'

'My Edna's gone down to Bakers' place. Not far. If Nora's there, they won't be long.'

Daniel pulled up a stool towards the settle and watched John's eyelids flutter and his mouth move. 'Mam.' Just the one word.

'Hang on, lad,' said Daniel, leaning towards him. 'We'll have you reet.'

A young man appeared at the door. 'What's up, Dan?'

'This lad, Colin,' said Daniel, pointing at the body on the settle. 'Found 'im at th' farm. 'E's badly. Edna's gone for 'elp.'

The young man had a full pint glass in his hand, holding it carefully as he came across the room. He looked down at the figure on the settle.

'Ehyup,' he said. 'I know him, it's John. Hang on a minute.'

He put down the glass on the mantelpiece above the fire and hurried out of the room. Daniel heard his voice in the bar. A minute later he was back, and another young man with him.

'See. It's John, the lad from the brewery in Ulverston. What's his name?'

'Pharaoh,' Daniel interrupted. Told me that himself before 'e passed out.'

'That's it. Pharaoh. Ulverston. He's a climber, not bad, too. Comes up weekends. Haven't seen him for a bit, mind. I think his mam died.'

'Said 'e's living at Boot,' Daniel added.

'Boot? Must've shifted. Always said he wished he lived nearer. Doesn't look good, does he? What's up with him?'

'Looks like pneumonia to me. Hurry up, Edna love. Phiz and I dinna know what to do for t'best.'

'Is Howard in, Rob?' said the first young man to his friend. 'Have a look for us. Said he was doing Hadrian's today. Should be down from Pillar now it's dark.'

Rob disappeared from the room, and Phiz returned with another pillow and a big grey blanket. Colin held John's head. Phiz tucked the blanket between John and the back of the settle and then laid it over him.

'Is Howard around?' said Phiz.

'Rob's gone to look for him. Lucky if he is. He might still be coming down. He and Mick stay out as long as they can.'

The men stood silently round the fire, watching the prone form in front of them. There were voices in the yard and Edna joined the group. 'Naybody there,' she said to Dan. 'House is dark. Mebbe in Whitehaven, on t'way back, who knows.'

'There's a doctor 'ere, but he's still out on Pillar. Just have to 'ang on, lad,' Daniel said to John but there was no response. 'What do we do, lads? Keep 'im warm, cool 'im down? What?'

'Beats me,' said Colin. 'Me gran had pneumonia, in our house when I was a little lad. She was in our front room, then she died.'

'Come on, Howard, where are you?' said Daniel, listening to John's laboured breathing. 'Could they 'ave gone down t'other way, into Ennerdale?'

'Nay. Stuff's still here, and the car.'

Edna looked up. 'Car, eh. That's handy. Couldn't 'ave the poor lad bumping all t'way down to Whitehaven in the back of our cart.'

'Hospital, you reckon?' said Daniel.

'Aye, have to be.' Colin said. 'He's bad. Can't just watch him slip away.'

'Who'll pay for that then?' said Daniel. 'It'll cost.'

The group stood, faces lit by the fire, and stared at John. They could all hear him wheezing, his lungs rattling with fluid and phlegm.

Edna spoke again. 'Can't just stand 'ere. I'll go back t'Bakers, see if I can find anyone. Tell them to get Nora 'ere when she gets back.'

They turned to watch her go, but no one spoke. Colin went back to the bar. Rob sat on a low chair in the corner and supped slowly at his pint. The clock over the fire ticked loudly. Below it the fire glowed red. Thirty minutes passed, forty, fifty. Phiz looked in, they shook their heads and he disappeared again. John stirred briefly but didn't wake.

Suddenly the front door opened, discarded boots thudded onto the pile in the corner of the porch.

'In there, doc,' said one of the voices, and a man entered the hot room. He ignored the others standing around, held out his arm and pushed them gently away, easing past them and dropping to one knee in a seamless movement.

'Thank God for that,' said Daniel. 'Glad you're 'ere, doc.'

'Who is he, do we know?' Howard Mackintosh asked, without looking up. He had one hand on John's wrist and stared at his watch. 'Need more light in here,' he said, to no one in particular. Rob and Daniel looked at each other, and Rob left to find Phiz, who arrived shortly carrying two oil lamps.

'One lamp over here,' said Howard, again without looking up. 'He's bad. Pneumonia probably. Do we know how old he is, where he's from?'

'Must be early twenties,' said Rob. 'Been coming up here for a few years, more often since his mam died.'

'What did she die of, anyone know?' Howard was trying to piece the bits of information together. It didn't look good.

'He didn't say much,' said Rob, holding the empty glass in front of him. 'Just said she'd died. Didn't want to talk about it I reckoned, so we left it.'

'Well, he could go the same way,' said Howard. 'Need to get him into hospital, but not tonight. Don't want to move him, but

115

no choice. First thing, I'll take him down myself. Is there a telephone anywhere?'

Phiz spoke from the doorway. 'Nearest's down at post office. Want us to phone now, or in morning?'

'Morning'll do. Call Whitehaven Hospital, ask for Dr Williams. Tell him I'm bringing a young man in, suspected pneumonia, no history. Give him the name, anything else you know. It'll take an hour or two, but we'll get there. Did you say there was a nurse somewhere around?'

'Nora Baker, lives down Ramside.'

'Ask her to be here by eight in the morning, if you can find her. He'll need some care while we're on the road, if he lasts the night.'

Howard wiped John's face, felt his forehead.

'Phiz. If you can find my bag in the room upstairs, can you bring it down? Need my stethoscope.'

By the time the bag arrived there more people crowding round the doorway, looking silently at the young man lying within.

'Can you all get out?' said Howard. 'The man's very sick and doesn't need you lot staring at him like an exhibit. Have some respect.'

The crowd dispersed. Daniel watched from the doorway, as the doctor did what he could. It would be a long night.

Chapter 15

John lay back on the pillows in the narrow hospital bed and stared to his left, to the window he could see over the two beds that lay between. These were both occupied by snorers. John cursed them both every night but the two of them neither knew nor cared. Jacob Phythian was a Whitehaven Hospital veteran, been in that same ward more times than he could remember. Everyone seemed to know him. His cough was relentless, harsh, terrifying. John wondered how much longer the man would live. The younger of the two, Stan Tilney, was thin and pale with an incongruously large tight stomach, like a pregnant woman. John didn't know what was the matter with him. Now though, in the early afternoon, they were both asleep, and mercifully quiet.

Beyond the window the air was pale with mist and cold. In the harbour, only a few hundred yards from the hospital, black water slopped against wharves and steps, and out beyond the protection of the harbour wall, white foam striped the sea. In his mind John saw the top of Bowfell sparkling where sunlight met frozen hail. He closed his eyes to keep the bright image in his mind, holding at bay the smells and sounds and sights of the ward where he lay.

It shouldn't be long now. How long had he been here? Almost three weeks they said, but he didn't remember the first days after they carried him in. The doctor who'd brought him down

Wasdale to the hospital had looked in on him a few days before. John didn't know him and after a few awkward minutes the stranger had gone back to the ward office to check his notes. That had been a couple of weeks ago. Now he felt stronger every day, and imprisoned. He was bored and restless. Long hours of doing nothing had emptied his mind, leaving space for memories to flit around, distracting and disturbing him like poltergeists. Memories danced in his head while he slept, the roar and taste of sea water, a blur of orange light reflecting off a lake.

During long days he found himself thinking about his mother, his real mother. She'd had him when she was younger than he was now. She must have made a choice about the sex. There was no baby without sex. What kind of woman has sex like that, risking a baby, without thinking? She must have been stupid, or thoughtless, probably both. Not fit to raise a child so she gave it away, to keep the family happy, to hush everything up. She might still be around, living a life somewhere, with other kids. She'd have forgotten about him, put it behind her. He wanted to do the same, but lying there day after day, it haunted him.

The young nurse had said he could go home so long as there was someone to take care of him. He'd mentioned Hannah.

'A relative?' the nurse had asked, smiling.

'No,' said John. 'My landlady.' It sounded so cold, but he didn't know what else to call her. He didn't want to say more, but he was sure that Hannah would look after him as well as Enid had ever done.

The nurse looked at him and smiled. 'Your landlady?' her voice rose a little. There was a slight pause. 'Where do you live?' the nurse continued, lowering her eyes to the little book she held in her hand. She felt for a pencil in the pocket of her apron.

'Up the valley,' said John, 'Eskdale, up the top, bottom of Hardknott.' The nurse shrugged.

'I'm from Maryport,' she replied. 'Don't suppose you know where that is.'

'Heard of it,' said John. 'On the coast is it?'

'No prizes for working that out,' she said.

'Well the place I live is called Boot, so what does that tell you?'

'Not much. Where did that name come from?'

'No idea. Never thought about it really. It's a long way.'

'How're you going to get there? Is there a bus?'

'Not sure. La'al Ratty, goes up the valley, but not much in the winter. I could find out.'

'What on earth is, what was it, La'al Ratty?'

'It's what we call the train, the little train that carries rock from the quarry to the coast. La'al means small. That's what everyone calls it.'

'Doctor wouldn't be happy with all that shunting about. You have to rest, or you'll have to stay here.'

'Can't stay here. I need to get out.'

'You've been very ill, tha knows. It could come back. You need looking after. Is there anyone we could telephone about getting you home, back to Boot, or wherever it is.'

'Telephone?' John laughed. 'No phones up the valley. There's one at the shop at Newton, I think. And there's a lady close by who has a car. Can't remember her name.'

'A car? That'd be just the job. We'd wrap you up well and you'd ride home in style. Might come with you meself, just for the ride.' She leaned forward and patted his arm. He smiled back.

The next day the wind swung round to the south-west and whistled through the gap in the window. After the early cup of tea, too weak for John's liking, the same young nurse appeared at his bedside.

'Her name's Miss Plane.'

'Who?'

'The lady with the car. In Newton. One of the doctors knew her dad. He's going to ring to ask if she could come and get you, take you home. Otherwise we'll have to keep you in a bit longer, until you're well enough for the journey. Can't spare an ambulance, not all the way up there.'

'She doesn't know me,' said John. 'Why should she help?'

'You'd be surprised what people do round here. You're not from round here are you?'

'Ulverston.'

'Well they do things differently there. Here we have to help each other. No one else will. No one ever bothers about the west coast. Not for years. Used to be one of the richest –' There was movement at the door of the ward, and she stopped abruptly.

'Ward round,' she said, straightening the covers on John's bed. 'Sit up properly, look lively and they might make that call and get you out of here.' She turned away and walked quickly back to the door and the ward office.

John endured the misery of the ward round yet again, peered at by a gang of young men of his own age, talked about as if he wasn't there. The doctor had said something about John being home soon, but that was all, and the cavalcade shuffled on to the next bed. The young nurse winked at John. He didn't know why. Rain was pattering on the long windows. They were on the first floor of what had been Whitehaven Castle, before the family who owned it had given it up and donated the whole place to be the town hospital. Generous right enough, but the place didn't really suit its new purpose. In the room where John and Jacob and Stanley lay there had once been colours and silks and servants and fine folk taking tea and conversation, looking out of those very same windows at ordinary people like the ones who now crowded the rooms. The rooms were too high, and the windows too big, letting in draughts, making it feel cold.

John lay back and let his mind wander to a place where the mist lay below him and he could see the bright outline of the high peaks above the cloud that lay in folds and drifts in the valley. He remembered the symmetrical peak of Great Gable, the Napes just showing above the blanket of cloud. Further over he could make out the ridges of Swirl How and the western slopes of the Old Man of Coniston. That day, alone on the silent hillside, he had turned with his back to the strong low sun for a moment and caught sight of a shadow, a figure, dark grey on the wall of mist below him and framed by a round rainbow. It gave him a shock, until he realised it was his own shadow. He raised his arms and the figure did the same, as if in greeting. That evening, snug in the pub he told someone what he'd seen. It was called a 'Brocken spectre', apparently, light refracting through the tiny droplets of moisture in the cloud.

He smiled as he remembered. How he longed to be out of here, away from the snoring men, the bustling town, back at the head of the beloved valley, with the people who seemed to be more like parents than his parents had ever been. And none of them were his real parent, the one who gave him away. He turned onto his front and buried his face in the lumpy pillow.

Next day was brighter, and sun poured through the great windows, catching pinpricks of dust in its rays. The young nurse appeared at his bedside just after breakfast.

'Well, it's all sorted out,' she said, pulling the covers on John's bed straight as she spoke. 'The lady, Miss Plane, is coming to pick you up tomorrow afternoon, when she's free. She's giving a message to the postman who goes up to – Boot, is it? – to tell the people you lodge with. So you'll be going home in style, and they'll be expecting you. Couldn't be better. I'm not sure you're really well enough, but if there's someone prepared to look after you, it should be alright. Don't suppose you're keen to stay with us much longer?'

'You're right there, nurse,' he replied quickly. 'Can't wait to get out.'

'I could be hurt by that, of course, but I'm sure you don't hate us that much.'

'No, of course … I mean –'

'I know.' She lowered her voice, as she eyed the two beds under the window. 'I'd be keen to get away from those two as well. They snore summat fierce.' She squeezed John's arm again, and smiled at him. 'I'll miss you, though. Not often we have such handsome young men in here.'

John felt his cheeks redden.

'Well,' she went on, looking around to make sure that no one saw her sitting on his bed. 'If I wasn't busy here I'd volunteer to come and look after you meself,' and with that she was off, walking a little faster than normal and without looking back.

John closed his eyes. He couldn't fathom women out, especially the young ones. They all seemed to tease him. One minute it was all business, the next she was squeezing him and smiling and whispering. He didn't know where to put himself. That girl at Hill House, she'd laughed in his face. And this one, throwing herself at him. Andrew would understand, he thought. Andrew understood women. He didn't say much, but John guessed he had something going on. Who was it, he wondered? Young probably, and pretty. Maybe more than one. Andrew would know what to say to the nurse, while he just stammered and blushed. Pathetic. 'Grow up John, for God's sake,' he said to himself. 'You're twenty years old, not a boy. Grow up!'

Once the end of his hospital sentence was close, waiting for release seemed to take forever. That night the hours dragged and snagged at his patience. Jacob's snoring woke him every hour or two until he got out of bed and walked unsteadily to the desk at the far end of the ward where a nurse was reading in the small circle of lamplight. He startled her, and apologised as she retrieved her book from the floor. 'Can't sleep,' he said, simply, jerking his thumb in the direction of the sound that seemed to echo round the old walls. 'Jacob, snoring.'

'Can't be helped,' she hissed. 'You must be used to it by now. I'll give him a poke and try to get him off his back, but you'll have to get back to bed.'

'What time is it?'

She peered down at the watch hanging by a pin on her breast.

'Too early. Ten to four. You can get a couple more hours before we come and wake you up.'

It was just twelve hours later, and John had been dressed and sitting by his bed since lunch, when he heard voices and a smartly dressed woman appeared with the nurse at the door. They walked down the ward towards him. The lady was wearing a grey coat, belted at the waist, a bright blue scarf hung loosely round her neck, and she was carrying blue gloves in one hand. He didn't like to look at her face, not while she seemed to be looking at him so intently. He stood up, steadying himself with one hand on the end of the bed.

'Mr Pharaoh?' she said, putting out her hand towards him. He shook it. The hand was dry and warm. 'I'm Agnes Plane, from Newton. I've come to take you home, back to Boot I believe.' The nurse stood beside the newcomer, smiling and nodding at John, as if wanting him to do something. He felt himself blushing again, and looked down.

'Yes,' he managed in reply. 'Very good of you.'

'Happy to help,' she said brightly. 'Do you have a bag or something, with your things?' She looked around.

'Just this,' said John, picking up the small bag he'd been carrying when he was taken ill, a lifetime ago. 'I was out walking

'… and they brought me straight here.'

'That's fine,' said Agnes, taking the bag from him, and slipping her arm through this. 'Sounds like you've had quite an adventure. You can tell me about it as we drive home. It's only a little car, but it goes well. Good day for driving actually, now that the mist's cleared.'

She turned to the young nurse. 'We'll be fine now, thank you. Come along, then, Mr Pharaoh.'

'Call me John please.'

'And you may call me Agnes,' she replied. 'Miss Plane sounds so formal, don't you think?'

And so they walked slowly down the curving staircase, across the tiled floor of the hall, out through the great door and down the steps, the smart woman and the shy young man, into the pale sunshine.

Agnes's car, a Morris, the same colour as her scarf and gloves, was parked up a side street and she opened the door for him, establishing that he was the patient and that she was in charge. She put his bag on the back seat, and slid behind the wheel beside him. As she busied herself with starting and manoeuvring down the cobbled street, he turned his head to get a proper view of her for the first time. She had a lively face framed by short golden brown hair, like pictures he'd seen in some of the magazines that were all he had to read in the hospital. Her mouth was quite full, and dark red. She sensed him looking at her and turned her head quickly towards him, just for a moment, before turning back to focus on the road ahead.

'Thanks again for doing this', he said. 'Definitely ready to get out of there. The noise at night, hard to sleep.'

'Yes, I understand,' Agnes agreed. 'We'll have you home in no time. Tell me again where it is.'

'Mill Cottage, opposite the old mill in Boot, up on the left.'

Agnes turned to look at him again. 'Hannah? Is that your land-lady? They said you had someone to look after you but I didn't know it was Hannah. How lucky for you, you couldn't be in better hands.'

'You know her then?'

'Of course, who doesn't in the valley? Knew her father too, God rest him. I was so glad she found herself a husband, and such a fine man. He has an injury from the war, doesn't he? Came from Broughton, have I got that right?'

'That's him,' said John. 'Fred lived in Broughton and met Hannah there. Don't think her dad was keen on them marrying but they waited and they seem very happy together. He's got one foot, lost the other in the fighting. Couldn't run the mill, but they've rigged it up to a generator and we have electric in the house.'

'Goodness,' said Agnes, 'How clever of them. And what a bonus for you, John.'

'Couldn't be better really,' he agreed.

They drove on in silence for a while, finding their way through the south side of the town towards Egremont. Agnes seemed quite at ease. John liked her confidence.

Away from the bustle of the town there was little traffic and Agnes took another sideways glance at her young passenger. A good-looking young man, dark, quite pale skin, long eyelashes clearly visible against the light through the car window. Faintest line of a moustache on his upper lip. He seemed very shy.

'Tell me a bit about yourself, John,' she said. 'What's a young man doing so far from his family?'

'Don't have a family, not close anyway,' said John, looking at the road ahead as they came down the long hill into Egremont. 'My dad died a while ago, and then my mam, in May. But she wasn't my real mam.'

125

'Oh dear,' said Agnes, while her mind digested this information. Not his real mother? What was that about? She looked across at John but he was staring ahead. 'I'm sorry to hear that, John. That must have been dreadful for you. Was there no one to help you with it all?'

'Oh, aye, my mam's sister and her husband lived close. They helped with the funeral of course, but when it was all over I wanted to get away.'

'Where did you live?'

'Ulverston. I worked at Hartleys, in the office.'

'The brewery, yes, everyone knows Hartleys don't they? Have a drop myself occasionally.' She smiled across at him. 'So how did you end up in this part of the world? Ulverston's not far as the crow flies, but it's quite a trek from here.'

'Saw it in the paper, a notice for someone to work at the quarry, same kind of job as before, but a step up for me. And there's the railway, too.'

'You mean the Ratty?'

'Aye. A bit daft mebbe, but I love trains, always have. Knew about the Ratty from the railway magazines.'

'It's seen better days, I think,' said Agnes. 'Before the post bus it was the only way for people to get around up there.'

'Needs some money spending on it,' said John. 'They're talking about it being sold, someone in Keswick. Just a rumour.'

Agnes slowed down as they went through Egremont. 'We could stop here if you need anything,' she said. 'The Co-op's still open. Once you get back you may need to rest up for a while.'

At the Co-op. John bought socks and a little ornament for Hannah's mantelshelf. It was good to be outside, away from the heat and smells of the hospital. He felt as if he was waking from a dream. Back in the car, he leaned back and breathed deeply, and the coughing didn't last too long this time. He ran his hand over his face. Not sweating, or only a bit.

'Right-oh,' said Agnes, easing the car back into the main road. 'Won't be long now. Oh, by the way,' she continued, as the car gathered speed again, 'I'm going to stop in Newton on our way through, if that's all right with you. I have to check something with Miss Whelan at the school. Do you know her?'

'Miss Whelan?'

'The schoolmistress,' said Agnes. 'Just a bit of WI business. Won't take a minute, I'm sure. Don't want to be too late getting you back. We've a committee meeting tonight I have to get back for.'

'Fine with me,' said John, settling back into his seat.

A little later, as they waited behind a flock of sheep and watched three dogs expertly herding them through a gate, Agnes continued her gentle interrogation of this young man who had dropped into her world.

'The doctor said they brought you in from Wasdale Head. What were you doing over there?'

'I walked over from Boot. Didn't feel great when I started but I didn't know I was really ill. It was probably the ducking in the sea that started it off.'

'In the sea?' Agnes looked across at him and then had to brake sharply as a dog leapt over the wall ahead of them in search of a stray sheep.

'When that steamer ran aground, last month down the coast. I was on the beach and tried to help but I got stuck in the water and someone had to haul me out. I was in a bad way for a while.'

'Good heavens,' said Agnes. 'That was you! I heard there was someone nearly drowned that day.'

John laughed. 'Not really,' he said. 'Just got knocked down by a big 'un and couldn't get up properly. Left me feeling pretty rough for a while. Then I got a cold but it got worse and worse. Thought

I was over it, so I set off to walk over, but … well, you know the rest.'

'You have been in the wars,' said Agnes. 'That's a lot for anyone to cope with. You must be very strong to have got through it. Your mother, moving up here, that awful experience and now getting ill. It would have finished some people off completely.'

John said nothing. She said he was strong. Not strong like Andrew, a different kind of strong. He liked that. And she was old enough to be his mother. Maybe it was just young women who made him feel so foolish. Mrs Barker, Hannah, this woman: he felt all right with them. Then he remembered the telling off Mrs Barker had given him after the funeral and looked away from Agnes, out at the fells ahead of them now that they'd turned up the valley. There was cloud on the top. It was growing dark already.

As they drove into Newton, Agnes slowed down. 'There's the school, straight ahead of us,' she said, 'and there's Miss Whelan. What good timing.'

Agnes began to pull over to the side of the road. John looked ahead. He saw a tall woman, dark hair blowing round her head. She put up one hand to brush it away from her face. Then the woman turned, back towards the open door and another figure emerged, ducking his head as he did so. John recognised him at once. It was the vicar, the one in the pub the night Andrew pulled him out of the sea. John hadn't seen him since, but the memory was sharp.

'Oh there's the vicar,' said Agnes. 'They're probably busy with something. And it's a bit late, so let's leave them to it. I'll see Miss Whelan tonight anyway. It'll keep till then.'

Agnes drove slowly past the school. Jessie Whelan bent her head to look into the car, and waved to Agnes. Lionel Leadbetter raised a hand too. John turned and watched them as they pulled away and out of sight.

'You really must meet Miss Whelan,' said Agnes. 'A delightful woman. Are you a churchgoer, John?'

'I used to be,' he said. 'My mother was very keen, Methodist.'

'Ah,' said Agnes. 'It's mostly Church of England round here.'

'That's all right. Since Mam died I've been going climbing at the weekends whenever I can. That's one of the reasons I moved up here. Church isn't for me, really.'

'We'll have to see if we can tempt you back,' said Agnes, smiling at him. 'We need young people like you. Did you get to the harvest supper? I wasn't there myself, but Miss Whelan was I think.'

'Didn't go,' said John. 'Didn't feel like meeting lots of new folk. Too soon. Andrew said I could go with him, but I didn't.'

'Andrew? Of course, you work at the quarry. It's a small world isn't it? That was the Reverend Leadbetter we saw back there. Andrew Leadbetter's in charge at the quarry for a while isn't he?'

'Aye, he is. I stayed with Andrew before I got this place with Hannah.'

'Well, well,' said Agnes, as they drove on up the valley in the gathering gloom. 'How the pieces of our lives fit together.'

CHAPTER 16

ANDREW DREW ON his cigarette. The tip glowed, echoing the glow of the fire that Jessie had lit in the small grate in her bedroom. She had guessed that Andrew would come to her that night, late, and she wanted them to be warm. Beside him in the bed Jessie lay on her front. She had covered herself with the blankets, but with his spare hand Andrew pushed back the covers, exposing her lower back and the top of her buttocks. He stroked her skin, loving its warmth and solidity.

'Look at you,' he said. 'Lying there like a wanton woman.'

She stirred, raising her bottom a little against his touch.

'I am a wanton woman,' she said, her voice muffled into the pillow. 'And it's all your fault. Before you came along I hadn't thought about sex for years. I was perfectly content, and now this. Shocking.'

'The only shocking thing is why it took me so long to get you into bed,' he said, stubbing out his cigarette in the little brass ashtray on the bedside table. 'Why did I waste my time with anyone else when I could've had you?'

He slid further down in the bed and turned towards her, pushing the covers away as he did so.

'Turn over,' he said. 'Let me look at you.'

She did so, holding a hand over her breasts.

He pushed her hand away.

'Don't cover yourself,' he said. 'Let me see.'

He looked at her body, rounded and plump below the waist, and then lay across her, taking her nipple in his mouth. She stroked the back of his head, still damp from the rain.

'You're sure no one saw you?'

He raised his head and lay back beside her, looking up at the ceiling. 'No one. God, woman, what you afraid of? I'm not used to creeping about, looking over my shoulder the whole time. I don't care what people say, even if they find out about us. I'm single, you're single, where's the problem?'

'That's not it, Andrew. You know that. I've got a lot to lose here. Things I care about.'

'I know, I know,' he said, 'your job and your reputation. But there's more to life than a job and a reputation in this place. It's a dump. Backward. Half the people here don't even have running water in the house, never mind a proper toilet. Still on oil lamps, no electric. You've been running that school for God knows how many years, answering to a bunch of old buggers who don't like you anyway.'

'Who doesn't like me?'

'They wish you were a man, Jessie, face it. If they could, they'd get rid of you. "Nice family man", that's what they want. Safe, boring, just like them. And as for my old man, he's just as bad as the rest for all his big talk about "the children". That new school isn't about the children, it's about him.'

'That's not fair. He does care.'

'I think different, and I know him better than you. Anyway, this place is going nowhere. I need to get away, should never have come back, and this time you're coming with me. How do you fancy Canada?'

He raised himself on one elbow and looked down at her, pushing a strand of hair away from her mouth.

'You're the one, Jessie. I know it, you know it. We both have the energy and the guts to get out of this place, to make something of our lives. We're both young.'

Jessie's eyes widened.

'Young? You're young, not me. I'm happy here, however you feel about it. I've got my friends, my work –'

'Friends? Who? That dried up old prude in the shop. Looks at me like I'm a hired hand? Swanning off to London all the time just so we know how rich she is? You can do better than that, Jess.'

'Leave Agnes out of this.' Jessie pulled the covers over herself. 'She's a good friend to me. Anyway, we've been over all this before. You think there's no problem with you and me turning up together in the Farriers one night and telling everyone that we're together now and isn't it grand.'

'Sounds good to me.'

'Well, it's not going to be like that,' she said. 'Look at me, I'm falling apart. I think about you all the time as it is, and long for you to come to me. Hearing your step on the stairs tonight, I felt sick with excitement. I know it's madness: it can't last. You want to be away and I need to stay here.'

'But you don't, you don't,' he said, taking her in both his arms and pulling her towards him.

He kissed her, hard. She didn't resist him, but then pushed him away. He lit another cigarette and went back to staring up at the ceiling.

They lay in silence for a while.

'Why me, Andrew?' she said, not looking at him. 'You could have anyone you wanted. Andrew Leadbetter, big and strong, good-looking, good earner.'

'Good fucker,' he added.

'Don't be crude. I wish you wouldn't talk like that.'

'I've had a few women, granted,' he said. 'But the one I want is you. I have to have you, Jess.'

'But why? I'm old and getting fat. I've got grey hairs. I'm nearly your mother's age.'

'Rubbish. You're the most exciting woman I've ever met. You're clever and funny and that arse – come here.'

'Not with that cigarette in your hand, you'll set fire to us.'

'Don't need a cig to set fire to you,' he said, holding the cigarette above his head and pushing his other hand down between her legs.

An hour later the fire was out and it was cold in the room. It smelled of cigarette smoke and Jessie wanted to open a window and clear the air. She turned and shook him.

'Andrew, you have to go. If you fall asleep properly you'll bump into someone in the morning when you leave, bound to. Come on.' She cupped his chin in her hand. He stirred.

'What time is it?'

'Late. Time you were gone. Where's the bike?'

'What?'

'Where's your bike. Where did you leave it?'

'Behind the pub.'

'Well, you need to go. I've got to work tomorrow, and so do you.'

He groaned. She pulled the covers back and he rolled to put his feet on the floor.

'Christ it's cold.'

'Then get your clothes on, quick.'

He pulled on his trousers, and picked up his shirt from the floor on the other side of the room where he had pulled it off earlier. His pullover was halfway up the stairs and his boots by the back door where he'd left them a couple of hours before.

She stretched out a hand and touched his back. 'When will I see you?'

'Next weekend. Are you going to the hunt ball?'

'Probably. Is it the same band as last year?'

'Think so. It'll be good. I've got to go, judging the hunt queen thing, you know.'

'Just up your street,' said Jessie. 'All those young girls on display.'

'None of them a patch on you, gorgeous. You could be in the running for the prize for the Best Lady's Head of Hair.'

'Go on,' she said, delighted.

Jessie lay back, watching him.

'I thought you wanted me just to spite your father,' she said.

He turned around and grasped her wrist.

'Don't you dare,' he said, fiercely. Spittle landed on her cheek and she blinked.

'Don't you dare start all that rubbish with me. My father's my business. He has nothing to do with this, with you and me. Yes I'm tired of creeping about. Yes I want him to know how I feel, and that you and I are together. Why not? But I want you because of what you are. You're the woman for me, Jessie, that's all I know. Just get used to it.'

She pulled her wrist away, and sat up. He pulled on his shirt, still with his back to her.

'Look,' she said. 'That was a stupid thing to say. I'm sorry. It's just that … I just don't understand, why me, even after all you've said. You know nothing about me, really.'

'And I don't want to. Just leave it. We'll just carry on like this for now if that's what you want. Leave the rest. But I can't wait too long, Jess. I need to get out and I need you with me. You have to decide.'

'Not now, not yet. Look, you need to go. I'll see you next week. If I draw the curtains in the back room, that means I'm expecting you. Be careful. Don't give me away, please, love. I'm not ready.'

He bent over the bed and kissed her again. 'Next week.'

She heard his steps on the stairs, the back door opened and shut quietly. Minutes later she heard his bike as it puttered up the hill past the house and away to his cold house at the quarry.

Chapter 17

Jessie and Agnes were walking back together from the committee meeting at the vicarage. Agnes was just about to tell Jessie about the interesting young man she'd taken from Whitehaven Hospital up to Boot when Jessie turned to her and they both spoke at once.

'Sorry,' said Jessie. 'Carry on.'

'No, dear, it's not important. What were you going to say?'

'It was just about the hunt ball next week,' said Jessie. 'I wondered if you'd want to go this year. Do you remember last year you said you'd never go again.'

'Did I?' said Agnes. 'I don't remember. What was that about?'

'I think it was the young woman who made such a scene. She must've had something to drink. She was shouting at that man, do you recall? Pretty unsavoury stuff. They had to practically carry her out.'

'Oh, yes, I remember now,' said Agnes, linking Jessie's arm. 'That was quite a scene wasn't it? Who was it? Anyone we know?'

'I think it was one of the McCallister girls from up the valley. The older one, can't recall her name. She's gone away, by all accounts. Manchester, or Leeds.'

'Just as well! You do such a wonderful job with the bairns, Jessie, but sometimes as they get older they seem to turn into creatures we hardly recognise. What gets into them?'

'Life, I suppose,' said Jessie. 'They realise they're not bairns any more and push against everything we've tried to teach them. They settle down in the end, most of them, anyway.'

'And some end up like poor Alice Kitchin,' said Agnes, as they reached the brow of the hill and started down again towards the schoolhouse and Applegarth. 'Tea, dear, or a spot of supper? I'm feeling peckish, so let's see what's in my pantry.' She squeezed Jessie's arm.

'Why not?' said her friend, as they quickened their pace down the hill.

Agnes found some cold chicken and some of her delicious green tomato chutney and they ate, side by side at the kitchen table. Afterwards they made tea and took it in the sitting rooom, to the comfortable chairs on either side of a fire that Agnes had poked back to life when they came in.

'You seem to have a new lease of life since you had your hair cut,' said Agnes. 'You're looking very well, dear, I must say. Very bonny.'

Jessie smiled: she knew why she might be looking 'bonny', and it had nothing to do with having her hair cut.

'I never thanked you properly for taking me shopping that day, Agnes,' she said, changing the subject. 'I do love that green jacket and I would never have bought it if you hadn't been with me.'

'What about the hunt ball?' asked Agnes. 'Time for another shopping trip, perhaps?'

'Oh no,' Jessie replied, shaking her head. 'I'm sure I'll find something to wear.'

As she walked back to the schoolhouse, Jessie wondered about Agnes. She'd been shocked by how much Andrew seemed to dislike her. Surely most people realised that Agnes meant well, even though she didn't really fit in the village. She was well organised and generous, but she spoke 'posh', and the car and

137

the clothes gave her away as having more money than most of the village put together. Surely that was no reason to dislike her.

The two of them had been friends for several years, ever since Jessie took over at the school. They enjoyed each other's company. Agnes was the only person, or at least the only woman, that Jessie could talk to about things beyond the village, about politics, ideas, the world in general. They argued of course about some things but that was enjoyable too, most of the time. One of their more troublesome differences of view had been about the abdication the previous year. Jessie really didn't care whether Mrs Simpson was divorced or not, and felt the king should be free to marry whomever he chose, but Agnes had stronger views about this, and about many other things. Much as she loved Wallis Simpson's clothes and style, she'd insisted that she really should go back to America where she belonged and leave the king alone. Agnes's brother, who was something high up in the diocese at Carlisle, had claimed the woman was the devil sent to tempt a hapless monarch. It was all very difficult.

'Sex,' Agnes had said, at the end of their discussion. 'Always a problem. Life would be so much easier without it, don't you think? If Edward had just married a good woman like his brother did, we wouldn't have had all that upheaval and unpleasantness. Marriage is good for men. Keeps them out of mischief. Not so sure about marriage and women, though. Look at you and me. Do we need to be married? So restricting from what I can see of it. My sister Gwen, there's a case in point. Just as bright as her husband but it was she who had to give up medical school to be his wife and raise his children.'

The memory of Agnes's views on sex and marriage came back to Jessie suddenly as she climbed the stairs to her bedroom and caught the residual tang of Andrew's cigarette. She could not bear to consider what Agnes would think if she knew.

They were still clearing away the card tables from the whist drive when Agnes and Jessie arrived at the Bower House the following Saturday evening. The band was setting up at the far end of the big room, and the bar was crowded. Jessie looked at herself briefly in the big mirror in the entrance hall. Agnes was right: she did look well. The purple dress she'd bought last year and never worn fitted her well, and the new hair cut still pleased her when she caught sight of it. She looked younger, but was still puzzled and wary about Andrew's reaction to her. This was why she didn't trust him: everything in this room was his real world – the people he knew, the women and girls who obviously wanted him, the socialising he was so good at. She was beginning to understand the jumble of her feelings for him, excitement and anxiety, desire and fear. What might he do tonight, or say? Why did she put herself through this?

Agnes pulled Jessie's arm and spoke into her ear above the noise in the bar. 'Excuse me a minute, dear,' she said. 'Someone I want to say hello to,' and she disappeared into the snug. Jessie waited, looking round. She wanted to check if Andrew was there without making it look too obvious that she was doing so. She spotted him, at the far end of the bar, pint mug in hand, deep in conversation. She watched for a moment, but he didn't see her. Or at least, he didn't acknowledge her. They were getting practised at deceit, Jesse thought. It was childish, but it excited her.

'Jessie,' Agnes called from the door of the snug, beckoning to her. 'Some people I want you to meet,' she said when Jessie joined her. 'Just through here, dear, in the corner.'

Jessie recognised the odd-looking couple sitting in the corner of the crowded room: she'd noticed them before and knew that they lived up the valley, but she'd never been introduced to them. The long-haired woman was wearing a strange collation of garments, layered, and brightly coloured. There seemed to be a problem with one of her eyes. The man sitting next to her looked younger, a brown intelligent face, bright eyes. They look happy, Jessie thought.

'Jessie, may I introduce you to Hannah and Fred Porter. This is Jessie Whelan, who teaches at the school in Newton. These lovely people live at the Mill Cottage, up at Boot. That's where I was going that day in the car, with that young man, d'you remember, when we passed you? A week or two ago. You were talking to the vicar.'

Jessie thought for a moment. 'I remember there was someone in the car with you, but didn't really notice. I meant to ask you, who it was. '

'It was John, John Pharaoh. He'd been really poorly in the hospital in Whitehaven and I was taking him to his lodgings – his home, he called it – up the valley at Boot. Mill Cottage, which is where these two live.'

'So glad to meet you both,' said Jessie. 'Is that the cottage opposite the mill, just over the bridge?'

'That's the one,' said Hannah. 'I've lived there all me life, but only a short while for Fred. 'E lived Broughton way afore that.'

'Welcome to the west,' said Jessie. 'Broughton's just a few miles away but sometimes it feels like another country.'

'It does that,' said Fred. 'Summat special about the west, over 'ere. Hard to put your finger on, but it's different.'

'I think it's the sea,' said Agnes as she and Jessie sat down. 'Not the estuary, or the bay like at Ulverston, the open sea. It's wilder here, more exposed, just a strip of land with the sea in front and the mountains behind.'

'Ages ago folk used boats to get about,' said Fred. 'Never ventured inland. Roads were too rough.'

'Exactly,' said Agnes. 'Did you come for the whist drive, you two?'

'Aye we did, but no luck. And we're not going to win t'spot waltz are we Fred, not with your one leg and me half blind,' said Hannah. 'But it's allus a grand night.'

'While I think of it,' said Agnes, 'let me explain to Jessie about the young man. How is he by the way?'

'Not bad. Something on 'is mind, making 'im restless when 'e needs to stay still a while and get better. Can't go back to work yet, doc won't let 'im.'

'This young man, Jessie,' said Agnes. 'He came from Ulverston to work in the quarry office, a few weeks ago now, wasn't it Hannah? Somehow he ended up being dragged out of the sea – of course you've heard about that, haven't you? The Leadbetter boy, Andrew, saved his life apparently. Anyway, he hadn't been at Hannah and Fred's for more than a few days when he was taken ill, pneumonia, probably a legacy of that awful time in the sea, and nearly died. The hospital asked if anyone could get him home, so I brought him in the car, that day we saw you.'

'I see,' said Jessie. How fragile our lives are, she thought. And fancy calling Andrew 'the Leadbetter boy'. No wonder he doesn't like her.

'Fred here is an artist,' Agnes was saying. 'He makes the most wonderful rugs, finest examples of hookie rugs I've ever seen. Colours, designs, just wonderful. Next time I go to London Fred's promised to give me some to take, to show to my friend who owns a gallery. Not easy to get them on the train but I'll manage somehow. They really need to be seen by more people.'

Jessie was about to ask Fred some more about this talent, but Agnes pressed on.

'And the other thing, dear, and this is just priceless, Hannah and Fred have used the water mill to provide their own electricity.

Can you believe that? What a step forward, when the rest of the valley is still in darkness, so to speak. So clever.'

'Heavens,' said Jessie. 'That is impressive. What a boon that must be for you all.'

'Makes such a difference in the evenings,' said Hannah. 'Fred can do 'is rugs and I can read without straining my eye so bad. I've only one eye, you see.' She pointed to her closed eye. 'Lost the other one when I was a bairn.'

'And I lost my leg in the war,' said Fred. 'What a careless couple we are, eh, Hannah?' And they both laughed.

'Will John be here tonight?' Agnes asked.

'Nay, we asked 'im, but not his kind of thing, 'e said. Said 'e were going to bed early. Good idea. Too much smoke in 'ere for his chest to cope with.'

'You really should meet him, Jessie,' said Agnes. 'Such an interesting young man.'

'I'd love to,' said Jessie. 'I often walk up the valley if the weather gives me the chance for some exercise.'

'Well, we're usually there, and you're always welcome, Miss Whelan. Come for tea. Always cake in the tin.'

Jessie and Agnes said their goodbyes and sat down to watch the hunt ball unfold in its usual way. The band played old favourites and the new songs of the day. A group of young women began to gather, and Jessie noticed Andrew and two other men sitting down at a table, ready to choose the hunt queen. On Friday evenings all through the season, as the hunt moved from village to village clearing out foxes, girls presented themselves to a panel of judges and a queen was chosen from among them. At the end of the season, at the annual ball, these village winners came together for the selection of the best, and tonight was the night. Families had come from all over the area to support their daughters. There was tension in the air as old village rivalries surfaced and the injustices of previous years were remembered. All Jessie could think about was Alice. She too had primped and posed for the men's scrutiny. She had smiled and teased, and then she had died. The Kitchins were not here tonight.

The chairman of the hunt called for order. It was a little after ten and the search for the hunt queen was about to come to its conclusion. The girls arranged themselves in a line across one end of the room. Andrew and two other men, both older than him, sat at the table and appraised the stock in front of them. Agnes whispered to Jessie, 'Any minute now they're going to look at their teeth.'

Andrew had kept his promise not to pay her attention and Jessie was relieved. She felt free to watch him closely as he and his fellow judges went about their task. She watched his face, saw the pale eyes run up and down each girl in turn. She noticed the girls colour slightly under his gaze. She wondered what he was thinking. Once, just once, she saw him smile, not a fresh pleasant smile but something different. It was a smirk, a knowing connection with the body of the girl he was looking at. It was as if he'd laid his hands on her, possessed her, although his stance behind the little table never altered. Jessie felt a flutter in her chest, a draught like a door opening.

When it was all over, and the winning queen had been crowned, applauded and congratulated Jessie and Agnes remained on their uncomfortable chairs by the wall while the band organised themselves and people streamed past them to the bar. Through the crowd Jessie caught sight of Andrew, saying something to the girl who'd won. She looked away as Agnes spoke.

'Reminds me too much of the auction market at Broughton,' said Agnes, 'the way those girls are looked at. Harmless enough I know but I still don't like it. Last century maybe, but not now.'

Jessie said nothing in reply, as the band had started again and the music made it harder to talk. People began to dance. Suddenly, someone stood blocking their view of the dancers, It was Andrew. 'Would you care to dance, Miss Whelan?' he said with mock politeness. Jessie felt herself flush. She rubbed her hands surreptitiously on the skirt of her dress.

'I …' she began. Agnes pushed her to her feet. 'Go on, Jessie,' she said, laughing. 'Dance with the young man. I'll keep your seat for you.'

The band was playing something slow. Andrew guided Jessie across the room to the other side where there was more space, and away from Agnes, who was talking to Caroline Leadbetter now, no doubt about her son's chivalrous attention to one of his parents' friends. How surprised they would have been to hear the words that passed between the two of them. Looking over her head, Andrew said very quietly, 'Jessie you're the best-looking woman in this room and I want you, right now.'

Jessie lost track of her feet and it took them a moment to find the rhythm again. She looked around, wondering who might be noticing them, and squeezed his hand slightly to urge caution.

'I mean it,' he continued, relentlessly. 'Looking at all those slips of girls makes me want you all the more. Can't we get out of here?'

'I'm with Agnes,' she said, speaking into his chest to mask the words. 'She wants to leave early.'

'Not yet, surely?'

'Don't know. Soon. She hates to see people getting drunk.'

'Typical. She's a tight woman. Needs a man.'

'Don't. Not here.'

'Can't you go to the ladies or something? There's a toilet in the yard. I could go out the other door. I just want a kiss. I won't jump on you.'

'Hush, for heaven's sake.'

'Please Jess, just this once. I'm bursting for you.'

She faltered. His desire for her shocked and tantalised her. Not since Clive had she felt the physical urgency that he brought to her. It was her other self, the one she remembered during those last few weeks she and Clive had together. That was so long ago. Surely it was gone for good, but here she was, hearing those same words, feeling herself fall for them again.

The band had stopped. People were applauding as they moved off the dance floor towards the chairs or the bar. Jessie looked up and whispered.

'The far end of the yard, where it's darker. Wait for me.'

Her legs felt like water. Andrew left her and disappeared into the bar as if nothing had happened. Agnes was still talking to Caroline. Jessie pointed towards the back of the hotel, Agnes nodded and waved. Jessie kept walking.

The 'other woman' was fully in charge now. Jessie the school-teacher would have called a halt to this before it ever started, but Jessie the lover kept walking, through the press of people in the bar and by the door, out into the cold air. It was damp, drizzling slightly. Jessie drew her stole up around her neck and looked around for the ladies toilet that was behind the hotel. She could always claim that the indoor toilet was occupied. It was dark as she turned the corner, away from the light in the yard. Andrew stepped out of the shadow and she ran into him. He caught her in both arms and steered her further away from the light. Jessie the lover kissed him on the mouth, and he held her very close. She felt hot. Her heart thumped.

'Christ, woman, I want you. Where can we go?'

'We can't. Not here. I'll be leaving soon. Make some excuse. Come to me later. I'll leave the door for you.'

'Don't go yet.' He was pushing a hand up her skirt, but she pushed back against him and stepped away. She heard a giggle, quite close, and leaned forward against him again.

'Don't move,' she said. 'There's someone there.'

A lower voice this time, murmuring. Then a girl's voice, rising to a muted squeak. More laughter. Jessie froze. She put her fingers over Andrew's mouth.

'I have to go,' she whispered directly into his ear. 'Later. Come later.'

He said nothing. She could feel irritation, anger even, from his body so close to hers.

He pushed her away, took her hand and pulled her after him round the edge of the wall, towards the yard and the light. She tried to pull free but he held her hand firm in his own.

As they reached the back door of the hotel he let go and pushed her ahead of him towards the entrance, his hand on her shoulder. Just as he did so, someone appeared in the doorway, silhouetted against the light inside. It was Agnes.

'There you are,' Agnes began to say, hesitating when she saw Andrew. Jessie burned. She could feel the heat in her face and knew that shame and confusion must be written across it. Agnes looked at her. Andrew brushed past them into the hotel without a word. The two women faced each other awkwardly.

'I was looking for you,' said Agnes. 'I thought you wanted to leave, so I guessed you were heading for the cloakroom, or the car.'

'The cloakroom was busy so I went outside,' said Jessie. 'Mr Leadbetter, Andrew, was out there too, having a smoke.'

'Ah,' said her friend. 'Do you have your things?'

'I'll get my coat. I'll meet you at the car.'

Jessie picked up her coat and glanced at herself in the mirror. She was flushed, but that could be the heat. There was no reason why Agnes would guess what was going on. What if she did? Would she say anything? Jessie had no idea what to do or to say. She heard men laughing in the bar, pulled her coat around her and went out to the car. Agnes was sitting waiting, looking straight ahead. Jessie got in and sat quietly, willing herself to be calm.

'Ready, dear?' said her friend, without turning round. 'Let's go home.'

Chapter 18

ANDREW DIDN'T COME to her that night. Jessie waited until sleep dragged her down. Grey dawn woke her. She shut her eyes tight against the light and against the recollection of that moment at the ball. Agnes knew, surely. Dancing with Andrew could have been innocent enough. But being together outside: that was too much. Agnes was an intelligent woman. She had London friends for whom affairs and adultery were part of life. Jessie could confide in her, as a woman, and ask for her understanding, or she could do nothing, just brazen it out. The whole thing was absurd. He was too young, too male, too needy. She was out of her depth, and sinking.

She made tea, took it back to bed and managed to sleep a little longer. It was after nine when she finally surfaced, her mind made up. She would carry on as if nothing had happened, which would either reassure her friend that nothing was amiss or force her suspicions to the surface. Jessie couldn't bear the dance of uncertainty. She wanted her affairs forgotten or made explicit, and preferably the former. In the spirit of normalcy, she got and dressed for church. Church on Sunday morning was her routine, and she would keep to it. Agnes would be there. Jessie would look her in the eye and talk about inconsequential things. They could talk about Hannah and Fred and their new lodger, whose name Jessie could not remember. That would be safe.

Jessie arrived a little late at the church, sat in her normal pew, and waved to Agnes as she always did if time did not allow for conversation. The vicar was his normal self, choosing for his sermon something about service to the community. Afterwards, as Jessie walked across the churchyard, Agnes caught up with her. Jessie remembered that it was her turn to offer hospitality after the service. 'Coffee?' she said to Agnes. There was no reply, and Agnes's face gave nothing away.

'Tell me more about the Porters.' Jessie used her brightest tone as they picked their way carefully through the farmyard beyond the churchyard gate. 'I've seen her, the wife before, I'm sure, but I don't remember where.'

'Aren't they an interesting pair?' Agnes replied, her voice and expression still precisely as normal. 'Apparently in Boot they call them 'the one-eyed woman and the one-legged man'.'

'Well at least that's accurate.' Jessie began to hope that nothing was amiss.

'Exactly so,' said Agnes. 'It's really immaterial what they look like. They are such a comfortable couple somehow. Clearly enamoured of each other, and with the time to be creative. I do so admire that, and envy them, too. Maybe I should follow suit, start being creative myself rather than just admiring it in others.'

'What would do, if you had more time?'

'More photography, for a start,' said Agnes. 'But then I think I would learn to paint. Caroline has a watercolour at the vicarage that she found in Whitehaven somewhere. It's just exquisite. A view from down by the viaduct, of the river with the mountains in the distance. Just a few birds in the foreground, quite lovely.'

Jessie thought for a moment, picturing the spot. 'That's where they found poor Alice's body ... The Kitchins weren't there last night, did you notice? I expected to see him, but not her. She's a sad soul. I think he beats her, you know.'

'So many men feel they have the right to treat their wives any way they choose.'

'And their children, too,' added Jessie. 'Makes me weep to see some of those poor bairns at school.'

'Stop it, Jessie,' she said to herself. 'Don't talk about men, or last night. Keep quiet.'

They walked for a while in silence, but Jessie found it hard to bear, and tried a safer topic.

'Are you going away over New Year?'

'Not sure at present. I'm juggling two invitations actually, one to Newcastle, to Gwen and family, and the other to London, which is unusual and could be a lot of fun. I think I may do both, Newcastle first and then London.'

'How are they all?'

'They're doing well, thank you. Wonderful boys, my nephews. They'll be away and gone soon enough. I feel I want to see as much of them as I can while they're both still at home.'

Jessie felt better. Everything was as it should be. Agnes seemed to have no questions about last night, no suspicions or assumptions. Conversation about the Newcastle family took the two women to Jessie's gate, and round to the back door, which was unlocked. 'Go on in,' said Jessie to her friend. Agnes went ahead, and Jessie waited a second to take a deep breath and steady herself before she followed her into the kitchen.

'Go through,' she said. 'See if you can rescue the fire.'

Jessie poured water into the kettle and set it on the range to boil for their coffee. She didn't hear Agnes come into the kitchen behind her.

'The fire's picking up now. Can I help?'

'No, that's fine thanks,' said Jessie, but Agnes remained standing in the doorway.

'He's a fine looking man,' said Agnes suddenly. Jessie did not turn to face her.

'Who is?' she said.

'Andrew Leadbetter,' said Agnes. 'I noticed when you were dancing together last night.'

'Oh, that,' said Jessie, a little too breezily. 'I think he was just being polite.'

'I'm not so sure,' said Agnes.

Jessie was determined not to react. She busied herself with finding the coffee in the cupboard, and a tray for their cups.

Agnes went on. 'Did you notice him while they were judging those girls, the hunt queens?'

'Not really, no.' That was an outright lie but Jessie was determined not to give anything away, anything at all.

'There was something about the way he was looking at them. Predatory.'

'Oh, surely not,' said Jessie, worried now by Agnes's persistence. 'No different from the other men, I'm sure. The whole idea is so bizarre, lining up girls like stock animals for inspection.'

There was a slight pause.

'Jessie,' said Agnes. 'Is there something going on with you and Andrew? Tell me. Tell me I'm wrong. Please.'

Jessie could not see the expression on Agnes's face, but she heard the tone and turned towards her. She was not prepared. The cups rattled in her hand.

'What do you mean?'

'You know what I mean.'

'No I don't. Explain. What do mean by "something going on"?'

'How clear do you want me to be? You are friends, I can see that, anyone can. You've been seeing him about plans for the school …'

'Only because Lionel insisted.'

'You've been talking together. Maybe he said something to you. There's something between you. I can see it.'

Jessie put the cups down on the tray. Behind her the kettle began to whistle on the range. Agnes was looking at her. There was accusation in her face, and pain too. Jessie tried to give herself more time.

'Go back in the sitting room and I'll bring the coffee through. We can talk properly in there.'

Agnes turned and left the room. Jessie leaned on the back of a chair and breathed slowly to clear her head. She would either have to lie, and keep on lying, or tell the truth and hope that Agnes would at least keep it to herself. That was the only choice. She made the coffee and carried it through. Agnes sat upright on the sofa by the fire, her hands folded in her lap. Jessie poured the coffee and handed it to her.

'If I tell you about it I want you to promise that it remains between us. I'm not proud of what's happened and I know how it might look. Will you promise?'

Agnes gave a slight nod of her head but said nothing. There was no retreat now. Jessie continued.

'Andrew and I are ... very fond of each other,' she said, fumbling for the right words.

'How fond?' said Agnes. Jessie realised she would not settle for euphemisms.

'He says he loves me. I've told him he's too young, that it could never work, but he still insists.'

'And what about you?'

'As you say yourself, he's very attractive man. I'm flattered, I can't help that.'

'But you haven't –'

'Haven't what?'

'You haven't ... been to bed with him?'

152

Jessie realised that this was more than a question. It was a supplication. The choice was still there. She could lie.

'Yes I have,' she said.

Agnes choked, spilling her coffee onto her lap. 'Oh no, no,' she cried, dabbing at the brown splashes with a small handkerchief. Jessie got up from her chair to help.

'Don't!' said Agnes, flinching away from her. 'Don't touch me.'

She put the handkerchief to her mouth now, covering it up, but Jessie saw tears in her eyes. Agnes struggled for breath.

'How could you? How could you?' she was almost shouting now. 'With him. With a man like that. He's an animal.'

Agnes turned away, gasping for breath.

Jessie got up from her chair once more but Agnes put a hand towards her, keeping her away, still without looking round. The only sound in the sunlit room was Agnes's sobs, gradually abating. She found another handkerchief and blew her nose.

'Why didn't you tell me?' Agnes's voice broke the silence. 'I thought we were friends.'

'We are friends,' said Jessie quickly, anxious to return to quiet talk, away from this fierce anger. 'It's just happened. I'm not proud of it. I was going to tell you, when I felt clearer about it. I need to decide. I was hoping for your help.'

'You've done pretty well so far without any help from me,' said Agnes, with a bitterness that surprised Jessie again. 'Not much left for me to help with, by the sound of it.'

Jessie looked hard at her friend. Agnes met her eyes. She looked hurt, angry, upset beyond all expectation. Jessie didn't know how to respond. She wondered if something more serious was the matter with Agnes.

'It's not so terrible,' she heard herself saying. 'We're both single people. These things happen. Yes, he's younger than me, but he knows his own mind, and so do I.'

'You chose this?' Agnes raised her voice again. 'You chose to have … relations with this man?'

'Yes, I did.'

'Oh God. I can't imagine. It's disgusting.' And Agnes started to cry again, holding the sodden handkerchief to her mouth and staring out of the window.

A gust of wind moaned in the chimney and the fire sparked suddenly. A burning coal tumbled onto the rug and Jessie scooped it up with the shovel, but not before a smell of burning wool escaped, acrid, into the tension of the room.

'After all these years,' Agnes's voice burst out again, unnaturally loud, accusatory. 'I thought I knew you. I thought we were friends. And all the time you were thinking about … that. I thought we would grow old together, you and I. Maybe even share a house when we needed to help each other, later. I never knew you. I never imagined –'

She got up suddenly, knocking the small table in front of her.

'I have to go. I can't stay here. I should have known. You've always had something about you. It was sex, that's what it was. I should have known.'

Jessie started to get up.

Agnes raised her hand again.

'No, don't touch me. I'm going. Leave me alone. Stay with your filthy lover. Don't speak to me.'

Agnes stumbled out of the room. Jessie heard the back door slam behind her.

Anger came first. Jessie sat and cried for a few minutes, not a sad, quiet crying but fierce and breathless. She could not believe that Agnes had spoken to her in that way, used words like 'disgust', and 'filthy'. How could she?

'You think you know someone, that they like and respect you,' she thought, 'and then something happens and all that is lost in an instant. Not just lost but replaced by such hatred. I'm the same person I was before.'

She got up to deal with the sputtering fire, and when that small distraction was over, more thoughts flooded in, more disturbing thoughts. Maybe Agnes's reaction was truly the way the world, or at least this world, would judge her. Maybe going to bed with a younger man, doing what she and Andrew did and enjoying it, maybe that was just unacceptable to everyone else. There were things she found difficult. The way Andrew talked to her when they were alone excited her, she had to admit that, but it was crude and shameful even, when she looked back on it. Sometimes his lovemaking was rougher than she wanted. Many women would find it impossible, but she wasn't 'many women'. She loved the manliness of Andrew, the lust and the strength, as she had loved it in Clive, too.

She had to admit that Agnes was right about something: there was huge risk for Jessie in what she was doing. No one would censure Andrew, or even be surprised. She knew he already had a reputation as a ladies' man, and was admired for it. But for her it was different. As a headteacher, even being female was a problem these days. To have any chance of keeping the job she loved, she had to be seen to be beyond reproach. What were the chances, realistically, of keeping this secret? She could trust herself. She doubted that Agnes would ever bring herself to mention anything about it to anyone. But Andrew? Could he keep quiet about it? Sometimes she felt as if he had pursued her because of what she was, not who she was. Could that be? Something he was trying to prove, to himself, or to his father? Would he blurt it out in a rage, or after a drink?

Andrew wanted to get away, that was clear. Maybe he sincerely wanted or expected that Jessie would go with him, and that would be the end of the problem. But her instinct had said from the start that they did not have a long future together. If she was going to start again, it would be on her own, not tied to a man who would still be in his prime when she was old and needing care more than passion. Was that how it would be, she wondered. If she ended this with Andrew, would there ever be a chance of love again, real physical love not some dry cerebral friendship?

Some clear thoughts were emerging. She would not talk to Agnes for a while, to let her calm down. Maybe Agnes would apologise for the outburst. Maybe they could be friends again, but certainly not yet. And she would have to talk to Andrew, to make him understand. She had to decide what to say to him. She would take a few days and then give him the signal by closing the curtains in the spare room, which he could see from the road. Until then, she hoped he would stay away and give her time to think. Her mind was clearer, but now the sadness came. This time she cried for lost youth, and lost love and lost friends, overwhelmed by loneliness.

Chapter 19

THE FOLLOWING WEEK passed in a haze of work, routine, distraction. Every night Jessie stayed at school as long as she could to avoid the emptiness of her own home, the beloved home that had been invaded by fear and anxiety. She could lose it all, the job, the house, her reputation and respect in the village, and for what? Did he love her, really love her, not just the lust that was so obvious and so inexplicable? Could she trust him to keep quiet about it, and for how long?

The weekend, when it finally arrived, stretched before her like a prison sentence. It was dark early, and by the time she walked the few yards from the school to her house on Friday afternoon the rain was slanting in from the south-east, cold and hard against her face. Even if she'd had anywhere to go, leaving the house again was a daunting prospect. She would rely on a good meal, a warm fire and the radio to distract and comfort her during the evening ahead. Tomorrow, with any luck, she could get out into the air and be able to think more clearly.

Food and warmth certainly helped, as did a couple of glasses of sloe gin, the remnants of last year's crop that would be replenished by the new vintage maturing in the dark recesses of her kitchen cupboard. At least for a short while she didn't have to talk to anyone, to explain or even defend herself. By nine o'clock

Jessie had almost convinced herself that Andrew was serious about going to Canada and taking her with him to start a new life there. He would settle down away from the pub and the hunt and young girls who brought out the worst in him. She would find a job in a Canadian school and be appreciated for what she could offer. They would be happy for a while, until the age difference between them became more of a problem and after that, who knew what might happen? But at least she would have known what it was like to love and be loved for the first time in decades. She deserved that. The prospect of a new life and love, made more attractive by the impact of the sweet scarlet contents of her third glass, lulled her into welcome sleep.

But it was a false prospect. With the damp dawn came disappointment and the same depression that had weighed on her all the previous week. Agnes's reaction had been extreme, but her caution was well founded. Jessie's rational being knew that she had more to lose than to gain from her association with Andrew, however exciting it might be. Her life and her future were here in this community, if not in this village. Her heart might yearn for adventure and romance like a love-struck teenager, but her strong head recognised the siren's call for what it was, an invitation to disaster. Jessie accepted her headache as a necessary punishment for foolishness and determined to treat it not with liver salts but with a good brisk walk.

Dealing with Agnes would clearly have to wait. For the time being she would seek company elsewhere, up the valley, and take advantage of the offer that had been made at the hunt ball, before Andrew's intervention had changed everything. It was a good step up to Boot to visit the Porters at Mill Cottage but if she set off early and strode out it would occupy her for most of the daylight hours, which was exactly what she wanted.

As it happened, Jessie didn't need to walk all the way to Boot that morning. The fish cart was going as far as Ganthwaite and Mr Mulholland was grateful for the company as he and his horse made their way up there. It meant a few stops along the road, and a slight odour that lingered on Jessie's coat for a while, but it cut her walk down to a couple of miles and brought her by around noon to the end of the lane running up to the mill and the cottage. If no one was in, it didn't really matter, she thought to herself: the walk would do her good with or without the company.

Nevertheless as she crested the little bridge Jessie was pleased to see the front door of the cottage open. On a summer's day it might be left open even if the house was empty but not today, when the wind was still strong and smelled of rain. Without sunlight to brighten it the brown bracken on the hillsides all around was dull, much of it already flattened by the weather. It would be months before the new growth struggled through. To her right she could hear the great water wheel turning but it was hidden from view behind the low slate buildings of the mill.

The steps up to the cottage door were greasy from the overnight rain and required some concentration. She heard Fred Porter's voice before she saw him, standing just inside the doorway, holding on to the door rather than his stick, which he rarely used in the house.

'Why it's the schoolteacher come to visit,' he cried. 'Come in, lass, and let's get this door shut. Hannah's been sweeping but the wind's blowing dust in, not out.'

Jessie looked up at Fred and they smiled at each other. There was something about this man that was reassuring, so unlike the unsettling affect that Andrew had on her. Fred was about Jessie's age, she guessed, maybe a little older but he seemed wise and comfortable with himself and with his wife, who appeared from upstairs wiping her hands on a red pinafore that reached almost to the ground.

'Well Miss Whelan, good to see ye,' said Hannah. 'I said to Fred, it's time we met Miss Whelan proper, after all these years of knowing her face but nowt else.'

'I was thinking exactly the same,' said Jessie. 'I know all the children and their families of course, but sometimes miss out on other good people who live around me.'

'Well we're reet glad you came to see us, aren't we love,' said Fred, taking Jessie's big coat from her to hang up behind the door which was now firmly shut against the wind and the coming rain.

'So, sit thisen down and gi'us all the crack,' said Hannah, taking off her pinafore to reveal a long patchwork skirt and green woolen cardigan.

'Not much to tell,' Jessie said. 'Just a plain old country school-teacher, you know.'

'That's rubbish for a start, eh Fred,' Hannah retorted. 'Plain old, my eye! We saw you dancing t'other night, showing those young 'uns a thing or two. Where did ye larn to dance like that I wonder?'

Jessie smiled at the memory. 'Actually, it was in the war, now I come to think of it. I was working in an aircraft parts place down in Chorley, and the girls I lodged with taught me to dance. And we practised too, every Saturday night when we weren't working.'

'So 'ow did ye get to be a schoolteacher then?' Fred asked as he leaned against the back door, filling the kettle from a large jug.

'After it was all over and the factory was stood down I got a place at a college near Liverpool and used the money I'd saved. It was hard, but worth it. When I was qualified I could come back to my roots, or closer anyway.' Jessie hesitated. The habit of secrecy was strong but she could tell that secrecy would be challenged in this house. Time to change the subject.

'But what about you two? What a bonus to have electricity up here while the rest of us are still doing without. Sometimes the west coast feels like the land that time forgot.'

'That's what comes of finding a very clever man and marrying 'im before anyone else snaps 'im up,' said Hannah, turning to laugh at Fred. ''E may have lost a leg but 'e's got a reet good brain. Dad never understood that.'

'He thought having one eye made ye stupid as well, love,' Fred's quiet voice came from the dark side of the room. 'We've neither of us 'ad much schooling, Miss Whelan, but we can still work things out.'

'Oh call me Jessie, please,' said Jessie. 'Unless you want me to call you Mr and Mrs Porter.'

Fred sat down heavily on a wooden chair at the table. 'I've a story for you Miss – Jessie, about how keen she was to be wed,' He pointed at Hannah, who laughed as she knew what was coming. 'We had to sign t'register like, when we were wed, and Hannah was supposed to sign 'er unmarried name, but she were in that much of an 'urry she started to sign 'erself Hannah Porter instead of Hannah Tyson. She'd to cross it out and start again. We laughed, didn't we, love?'

Jessie looked at them. 'When did you two meet?' she asked.

'Well it was Dad's sister Mattie,' said Hannah. 'She always told me dad to go easier on me, and to stop blaming me for Mam's death. Mam died having me ye see, and 'e never really got ower it. Given a choice, 'e'd have taken 'er over me any time. Anyway, I must have been mid-twenties, summat around that, and 'e were getting worse, 'ardly let me do anything except look after 'im and 'ouse. I were ground down by it.'

'You were that, love,' Fred chipped in. 'She were a lovely lass, Jessie, and treated bad. 'E didn't mean it I reckon, just didn't think of anyone save himself and his own troubles.'

'And 'e worked 'ard,' said Hannah, 'too 'ard, looking back on it now.'

Hannah broke off to find some gingerbread in one of the tins on the shelf, leaving the story hanging. Jessie took a piece of the proffered gingerbread and waited.

'Where was I?' said Hannah.

'Mattie,' said Fred.

'Oh, aye. Well, Dad's sister Mattie lived in Broughton. She came to visit and gave me dad a right rocket about the way 'e were treating me. I were upstairs but I could 'ear them going at it 'ammer and tongs.'

'She were fierce, that Mattie,' Fred added. 'So 'e didn't stand a chance.'

'Well it ended up that Mattie got one of 'er lasses, a bit younger than me she were, to swap with me for a full month to give me a break from looking after me dad.'

'And to get the lass away from that lad she was seeing, the big lad, Hewer, they called 'im.'

'That's it!' cried Hannah. 'I'd forgotten that bit. Dan Hewer. They married in the end but didn't last. She ran off with that bugger from Gawthwaite, what's 'is name? Doesn't matter anyway. Gertie they called her. She came over 'ere, and I went there, to Broughton. It were market day that first week I were there, and I was watching all t'folk and I saw this man, 'andsome as auld Nick, sitting on the steps by the cross in the square, whittling or summat, just sitting there, and that was it. Saw him smile, corn-flower eyes, lovely hands, curly hair, that was it. Smitten. When 'e stood up 'e only had one leg, but too late. I'd 'ad it by then.'

'What did your father say?'

'Didn't tell 'im, did I. Me and Fred kept it dark as long as we could. It were that stupid Gertie, blurted out summat to me Dad about me man only having one leg and there were 'ell on. 'E gollered and radged. No way we could wed with that going on, so we 'ad to wait. Wait to wed, not for anything else, eh, Fred.'

'Give ower love, in front of company.'

'Anyway, 'e died, me dad, God rest 'im, and 'ere we are, 'appy as pigs in you know what. It were meant to be, no question, so we just 'ad to take the chance when we got it.'

'And you never found someone?' Fred asked, looking across at Jessie. 'Handsome clever woman like you. How did that 'appen?'

'War, was it?' said Hannah.

'Me and a million others,' said Jessie, glad to have such a simple explanation offered to her. 'Not in France, but in the shipyard of all places. He was helping build an airship and he fell. Banged his head on the side of the dock and that was that.'

They shook their heads at the injustice of it all. Jessie let the silence swallow any further explanation.

Hannah reached for her pinafore. 'Looks like lunchtime already and 'ere we are raking over auld times and no sign of our John. Where did 'e say 'e were going, Fred?'

'Just up to Hardknott, he said, and straight back. Should be 'ere soon.'

'I'll get food on table and he'll walk in, you watch. Needs his food, that's for sure. Much better than 'e was, but still not reet. Too thin for 'is own good, and broods a lot. Spends too much time on 'is own, 'appen. Young people need company.'

'Is he back at work yet, after his time in hospital?' asked Jessie.

'Doc says no, not yet. 'E were really bad, nearly died, they said. Lucky that doctor was up there at the Wasdale Head that night and got 'im straight into hospital. Says 'e might go and see his aunt and uncle in Ulverston, something to do with his mam's death. Dinna know what'll 'appen about the quarry job. 'E doesn't tell us much.'

Fred glanced out of the window at the front of the house.

'Looks like 'im coming over bridge now. You were right Hannah, he must've smelled that cheese.'

Jessie got up to help Hannah put plates and knives on the table. The sound of the door opening made her turn towards it. The young man's shape was outlined against the light, bending his head in the low doorway, and she couldn't yet see him clearly. He was wearing a hat pulled down low over his eyes, and a woollen jacket with the collar turned up against the wind.

As she watched, the man stood up straight and pulled off his hat. Jessie caught sight of the dark hair, the face, the shape of the shoulders. She gasped, put a hand to her open mouth and then fell heavily, straight down onto the flagged floor and a rug the colour of blood. For a moment three people stared at the woman lying on the floor, watching as she stirred slightly. It was John who moved first, holding his arm out to keep Fred away before he too lost his balance.

'Who is it?' John asked, as he pushed away a chair and knelt down beside Jessie.

'Miss Whelan, schoolteacher from Newton,' said Hannah. 'We saw 'er at the hunt ball and she walked up to visit.'

'Is she ill?' asked John, and then turned his attention to Jessie as she struggled to raise her head. 'Get us some water, Hannah. She's just fainted.'

Hannah poured some water into a big mug and brought it across.

John helped Jessie to sit up, and supported her while she drank from the proffered mug. He took the mug from her but Jessie kept her head down.

'I'm so sorry,' she murmured. 'I don't know what happened. I was getting up and then everything went round and blurred and down I went. I'm fine, really. If you could let me lean ...'

John took her elbow and helped her as she got slowly to her feet, then guided her back into a chair. Still Jessie did not look up.

'My bag?' she said, looking around.

'It's 'ere, pet,' said Hannah. Jessie found a handkerchief and wiped her mouth. She pulled her hair back from her face and breathed in and out very slowly, her eyes focused on the square of light from one of the windows. John and Hannah and Fred waited while their guest recovered her composure.

'That's better,' said Hannah. 'Bit more colour in your cheeks. For a bit there looked like you'd seen a ghost. Now you need a cuppa, strong and sweet. John, love, sort kettle out, will you?'

With John busy across the kitchen, Jessie at last was free to raise her head, and she did so, stretching her neck from side to side. She checked her hands and knees. They would bruise no doubt but no skin broken, no blood anywhere.

'No harm done,' she said. 'Must've got up too quickly, you know. I'm fine, really.'

'That 'appened afore?' asked Fred.

Jessie lied without compunction. 'Yes, once or twice. Maybe it's time I asked Dr Dawson to have a look. Could be just my age, you know.'

Hannah and Fred looked at each other.

'Here's that cup o' tea,' said Hannah, 'and then what's the best, miss? You could lie down upstairs for a bit. John could 'elp you.'

John was stirring sugar into Jessie's tea.

Jessie reacted quickly. 'Oh no, really,' she said. 'A cup of tea will set me up right I'm sure. Need to be home. Not sure I can walk back though, feel a bit unsteady.'

Hannah turned to John. 'Give us that tea, our John, and go down to t'pub. Tell George we need a nag an' cart to tek Miss Whelan back to Newton.'

John did as he was told, pulling his hat back on as he left.

Now Jessie could relax a little more. She sipped her tea, grateful for a reason to say nothing for a few minutes. Hannah gestured to Fred silently over Jessie's bent head, pointing upstairs.

'You really should lie down for a while, Miss Whelan.' he said. 'We'll be worried if ...'

Jessie was determined. 'No, no,' she insisted. 'I'll be fine, going home in style. I'm only sorry I couldn't stay longer. I'm so grateful to you, so kind. Sorry to give us all such a shock.' She smiled up at them, and got carefully to her feet.

When the door opened again Jessie was ready this time, not looking at John's face as he entered, concentrating on finding her coat, reassuring Hannah, finding a comb to restore some order to her appearance. Mercifully George had responded to the urgent summons, and within a few minutes they could hear the horse's hooves on the bridge.

'There it is,' said Hannah. 'Take Jessie's arm, John. Them steps are slippy when it's wet. Don't want any more accidents.'

Jessie let John help: she had no choice. Hannah and John together pushed Jessie up on the seat. George took up the reins, and coaxed the horse to negotiate the tight turn in the space beside the mill. Jessie smiled and raised her hand briefly as they moved slowly down the lane.

'You alreet, miss?' said George. 'John said you've 'ad a fall.'

'I'm fine,' she said again. 'Just fainted. Silly. Not enough breakfast, probably. So kind of you, George.'

Her mind was reeling. She took no notice of the shadows of clouds as they swept across the valley floor, or the buzzard sitting on a fence post watching as they passed. When they reached the schoolhouse, George helped her in and then she was alone. Upstairs she lay on her bed, willing herself to sleep, to blot out the maelstrom in her head, but the questions whirled.

Was it him? The young man looked so like Clive, but could it be just a chance, or her mind playing tricks? Or could he be someone related to Clive, but not to her? Clive had sisters, she remembered that. They could have children who looked like

166

Clive. The name, Pharaoh, meant nothing to her. Her mother would know, or Aunty Barbara, but they were both gone. No one to ask, no way to check, without asking the young man himself, but she dare not reveal herself. If it was him, that person she'd not seen for twenty years, what would she do? And what was he doing, living so close? Just coincidence, or was he tracking her down? Would he want to punish her for what she did all those years ago?

The uncertainty paralysed her. She had no idea what to do. The only safe thing for the time being was to do nothing, to wait. Agnes had talked to the young man, but how could she check without telling Agnes what she should have told her years ago and never did. And now it was too late, even for that. Agnes had cast her off. 'Disgusting'.

Jessie turned her face into the pillow and wished for it all to end.

Chapter 20

'Uncle George, over here.'

It had taken a minute or two for the steam and smoke to clear before John was able to see the familiar short figure standing on the platform at Ulverston station, under the yellow cone of light from the lamp. John put down his bag and waved, and George smiled as he walked towards him.

'By 'eck, you picked a rotten night for a journey, our John,' said George, as he shook the young man's hand.

'Aye, not much to see on the way down,' said John. 'I can carry that,' he added as George picked up the bag. 'I'm much better now.'

'More than my life's worth to let her see you carrying a bag, lad,' said George, nudging John away. 'We've been right worried about you I can tell you, Anne and me. You nearly drowned and then so poorly and so far away, having to be looked after by strangers. Worried sick, we were. Now there's no rush, so take the hill slowly, and we can always stop on the way, for a rest.'

George winked at him, and John knew full well that the 'rest' was more likely a chance for them to have a quiet beer together before they faced Aunty Anne.

They walked side by side slowly up the steep hill to the gas-lit main road.

'Street lamps!' said John. 'It's like another world here, Uncle George. Over in Boot it's moon and stars or no light at all at night. Never known darkness like that. Like having a thick blanket over you. Can't see anything, not even your hand in front of your face. So dark that you could walk into a wall, or off a bridge. And cars here too,' he added as they reached the road. 'Only two people I know up there who have cars are the lady who brought me home from the hospital and the vicar. He's got an Armstrong Siddeley, would you believe? Folks think he's a bit mad.'

'You mentioned that woman in your letter,' said George. 'What's 'er name again. Miss Plane was it?'

'Aye, that's it. Really kind of her I thought, but people help each other out more when they need to. 'Appen that's the way it works in the country.'

'You've picked up the talk, too', said his uncle. 'Don't know what Enid would have said about words like " 'appen". Here we are, lad. The Locksmiths. Nice quiet little place. There was a crowd of Vickers blokes got off the train ahead of you but they'll be heading for the King's Head down the town. Best to keep out of their way when they're escaping from the drink police in Barrow. They can get fined there you know, for drinking. Vickers run that town like Mussolini runs Italy, all rules and do as you're told.'

They found a table by a bright fire in the snug and George bought a pint of Hartley's best for himself and a half for John. They sat in silence for a few minutes, enjoying the warmth and the quiet.

169

'Now then, lad,' said George finally, 'before we get back to Church Walk and Anne plagues you with questions, tell me a bit more about what happened on the beach. You might need to spare Anne the details, but you can tell me. You didn't say much in the letter, just that you had some trouble and some bloke pulled you out of the sea. But what were you doing there in the first place? That's what we couldn't work out.'

John told the story again, answering George's questions as patiently as he could. He left out the fact that he'd thought he was going to drown.

'So the bloke who pulled you out turns out to be your boss at the quarry? That might be tricky, mightn't it, feeling that you owe him, you know.'

'That's right, Uncle George. Took me a while to think about that, but you're right. I don't feel comfortable with the bloke. And he's a strange one too, I reckon. Moody. Wouldn't like to be around him when he's drunk. That's why I needed to get out, find somewhere else to live.'

'And what's this place where you're living now. Boot, is it?'

'Aye, up the other end of the valley from Newton. Quarry's about half way up the valley and Boot's another couple of miles beyond that. When I start work proper I might get a bike, even a motorbike. Went on Andrew's motorbike when he took me back to his place, and I was scared to death, but that's because he went too fast. Great way to get around. I've got lucky with the people I'm living with. Hannah and Fred, the one-eyed woman and the one-legged man they call them, because they are! They're so easy with each other, somehow. They talk about anything. It's been a revelation for me after living with Mam – Enid – all those years. They even talk about sex.'

George put down his pint and looked at John. 'They're not, you know, funny like, are they?'

170

'Not sure what you mean by funny, Uncle George, but they're good people, I know that. Honest, kind, happy in themselves. Don't care about money or appearances.'

'Well that's good, John. But don't mention that sex thing to Anne. She's Enid's sister, after all.'

The house in Church Walk was as warm and welcoming as it had always been. Anne Youle was so pleased to see him that she didn't chide her husband for stopping off on the way and making them a bit late for dinner.

'John needed a rest,' George said to her, 'and then we got talking about all his adventures. Makes our life sound pretty quiet by comparison.'

'Quiet but safe,' said John. 'Lovely to be back, Aunty Anne.' Anne gave him a hug for the first time since he was child, and they sat down to a delicious meal.

'Pork!' said George, 'and it's not even Sunday. You can come again, lad.'

An hour or so later, Anne and John sat together in the front room while George did his duty with the washing up. Anne demanded as many details about everything that had happened as John could find the energy for. The journey, the beer and now a big meal had made him so tired he could hardly keep awake. But he had to tell them the reason for his visit: it might take them a while to decide how to respond. He'd thought carefully about what he wanted to say.

'While you're both here, and before I get too tired to think,' he said, facing them both, 'I've been thinking about my mother, not Enid, my real mother. I want to find out who she was, and why she had to give me up. At first I wanted to punish her, but now, well, I just want to know. You two are my best hope. Enid and Arthur have both gone, and I'm sure Enid never meant me to know that I wasn't their child. She was dying and her mind had gone and it just slipped out, by accident. But now it's out I can't forget it, and I'm going to look until I find her. I know you promised Enid you wouldn't talk about it, but they're both gone and I'm here. You have a think about it. There's no rush. The doc won't let me go back to work, and I reckon they'll sack me pretty soon. There must be something you can remember. I'm asking you to help me.'

The fire crackled in the grate. Anne and George looked at each other. 'We promised, George,' said Anne. 'She made us promise.'

'I know she did, love,' he said, taking hold of her hand, 'but that was a long time ago. And our John's here now, with his life ahead of him. If it was me, I'd be asking questions, and you would too. You and Enid talked about it, you must have done. That's all he wants. We have to help him.'

Anne's eyes filled with tears.

'I know, I know.' She turned to John. 'He's right, John. But she didn't tell me much, really. Little things I picked up, but I've tried to forget them over the years because that was what she wanted. If Arthur had lived – but he didn't – and after he was gone she got even more determined that it'd never be mentioned. She'd be turning in her grave right now if she could hear us.'

'That's it, Anne love,' said George. 'She's in her grave, God bless her. Time to move on.'

George turned to John. 'Too late to do any more tonight. Give your Aunty Anne a night's sleep to think it all through and we'll talk tomorrow. Might even be able to find some stuff that would help you. Loads of boxes in the loft that we brought from Barrow when we moved and never looked at since. I'm not on till ten tomorrow so I could get up there first thing and you and Anne can have a good rummage around while I'm out.'

The following morning John held the ladder while George climbed up into the loft and Anne shouted instructions about where to find the box she was looking for.

'Right away down, in the corner,' she shouted, as drifts of dust floated down from above.

'Pretty mucky up 'ere,' came George's voice, 'Good job I didn't put me work clothes on yet.'

'Can you see it?' called his wife. 'It's a big tea chest. Newspapers on top probably, just to keep the dust out.'

'Found it!' called George. 'There's another box inside it.'

'That's the one,' said Anne. 'Take it out carefully. Is the key in it?'

'Aye, there it is, after all these years. Newspapers dated 1921, that's when we moved here. What's in it?'

'All sorts,' said Anne, as George handed the box down to her. 'Stuff from the Barrow days, before John was born, and afterwards. Might be something that would help him.'

'Let me,' said John. He took the box from her and looked at it. Maybe here would be the clues he so badly wanted. He already had that fragment of a letter he'd found after the funeral. It was tucked safely in the side pocket of his bag upstairs. On its own, it wasn't enough. Maybe, just maybe, he could soon start his search in earnest.

CHAPTER 21

WHEN GEORGE HAD left for work, Anne and John made more tea and took it into the front room with them. Anne had dusted off the box and it sat on the table in the window.

'Go on, love,' she said. 'This is for you. You open it.'

John thought for a moment.

'Before we start, I want to show you the only clue I've found so far. It was in Enid's house, our old house. I turned the place upside down after she died, hoping to find a box like this, labelled "Clues for John when he looks for his real mam", but of course there was nothing. The will was there, but nothing else except this,' he said, taking an envelope out of his pocket. 'I found it stuck at the back of a drawer upstairs.'

'What is it?' Anne asked, looking at it carefully.

'Looks like the first page of a letter. The rest must have been thrown away and this got left behind.'

John removed the page from the envelope and held it in his hand. Just looking at it made his heart bump. He remembered when he'd found it, how angry he was with Enid. And when he read it again at Mill Cottage he was angry still, but this time with the woman who'd given him away. That seemed so long ago now. Now he wasn't so angry, just curious.

'My glasses are upstairs.' Anne tapped her pockets in vain.

'Can you read it to me?'

John read the familiar words, and Anne listened carefully.

'Just a minute,' said Anne, leaving the room to return with a piece of paper and a pencil. 'Now read it again.'

This time she started to scribble. When he'd finished a third read through, she looked at what she'd been writing.

'This is what we know. The arrangement about finding a home for you was made quite a while before you were born by the sound of it. Someone who knew Enid very well – knew all about her and Arthur wanting a child – also knew your real mam's aunt. That person lived in Furness Road. You know where that is?'

'No,' said John. 'Don't know Barrow very well at all.'

'Well it's close to where Enid and Arthur lived in Bridgedale Road. The person who wrote this letter lived close by. Enid and Arthur went to St Luke's. So church is a connection, and the choir. Is that all there is?'

'That's it, just stops in mid-sentence. No name.'

'The only name we have is Thompson, which must mean that your mam, the daughter, was called Thompson, too. Well, that's a start. Now what we have to look for in this box is anything about the choir, or anyone called Thompson. I'm going to need my glasses, aren't I? Can you get them for me, pet, on the bedside table. Don't need them for anything but reading, but I need them now.'

When John returned with the glasses, Anne was still waiting.

'You open it now,' she said.

John put his hand over his mouth.' I'm feeling a bit sick, actually. Just nerves I think.'

Anne looked at him. 'I can't imagine what it must be like,' she said.

John turned the tiny key and lifted the lid of the box. It was full of papers. The first items he looked at he handed to her without

175

comment: school reports from Anne's childhood, and some from her children. There were photos too, and Anne laughed as she remembered people and places from long ago. She handed one to John.

'Look,' she said. 'Enid and Arthur while they were courting. They walked out for a long time before they got engaged. Before the war we all thought we'd live forever. We had no idea what was coming. Look at the hat, isn't it priceless! They look happy, don't they? They were happy, I'm sure. It was only in the later years that she got so – you know – pinched. Nothing was ever right for her somehow. When you arrived I thought she'd be cheerful again, but no, or only every now and then. Little things bothered her a lot, too much. Looking back I wonder when that illness and the trouble with her memory and such really started. When you were still at junior school she sometimes said some odd things, but I didn't think much of it at the time. It was when Arthur died that she really seemed lost. After that, she was never the same.'

'That's how I remember her, I'm afraid,' said John, as he looked at the photo of the far-off stranger who had pretended to be his mother. 'Nothing was ever right, like you said. She seemed disappointed in me. Wanted someone livelier I suppose, more confident, cleverer even. And all that time I wondered why I didn't fit, if you know what I mean. And she knew, and she said nothing.'

'Keep going, love,' said Anne. 'Photos are always helpful, if we can sort out who everybody is.'

John looked a little further and picked out another photo. It was of a group, maybe thirty or so, men at the back and women nearer the front, with another man standing alone to one side. Some children sat at the very front, on the ground, legs crossed. Looked as if they were on a beach, or a ship with the sea behind them. John turned the photo over. 'Choir trip to Blackpool, June 1914', he read, after squinting at the tiny writing for a moment.

'There are lists of names too, but really faded. Must've been in pencil. Can't read most of them. 1914. Three years before I was born.'

Anne peered at the photograph and then turned it over to look at the names. 'Enid was in the choir. I wonder ... Let me see.'

'It's no good,' she said, 'Can't see the faces, never mind the names, even with my glasses on. It's a terrible thing getting old. You have another look, John. No, better still, I think there's a magnifying glass in the bureau drawer in the back room. Can you fetch it for us?'

Anne still had tight hold of the photo when he returned a minute later with the magnifying glass in his hand.

'Can I see?' he said.

'Of course, pet. Here am I, hogging the thing. You have a look. See if you can see Enid. Maybe she wasn't there, but why should she have given me the photo if she wasn't on it?'

It wasn't the people John noticed first, but the name on the lifebelt hanging on the wall behind the group.

'Who's Lady Moyra?' he said to Anne.

'The *Lady Moyra*,' said Anne. 'Well, well. It's the name of the ship. Let me look. Give me the glass a minute ... Of course.' She looked up at John. 'They were going to Blackpool on the *Lady Moyra*. It was a paddle steamer, took folk across Morecambe Bay. Barrow people loved that trip, specially in the summer. It all stopped when the war started. I think they took the ship for minesweeping. So the choir went to Blackpool.'

She looked again. 'There she is, ' she cried out, 'there's your mam, Enid. On the right there, can you see? Here.'

She handed the photo and the glass back to John who turned towards the window for more light.

'On the right, near the front,' said Anne, leaning over. 'She's wearing a hat and a shortish jacket. Can you see?'

John could see. The woman who called herself his mother, before she had ever seen him, before he'd been born to someone else, before she and Arthur grew so desperate that they took someone else's baby as their own.

'She looks sad,' he said. 'Even on the trip, she looks sad.'

'She was sad a lot of the time, before you came. Even afterwards, too. Nothing was ever quite right. It's a curse, wanting things to be perfect. Poor Arthur tried so hard to make her happy, but he didn't really know what to do. I always thought he agreed about adopting you just to please her, and then it was him who loved you so, more than he ever expected he told me. Quite shocked him, I think. Never thought of himself as the fatherly type, but he loved you, John, he really did.'

'Do you have any more photos of him, Aunty Anne? I found one of their wedding in the house, but it was awful. They both looked scared stiff.'

'We'll have a look in a minute, but let's see what else we can find in this one first. Must have been a weekend, or a school holiday. Look how many children there are. And some older ones, too, although they could've been in the choir themselves. Look at this girl, just off to the side. On the other side, away from Enid. Lovely, isn't she? About your age maybe, or younger. Hard to tell.'

John looked, then took the glass and looked again. He saw a tall young woman, with full dark hair. No hat, and the hair blew around her face. She was wearing a white blouse, tucked into a dark skirt. Her eyes were half closed against the sun. He handed the photo back to Anne.

'So we know Enid was there,' she said, 'and twenty or so other people. Let's assume this was the whole choir, plus some children. I think the man at the front must have been the organiser, maybe the choirmaster. Something about the way he's standing. Looks as if he's in charge. I wonder who he was.' She turned the photo over and peered at the faded markings. 'There's a name in the bottom left corner on this side, in the same place where the man is standing. Must be him. Mr Cram, no, Mr Crane.'

Anne picked up her little notebook.

'Let me write some of this down before I lose track,' she said. 'Choir trip to Blackpool, 1914. The *Lady Moyra*. Mr Crane. I'll put choirmaster, question mark. Can't be sure of anything yet. But it's a start. If we're right, Mr Crane was the choirmaster at St Luke's in 1914. That's three years before you were born, and we think that someone in your real mam's family knew Enid through the choir. Three years. Things could have changed, of course.' She thought for a moment and scribbled some numbers on the page of her notebook.

'Have another look at Mr Crane,' she said to John. 'How old d'you think he looks?'

'Hard to tell,' said John, moving the magnifying glass forward and back to get the right focus. 'Forty maybe? I can never tell ages by looking at people.'

'Well if he was forty in 1914, that would make him too old for the war, and if he lived through that he would be sixty-three now, or thereabouts. Could be still around. I bet he could tell you a few things about the people in that photo.'

'But if I'm wrong, and he was older, then –'

'No good speculating,' said Anne firmly. 'It's just a clue so far, nothing more. At least we know it was St Luke's and the church will still be there. Churches have records don't they? Do you know where it is? Doesn't matter, I do, so we know you could go there if you wanted to.'

John turned the photo over again and looked at the names written so faintly on the back. There weren't as many as the people in the picture, so it was only some of the names. They didn't seem to correspond to the placing of the people in the picture either, so he couldn't connect a face with a name. He put the photo down and leaned back on the chair. His aunt leaned over and put her hand on his shoulder.

'Here am I, prattling on,' she said. 'It must be so strange for you, not knowing.'

'It is,' he said, leaning away from her touch. 'Can't describe it really. Too much to take in. Can I keep this, Aunty Anne?'

'Of course you can, pet. Means far more to you than to me.'

'I didn't find anything like this in the house. Maybe Enid just got rid of anything from those days. They cut themselves off, just to stop people asking questions about me. And I was a disappointment, I know that now.'

Anne leaned forward towards him again, looking into his face.

'You were never a disappointment, our John. Arthur told me that having you was the most wonderful thing in his life, truly. They were just, you know, closed up about emotional things. Never heard them say things to each other about how they felt. It was all taken for granted. When you got that job at the brewery, Enid was proud as punch, they both were.'

'But they didn't say that to me,' said John, looking at his aunt now, tears in his eyes. 'We never talked, not like you and I are doing now, not like I can talk to Hannah and Fred, and I've only known them a few weeks.'

'I think that's a difference in you, since we saw you last,' said Anne. 'George and I have both noticed it. Since you moved away you seem happier, somehow, despite all that's happened.'

'Happier? That's not it. I just feel more myself, even though things have been hard. Maybe –'

'Enough "maybe's",' said his aunt. 'I'll make us a drink while you keep looking through that box. Who knows what else there is? You carry on, I won't be long.'

John put the choir photo to one side, and took more items out

180

of the box. More snaps of Enid and Arthur, looking quite relaxed. He put a couple to one side. Some studio photos of young men in uniform, some with names on the back, but nobody he recognised. There was a programme from a concert at Barrow town hall, a booklet of Christmas carols, a newspaper clipping about an airship accident in 1911. Then there was something else about the choir, from 1916 this time. A concert programme. On the back were printed the names of all the choir members. He looked down the list of sopranos, then the altos. There she was: Mrs E. Pharaoh.

He scoured the other women's names: Caddy, Booth, Steele, Hardman, Gregson, Moodie, nobody called Thompson. He might have to track all these other people down, just to see what they knew, to find whoever wrote that letter. Where to start?

When Anne returned, John showed her the programme. 'You know, I remember that concert,' she said, smiling at the memory. 'George came too, and we enjoyed it. There was a tenor, what was he called?' She looked again at the programme. 'That's him. Alexander Benson. He was such a good-looking fellow, George teased me about it for weeks. Isn't it funny what you remember? Feelings more than facts.'

The programme was placed carefully with the photo for future use, and they looked together at each of the other items, but found nothing else of interest. When the box was finally empty, John felt empty, too. He'd hoped for so much more: something specific, a letter maybe, with names and dates that they could fit into a jigsaw and make sense of.

'Well, that's been useful, don't you think?' said Anne cheerfully. Maybe she expected less, John thought to himself. He tried to feel more positive.

'So what's next?' said Anne.

'Have to go to Barrow I think, don't you? I need to check out

Furness Road, and try to find Mr Crane, the choirmaster.'

'Try the church, St Luke's. They keep good records usually, and the vicar may know something himself.'

'But it was twenty years ago. We know Enid was in the choir, but who was the woman who wrote that letter?'

Anne smiled encouragement at her nephew. 'You'll just have to keep going, John, follow up anything we've got so far. Things'll make more sense when we know more. It'll take a while.'

When George came in from work that evening, Anne and John were able to report some progress. They showed him the items about the choir. George looked at the photo long and hard. 'Just think,' he said. 'This might be it. One of your real mam's relatives might be in this picture. Family likeness. Let me look again, with the glass.'

After a few minutes he put it down. 'I don't know,' he said. 'I can see a chin here, or a mouth there, that could be related to you John, but it's all so …' He shrugged. 'Sometimes it's the voice that shows the likeness, or the way someone walks. Or the way they think. All we've got is this picture.'

George looked at his nephew, then reached across and patted his arm.

'This must be hard for you, lad. You alright with it?'

'I'm alright Uncle George, honest. I've thought about it for a while. Before I got ill, before I left Ulverston actually, I was so angry with Enid and my real mam that I just wanted to disappear. But you can't be no one. We all come from somewhere, don't we? Lying in the hospital, I had nothing else to think about. I just wanted to find out, you know, who I am. Once you start on that, you can't stop halfway. I have to keep going while I have the chance.'

'So where next?'

'Well, Barrow sounds the most promising, so I'll go there.

182

Maybe Carnforth after that, but I'm not sure that'll give me anything. Post Office told me there was nowhere in Carnforth called The Oaks. Most likely the place has changed, things are a bit different now. So I'll go to Barrow. Anne reckons I should go on Sunday and talk to the vicar at St Luke's. More likely he'll know about who was who twenty years ago. Things move more slowly in the church you reckon, don't you Anne?'

'That's what I'd do, John. And it's easy, isn't it? Just a step from the station to St Luke's. If you go mid-morning on Sunday you'll find someone there.'

They sat quietly for a few minutes, the three of them, each thinking their own thoughts about the past, and family, and attachment, and loss.

Anne broke the silence.

'What if you do find her, John love. What then?'

John looked at her. 'I don't know,' he said. 'I'll be happy, I know that.'

'But what if she … what if she's not happy. Have you thought about that?'

'But I'm her son,' he said. 'Of course she'll be glad to see me. Won't she?' John looked across at George, appealing to him.

'Well, I'd hope so of course,' said George. 'I'd be happy, I know that.' They smiled at each other.

'But, it's not that easy,' Anne insisted. 'Poor lass, she must've been in a terrible state, when she … you know. But that was twenty years ago and things are different now. Still, she might be married, might have kept this secret all this time and all of a sudden, there you are.'

'But it's 1937, Aunty Anne,' said John. 'You told me yourself that the war changed everything. People don't have secrets like they used to in Victorian times.'

'Well, maybe,' Anne said, regretting she'd raised doubts in his

183

mind. 'But if you want to find her, love, that's what you must do.'

'What if it was you, Aunty Anne? What would you do if I turned up saying I was your son that you gave away when I was a baby?'

'Yes, Anne,' George chimed in. 'What would you do?'

The answer Anne gave them was not the truth, but it was what John badly wanted to hear.

Chapter 22

RAIN BLEW IN from the Irish Sea, whipped across the fractured surface of the dock and swirled into the town. The side door of St Luke's church on Roose Road faced away from the wind and the dozen or so people who emerged from it around eleven-thirty that Sunday morning waited in the doorway to turn up their collars and pull down their hats before stepping out into the misery of the morning. John was standing in the shelter of a doorway across the street, watching. He'd been waiting there a while, not wanting to interrupt whatever was going on inside. He didn't belong there.

A few more minutes passed, and a lone figure appeared at the door. A man, young and slight, with a loose grey coat over the long black robe that marked him out as the vicar. He put on a black hat and turned around to lock the door behind him. John took his chance and crossed the street. Not wanting to stand too close, he waited in the middle of the pavement, where the rain caught him full in the face. The young man turned and faced him, startled for a moment. John struggled to find words.

'Can I help you?' said the vicar. 'Are you all right?'

'Yes, yes,' said John. 'I'm fine. I just … I want a word. Can we talk a minute?'

The vicar turned back to the church door and unlocked it.

'Come in, do. Far too wet to stand out there.'

Inside the church it was quite dark and surprisingly warm.

'Don't want to turn all the lights back on. We'll go in the vestry. Just follow me. Can you see?'

'Yes, thanks,' said John, following the man down the side aisle towards the far end of the church. The man found a door and opened it. 'In here,' he said, reaching for a light switch that snapped on, flooding them both with harsh white light. John blinked.

'Sorry about the mess. We had to find the crib, needs a good clean before Christmas, and it was right at the back of the cupboard. Haven't had the chance to put everything away. There's a chair behind you, just move that stuff onto the floor.'

John placed a pile of sheet music on the floor and pulled the small chair towards him. The vicar sat on the larger chair by the cluttered desk and gave John his best pastoral expression.

'That's better.' The vicar's voice and face had both softened. 'Now, what can I do for you? Are you sure you're all right? You look very pale. Nothing to offer I'm afraid. Communion wine not quite apropos.' He smiled, friendly but concerned. John liked his anxious face.

'No, really,' said John. 'I'm fine, really. Been ill, that's all, getting better now. But, I –'

'Yes?'

'I'm not sure you can help. You look too young – no, I don't mean – it's just that I'm looking for someone, from a long time ago, twenty years ago.'

'A bit before my time, true,' said the vicar. 'I'm Peter Blount, by the way, vicar of St Luke's. Welcome.'

'And I'm John Pharaoh,' said John, holding out his hand. The two men shook hands and laughed. 'Seems to be coming out backwards somehow,' said John. 'Can I start again?'

'Start wherever you like,' said Peter.

186

John took a breath, to collect himself and to remember how best to tell his story.

'Well,' he began, 'Twenty years ago, before I was born, the lady who adopted me came to this church. The sister of my real mam's mam was in the choir, at least we think she was, but we don't know her name.'

Peter Blount looked blankly at him. He didn't seem to have heard. 'Twenty years ago I was still at school,' he said, holding his hand four feet off the ground, ready to pat his younger self on the head. 'I can tell you who the vicar was here then, twenty years ago you said?' He stood and turned to a row of books on a shelf, peering at them and then pulling one towards him. 'Hang on a minute.' He opened the book with care and turned pages, glancing at each one. 'Here it is, 1910 to 1919, Reverend Arthur Hutchinson. Oh dear.'

'What is it?' said John.

'He died, in the 'flu outbreak after the war. December 1919. What a shame. It was a dreadful time. I lost an aunt …' The vicar shut the book and put it back on the shelf. 'So I can't help you there. But it was the choir, you said, right?'

'Yes. Look –' John reached into the inside pocket of his wet coat and took out a brown envelope. While the vicar watched he opened the envelope, took out the contents and laid them gingerly on the corner of the desk. With the tips of his fingers he prised the damp papers apart until he found what he was looking for.

'Here it is.' John handed the photo across to the man in black.

'What's this?'

'In the front corner of the picture, do you see? The man in the hat. We think that must be the choirmaster. He looks as if he's in charge.'

'Where are they?'

'On a boat, going to Blackpool. Some of the names are on the back. The man's name looks as if it's Crane or something. It's very faint.'

'Mr Crane! Of course. He was here for years. Well, well. Let me look again.'

The vicar held the photo nearer to the dirty bulb that hung from the yellowing ceiling of the vestry.

'Yes, that's him. Well I never. What year was this?'

'It was 1914, according to the scribble on the back. Must have been before the war came. The boats stopped after that.'

'Let me think. I came here in 1932, and he'd just retired as choirmaster. That's what, twenty years or so after this was taken. He was probably about sixty, maybe more, when he gave it up. That looks about right. He might have been forty, maybe forty-five, in this picture.'

Peter Blount held the photo up again. 'Look at them all. Not a care in the world. What a terrible folly it all was. So many taken, so many widows. And for what? Oh dear, now I've forgotten what you told me. There's someone in this picture who's important, isn't there?'

'Someone who knew my mother, my adopted mother, well enough to tell her about the baby, about me. We think that my mother was called Thompson. The one who adopted me was called Enid Pharaoh, and she was on the trip, too. Here.' John pointed to Enid.

'Goodness, how complicated,' said the vicar, trying to hide his confusion. 'That's very personal, yes, indeed.'

John persisted. 'I was given away, adopted, when I was born. I found out just a few months ago. And now I want to find my real mother. This was all we could find, this and half a letter.'

'A real mystery,' said the vicar. 'Goodness … and now you think that Mr Crane might remember something. What other clues do you have already?'

'That's it. This is all we have really, apart from the letter.'

'A letter? That must help, surely?'

'But it's only half a letter. We don't know who wrote it. It mentions the name Thompson, and a reference to the choir, at this church.'

'I see,' said the vicar, trying to keep up. 'I'm sure you've worked all this out. And you think it would it help to find Mr Crane? I'm sure I would have heard if he – if he was no longer with us. He retired as we know, but maybe he stayed locally. I don't know but I'm sure we could find out. Mrs Finn was here this morning. She's been with this church for forty years, she'd know. She lives just round in Gloucester Street, a few minutes away. What time is it? They may be having lunch but I'm sure she'd be willing to talk if I came with you. Do you have time?'

'Oh yes, I've come specially. But what about you?'

'Nothing waiting for me except an empty vicarage, unfortunately. I was married but ... So let's go, shall we? Just a few minutes. We'll get wet, but it's only water after all. Won't do us any harm. Don't forget that photo. Put it somewhere safe.'

They walked together back to the church door, stepped out into the wind and rain and the vicar locked the door behind them. He took John's arm and propelled him across the street and down to the left. They turned right at the bottom and then crossed the street again, heads down against the rain, making a car screech to a halt.

'More cars all the time,' he said as they reached the safety of the other side. 'Can't get used to it. They seem to go so much faster than horses, don't you think?'

'Only ever been in one car,' said John. 'Not long ago, actually. Exciting. I loved it.'

'Too noisy for me,' said the vicar. 'Here we are. Thirty-seven. That's the one.'

He knocked on the door and they waited. John felt inside his coat for the envelope.

The door opened, and the glorious smell of roasting beef enveloped them before being whisked away on the wind.

'Oh, it's you, vicar,' said a short balding man, red-faced with a perfectly round red nose. He was wearing a waistcoat and braces holding up trousers that were slightly too short. 'Have you come for lunch? She didn't say 'owt about it, but come away in, both of you.'

The vicar stepped up into the narrow hall, and John followed, closing the door behind them. They stood, waiting to see what to do. 'Hang on,' the vicar whispered to John. 'It's obviously lunchtime. With any luck …'

A woman emerged from the room at the end of the narrow hall. She looked flushed and reminded John of Mrs Barker.

'Vicar,' she said. 'Is there anything wrong? I've only been home a few minutes.'

'No, nothing wrong, Mrs Finn, nothing at all. So sorry to intrude at lunch time, but this young man …' He turned, revealing John standing quietly behind him.

'John Pharaoh,' said John, extending his hand, which Mrs Finn grasped. Her hand was damp. 'Very pleased to meet you.'

'Likewise, I'm sure,' said the woman. 'Any friend of the vicar's. Come in the front room, the pair of you. Can't stand here like folks at a funeral. Arnold,' she shouted towards the back room, 'Just take the potatoes off the heat and turn the oven down a bit.'

She ushered them into the front room. It reminded John of Enid's parlour, rarely used.

'So sorry to bother you right in the middle of it all,' said the vicar again. 'Would it be better if we came back later?'

'Not at all. Any road, now you're here, you'll stay, won't you? Our Betty and her man often come on Sunday but they're away to Lancaster today to his folks, so there's plenty to go round. You need feeding up, vicar, and your friend looks as if he could do with it, too. Whatever it is can wait for a while I'm sure. Everything's nearly ready. We'll eat in the kitchen if you don't mind. Warmer than here on such a miserable day.'

'But –' began John, hesitating as he felt the grip of the vicar's hand on his arm and heard Peter Blount's voice speaking over his own.

'What a kind offer, Mrs Finn. We'd be delighted, wouldn't we, John?' It sounded like a question, but was more of a statement. John nodded.

'Grand,' said Mrs Finn, and the three of them smiled at each other. The smell of the beef made John's mouth water.

Two delicious courses later, they left Arnold clearing the table and went back into the front room.

'Now then, food's eaten and time for talk,' said their hostess. 'What's brought you both here?'

'Well,' said Peter Blount, 'I was just locking up after the service, just after you left, and this young man appeared with such an interesting tale to tell that I wanted to help him straight away. No time like the present, eh, John? Do you want to tell Mrs Finn what it's about? Start at the beginning, it might be easier that way.'

John told his story again. He remembered the photo in the pocket of his coat that was now hanging in the hall and excused himself to fetch it. As he did so, Mrs Finn raised her eyebrows to the vicar, who nodded his reassurance. John returned with the photo and handed it to her.

'We think it's the choir trip to Blackpool, in 1914, before the war started,' he said, as she peered at the photo before taking a pair of spectacles out of the pocket of her skirt. 'The man at the front is Mr Crane –'

'So it is, indeed,' said Mrs Finn suddenly. 'Look at him there, so young! And look, there's Eileen Robinson too, and her little one. What was her name, Mary. Mary Robinson. What year? Why she must be nearly thirty now. What a sweet child she was then. And Caroline. Caroline, what's her married name I always forget. Wonder where she is now, not seen her in years –'

'Do you remember a family called Thompson?' John interrupted with an urgency that caused the vicar's smile to become a little strained.

'Thompson, Thompson,' said Mrs Finn. 'Hang on a minute.' She raised her flushed face and shouted towards the door. 'Arnold, Arnold!'

'What?' came the voice from the kitchen.

'Remember Barbara Skinner. Big woman. Bossy. What was her sister called, the funny one?'

'Thompson,' Arnold replied without hesitation. John's stomach tightened.

"First name?"

'Hold on, it were a long time ago. Let me think. I'll be there in a minute.'

Mrs Finn turned triumphantly to John and Peter. ' Well, we're getting somewhere now! And you're looking for your mam? There she is!' She pointed a red finger at the edge of the photo.

'Where?' John seized the photo, his heart thumping.

'Your mam. There she is.'

John looked at the image of Enid. 'You mean Mrs Pharaoh? Yes, I know she's there. I'm looking for the other one.' His voice faded.

'What other one? Oh, your real mam. Hold on a minute, ' said Mrs Finn, 'Let me see again.'

John held out the increasingly battered photo and sank onto a chair. This was hopeless. He was going round in circles. But Mrs Finn continued peering at the photograph. 'Yes, there's a few people on here I don't know at all. Must have opened up the trip to families or something. Makes sense. I'd just forgotten about that. We do things differently now, don't we, vicar. The war changed everything.'

'I'm sure it did, indeed, Mrs Finn,' Peter Blount replied, wondering about what to do with the angry and miserable young man he seemed to have inherited. 'Is there anything else you can tell us, I wonder?' he said, catching her eye and nodding towards John, who was sitting forward now with his head in his hands.

The woman looked down at him and shook her head. He tried again to salvage something.

'If I understand this right, John's mother must be the daughter of Mrs Thompson, and the niece of Mrs Skinner. I wonder if either of them is in this picture?'

With admirable timing, Arnold Finn put his head round the door, saying, 'Washing up's done. And I remembered! Cora Thompson, that was Barbara Skinner's sister. You remember, you never liked her, said she fancied herself. She died, big funeral. Must be five years ago or so. What about her? What's going on?'

'Don't just stand there gawping,' said his wife. 'Come in properly and look at this.' She pushed the photo into his hands. 'Can you see Cora Thompson? It's a choir trip but she might not have been in the choir, so –'

'Give me a minute. Still don't know what all the fuss is about,' said Arnold, casting his tiny eyes over the photo, The small group waited anxiously, watching Arnold Finn. John wanted so badly to get out.

'There!' Arnold's red face lit up like a beacon. 'Cora Thompson. Typical. Not in the choir but she wangled her way onto the trip. There, right hand side. Look at the hat!'

'Show me,' said John, getting up suddenly and towering over Arnold's smooth head as he peered at the photo.

'There,' Arnold said. 'Standing at the end of the row, next to that girl with the hair blowing all over the place. Must have been windy. Hang on a minute. What's going on? I've missed everything. What's all this about?'

Peter couldn't bear to hear John tell his story yet again, and began to tell it himself. John who was still examining the photo suddenly interrupted.

'What about the daughter, Cora Thompson's daughter?' he demanded, looking directly at Arnold.

'Well, there were two that I can remember,' said Arnold, finding himself under discomforting scrutiny. 'Could have been more. The older one didn't go out much. Went off to college, somewhere. Can you remember, love?'

Without waiting for his wife to respond, Arnold Finn continued. 'Elder one had just gone to college, so she must've been eighteen or so when the war came. Apple of her mother's eye that one. Barbara went on and on about that college. You'd think she'd gone to Oxford they way they carried on. Now the younger one, she was different, bit of a madam. What was 'er name, oh aye, Betty, no Beattie. Beatrice probably. She got married and went off to New Zealand, or Australia, somewhere down there. Maybe she got into trouble. She was, you know, a big girl. No one ever said owt, but then they wouldn't would they?'

Arnold beamed at his wife, enjoying the unusual position of being the centre of attention. 'All right then, Mr Memory,' she said. 'What about the other one?'

'Bloody – begging your pardon, vicar – blimey, why me? Can't you remember anything?

'I can remember Barbara Skinner going on about one of them going to college,' said his wife, 'but not the names. You remembered the younger one's name, what about the other one?'

'Mary, was it? Polly? Now there was a Polly, 'pretty Polly' we used to call her, but she was a Carson, lovely girl … One of the Thompson girls, eh, up the duff, who'd have thought it. Bet that gave old Cora a shock, and that Barbara, well –'

'Oh, for heaven's sake Arnold,' said his wife, swiping at him with the back of her hand. 'Have some respect. This young man thinks that one of those girls was his mam.' She pointed at John, who felt as if he were going to burst.

'By 'eck,' said Arnold, as the information began to sink in. 'So you think one of the Thompson girls was, y'know …' He too pointed at John, opening his eyes wide. 'Give me another look.'

As Arnold reached for the photo, John made a strange strangled noise and threw up his arms with such a jerk of frustration that the three other people in the tiny room stepped away from him, alarmed.

'There now, John,' said the vicar hurriedly. 'This must be very hard for you. Mr and Mrs Finn have been very helpful, but maybe it's time we were going.'

He looked meaningfully at the Finns, who moved away from the door simultaneously as he steered John towards it. Mrs Finn raised her finger to Arnold's face yet again and followed them out into the narrow hallway, trying in vain to get to the front door ahead of them. John opened the door and stepped out into the street as the wind hurled rain into their faces. The vicar followed, pulling on his hat. He turned back to Mrs Finn who had half closed the door and was peeping round it.

'We'll go. Let him calm down, poor lad. Thanks for the lunch, much appreciated, and for the information. Really, um, useful. Best if we say no more about this. We'll find Mr Crane next – but where is he? Do you know? Forgot to ask.'

'Grange-over-Sands, with his sister. Fernleigh Road, big nursing home. Haven't seen him in a while. So sorry about Arnold, vicar, hasn't the sense he was born with sometimes.'

195

'Not to worry. We'll just leave it, and look for Mr Crane next. Thanks again. You go in, you'll catch your death.'

The door closed and Peter took John's arm as they walked heads down against the rain, back towards the cold vicarage.

CHAPTER 23

THE TINY OFFICE in the main quarry building at Beckside looked as if a strong wind had torn through it, scattering papers at random around the room. The bits of slate that Andrew used to hold different piles of paper down in their appointed places were scattered untidily across the table top that served as his desk. Andrew threw himself back in the rickety chair and shouted.

'Ted!' No response.

'Ted, get in 'ere, now!' Still no response.

Andrew pushed back the chair, reached the low door in two strides and bellowed out into the yard.

'Ted! Where the 'ell are you? Get in 'ere, now.'

A door on the other side of the yard opened and Mick Arkwright, one of the labourers, looked across.

'I'll get 'im, boss.'

Andrew turned back into the chaos in the room. He picked up as many papers as he could and tried to form them into one big pile. He put the pile in front of him, sat down and began looking at each paper in turn, starting new piles in a miserable attempt to restore some sense of control. Ted came in from the yard, rubbing his hands on the front of the old jacket he wore at work in the winter.

'By 'eck, boss, it's raw. I'm nithered.'

'You'll be more than nithered,' said Andrew turning towards him. 'Where the hell have you been?'

Ted pointed towards the door but Andrew cut off whatever explanation was about to follow.

'Look at this lot. How did things get in such a mess? We're running a business here, not making a paper trail. Who's looking after this lot, or not looking after it?'

'That's what we got the new lad for, boss. But 'e were nae good to us, never 'ere, and now e's got 'is cards.'

'Well we need someone,' Andrew was shouting again now. 'I can't do all this. We need to get the money in, and how do we know who to ask for it? If we can't get someone else pretty damn quick you'll have to tidy this lot up yourself!'

Ted stared. 'Cannut. Learned nowt at school, me. Couldn't even read most of that lot, never mind know what to do with 'em.'

'Well get us someone else, dammit, or I'll make you do it, and blame you if it's not right. Right?'

'Aye,' said Ted. 'But –'

Whatever Ted was going to say was interrupted by the sound of a car horn that echoed first around the buildings and then off the slate wall of the quarry itself.

'Fuck!' Andrew's anger burst over the room. 'Get out there, quick. Tell him I'm not here. Quick, man.'

Too late. Before Ted reached the door the space was filled by Lionel Leadbetter's large bulk, ducking his head, his long coat almost reaching the dusty floor.

'There you are,' he said, taking off his hat as he made out his son's shape sitting at the desk. 'Paperwork Johnny now, eh?'

Ted escaped. Andrew pushed back the chair that toppled backwards this time and lay where it fell.

'What?' Andrew's voice was bitter. 'We're busy here. What d'you want?'

'Just a chat, my boy, won't take long.'

'Don't "my boy" me here, not at work. Not anywhere. I'm a grown man.'

'Of course, my apologies,' said Lionel, bending to pick up the chair, which he pulled towards himself and sat down. 'Just need to check with you about the new school. Won't take a minute.'

'Christ,' said Andrew, 'the bloody school again. What new school? There is no new school. It's not going to happen.'

His father looked up at him from the fragile chair that had now disappeared under the folds of his coat.

'No need to blaspheme,' he said, quite mildly, as he felt the wave of Andrew's frustration breaking over him. 'I'm consulting with Sir John, and then with the bishop, to try and get the diocese to help. Caroline tells me that may be the best way. I need to check with you about costs before I go, that's all.'

Andrew's anger would not be soothed by his father's unusual reasonableness.

'Just look what we're dealing with here,' he said, sweeping his arm towards the mess on the desk behind him. 'Up to our back-sides in paper, no one in the office to help since that boy they sent us got ill and disappeared. I'm trying to run the place single-handed and you waste my time with this bloody pipe dream.'

'How is the boy?' Lionel leaned forward a little.

'Forget the boy,' Andrew was shouting again now, 'and forget the bloody school! Tell the bishop if he wants a new school, he can build it himself. Now I need to work, so get out and let us get on with it. And take that machine with you out of our yard.'

Lionel stared at him for a minute and then got to his feet, head bent against the low ceiling and clearly taller than his son. The mild demeanour was draining away.

'Now look,' he said, still quiet, but with slow deliberation. 'We've had this conversation before. You may be running this miserable place for the time being, but you don't make the decisions around here. Skeffington says he wants the school, just like I do and most of the village. He owns this quarry, and all the stone that you fellows dig out of it. What he says, goes. He expects me to sort it out, but a word from me, and you'll be dealing with him, not me. Think on that.'

'Skeffington's in business, like me, and not like you.' Andrew came back at him in the same fierce tone. 'He keeps you running around. Knows you've nothing better to do. If he thinks your schemes might interfere with the profit from this quarry, that's the end of it. No school.'

'But the village wants it, Skeffington knows that.'

'Ha! That's a laugh. You don't hear what they say in the Farriers. Most of the blokes in there couldn't give a damn about a new school, and sure as hell won't lift a finger or pay a penny to make it happen.'

'Miss Whelan says –' said Lionel, changing tack.

'Miss Whelan knows who pays her wages. She's going along with it to keep you happy, to keep her job. She's told me herself.'

'Oh, so you two are plotting behind my back now, are you?'

'What Jessie and I say to each other is between us, and don't drag her into it.'

'Jessie, is it? Where's the respect, young man. She's old enough to be your mother. It's "Miss Whelan" to you.'

'If you –' Andrew began and stopped, turning away. 'Look, just leave us alone. Tell the bishop anything you like. You're not getting the stone for the school from here unless you pay for it, a real price. And you're not getting my time, either. If that's the end of the new bloody school, so be it.'

'We'll see about this,' said Lionel, putting his hat back on and heading for the door, bending to get through the small space. But then he turned back and stood upright again. He peered into the dark of the room, made darker by his body blocking the light.

'You can rant and rave all you like. You're an employee here, that's all. You'll do as you're told, and you'll treat me and others with more respect in future. Good day to you.'

He disappeared through the door. Moments later the engine of the Armstrong Siddeley roared into luxuriant life. Andrew picked up a stray lump of slate from the table and hurled it at the door. It skittered across the yard outside. Ted, who was heading towards the office, turned quickly away and ducked into the outhouse before his boss could see him.

Andrew left the quarry early that evening and headed for the Farriers. It was Friday, the end of a bad week. He rode the bike faster than the narrow lanes would tolerate and narrowly missed a cat as he swept down the hill into Newton, past the schoolhouse. It was quiet in the pub as Elsie Eilbeck pulled his pint, which he downed in two long gulps, and then another.

'Bad day?' she asked, hoping for something interesting in response. It had been a quiet week and she wanted something to cheer her up.

'Bad enough,' was all she got. Andrew put his empty tankard down noisily on the bar.

A couple of other drinkers had come in, and the talk shifted to rugby. They talked across him and Andrew took his drink to the shelf in the corner and stood leaning against it. 'Bloody man,' he said to himself. Elsie noticed, but said nothing. Andrew stood and drank steadily. The frustration and humiliation of the day seethed. Other drinkers felt his mood and avoided him. Even Elsie knew to leave well alone: it was a mistake to cross young Leadbetter in drink.

When Andrew walked unsteadily out into the pub yard well after ten, the cold air hit him hard. He looked at the bike, at the stars over his head, at the cloud of his breath in the frigid air.

Down the road, just in his sight, was the schoolhouse. Downstairs was in darkness, but upstairs he could see that the spare room curtains were drawn. He knew what that meant. At Jessie's window he could see a faint glow. He pictured the warmth of the fire in the soft room, the bed, her body. Despite the drink, maybe because of it, he felt the familiar stirring.

Determined, he walked along to the house, steadying himself on the wall. Round the back. The door was unlocked. He went in, closed the door silently behind him and took off his boots. Careful. No noise. He wanted her drowsy, unresisting. He wanted her now.

Chapter 24

Jessie was sitting up in bed reading, a dark blue dressing gown round her shoulders. It was Friday evening, a little after ten, the end of another busy week. She had gone up early to read. The fire was warm in the grate. The crackle of burning coal and the soft tick of the clock on the landing were the only sounds.

She heard something. Footsteps on the stairs. The bedroom door creaked.

'Andrew?'

'Expecting someone else?'

'It's late.'

'Been in the Farriers.'

'I can smell it.' Fumes of beer and tobacco filled the space between them. She put down the book on the covers beside her and looked at him.

'I think you should go home.' Her voice was quiet. She watched him.

'Curtains were drawn. That means come on in. Can't go home. Can't see straight.'

'Straight enough to get down here, though. Did anyone see you?'

'No idea! Christ! I'm sick of this. Ashamed of me or summat?'

Andrew stood just inside the door. Jessie sat still, covers pulled round her. Neither of them moved. The small fire hissed.

'It's late,' she said. 'I did want to talk to you, but you're in no fit state. I can make you a drink, but you need to go home.'

'Look,' he said, lowering his head. 'No one saw me, alright? Your precious reputation is safe. I'm tired and I'm pissed.'

Jessie pushed back the covers off her bed, put her feet to the floor, stood and pulled the gown around her. The light from the fire and the oil lamp beside the bed glowed on her hair and the side of her face. Andrew leaned against the wall.

'I said I'll make you a drink,' she said quietly. 'That means going downstairs. So you sit down, out of the way, and I'll bring it up. Or come down with me and put your feet up on the sofa for a few minutes.'

'I'm not going anywhere, staying right here. And you're staying here with me. Forget the drink. Had enough drink.'

Jessie walked towards him. He did not move. She reached to push him gently away from the door. He grabbed her hand and pulled her towards him.

'Stop it, Andrew!' She twisted away from him. 'You're drunk and you're hurting me. Get off me.'

'Get off me,' he mimicked her voice. 'That's not what you said last time.' He fumbled at the tie of the gown at her waist, pressing his other hand against her breast.

She pulled back away from him and the tie tore. Her gown fell open and she struggled to hold it. He stepped towards her again, reaching for her. 'Come 'ere, woman.'

'You're drunk,' she said again.

'Not too drunk to give you one. You know you want it.'

Jessie stepped back. He reached for her, losing his balance. She braced herself against the foot of the bed behind her, and waited a moment. Her mind was racing.

'For goodness sake,' she said, 'sit down, before you fall down.'

She slipped past him towards the stairs, holding the gown around her. He caught the hint of lemon in her hair. He reached out for her, but she was gone. He slumped into the little chair beside the fire and closed his eyes.

Downstairs, Jessie waited for the kettle and mixed some coffee in a mug. Her heart thumped: her mind was working quickly.

'Never seen him quite so drunk before,' she said to herself. 'More boyish than ever. Ridiculous, talking like a gangster in a movie. Should be angry with him, but … he'll settle down. Probably something to do with Lionel, usually is when he's like this. Must have been bad, whatever it was. Never spoken to me like this before.'

'Come on, Jess,' she spoke out loud, sharply. 'He's drunk. He has to go. That's all.'

She pushed open the bedroom door and he stirred in the chair. She put down the mug and pulled the gown around her once again, standing out of reach.

'Here's what you need. Drink it, you'll be right to drive home. Come on. You can't stay here.'

'Sound like me bloody mother,' he said without opening his eyes. 'Drink it up,' he mimicked her again, 'there's a good boy.'

'Well, I'm almost old enough,' she said lightly.

He pushed himself up in the chair. 'That's what *he* said. "She's old enough to be your mother." Said I should respect you. I nearly told him, right then, told him how you spread yourself for me, the noise you make when I fuck you.'

The words hit like a punch. She waited a moment, pulling herself together.

'What did you say to him?'

'Nothing. I said nothing.'

Jessie looked at her lover. 'Is that what you think of me?'

'I fuck you. You make a noise. What's wrong with that?'

'You'd better go. Now.'

'Upset? Just 'cos I said "fuck"? That's what we do. You love it, I know you do. I can feel it. You want it as much as I do.'

'Get out!'

'Plenty other women out there. They all want it. Young girls, flaunting themselves. I know what they want, and they get it, too. Even that bitch, Agnes.'

'Andrew, that's enough.' Jessie tried her schoolteacher voice, struggling to keep calm. He must not see that she was afraid of him.

'Yes teacher, no teacher,' he mocked her. 'All right, all right, I'm going. Just one kiss and I'll go. Come on, Jess. That's all. I'll be good, teacher, promise.'

She hesitated. He smiled at her, picked up the coffee and drank some of it, wincing as it burned his mouth. Anger flared again and he threw the mug down onto the floor at his feet. The coffee arched towards the fire, splashing in heavy drops onto the carpet.

'I'll get a cloth,' she said quietly, turning towards the door.

'Leave it!' He shouted, lurching towards her. 'Let it lie. Didn't come for a drink, I came for you.' He caught her arm as she turned, pulled her towards him, seized her other shoulder and pushed her back towards the bed. She fell back, pulling him to his knees.

'Fuck it, Jess,' he said 'Give over, just lie still. I won't hurt you.'

But he did hurt her. Pushing up from his knees, he heaved her body up onto the bed and held one arm across her neck while he struggled with his belt. She tried to cry out but his arm was choking her. Her mouth was open but she made no sound. He pushed her legs apart with his knee and forced himself into her. The pain was sharp and shocking. She struggled but his full weight was on her now. He pushed harder, forcing a hand under her hips to hold her under him. He finished quickly, and loud, then lay panting. The weight on her chest made it hard to breath.

206

She stretched her back to find some air, gasping, trying to move her legs, to force him away.

As his body relaxed she pushed hard against his shoulders, straining to release her hips. He slid out of her and she pushed again, with her body as well as her arms, breathing hard to fill her lungs.

'Get off, get off!'

He slipped to the floor, and leaned back on his haunches. Jessie scrambled down the bed away from him. On the other side of the room, she stood, pulling the gown down around herself, pushing the hair off her face. Tears were in her eyes, but she wiped them away.

'Get out of my house. You hurt me. Get out!' She shouted at him, reaching for breath between the words.

Andrew got up slowly, pulled up his trousers and rubbed his face with his hand.

'Away with the fuss, for God's sake, you'll wake the whole village. That's all I wanted. Where's the harm, just a bit of sex, that's all.'

She said nothing, both arms stretched in front of her, warding him off.

'I'm going, don't fret. Sorry about the coffee.'

He walked unsteadily across the room, out and down the stairs. Jessie heard the back door close behind him and sank to her knees.

CHAPTER 25

FOR A LONG TIME after Andrew left the house Jessie knelt on the floor, leaning against the bed. The fire died slowly in the grate beside her and the room grew cold. She did not sleep, but closed her eyes, trying to blot out what had happened. It was the cold that roused her at last. She pulled herself up and went slowly, painfully, down the stairs. The water in the kettle on the range was still warm, and she poured some into a bowl, took a cloth from the sink, soaked it in the water and then pressed it first to her face and then, with more difficulty, between her legs.

She needed a drink. There was a bottle of whisky somewhere but she couldn't remember where and had no strength to look for it. She put the kettle back on the range to heat and sat on a chair to wait. Her legs felt weak. Her mind swarmed. Minutes passed, marked only by the insistent ticking of the clock in the hall. As she poured boiling water into the teapot some of it dribbled unseen onto the floor. She needed to go back to her bed, to reclaim it, and forced herself to climb the stairs. She sat on the edge of the bed. The book that she'd put down an hour before slid to the floor. Then the tears came, sliding unhindered down her face until she wiped her eyes with a corner of the sheet.

Disgust. She felt it now, not about Andrew, but about herself. She had deceived herself, pretended that he loved her. She wanted to be desired after all the years of loneliness. For a little while she had felt like a woman, doing the things that women do, thinking about a man, waiting for him to come, loving his hands on her, feeling filled up by him, complete. But it was a sham. Whatever he felt for her, it wasn't love, couldn't be. He wanted to own her, to show her off to his wretched father. He had taken her tonight because he could, because he wanted to, because she couldn't stop him.

She put down the cup and lay on her side, her legs pulled up like a baby in the womb. Alone. There was no one she could turn to. Not for help, she didn't need help. Just for comfort. He'd come inside her: she knew that and what it could mean. Last time, all those years ago, she'd told herself it would be all right. Just one time, she couldn't get pregnant from just one time. But she'd been wrong then. She was older now, less fertile, but it could still happen. What to do? She didn't know. A wave broke over her. All she'd worked for, all these years, all at risk because the man was drunk and she didn't have the sense or the strength to throw him out. She could have ended it earlier, so why hadn't she? Flattered. That was the problem all along. After all the years of feeling invisible, a man had noticed her, a young man, strong and passionate.

Jessie covered her eyes again. Regret. Shame. Humiliation. She had to face a truth about herself. If Andrew had been a respectful, respectable young man she wouldn't have wanted him. She wanted him because it was exciting. The secrecy of their affair gave her a thrill she hadn't felt since she'd lied to her mother all those years before, since she and Clive had made love in that empty house while the storm crashed around them. The impulse had been hers as well as his, then and now, except that tonight it was drink that had fuelled Andrew, not love for her. Sex. That's what he wanted tonight, and he thought she wanted it, too.

If there was damage, it was already done. It wouldn't happen again. She'd already decided to end it when she'd drawn the curtains three days before to signal she wanted to see him, but he couldn't have known that. He probably thought … She stopped herself, but the idea persisted. He thought that the drawn curtains meant sex, as it had done before. That's the message she had given him. And he'd been drinking. Anything could have set him off. She knew he was a drinker. What was she thinking of, letting him into her life, into her body?

She lay still a while, feeling her stomach. It might be weeks before she could be sure. If the worst happened she would deal with it then. Nothing to do now, not about that. About Andrew? She would do what she'd planned. No use making a drama out of what happened tonight. He was drunk, he'd forced himself on her. He was wrong, but she knew he wouldn't understand. He'd probably done it before, in drink, with someone who he thought was wanting it, even though she struggled and said 'No.' She shut her eyes against the thought. What did that make her? A slut? A fool?

When Jessie woke, grey light filled the room. It was cold. For a few precious moments drowsiness blocked the pain of the previous night, but then it flooded back and she closed her eyes again. She was still sore. As she stretched for her watch from the bedside table she felt the pain in her arm from his grip. Her head throbbed. She wanted to stay quite still, to be invisible and rebuild herself without the scrutiny of neighbours. But Newton was too small for invisibility. Even curtains closed for too long would be noticed. She had to protect herself. If she drew the curtains and lit a fire all the outward signs would be normal. It was Saturday. No school, no public face was required of her. She could hide for a while behind a headache, or a sore throat, anything to keep others away until she was ready to face them.

She didn't want food, but she needed it. Bread and jam. The thought distracted her and she got out of bed, forcing herself through the stiffness, and reached for the gown. The torn tie reminded her and for a moment she faltered. But only for a moment. She stood straight and took a deep breath, then another, before going downstairs. Bread, jam, tea. Normal, nourishing. She laid and lit the fire in the small back room, dressed warmly, and thought about what to do. For a while thoughts jumped and swerved in her head, doubling back on themselves, stopping suddenly before veering off again, like cows in a field disturbed by a dog, fearful and confused. Back to bed, to stop herself thinking.

When she woke again it was mid-afternoon and the light was already fading in the west, a shaft of late sun picking out the tops of bare trees that thrashed in the southerly gale. In the quiet of her room upstairs in the cold schoolhouse Jessie reached a conclusion. Andrew was lost. She just needed to work out how to rid herself of him without exciting comment. What she needed now was the company of women, undemanding friendship and support. There was only one person she could turn to: Agnes. Steady, respectable, disgusted Agnes.

By the time Jessie had washed and changed it was almost dark, though still only mid-afternoon, just two weeks off the shortest day. She found her long coat, pulled a wool hat down over her hair, took her big torch and set off on the familiar walk to Applegarth. It was good to move. The wind calmed her. In the winter with the trees shorn of leaves the view down the drive to Agnes's house was clearer than earlier in the year, and as she passed the gate Jessie could already see the glow in the window that meant that Agnes was at home. Normally that knowledge would have been a pleasure. This time the likelihood of seeing Agnes, so soon after the awkwardness of the previous week, made her anxious but she was still sure of what she needed to do. When she saw

Agnes peep round the half-drawn curtains to check who was at the door, Jessie turned and smiled.

Agnes's sitting room was warm and softly lit. The red of the fire and the dark gold of the brass oil lamp burnished the scarlet of cushions and curtains. Agnes was clearly surprised, but said nothing beyond an invitation to enter. She closed the door quickly against the wind and followed Jessie into the room.

'Jessie,' she began, but stopped when Jessie raised her hand.

'No, don't say anything. I have some things I have to tell you and they won't wait. I might lose my courage. Please, and before you ask, I don't want any tea. Just sit here and let me talk to you.'

'Very well,' said Agnes after a short pause. 'Talk to me.'

Jessie began to speak, so quietly that Agnes had to lean forward on the sofa to hear what she was saying.

'We've known each other how long? Ten years, more, since I came to Newton, and been friends for most of that, but we've never really talked about our lives, about the things that matter.'

'But –' Agnes began again, and again Jessie cut her off.

'You may think we've told each other all there is to know. Maybe you have, but I haven't, not to you, not to anyone in this village. As far as you all know I'm the schoolteacher who's led a quiet life. That's maybe why you were so shocked that time, because it wasn't what you expected, contradicted what you thought you knew.'

She looked up, expecting Agnes to say something, but there was no sound except the hiss of the lamp. She took a deep breath and continued.

'Twenty years ago I was living in Barrow. It was wartime and the town was like the Wild West. The ironworks, the shipyard, thousands of people coming in from all over the place. My mother rented rooms. I was at college, in Ambleside, coming home for holidays and some weekends, when I could afford the train fare.

Mam just wanted me working, out of the house, out of her way, at least that's how it felt. Anyway, I met someone. He worked at the shipyard. He was clever and funny and I loved him right from the start. We – I fell pregnant. We knew were going to be together and we had it all planned. We would get married, I would have the baby and finish my teaching course if they let me and we would have a life together. We were young, I was just twenty, but I was sure.'

'What did your mother say?' asked Agnes.

'Oh, she was more angry than upset. This wasn't part of her plan. She thought I would get a job somewhere and send money back, or live at home and pay her back for letting me going to college. She was like that. She calculated everything. She was afraid there'd be no recompense for her "sacrifice".'

'I remember when she died,' said Agnes quietly. 'You didn't grieve for her as I thought you would.'

'I know. I wish I had done, but I couldn't. There was too much hurt still between us. She – she said – it doesn't matter now, but she said some terrible things. She wanted me to get rid of it.'

'But I thought you said – '

'Oh, he died, you see. That's what changed everything.'

'Who died?'

'Clive, my … fiancé. He worked at Vickers, on the airships, and he fell. No one told me. I read it in the *Barrow News*, that was the first I knew about it.'

'Oh, my dear.' Agnes knelt beside Jessie's chair and held her hand, but Jessie took it away.

'It's not finished. Let me finish. Sit back where you were, or I might not be able to do this.'

Agnes sat back on the sofa again, finding a hankie under one of the cushions.

'Clive died. An accident they said. That's when Mam tried to

213

make me get rid of it. When I said I wouldn't, I couldn't, the two of them, her and her sister, started going on at me about having the baby adopted. They said no one would ever give me a job, that my life would be ruined, that it would be no good for the baby. All the things you'd expect them to say.'

She looked at Agnes, searching for understanding or acceptance but saw nothing except the calm face. She guessed that Agnes would have agreed with Cora.

'So I had the baby,' Jessie continued, as if she was relating a story about someone else, 'in a home for unmarried mothers in Carnforth. It was a dismal place but they weren't unkind. Some of the other girls were in a far worse mess than me, so young, at least they seemed like children. Four days after the baby was born some people came – my mother knew them, or her sister did – and they took him away. I didn't see them. No one told me who they were and I didn't ask. I turned my face to the wall and got through it somehow.'

The flow of words faltered. The two women sat facing but not looking at each other. Worlds apart. Agnes held the hankie to her mouth. She was trying not to judge, trying to understand.

'What you must have gone through – I can't imagine,' she said. 'Why did you never tell me?'

'All sorts of reasons,' said Jessie. 'I buried it all deep and as time passed it was easy to keep it like that. I built a new life for myself, and the past didn't fit with it, so I let it go. And I never knew how people might take it if they knew, what they might say. It's so easy to judge isn't it? I do it myself sometimes and then catch myself, jumping to conclusions without knowing what I need to know. If we trust people, we have to trust their past as well as the present. We have to assume that they acted for the best at the time, whenever and whatever was done. Don't you think?'

'You're asking me?' said Agnes. 'When you confided in me

about Andrew, I judged you. I didn't know anything about it, not really, but I had my two penn'orth. I was shocked, I admit. I wish I hadn't said what I said. I wanted to tell you that before, but, well, I didn't. I'm sorry, Jessie, for what I said.'

Jessie took a deep breath.

'More things have happened. I don't think I can deal with them alone.'

Still Agnes seemed impassive. There was a silence that seemed to last for a long time.

'Are you sure you want to confide in me, Jessie? I may let you down. I may not be able to deal with things myself, never mind help you.'

Jessie considered this.

'Well there's something connected to what you know already. I need your advice, your calm good sense.'

'Try me.'

'I told you about the baby, and Clive'.

'Yes.'

'Well I went to see the Porters, up at Mill Cottage, just after the hunt ball.'

Agnes eyes flickered just a little, but she said nothing.

'We talked for a while, and then their lodger came in. You've met him.'

'I have indeed,' said Agnes. 'A nice young man, I thought. Quiet, well-mannered.'

'Can you remember what he looked like?'

'Yes I think so, it wasn't very long ago, although I've not seen him since that day I brought him back from Whitehaven.'

Jessie fumbled in her bag and brought out an envelope. She drew from it a tiny photo.

'Look at this,' she said to Agnes. 'Does this young man look like John Pharoah?'

Agnes reached for her glasses and put them on before taking the photograph from Jessie's hand. She leaned towards the oil lamp.

'Why, yes,' she said. 'Where did you get it?'

'It's not John,' said Jessie. 'The photograph is of Clive Whelan, my Clive when he was about the same age as John is now.'

Agnes looked up. 'Oh, my dear,' she said. 'You think … you think that John is Clive's child, your child?'

'I don't know. The likeness is uncanny, you can see that yourself. When I saw him at Mill Cottage I fainted, dropped to the floor like something out of a Brontë novel. I said I'd had a dizzy turn or some such thing. Covered it up. But it was this that made me faint, I know it.'

'What are you going to do?'

'I want to be sure, but don't know how, without telling him the truth. What if I'm wrong? Clive had two sisters. I thought maybe John could be related to them, part of Clive's family but nothing to do with me. That's possible isn't it?'

'Of course it is. Or it could be just a coincidence.' Agnes looked again at the photograph.

'And even if it is him,' Jessie went on, 'what do I do then?'

Agnes looked at her. 'What do you want to do?'

'I don't know.' Jessie hung her head. Her eyes filled with tears. 'It was twenty years ago. All I wanted was Clive, and he died. I never really wanted this baby. Even when he was inside me I tried to detach myself. I knew he would be taken from me, and that was what I wanted at the time. It was selfish, I know, but I was young and that was what I wanted, to get away from my mother and Barrow and make a life for myself, without Clive if that's what had to be. But I didn't want anyone else, anyone to be responsible for, and I still don't.'

Tears were coming fast and Jessie wiped her eyes ineffectually with her sleeve. Agnes went to find another handkerchief and came back with it. Jessie wiped her face and blew her nose. She looked at Agnes. 'You said I was disgusting for having Andrew. What must you think of me now? Don't tell me please, just help me to think about this. I don't have to do anything, after all. He doesn't recognise me, why should he? But I wonder if he's trying to find me? Maybe if I moved away …'

'Could you do that, really? Just leave without telling him?'

'I don't know. I love my life here, my work, the children. That could all be lost.'

Agnes hesitated. 'It could all be lost anyway, if –' Her voice faltered and she looked away. 'You know what I'm saying.'

'Andrew? That's over,' said Jessie. 'You were right. Don't ask me any more about it. I'm sure you don't want to hear it."

'Thank God,' said Agnes. 'My dear, I've been so worried. I was shocked. I'm so sorry. You needed advice and I – I can't remember exactly what I said that day but I know it was horrid and I'm sorry. Let's leave it there. Now you may not want anything to drink but I must. I won't be long. Look after the fire, I'll be back in a minute.'

Jessie leaned back on the soft cushions in the comfortable room. She had come here to tell Agnes about Andrew, but she couldn't. What was the point? Nothing Agnes could say would change it. She would talk to Andrew in her own time, tell him what he'd done and that it was over. After that, who knew? And for the other thing, why would Agnes know what to do any more than she did herself? Even with a friend, she was alone.

CHAPTER 26

TWO FIGURES EMERGED from a shaded path and turned left on to the promenade towards the station at Grange-over-Sands, the low winter sun shining into their faces. Beyond them the incoming tide advanced at the same pace, creeping over mud flats and salty grass banks. Eventually it would reach the base of the promenade, filling the massive basin of the bay. Overhead small white clouds scurried across a pale blue sky. Turnstones skittered at the edge of the tide, feasting on whatever the encroaching water might provide.

John Pharaoh, the taller of the two, was pale faced, his dark hair blowing over his eyes from the following wind despite all his efforts to keep it under control. His shoulders were hunched against the cold and his hands forced deep into the pockets of a long coat that flapped around his legs. Beside him was an older man, walking with a brisk energy. He wore a hat pulled well down and a yellow hand-knitted scarf peeped from the collar of his coat.

The man's face was lean and ruddy, eyes watering slightly in the cold air that buffeted them both.

For a few minutes neither man spoke. John had been up early to catch the train from Ulverston, unsure how long it would take to track down the man he was looking for. He was impatient to do so after a week and more in the house in Church Walk, laid low with a heavy cold and his aunt's insistence that he should not risk his health again after the soaking in Barrow. Time was passing. It was nearly Christmas, he wanted to be back at Mill Cottage, but he had to see Mr Crane before going all the way back there, round the Barrow peninsular, north again and then the final trudge up the valley. At least it had been easy to find the place on Fernleigh Road. Everyone knew Miss Crane.

John was relieved to see that Isaac Crane was not an 'inmate' of the home, and seemed to be in robust health, both physically and mentally. He was having trouble keeping up with the older man, leaning forward to catch what he was saying, as the words were snatched away by the wind.

'Every day, about this time, I take this walk,' Isaac Crane explained. 'Every day it's different, different tide, different light, different things to see in the gardens by the station. I love it. Keeps me fit. Keeps me out of the way, too. Martha's busy time.'

'Martha?'

'My sister. You'll meet her later, I'm sure. Sorry I rushed you out of the house. Like to keep to the same routine, you see. Leave the house before ten, that's the idea. Good walk, pick up whatever I need in the town, back in time for lunch. Rain or shine, every day.' Isaac Crane stopped and faced out across the bay. 'See the tide? If we were out there, it would overtake and overwhelm us. So many people get caught. Can't outrun the tide in Morecambe Bay. Power of nature, eh? Can you see the rain out there, too? It'll miss us, with any luck. No hat?'

'No,' said John, trying in vain to control his hair. 'Never thought.'

'Never thought you'd be dragged out by some mad old man,' said Isaac. 'Probably thought I'd be in my dotage, did you?'

'Not at all, Mr Crane.' John lied: that was exactly what he'd expected. He wondered how much longer they would march along before he could sit down.

'You didn't say much in the letter, and it's hard to talk properly out here in the wind, so we'll head for the café across from the station and talk there. Alright with you?'

'Fine, thanks. Will that be long?'

'About seven minutes,' replied his companion, 'Or possibly eight, depending how energetic we're feeling.'

'Let's call it six then, with this wind behind us,' said John, and they laughed and pulled their coats a little tighter around them.

It was warm inside the café, and steam condensed on the windows, running down into little pools on the windowsill. They ordered toast and a pot of tea and waited.

'Now then, young man,' said Isaac, 'You'd better start at the beginning. I gathered from your letter you're interested in my time at St Luke's during the war, is that right? About the people in the choir?'

'I know it sounds strange, Mr Crane. It all started with this,' said John, taking from his pocket the brown envelope containing the photo of the choir's trip to Blackpool. 'Before I ask you about this photograph, let me explain why I'm interested in it.'

John stopped while the waitress put a large plate piled high with buttered toast in front of them, and loaded the small table with teapot, hot water, milk, sugar, teacups and saucers.

'Leave the tea to steep,' said Isaac, sensing the tension in the young man. 'I'll just pour for us both when we reach a natural break. This is about your mother, you said.'

'Well, two women actually.' John was getting used to telling this tale, making it clearer for people. 'One of the women was my real mother, the one who gave birth to me, and the other was the one who adopted me. I thought she was my real mother until very recently.'

Isaac looked closely at him.

'How did you find out about it?' he asked. John expected him to pour the tea but he didn't.

'My adopted mother told me herself. She didn't mean to. She was … very ill, and she thought that I was my father – her husband – and started to talk to me about how I was adopted, just after I was born.'

'That must have been a shock.'

'Yes, it was. All of a sudden you realise you aren't who you think you are. Don't know who I am really. That's what I'm trying to find out.'

'What's this got to do with the choir at St Luke's?'

'Well, my mother who brought me up, the one who was ill, she died.'

Isaac murmured something in response as he stirred the teapot, but John didn't respond and carried on.

'After she died – her name was Enid Pharaoh, by the way – I searched the house looking for any information about where I'd come from, but the only thing I found was half a letter that mentioned the choir.'

'And you think the choir was my choir, the one at St Luke's?'

'That's what my aunt told me, my adopted mam's sister. They live close by, in Ulverston.'

'So how did you track me down? It's a while since I left Barrow.'

'I went to St Luke's and met the vicar there now, Mr Blount.'

Isaac Crane helped himself to a piece of toast. 'Don't think I've ever met him.'

John went on, 'No, he's only been there a few years, since you left. But he took me to see some other people, Mr and Mrs Finn,'

'Ah, yes, Honoria Finn, I remember her. She was a regular at church, and he came occasionally. They knew everything and everybody, enjoyed the gossip like some people do.'

'Well it was Mr Finn who remembered most.' John hesitated, remembering the excruciating conversation in the front room, and Mr Finn's gleeful thirst for scandal. 'Anyway, the letter mentioned the surname of a woman whose daughter was having a baby –'

'Thompson,' said Isaac suddenly, 'Cora Thompson.' He spoke the name quietly, and sat quite still, a piece of toast halfway to his mouth.

'There was a sister, too,' said John, aware that his heart was beating very fast.

'Yes, Barbara. Barbara Skinner.'

'That's right,' said John. 'But – '

Isaac put down the toast and looked at John intently. 'What year was this John? When were you born?'

'Nineteen seventeen.'

'The photo. Let me see it, please.'

John noticed that the old man's hand was shaking as he held the photo close to his face. Isaac patted his pockets, then stood up abruptly and headed towards the counter, still holding the photo. A moment later he returned with a magnifying glass and used it to look once more. As he raised his face, he looked pale and anxious.

'John, let me be sure about this. You think that Cora Thompson and her sister Barbara Skinner had something to do with arranging for you to be adopted.'

'That's what it sounds like, from what I know so far.'

'And this was in 1917?'

'Yes, early in the year.'

Isaac Crane sat back in his chair. He rested his hands on the

222

small table in front of him, then found a handkerchief in his pocket and patted his forehead. He seemed unwell.

'John, will you excuse me?'

John had no time to respond before Isaac stood up yet again, steadied himself for a moment, and then walked away, this time towards the stairs and the sign depicting a pointing hand. Left alone at the small round table, he took a bite out of a glutinous piece of toast and poured himself a cup of tea that was over-brewed and dark brown in the delicate cup. He drank the tea and waited. Maybe this was all a waste of time.

John was filling the teapot with fresh hot water when Isaac returned to the table a few minutes later.

'I think there may be something you need to know, young man,' he said gravely. The tone of his voice made John look up.

'What?'

'Something that happened before you were born.'

John's heart raced.

'They came to see me,' said Isaac.

'Who did? Who came to see you?'

'Mrs Skinner and her sister, Mrs Thompson. They came to my house one evening, after New Year, in 1917, after the busy choir season was over. I was surprised to see them at my door. I knew Barbara, of course, from the choir, and I'd met Mrs Thompson but …'

'What did they want?' John interrupted.

'They wanted my advice. I asked why they didn't talk to the vicar, but they said they wanted to talk to me, in confidence. They thought I wouldn't, well, judge.'

John couldn't wait to hear more. 'It was one of the daughters, wasn't it, in trouble, having a baby? Tell me!'

People in the crowded café heard the urgency in John's voice and looked across at them.

'Not in here,' said Isaac. 'Let's talk outside, more private.'

Isaac whispered something to the woman at the counter, who nodded. John stumbled across to the door and yanked it open. He waited for Isaac in front of the café, unaware of the faces inside turned towards him, like the audience at a play. When Isaac joined him, John seized him by the shoulders. The audience inside the café caught their breath.

'Tell me,' said John.

Isaac held John's wrists and gently pushed him back, wishing he were tall enough to put his arm round the boy's shoulders. Out of the view of their audience, he found a bench and eased John, unresisting, onto it.

'You know,' said John. 'For the love of God, tell me, please.'

'Cora Thompson had two daughters, Jessie and Beatrice.'

'Which one was it?' asked John

'It was Jessie,' said Isaac, 'the eldest. That was what they found so difficult. Jessie. The brightest, the one with the future. "Thrown away," they said. "All that future thrown away." Mrs Thompson, your grandmother, she cried I remember. She was angry and upset. Barbara was the calm one.'

'Jessie Thompson,' said John. 'My mother.'

'Yes, John, she was. They persuaded her to go to Carnforth and have the baby there, out of sight. Mrs Thompson, for all she said, was as much ashamed as upset, I have to say.'

'Why you? Why did they want to talk to you?'

'They wanted to know about the Pharaohs, Enid and Arthur. They knew that I'd known them for many years. Arthur and I went to the Grammar together, way back. And Enid and her family lived in the next street. I knew they'd wanted children ever since they married, Arthur told me so himself. I knew that they were good people, and I said so. Barbara, your aunt, wanted to know if they'd be willing to adopt the baby that Jessie would have.'

John stared at him. 'And did you? What did you say?'

'I told them that they should make the approach themselves. Adopting a child is a huge step. I told them that. I asked why they couldn't keep the child, bring it up within the family.'

'And why couldn't they?'

'Cora said she couldn't possibly manage to bring up a child, with her husband gone, and the whole street watching. That's what she said. And they were sure that it would be impossible for Jessie, too. She couldn't keep the child and be allowed to teach. I don't know how true that was, but that's what they told her, I'm sure. She would have had to choose. A terrible choice for a young woman, even one as strong as Jessie.'

'You knew her too?'

'From the Sunday school, when she was a child, and then watching her take charge of some of the younger children. She was a natural teacher, even then. Such a lovely young woman.'

'And what about the father?'

'The father of the child? Your father? I don't know, John. If I did, if they'd said, I would tell you, but they never told me and I didn't ask. Maybe they didn't know themselves. I don't know, truly. I do know that your mother, Jessie, wouldn't ... wouldn't have given something so precious to someone she didn't – care for.'

John put back his head and closed his eyes.

'Oh, my poor boy,' said Isaac. 'I'm so sorry you've had to wait so long. I can't imagine ...'

Suddenly John remembered the photo in his pocket. He fumbled for it with his gloved hand, pulled it out and tore off his glove in frustration to get hold of the battered paper without damage.

'Here,' he said. 'One more thing, please. You looked at this before, but you didn't say anything.'

'I wanted to be sure.'

'So look again now and tell me. Is she there? Is Jessie Thompson there?'

Isaac Crane didn't need to look. He'd seen her straight away.

'She's there. The girl at the end of the row, hair blowing over her face. That's her, Jessie. Such a lovely girl. I wonder what happened to her?'

John looked at the photo in his hand and touched the image of his mother.

CHAPTER 27

IT WAS COLD, very cold. The temperature had been dropping since the pale sun had sunk exhausted below the western horizon, at its most southerly point of departure. From the next day the point of sunset would begin to travel northwards again, slowly, inch by inch along the horizon. The group of women gathered outside the village hall stamped their feet and rubbed their gloved hands as they waited under the stars. A small cloud hung round them, rising slowly into the freezing air. The ladies from Newton Women's Institute were going carol singing.

The door of the schoolhouse opened, and the women turned towards the sound. Jessie called from the doorway.

'Come and wait inside, we can watch from the window.'

Gratefully, they crowded into the warm sitting room. Agnes had a few carol sheets and handed them around. They talked about which carols they could all manage, and which verses to leave out.

'Are we expecting anyone else, do you think?' she said, putting the rest of the sheets into her handbag. 'Bit thin on the ground tonight. Too cold for some, and it's a bit slippery underfoot.'

'And they're plucking tonight up at Tawbank,' said Frieda Satterthwaite. 'That'll take a few out.'

It was nearly eight when they reached the end of Tawbank

Farm lane. They had sung well at various doors around the village and debated whether they should call it a night. The moon was rising above the line of the fells to the east, improbably golden.

'Are we going down to the farm?' asked Jessie. 'They might be finished in the barn by now, worth a try. If they're still working they'll be glad of the interruption. Hard work, plucking.'

'Let's give it a go,' suggested Agnes. 'We're warmed up now and it's not far. After that we can go home.'

They straggled down the lane that was pitted with small frozen puddles, and reached the farm door. No light there. No sign of life.

'In the barn,' said Maggie Adamson. 'There's the light. They're still at it.'

Indeed there was light, seeping round the door of the barn across the yard as it stood almost closed against the night and the cold.

Agnes pulled open the barn door. A swirl of feathers rose gently on the air, catching the light from lanterns strung around the barn. Turkey feathers, some dark, some light, drifted around the barn like mottled snowflakes. One knot of women stood at the door, looking in: the other women sat on straw bales, legs apart, holding the half-plucked birds like small, white cellos. All the women stared at the feathers, mesmerized. Jessie held her breath.

'Close the door, quick,' cried a voice. The singers shuffled into the barn and pulled the door closed.

'We thought you might come,' said another voice from beyond the veil of feathers. 'We need a break. Sing us something. We can join in.'

And so the women sang together as the feathers sank slowly onto their coats and aprons and shawls. 'In the bleak midwinter, frosty wind made moan,' they sang, and in the neighbouring barn cattle lifted their heads to listen.

'Ee, that was grand,' said Nellie Kitchin. 'Our Alice, she had a lovely voice …'

'There now,' said another, putting an arm round Nellie's shoulders. They all remembered Alice.

'We're nearly done wi' these birds.' Janet Lowery's voice filled the brief silence. 'Just a couple left. Farm door's open. Go in and put kettle on. We all need a drink. Get the place warmed up for us, we'll be there in a tick.' She pulled another dead bird off the pile at her feet. Jessie turned and opened the door again, more slowly this time, and the singers picked their way across the frozen yard.

Alice. Jessie hadn't thought about her for a while, but there she was in her mind's eye, singing in the school Christmas play not many years ago. Such a sweet voice she had, and so self-aware, looking not at the back wall of the room as other children had done but boldly at her audience, smiling at them, confident, fearless. And now she was gone.

They sat together, the women of the village, and drank tea in the cluttered kitchen, huddled round the range for warmth. Branches of holly brightened the walls, stuck behind curtain rails and round the frame of a faded photograph. The farmhouse was three hundred years old, Jessie remembered. All those years hovered in the air they breathed.

Each of the turkey pluckers had a bird to carry home, and the singers offered to help as they trudged back down the lane towards the village.

'Bring your bird back to the schoolhouse, Nellie,' said Jessie. 'We'll leave it outside in the cold and you can send the children up tomorrow to carry it back. No point in you struggling with it on your own.'

By the time they reached the schoolhouse they both had wet feet and cold hands.

'Drop the bird in the porch and go in,' said Jessie. 'The door's open. I'll stir the fire up and we'll get your shoes dried off a bit. Will the children be alright for a bit longer?'

'Bill's in, miss. Asleep by now, likely.'

'Not "miss" please, Nellie. Makes me feel so old,' said Jessie, smiling. 'Call me Jessie, won't you? Here, leave your shoes in the hearth and I'll get the fire going. Not quite dead yet. I've got some sloe gin, this year's brew and just ready. Have a wee drop before you go. You can test it for me. Sloes seemed a bit hard this year, in that hedge down by the river. Someone got there before me, got the best ones. Let's see if it's drinkable.'

Jessie had pricked the sloes, added sugar and cheap gin and left them for three months, turning the jar occasionally. The liquid shone crimson in the tiny glasses and smelled of autumn. They sipped and smiled.

'Good stuff, miss,' said Nellie, licking her lips.

And so they sat a while, warming their feet, sipping their drinks, enjoying the peace of the night.

'It'll be hard for you, Nellie, the first Christmas without Alice.'

Nellie looked at her, but said nothing.

'My sister Bea went to New Zealand, many years ago,' Jessie continued. 'Not seen her since. We weren't close, but I miss her most at Christmas.'

'Still can't believe our Alice is gone,' said Nellie. 'We 'ad our moments, but she meant no 'arm to no one. Lively as a lark, she was. She'd 'ave been with us for a day or two at Christmas, bossing us all about. Grand with the kiddies, such a help to me.' She paused. Jessie said nothing. 'Stood up to 'er father too, that's the trouble. Made 'im real mad at times. That was the hard part. Got worse after she went to th' Hall. Got ideas above 'erself, mixing with that lot.'

Jessie remembered something. 'Mr Alex was fond of her, she said.'

'Oh, she told you about that, did she? 'Ad some daft idea that he was sweet on 'er, wanted to – you know – marry 'er or summat. Daft. Old man'd never –'

'Bill, you mean?'

'Nay, t'other one. Sir John. All very polite and such, but that's it. Let his precious son bring a village lass into t'family? Nay. Never.'

Jessie had to ask.

'Nellie, did you know?'

'About Mr Alex? Told me 'erself.'

'No, not that. About … the baby?'

Nellie got up suddenly, shouting down at Jessie as she did so. 'A babby? Our Alice? Nay. When? Did you know? She never said owt, never told me.' She put her hand to her mouth and sat down again.

'I'm so sorry, Nellie. I thought she must have told you. I urged her to. She came to see me, you see, just a week or two before. She just blurted it out. Not asking for help. Said she knew what to do. I tried, Nellie, believe me. I tried to get her to talk to you. I hoped she did. She said she couldn't, that her dad would –'

'Oh God,' said Nellie, holding one hand to the top of her head. 'A babby. Dead with its mam. Why did no one know, at the inquest, all that talk? And you knew and said nothing.'

'I couldn't, Nellie. I thought you and Bill would know. You could have said something, but no one did. Why make more upset and grief?'

'What about the father? Someone must know that they … you know, that they'd had her, like. Not Mr Alex? Surely not. Turning up at funeral bold as brass, the bastard. Bill'd kill 'im. I'd do it meself.'

'We don't know that, Nellie. Don't say anything to Bill for pity's sake. We don't know who it was.'

'What did she say? Did she know who it was? She must've

known, unless – oh, the little – more than one? How could she?'

'I'm not even sure she was telling the truth, Nellie. She seemed to think she could get whoever it was to take her because of the baby and then … It's what young women do sometimes, to get what they want. You know how it is. Maybe she made it all up.'

'She could do that, God knows,' said Nellie. 'She could lie straight out, bold as brass. We'll never know now. That inquest, just covered everything up. Police weren't bothered. Just another poor lass from t'village, no one special, not like those bloody Skeffingtons.'

'What about the young woman, her friend,' said Jessie, 'the one she was with that night, the Monck girl? What's her name, Phyllis? Maybe she knew something. Girls talk to each other, don't they, tell each other secrets?'

'She's a madam, that one,' said Nellie. 'No better than she should be, so they say. Standing up there, smiling at the coroner like butter wouldn't melt. She's at th' Hall as well. Started before our Alice. They could've got 'er to say what she did, covering up like. Paid 'er.'

'We don't know that, Nellie. Maybe the Skeffingtons had nothing to do with any of it, not Mr Alex, not Sir John. Maybe it was someone else. Maybe nobody. We don't know.'

'We can ask, though. We can get that Phyllis on 'er own and ask all the questions that should've been asked at the inquest when we were all too upset to say a word. She's still there, I know that. Saw 'er mam at market last month sometime. Allus lets on to me. Could've been 'er that lost a daughter …'

Nellie stopped. She put a hand to her mouth. A tear ran down the side of her face. 'Sorry, miss. Look at me. Too late for tears. She's gone, never coming back. It's the gin talking.'

'You cry if you want to, Nellie,' said Jessie. 'I'm sorry I raked it up. I just … wondered, you know, if she ever told you. She would have done, of course, if she hadn't been so frightened.'

'Of 'er dad? Aye, she were right to be feared of 'im. I am meself sometimes. Men. They get away with it, every time, knock up a lass and just walk away. Not right. It's the women who 'ave their babies, feed everybody, manage everything, get knocked about. It's not right.'

Jessie waited while the anger faded. The fire was dying and the room was cold. Nellie pulled her shoes out of the hearth and her shawl from the back of the chair behind her. She sniffed. 'Have to go, miss. Bill'll notice if I'm real late. We need to talk to that Phyllis. You 'ave to come, miss. You can make 'er tell us what she knows.'

'I doubt that, Nellie, but of course I'll come with you. If it stays clear and cold like this we can take the river path: no mud, easier under foot. When, though? It's alright for me, I'm going to Agnes Plane's for Christmas, but you will have so much to do.'

'I'll manage an hour or two. Bill doesn't finish till Christmas Eve. Our Mary can look after the two young 'uns. Plenty to keep 'em all busy.'

'We could send a message to the Hall,' Jessie began.

'Nay, miss,' said Nellie with unusual determination. 'Don't give that Phyllis time to prepare a story. Catch 'er on the hop. She knows something, I'm sure of that.'

CHAPTER 28

THE RIVERSIDE PATH to Skeffington Hall was as hard and dry as Jessie had predicted, and the two women were walking up the long drive with plenty of time to do what they had to do before the mid-afternoon dark would overtake them. A familiar car passed them as they walked and Jessie raised her hand in greeting to the vicar, but Lionel was looking straight ahead and did not even see them.

'Was that th' vicar?' asked Nellie, stepping out of the ditch that had protected her from the speeding car.

'I believe so, but he didn't see us.' Jessie sometimes got a glimpse like this of how Lionel was viewed by many of Newton's inhabitants.

'Don't believe in them cars, miss. Folk don't need to go as fast as that to get things done. So noisy, too.'

'You're right I'm sure, Nellie. When I was in London – '

'London, miss? You've been to London?'

'Just the once, Nellie. With Miss Plane. She has an aunt there. So many cars. That's the first thing you notice.' They'd arrived at a fork in the drive. 'Back door I think, don't you?'

Ahead of them stood the Hall, faced with large sandstone blocks, probably taken from the Roman fort down by the sea centuries before. Jessie loved this house, the way it sat comfortably in the landscape as if it had always been here, and the wonderful view up the valley from the terrace at the front. The tradesmen's entrance at the back was much less grand, with no view at all, but it was the best place to find the girl they were looking for. Jessie stopped and held Nellie's arm as they approached the door.

'Now we'll have to be careful with Phyllis, Nellie,' she said. 'I know you think she knows something about the night Alice died, but we can't be sure of that. If she knew something and didn't tell the coroner, that could be very serious. Can't expect her to just tell us the truth now, just because we ask her to.'

'I won't fly at 'er, miss, though 'eaven knows I'd like to. She and our Alice was thick as thieves, right back to being young 'uns. Told each other everything. She knows summat, I'll swear she does. Why did she lie? Must be covering it up for some reason.'

'And it must be important to her, that's what I'm saying,' said Jessie. 'So let's just be friendly and see what happens. Alright?'

Jessie waited until Nellie nodded assent before she pulled on the bell rope that hung at the side of the door. They waited. A face appeared at a small window just above their heads and then the door swung open. The young woman who opened it was about the same age as Alice. Even looked like her, thought Jessie with a start. Maybe it was just the uniform that made young girls in service all look much the same.

The girl recognised Jessie and blushed.

'Good morning, miss,' she said, smiling. 'You've not seen me for a year or two. Elspeth, miss, Elspeth New.'

'Good heavens,' said Jessie, 'So it is. How are you, Elspeth?'

'I'm well, thank you, miss.'

'And your mother, how is she … coping?'

'Well as she can, miss. It's been 'ard, you know, since –'

'Of course. Is your father still at home?'

'Nowhere else to go, miss, since 'e's lost his sight. Cannut do

235

'owt for 'imself. I give Mam what I can, and James too. He's at Eskmeals now, just started. Not much, but it all helps with the young 'uns.'

'Elspeth!' a voice bore down on them from the room behind the door. 'Who is it? Why's that door still open, making the fire smoke?'

Elspeth flinched. 'Better come in, miss.'

'Thank you, Elspeth,' said Jessie with due formality. She and Nellie stepped up into the hallway and Elspeth shut the door behind them. 'Follow me, please,' she said, leading them through a door into a huge kitchen.

'Who is it, Elspeth?' said the owner of the voice, Mrs Hodgkin the housekeeper who Jessie recognised from church. 'Oh it's you, Miss Whelan. Round the back?'

'Yes, Mrs Hodgkin. I thought it more apropos. Good morning to you, by the way. It must be a week or two?'

'It has been that long, Miss Whelan, indeed. I'm a martyr to my chest, and it's been bad lately. Nothing worse than coughing in church, I always say. So rude.'

Nellie and Elspeth watched this brief encounter with interest. Neither of them had ever heard Mrs Hodgkin speak so politely to someone 'round the back'.

'Have you met my friend, Mrs Kitchin?' said Jessie, responding to the mood of ladylike conviviality.

'Oh my, it's Alice's mother, is it?' said the housekeeper. 'A fine young woman, your Alice, Mrs Kitchin. We miss her downstairs, don't we Elspeth?'

'Yes Mrs Hodgkin, we do.'

'And what can we do for you, Miss Whelan? What brings you here, both of you, and at this end of the house?'

'I do apologise for this intrusion, Mrs Hodgkin. We would like a word with one of your girls, and thought it better to see you rather than someone else in the house about it. It's a private matter, but rather urgent.'

'Private, well. We don't encourage the girls to have callers while they're at work, but I assume it's important to bring you both up here. Nothing serious I hope?'

'No, no,' said Jessie, who could still lie convincingly when she had to. 'But we would be so grateful for a little time with – oh I didn't say – with Phyllis, Phyllis Monck, if you would be so kind as to ask her.'

'Phyllis,' Mrs Hodgkin's expression altered just a little. Was she surprised, or not, Jessie wondered. 'Yes of course. Elspeth, run upstairs and fetch Phyllis, there's a good girl. She's in the blue bedroom, or she should be. Now will you take some tea, Miss Whelan, Mrs Kitchin, while you wait?'

Jessie glanced at Nellie before she declined the offer.

'That's very kind, thank you, Mrs Hodgkin, but Mrs Kitchin and I can only stay a few minutes. We've walked across and the dark draws in so early.'

'Well, come through to my parlour,' said Mrs Hodgkin, 'while we're waiting. Warmer in there and we can sit down.'

And so they sat. Mrs Hodgkin wore her best expression of benevolent curiosity but Jessie wasn't tempted to say anything more about the purpose of their visit. Instead she asked, 'Was it the vicar we saw leaving as we came down the drive? He seemed to be in a hurry.'

'Indeed it was,' replied the housekeeper. 'He came to see Sir John, but he's in Cockermouth today and the vicar couldn't wait. Seemed to be in a hurry over something. Such a busy man, always.' She turned towards the door as it creaked. 'There you are, Phyllis. Go and wash your hands, girl. These ladies would like a word with you, but not with dirty hands like that.'

'Yes Mrs 'odgkin. Sorry, miss,' said Phyllis, hurrying away.

'I'll leave you to it, Miss Whelan, ' said the housekeeper, with obvious reluctance. The vicar calling, now the schoolteacher, both unexplained. There were too many things happening this morning that she didn't know about.

Jessie and Nellie sat on the small chairs either side of the fire-place, leaving a hard wooden chair between them for Phyllis when she returned.

'I expect you'd like to know why we want to talk to you, Phyllis,' said Jessie, as Phyllis sat down. 'You know Mrs Kitchin, I'm sure, poor Alice's mother.'

'Yes, miss,' said Phyllis, looking down at her clean hands. She knew Nellie Kitchin all too well.

'Well,' Jessie went on, 'Mrs Kitchin and I have been thinking about the way poor Alice met her death in May, just before coronation day, do you remember?'

'Oh, yes, miss.' Phyllis's voice had dropped to a whisper and a red blush was clear on her cheeks even in the gloom of the small parlour.

'You were probably the last person to see her alive, Phyllis. Her mother and I, we both need to know more about what happened that night, more than what came out at the inquest. That's why we want to talk to you.'

'Why now, miss? It were months ago.' Phyllis raised her head, but still did not look at Nellie, not a flicker.

'You know, I'm not sure, Phyllis.' Jessie could hear her herself, sounding like the teacher. 'Maybe something about Christmas coming. It's always so hard you know, the first Christmas after … after you've lost someone dear to you. So many memories. Nellie and I were talking about it the other day, weren't we, Nellie?' Nellie nodded, but said nothing. 'And we both said, almost together, that we wished we understood more about that night, and what happened.'

'I told 'em, miss, the coroner and all them folk. I told 'em what 'appened.'

'Yes of course, you did. We were all there, weren't we? And I expected the coroner to ask you some more questions but they all seemed so sure that Alice had just slipped and fallen into the river. No one else around who could have helped her. She must have, well, she must have called for help or something, don't you think?'

'Don't know, miss, I'm sure.' Phyllis's head was down on her chest again.

'Well we thought we'd just come up and ask you about it ourselves, before we all get involved in Christmas. And we didn't want to interrupt your break with your family.'

'Only Christmas Day, miss, that's all they give us.'

'Exactly,' said Jessie, reasonably. 'That's why we've come today, just for a wee chat about it, just to set our minds at rest.' She looked across at Nellie, who was struggling to keep quiet, and shook her head slightly. She thought that Phyllis might tell them more if they took it very slowly.

'Now,' Jessie went on, 'you were with Alice at the dance in Ganthwaite that night, weren't you?'

'Yes, miss. We all went.'

'And was Alice with anyone there, apart from you and her other friends from the Hall.'

'No miss. We were all together. There were village folk there, like, but no one ... Alice wasn't with no one, miss.'

'Did she have any special friends, Phyllis? A young man perhaps? She didn't tell Mrs Kitchin anything.' Jessie looked at Nellie who was watching Phyllis very carefully. 'But then we don't always tell our mothers about these things, do we?' She smiled at the bent head. Phyllis looked up again, but not for more than a moment.

'No, miss. Alice didn't 'ave a young man. She'd've told me. I would've known.'

'Of course you would.' Jessie hesitated. 'Phyllis, Alice told me that Mr Alex was very fond of her.'

'Our Mr Alex, miss?'

'Yes, Alex Skeffington, that's what she said.'

Phyllis turned her head to one side, trying without success to stifle a laugh.

'She said that? About Mr Alex?' She dipped her head and looked about, nervous at the mention of the young master's name in his own kitchen.

'Yes, she did.'

'Well, I – sorry to laugh, miss, but Mr Alex, he's such a ... well, he's engaged to be married, miss, to Miss Ramsden. He couldn't.'

'It is possible that Alice was wrong about that. If he was, you know, kind to her, she might have misunderstood.'

'She did like Mr Alex, I know that,' said Phyllis suddenly, almost gleefully. 'But ...'

'But what?'

'Well, Mr Alex wasn't at the dance, was he? No posh folk at Ganthwaite.'

'No, of course.' Jessie hesitated a moment, long enough for Nellie to interrupt.

'You said that you and Alice left together.'

'Yes,' said Phyllis, clearly worried about talking to Alice's mother rather than the schoolteacher. The thought of Alice's father was worrying her, too.

Nellie was unconvinced and her voice rose as she continued. 'Now look, Phyllis. I've known ye since ye were a babby. Don't lie to me. If ... if you're not telling th' truth it could be ... well, you'd better be telling us th' truth, my girl.' She glared at Phyllis. 'I know my Alice.' Her voice sank to a fierce whisper as Jessie put a finger to her lips and looked towards the door. Mrs Hodgkin was certain to be close by, hearing as much as she could.

'Look at me, Phyllis,' Nellie whispered. 'Did you and Alice leave together, like you said? Was anyone else with you who might've seen summat?'

Phyllis said nothing more. She hung her head and took a hankie out of her pocket.

'You have to tell us, Phyllis,' said Jessie, imploring the girl to say something. Nellie was clearly ready to threaten her, or worse.

Phyllis looked up, her eyes bright with tears. 'But I promised,' she began.

'Promised? Who? What did you promise?' Nellie demanded. 'Look,' she said, her head very close to Phyllis. 'Look, she was my daughter, my eldest, and she could be a madam, I know that. What did she make you do? We don't blame ye, do we Miss Whelan, we just want to know what 'appened. You promised Alice but she's dead, and we're 'ere. You're 'ere. You're carrying something for 'er aren't you, but she's dead. She died that night, drowned like a rat in a dyke. And I'm 'er mam. Tell me!'

'She made me promise,' sobbed Phyllis. 'She was going to meet someone, but she made me promise I wouldn't tell. After – when they found her – I 'ad to keep me promise. For Alice, as her friend. So I did. I said she'd been with me, and no one asked me, so …'

'So she went to see someone, on her own, after the dance?'

'Yes, miss.'

'And who was it? A man? I knew it!' Nellie sat back suddenly, clenching her fists.

Phyllis shrank back into the chair. 'Yes, miss.'

'Who was it, child?' Jessie could see that Phyllis was struggling.

''E said if I told anyone, I'd get into trouble, that I'd lose my place, that I could go to prison even for not saying anything before.'

241

'Who told you that? The same man?'

'Yes.'

Nellie seized the girl by the arm and twisted her round.

'Who was it, you little bitch?'

Phyllis pulled away, but the tears didn't stop.

'It was Andy,' she hissed at the two women, hating them, hating herself. 'Andy Leadbetter. He met 'er, by t'river, after t'dance. She wanted to meet 'im. She wanted 'im, she told me. And I wanted 'im, too,' she sobbed. 'It's not fair.'

CHAPTER 29

THERE WAS NO ONE home at the Church Walk house in Ulverston when John got back from Grange, but the back door was open as always, and he revelled in the silence of the house. It was windy, but not as much as on the exposed promenade where he'd walked with Isaac Crane. The house was cold. George was at work and Anne must have gone out without lighting any fires. Winter sunshine brightened the house but didn't warm it up, and John kept his coat on while he made a drink. He was glad to be alone. He wanted to think. Aunty Anne meant well, but her concern was exhausting.

Jessie Thompson. John couldn't get the name out of his mind. And the picture. She had been in the picture all along and he hadn't known. She looked so young. Only forty or so, even now, still young. She'd given him up for her job, or that's how it looked. There had to be a reason, but this was more like an excuse. He tried to imagine the pressure she must have faced: 1916 was different world. He hadn't learned much at school about it, but he could see just by looking at that photo how much the clothes had changed since then. No more skirts to the ground these days, no more big hats, pinched waists.

Poor Jessie, he thought. Up against her mother and her aunt. They must have pushed and nagged her, and worse. What did it take for his mam to be packed off to Carnforth in shame and watch someone else take him away, her child? John didn't often see the world from someone else's viewpoint, but he did now and the hurt was unbearable. He sat at the kitchen table, forehead leaning on his fist. Why did Enid have to say what she'd said and set this whole thing in motion? He wasn't happy before, but he was surely more content than he felt right now. 'Be grateful,' Mrs Barker had said. 'Many people have it worse.' True. He had money and his health was improving, although much of the time he felt wretched and he wanted it to be over. Still, he couldn't stop now. He knew who he wasn't, but the truth was still blurred and obscure. All he had was a name and an old photo.

The clock on the wall said nearly noon. Anne might be back soon, or George home for his lunch. They would want to know what he'd found out. He had to decide how much to tell them. Keeping things to himself would take more energy, but John desperately wanted to do so, to stay in charge of it. It was his life. He wasn't even related to these two, not by blood. He had to decide what to do, where to go next. It was nearly Christmas. Did he want to stay here, in Ulverston?

First things first. Before he was disturbed, and as a way of clearing his head, he took a small notebook from the inner pocket of his jacket, took off his coat finally and sat down to write in a small meticulous hand the things he'd found out in the past few days. After only a few lines he stopped writing and thought about Arthur. He was well over forty when John arrived. Did men of that age want babies as badly as women? John knew that older women were less likely to have babies but he wasn't sure at what age it would be impossible. Anyway, they got the chance of a baby, and they took it. That was brave of them, he thought, with unusual generosity towards his adopted parents. It must have been hard, to have a baby so late, when they were so set in their ways. Everything would change. Or maybe they expected the baby to fit in with them. He'd always felt that as a child: not unwelcome, but a bit of a nuisance. Maybe they were disappointed, not in him but in the idea of being parents. But Arthur had been so kind, so willing to have fun with him and do the things that boys like to do. It wasn't just 'duty'. Arthur had loved him, he was sure of that.

Without warning, sadness welled up inside him, up from his stomach to his head and eyes. He wept without control, the tears oozing through his fingers and down onto the table, onto the little notebook, staining the pages. John pushed it to one side, found a handkerchief, wiped his face and blew his nose. He would write more, but not yet. He couldn't bear any more for a little while.

When Anne and George came into the house an hour later, together, John was asleep upstairs. They noticed his coat in the kitchen where he'd left it.

'He's back,' said George. 'Our John's back from Grange. That was quick. Maybe that chap was no use to him, the choir chap he was going to see. All too long ago. Poor lad. Must be awful, knowing bits of things but not being able to fill in the gaps.'

'We're back, John,' called his aunt up the stairs. 'Are you there?'

'He might be sleeping,' said George, pulling her back into the kitchen. 'Leave the poor lad alone and make us a brew. And how about some lunch, too? I've got be back in twenty minutes or old Monty will be on at me again. Bloody nerve, that bloke. Think 'e was never late the way 'e goes on at me.'

George was on his way out of the house back to work when

John came slowly down the stairs. He'd heard them, but wasn't ready to face them both. He needed more time to think.

'There you are, John,' said his aunt, putting her apron back on again. 'Sit yourself down and I'll get you some lunch. You must be starved. George and I went to the bank, stuck in a queue. Why does everyone go at lunchtime? There was only one teller serving and the line was right to the door. How long have you been back? Was it the eleven-fifteen you got? Have you been asleep? Didn't get much rest last night, did you? I said to George, you were up half the night, pacing about, up and down the stairs. You must be exhausted –'

'It's alright!' John cut across her. It sounded rude but he had to stop her talking, just for a minute. If she didn't stop he'd have to get out. He couldn't stand it. 'It's alright, really, thanks Aunty Anne,' he managed to say, and avoided the urge to put his hands over his ears. 'I went to have a rest, I'm fine now.'

'Of course you are, love,' she said. 'George and I are just concerned about you, you know. Must be hard for you …'

'Yes, yes,' he said, a little too abruptly. 'But I'm fine, just a bit tired, all this running around, talking to strangers. Never was very good at it.'

'And how's it going?' she went on, unaware. 'What have you found out? Was that chap helpful, the one from the choir? Sounded as if he might be a bit ga-ga, in a nursing home like …'

John smiled. 'Oh no, not him. He was just staying there, with his sister. She owns the place. Nothing wrong with Mr Crane. Fitter than me. He walks along the prom at Grange every day, rain or shine. Sunny out there this morning, but cold, the wind …'

'You see, that's why we worry, love. You were very ill, not long ago. Got soaked through in Barrow and here you are, out again in all weathers. Maybe you should wait now, till the weather gets better, when the spring comes.'

'I've waited long enough,' said John, more firmly than he intended. There'd been enough talk in this house about his delicate health. He wasn't a child and he was tired of being treated like one. 'Once I decided I wanted to know more, I had to do it. Couldn't wait. Still can't.'

'So he wasn't much use then, this chap?'

John hesitated. 'No,' he lied, after a moment's pause. 'Nice enough bloke, willing like, but couldn't help much.'

'But what did he tell you?'

'Not much, as I said.' The lie was getting easier. 'We talked a while, then went for tea in a café behind the station and I got the train back here. That's alright. I didn't expect much really. It's all so long ago. Why should people remember just because I want them too?'

'Yes, but –'

'No,' said John. 'It's alright. I'll leave it a while, have another think about it. There's no rush really, just me being …'

'Curious. Of course, love. Of course you are.'

John picked up his little notebook from the table and went back up the stairs, murmuring about something he'd left up there. He would be relieved to get away from this woman who kept finishing his sentences for him. He was already thinking about the next train to Barrow.

By mid-afternoon he was heading north on the train, just by the place where he'd nearly drowned a few months before. The day was darkening under a low ceiling of cloud that slid across the sky from the north-west. The sea was grey and flat as slate, despite the wind earlier in the day. In the crowded carriage cigarette smoke hung thick and blue in the air. John felt his lungs itch, and he pulled down the window to look out at the sea and suck the freshness of it into his body.

The few people who got off the train at Newton quickly disappeared, hurrying home to families and familiarity. Standing on the platform with his bag John felt suddenly alone, terribly alone. He had no idea how he would get back to Mill Cottage. There'd be no more trains up the valley at this end of the day. It wasn't raining, mercifully. He pulled his coat around him, tightened the scarf Anne had insisted on giving him, shifted his bag to the other hand and set off walking up the hill towards the main road. If it stayed fine he could get quite a long way before it was too dark, and then his eyes would adjust. It would be all right.

He hadn't walked more than a mile when a horse and cart slowly caught up with him, going the same way. It was Peter Sim, the landlord from the pub in Ganthwaite. 'You going my way, up to Boot?' he called down to John from his perch behind the horse.

'Aye,' said John. 'Mill Cottage.'

'I 'eard you were there. Alright is it?' asked Peter, as John climbed up beside him. 'Rum couple those two, I've 'eard.'

'Hannah and Fred you mean? Aye, they're funny like, but grand to live with. Very easy-going.'

'That's what I 'eard,' said Peter.

They talked as they rode up the dark valley together, of the weather, and the plans for the new school. Peter thought the school was exactly what the village needed, but he doubted it would ever get built.

'Folks have enough to do round 'ere, without volunteering for things. Vicar can bang on all he likes about Christian duty and all that, but schools shouldn't be run like that. It's the country that needs the schools, to get young people educated and into work when the work's to be 'ad. Nowt to do wi' church. If this were Carlisle or even Manchester, we wouldn't be messing about like this.'

John agreed. It was the church, he was sure, that made Jessie feel ashamed about her baby, about him, and shut her away, hushed everything up. And it was the church and that precious 'respectability' that had made Enid deny where he had come from, right to the last.

Finding themselves of one mind on major issues of the day, the two men continued in amiable silence, interrupted only by the crackle of wheel rims against stone and the rhythmic clopping of the horse. Above their heads the skyline glowed fierce as the moon rose, flattened and deep orange over the black line of the ridge. Stars appeared slowly, more and more, some steady, some twinkling, some clustered together so close that the band of the Milky Way was soon clearly visible if the two men had craned their necks back to see it, which neither of them did. The white noiseless ghost of a barn owl reared in front of them, disappearing behind the wall as suddenly as it had appeared.

Before long the faint light of oil lamps appeared in houses and farms along the way. Peter dropped him off at Hill House and John walked from there up the lane and over the bridge towards his home. He guessed that Aunty Anne had been appalled by his accounts of life at Mill Cottage. She'd said something about John settling down in a 'proper house', finding a 'nice girl'. To John, though, Mill Cottage felt like home. As he pushed open the door, saw the familiar glow of rugs on slate flags and smelled the remnants of Christmas baking from the range, he was glad to be back. Hannah and Fred were glad he was back too: another pair of hands and legs to help with the jobs, someone to bring them news of the world beyond the valley, someone who liked them as they were. They asked how he was, and how he was feeling, but nothing more. John told the same lies he'd told in Ulverston. They ate supper, opened the beer that Fred had brewed for Christmas and stayed up late till the log basket was empty and none of them could be bothered to fill it.

As the moon shone higher in the sky casting white light across fields and walls and streams, John lay on his side in bed, looking out of the little window, listening to Hannah and Fred making love in the next room. He was used to it now and found the muffled noise comforting. It was love, not just sex, that made that sound. He hoped it had been love, that had made him, too.

Jessie. His mother's name stirred a memory at the back of his head. It flickered for a moment, then was lost in sleep.

As he sat at the table the following morning, mug of tea in hand, Hannah turned around from the sink to speak to him, holding a delicate cup in her hand.

'Forgot to tell you last night,' she said. 'Fred's beer, make you forget your own name! Never use these cups normally, they were me mother's. Anyway, got one out for a visitor we had, t'other day while you were away. Couldn't think who it could be when we heard car coming up t'lane. It was that woman from Newton, the posh one, the one who brought you back from hospital.'

'Miss Plane?'

'That's the one. Funny business,' Hannah continued. 'Never really told us why she'd come. Maybe just for a run out. It were a grand day, reet enough. She drove that car over Hardknott last year, did y' know? God knows why. Just for 'ell of it, Fred reckons. Any road, there she were, all dressed up. Maybe that's her usual. Must 'ave her own money. Lovely colours. Fred says he'd like a rummage in 'er wardrobe, when she chucks things out.'

John was half listening, wondering where all this was going.

'Turns out she came all this way to ask after you. Very disappointed you weren't 'ere, so she said. But happy that you were recovered. Hadn't seen you since that day she brought you home in the car.'

'Aye, I remember that,' said John. 'I'll have a car one day, I'm determined. Once I get another job, get earning again.'

'And afore y'have a lass to spend all y'money,' Hannah laughed.

'Nay, Hannah,' he said, 'My lass'll bring home money, too. Modern lasses … not like th'old days. That Miss Plane. She pays 'er own way, wherever the money comes from. Nice woman, in a posh kind of way, but not stuck up. I like 'er.'

'She likes you too, by t'sound of it.' Hannah stood with her back to the sink now, wiping her hands on her apron. 'She asked how you are, in yourself, like. Asked where you were, too. I told her you 'ad family in Ulverston, and she asked about that. Questions, questions! Maybe just making conversation. Have to talk about summat, don't you, when you're in someone's 'ouse, drinking tea out of best cups.'

'What else did she say?' John was curious now.

'Nothing much. She knew, you know, about your mam, and how you were adopted.'

'Told 'er that meself, in the car that day.'

'Asked if you'd ever tried to find your real mam. Funny question, I thought, for a stranger to ask. Nearly said to mind 'er own business. I just said I didn't know. She said no more about it after that. Just finished her tea and went off again …' Hannah paused. 'No I'm wrong,' she said. 'Before she went she told me to tell you that if you ever wanted any 'elp, she has the car and she's getting one of them telephones and you were welcome to use them, summat like that. Fred was 'ere, he might remember. Bit rum, I reckon. 'Appen you said more to 'er than you recall. You were still pretty shook up after being so ill, in hospital, all that.'

John tried to remember the trip in Agnes's car. He couldn't remember telling her very much. Something snagged at his mind.

Chapter 30

'Have you seen Mr Leadbetter?'

Jessie's voice seemed to bounce off the walls of the quarry yard. The man she had called out to looked familiar but she didn't really care who he was. All she wanted was to find Andrew before her courage failed.

'Miss Whelan, isn't it?' said the man. 'Long way from the school up 'ere. Arkwright's the name. You had our two, ages ago.'

'Of course, Mr Arkwright.' said Jessie, suddenly connecting the name with two children from a decade before. 'I remember your two, of course. How are they now?'

'Grand, thanks,' said Mick Arkwright. 'Good of you to remember, miss. Good memory, eh, goes with the job.'

Jessie smiled. 'Is Mr Leadbetter around?' she asked again, trying to keep the urgency out of her voice and to find the words she'd rehearsed as her reason for being there. 'I was taking a walk up here and I could do with a word about the school, the new building, you know.'

'Aye, I know,' said Mick. 'Is it going ahead? Boss hasn't said much about it lately.'

'That's why I need a word,' said Jessie, brightly. 'Is he here?'

'Might've knocked off early like, being Christmas Eve an' that, aye. I'm on me way mesen. Too dark to do owt. Try the 'ouse,

252

miss, 'appen 'e's there, like. 'E'll be down Farriers later if that's any good. Any road, I'm off. I'll wish thee a good day, for tomorrer, like.'

'And to you Mr Arkwright, thank you. And to the family, of course.'

'Aye, reet enough,' said Mick, touching his cap to Jessie as he picked up his bait box and walked across the yard and out to the lane.

Jessie waited, listening, but could hear nothing but the roaring of the swollen beck and the wind in the trees. She'd waited all day, pretending to be busy, baking, just to pass the time before she was due at Agnes's house for their Christmas together. It was mid-afternoon and nearly dark when she finally decided what to do about Phyllis's revelation; all the way from her house to the quarry she'd regretted the decision but she seemed unable to abandon it. She should have been as shocked by Phyllis's words the previous day as she pretended to be, but the possibility that Andrew had something to do with Alice had been on her mind for a while. Maybe it was something Nellie had said, or maybe just the expression on Andrew's face that night at the Bower House, the way he'd looked at those girls. She could believe that Andrew had been with Alice, but surely he didn't harm her.

Jessie needed to find a reason to forgive him. She wanted Alice to be a liar, or Phyllis, and both of those were possible. And she wanted Andrew to be appalled when he realised that he'd attacked Jessie, to be contrite and beg her to forgive him. She wanted to forgive him. He was the only one since Clive who'd wanted her. There'd been others who'd admired her, respected her, but no one as demonstrative as Andrew. She was terrified that he, of everyone she knew and who knew her, he was the one who truly understood the secret side of her, the side she had kept hidden. She'd always known it was there, the part of her that lied, and yearned for the touch of a man. Andrew had seen it. That night when he first confessed how he felt, just a few weeks before, she should have told him 'No,' right at the start but she hadn't. She'd thought about it for days, about whether to give in to him, and then she'd done it. Everything that had happened since, she had brought on herself. And still she wanted him. If she could see him, ask him about Alice, give him the chance to explain, to be sorry, then maybe she could still have him.

She turned off her torch and sat on a slate bench in the quarry yard, shrouded in her big coat and a hat pulled down against the cold. It was late afternoon, dark already and there was no one about, here or on the road as she walked up. Then she saw the light: just a gleam, no more, in one of the downstairs windows of the house across the yard. As she watched, the light moved from one window to another, a lamp carried by someone who cast a black shape on the far wall of the room. The door opened. She shrank back but the light shone in a long beam towards her, caught her boots in its glare and then moved slowly up to her face. She wanted to look down, to hide, but she could not.

'Who's that?' Andrew's voice echoed off the hard slate walls of the yard. He started to walk across towards her, carrying the lamp high. She looked into the light.

'Jess?' he said, stopping a few yards from her. 'Jess? What are you doing here, lass, sitting in the dark? It's bloody cold out here, come away in. I've lit a fire.'

'No,' she said. 'I can't. I can't.' Her voice tailed away. The words she'd rehearsed turned to dust in her mouth.

'For God's sake, lass, just get in here before you freeze,' he said, moving forward again, holding out his hand to her. Jessie stood, still leaning back against the wall, feeling the edge of the bench behind her legs. Before he reached her she twisted away from him.

'Don't play silly buggers, for God's sake,' he said, his voice quieter now. 'I won't hurt you. Just come away in and sit a while. It's good to see you, but it's been a sod of a day and I can't be arsed flitting about like this. We can have a drink, there's some whisky somewhere.'

'No,' she said again. 'You said before that you wouldn't hurt me, but you did.'

'What're you on about?' he said. 'Are you coming in, or not?'

She hesitated. She could see him clearly now in the light from his lamp that he still held up at shoulder height. She couldn't see what he was thinking. Was it possible that he did not remember that night? He'd hurt her, whether he'd meant to or not. She knew that she should stand her ground, or walk away, but instead she stepped carefully round him, out of reach, and across to the open door of the house. As he followed her, the shadow sharpened across the cobbled ground. She was not afraid of him now. He was sober and calm and she was certain he would not hurt her. She would tell him about Phyllis and then decide what else to say. They were adults after all.

Inside the depressing house she heard the crackle of the fire to her left and walked towards the glow. The room was almost bare of furniture, just a table covered with a newspaper in the centre and one chair next to it. How could he live like this? She took off her hat and shook her head, put the hat in her pocket and held out her hands to the fire as she heard the door close and his footsteps. She turned quickly to face him.

'Stay there,' she said. 'Just listen to me. Don't come any nearer.'

'All right, lass, if you say so. Grand to see you. Best thing I've seen today, that's for sure.'

'Stop,' she said. 'Don't say any more. I have to say some things and then you can talk.'

He smiled. 'Well, it's the schoolteacher again, haven't seen her for a bit.' He moved a step towards the fire, but then stopped, seeing her face. He hung the lamp on a hook at the end of the mantelpiece and it swung there, shadows bending and curving around the bare room. 'Go on then,' he said. 'Get on with it, whatever you're trying to say.'

'I went to see Phyllis, up at the Hall,' said Jessie, watching Andrew's face intently, lit by both the fire and the swaying lamp. The smile hardened.

'Phyllis who?' he said.

'You know Phyllis,' said Jessie. 'She told us, about what happened the night Alice was drowned.'

'Whatever she said, she's a lying bitch,' he said. 'Always has been. You know that, you had her in school, and that Alice, too. Couple of silly tarts, the pair of them.'

'One of them's dead,' said Jessie. 'Drowned like a rat. And you were there. Phyllis told us. You were at the dance, that night in May.'

'Aye, I was,' said Andrew, less relaxed now, 'and so were plenty of other folk.'

'Phyllis said that Alice wanted to talk to you, and that was the last anyone saw of her.'

For a moment Andrew stared at her, then looked away. He ran a hand through his hair, then reached for the mantelpiece and leaned against it. It was a few moments before he spoke again. Jessie watched him carefully.

'Alright,' he said finally, 'So I was there. Alice Kitchin was a stupid girl who thought I'd fall for the oldest trick in the book.'

Jessie interrupted. 'She told you she was expecting, didn't she?'

'Aye she did, must think I'm a real fool. Some silly girl says she's knocked up and what am I going to do about it. All right, I'd had her, but me and a few others. She didn't want the useless boys she'd laid down for and decided to have a go at me. Well I'm no fool and I told her so.'

'So you did see her, after the dance.'

'Aye, I saw her. That lying bitch Phyllis set it up.'

'Where did you meet her?'

'Where she said, on the path by the river. Bloody silly place. It had rained for hours, path was slippery as hell. I had the dogs with me. I knew she was feared of them, but that wasn't why … I just had them out, on a rope like, not loose. I had no idea …'

They stood facing each other, the fire between them. Jessie wanted to stop, to sit down and talk to him like she used to, but she could not, would not, not now.

She said nothing, and he went on.

'She started shouting. Said she was late like, and the bairn was mine and she was going to tell her dad and he would make me marry her. Dogs were fretting when she started shouting, then they pulled towards her, barking, and she backed up quick and slipped and went down the bank. Just like that, she was gone. The dogs were carrying on something fierce. It was pitch black, no moon. River was in flood. Caught a glimpse of her, the white of her face, heard her screaming but she went down and there was nothing, nothing to see. I ran, further downstream, but what with the water and the wind I couldn't hear her. Nothing I could do, Jess. That's how it was. She was gone, nothing I could do.'

He looked at her. 'So now you know,' he said, running his hand though his hair again. 'I'm not lying to you. It was an accident.'

'So why didn't you say anything, tell anybody? You have no idea what poor Nellie went through. When we went up to the Hall …'

Andrew looked up sharply. 'Who went to the Hall? Who was with you?'

'Nellie,' said Jessie. 'Nellie Kitchin.'

'Christ, woman,' he said, twisting away from the mantelpiece. 'What does Nellie think?'

'That you got Alice pregnant and then pushed her into the river to shut her up. What else could she think after what Phyllis said.'

'But she must know Phyllis is a liar.'

'Maybe, but Nellie lost her daughter and she wants someone to blame.'

Andrew looked up at the ceiling of the dismal room. 'Oh God,' he said quietly. 'She'll have told him. Bill Kitchin is a wrong 'un. He'll come after me.'

'I asked her not to tell him, until we were sure.'

Andrew snorted. He knew there was little chance that Nellie would keep this to herself. He leaned forward towards Jessie, more urgency in his voice.

'When was this, when did you go up there?'

'Yesterday,' said Jessie. 'I told you. Nellie and I talked after we'd seen Phyllis and she agreed not to say anything to Bill until we'd seen the constable, after Christmas.'

'He'll kill me,' said Andrew. He caught Jessie's expression. 'Bill, you know what he's like. He'll come after me. Could be coming right now.'

'Is that all you can say?' Jessie was shocked. 'You watched a girl die, and all you're bothered about is her father coming after you?'

'I've been through all that, months ago. She was gone, nothing more I could do. No point in making it worse. Nobody knew anything about the bairn, if there was one. No gain in raking that up. So I kept quiet, better for everyone. And now it'll all come out. Why couldn't you just keep your nose out of it?'

'I knew about the bairn, too,' said Jessie. 'Alice came to see me. She told me she was expecting and wanted me to help. I urged her to tell her mother, but she knew what her father would do if he found out. You can't blame me for this mess.'

She paced across the small room, suddenly furious with him, then turned back to face him. 'Look at you, feeling so sorry for yourself. You can't keep your hands off, can you? I saw you, that night at the Bower House, looking those girls up and down like slabs of meat.'

'I told you,' he said, 'It wasn't them I wanted, it was you, from the very first time I saw you. That hunt queen thing, that's just how it is here. Means nothing to me, or them either.'

'I know you said that,' she said. 'I believed you. I was flattered, God help me. I thought you loved me. And then that night – '

'What night?'

'The night you attacked me.' Alice was forgotten, despite all Jessie's resolve to deal with that and nothing more. The hurt and shame she'd tried to control filled her mind and spilled out in words.

Andrew was on his feet, and she backed towards the door.

'I never attacked you. I wouldn't.'

'You did. You were drunk. I tried to send you away but you wouldn't go. You attacked me. You hurt me. I was ashamed, but you did it. Took me like, like a whore.' Jessie choked on the word.

'I never,' he began, then stopped and took a step towards her.

'Don't,' she cried. 'Keep away from me.'

'I never meant to hurt you. It was that Friday wasn't it? It must have been. I'd had a row with the old man, then I went to the Farriers. Can't remember how much I had to drink, too much. I saw the curtains closed in the back room. I wanted you, Jessie. I want you now.'

'No,' she said. 'No!'

'I thought you wanted me, Jess. That's what the closed curtains always meant. I don't remember anything. What did I do?'

'I told you to go away, as soon as I saw you I knew it was no good. I said no, but you – you *forced* me.'

'But I couldn't hurt you, Jess. I was a bit rough maybe, but you told me you liked it, when I was, you know, forceful. Did I hit you or something?'

'No you didn't, but you hurt me. I tried to get you to stop but you didn't.'

Andrew took a step towards her again but stopped himself.

'Jess, Jess,' he said. 'I know I'm rough sometimes, but I could never hurt you. You're precious to me. You've got to believe me. I know it looks bad, with Alice and all, but I love you Jessie, I always have.'

For a moment she hesitated, her resolve to be strong beginning to ebb away. The fire crackled in the hearth. Suddenly dogs began to bark outside. Andrew turned towards the door, then bent to pick up an axe from the log box. He stared at her. She could see the alarm in his eyes.

'It's him,' he whispered. 'He's come for me.'

'Who?'

'Bill Kitchin. He thinks I killed his kid. The dogs can smell him. Keep still, woman, for God's sake. If he comes, tell him I wasn't here, d'ye hear me? Can you reach the lamp? Turn it down, right down. That's it. Now don't move. Whatever happens, don't come out, whatever you hear. Stay here. He won't harm you. It's me he wants.'

'But you didn't kill her,' she whispered.

The only light in the room was the red-gold glow of the fire. Jessie stood quite still, hardly daring to breathe while the dogs' barking rose to a frenzy, and the animals yanked at the chain that held them close to the wall across the yard. Andrew looked around, the reflected red light from the axe blade dancing across the wall.

Then they heard it, a faint sound. Andrew ducked down below the level of the window and gestured wildly for Jessie to do the same.

'What was it?' she whispered. 'An owl?'

He put his finger to his lips. They crouched together, close enough to touch.

This time they both knew it was a voice, unmistakable when the furious barking stopped for a moment.

'Hello,' called the voice, closer but still faint and pleading. It was a woman. Almost at once the latch on the door into the yard clicked up and the door began to open inwards, towards them.

It was Jessie who saw her first. 'Nellie!' she cried. 'Come in, close the door. Thank God. How did you know I was here?'

'It ain't you I were looking for, miss,' said Nellie, pulling the edge of her shawl around her face, 'It were 'im.' She gestured towards Andrew who was still crouching on the floor like a tiger about to spring. Outside the dogs' panic had begun to subside.

'Who's with you?' said Andrew. 'Is he here?'

'Bill, you mean?' said Nellie. 'Nay, e's at 'ome, sleeping it off. But, 'e'll be 'ere tomorrow. I cannut stop 'im.'

'What did you tell him, Nellie?' said Jessie. 'You promised me you wouldn't – ' and she stopped as Nellie pulled back the shawl from her face. In the glow of the fire the blood on the side of the woman's face showed dark and one eye was almost closed.

'Oh God,' said Jessie, getting up to take a closer look. 'Was that him? What happened? Andrew, for God's sake, get Nellie a chair. And something to drink, water, tea, anything.'

Andrew left the room by the other door into the dark kitchen behind, leaving the door open to give himself just enough light. He came back with a wooden chair, placed it by the fire and left again. Jessie lowered Nellie carefully into the chair and knelt beside her, stroking her hair away from the damaged eye.

'Tell me Nellie, while he's not here, what happened?'

'Someone told our Bill that you and me, that we'd been to th' Hall, to see Phyllis. When he got back from work he turned on me, wanted to know why, what she'd said, what she knew about our Alice. He were raging, miss. I tried to do what you said, miss. Told 'im that Phyllis had told us nowt, and any road she's a liar. Then 'e 'it me, miss. I managed to get 'im to calm down a bit, 'e allus calms down after, and got 'im a drink, and then 'e started drinking proper like, crying about Alice. Said whoever it was got our Alice in trouble 'e'd kill 'em, and din't care what 'appened. I kept on putting drink in front of 'im till 'e went to sleep. I 'ad to warn Andy, miss. I knew Bill would find 'im and kill 'im and then where would me and the bairns be, miss? Who'd look after us then?'

Andrew was standing at the door, holding a mug in his hand. Jessie got up from Nellie's side, took it from him and handed it to Nellie.

'Bill did this,' said Jessie to Andrew over Nellie's bowed head. 'She didn't tell him, but he could still beat it out of her. She came to warn you. He'll kill you, Andrew, and she's afraid for her children.'

'Christ,' he said. 'What a mess. And all because of that lying bitch.'

'Stop it!' cried Jessie. 'This is Alice's mother. Don't you dare blame Alice for all this. You treated her and those other girls like meat, what do you expect from them? Alice lied because she had to, to get what she wanted from people like you. She's dead, poor girl, and all you do is worry about yourself. Now it's caught up with you. It'll all come out. Just get out while you can. Nellie's given you that chance, so take it.'

'What about you?' said Andrew. He stepped towards Jessie and put both hands on her shoulders. Jessie pulled away from him, shaking her head as Nellie looked up.

'I'll check the yard,' said Jessie. 'Go and get the things you need. Where's the bike? Fuel?' Andrew nodded. 'So go, before the weather gets worse. Nellie and I can leave after you and no one will know. Don't tell us where you're going, then we don't have to lie.'

'What about my mother?' said Andrew.

'She'll worry, just like Nellie did when Alice disappeared. But you can write to her, tell her you're all right. You won't be drowned like a rat in the river.' Jessie spat the words at him, and he turned and left the room again without speaking.

Jessie turned back to Nellie.

'That was a very brave thing you did, Nellie. Andrew has the chance to get away. He told me what happened with Alice. He says it was an accident, that she slipped and he couldn't save her. I know, why didn't he say anything? Same reason he's running away now. He's afraid, Nellie, of your Bill. If Bill can attack you like this, what would he do to Andrew?'

'He'd kill 'im,' whispered Nellie. 'I know 'e would.'

'So Andrew will get away. It's for the best, Nellie, truly. I'll talk to Bill, tell him we don't know where he's gone, tell him to leave you alone.'

Before Nellie could speak, Andrew came back into the room, a bag slung over his shoulder. Jessie squeezed Nellie's hand.

'I'll check the yard before he goes,' she said. 'Then I'll walk you home. Bill will never know what you did. And Andrew will owe you his life,' she added, looking hard at Andrew as she did so.

'Thank you, Mrs Kitchin,' said Andrew. 'I didn't hurt Alice, but I couldn't save her. I'm so sorry.'

Nellie waved him away miserably and fingered her face as she turned towards the fire. Jessie pushed past him, out into the yard, and the dogs began to bark once more. Light snow was drifting slowly down, catching the dim light from the window.

'No one here,' she said, turning back to Andrew. 'What about the dogs?'

'Chancer! Gunner!' Andrew shouted from the doorway. 'Quiet!' The barking stopped and they could see the dogs' tails wagging slowly as they recognised the voice. Andrew put down his bag, strode across the yard, released the dogs from the chain and led them to a shed in the corner where he pushed them in and bolted the door from the outside. 'Someone'll find them,' he said, picking up his bag again. 'I'm going,' he said. 'You know I wanted to anyway, before all this started. Need to get away from the old man once and for all, and the quarry's going down fast. If that useless boy had sorted out the paperwork we might've survived but it's too much of a mess now.'

'Where will you go?' Jessie whispered, standing well clear of him still. 'Quietly, don't let Nellie hear.'

'Canada, of course. I told you that. Asked you to come with me, remember? I meant it, Jess. Will you come, once I'm settled?'

'You hurt me, Andrew. You may have forgotten, but I can't. It's finished now.'

He bent towards her.

'Don't,' she said, stepping back. 'Don't touch me. Just go.' She turned away and went back into the room where Nellie was still sitting by the fire. A minute later they heard the engine of Andrew's motorbike fire and roar, then settle into a steady thud as he guided it carefully out to the road and away.

Chapter 31

It was just before midnight. A gloved hand was beating on the door of Mill Cottage. John heard it first, and the muffled voice. When he opened the door, Agnes Plane was standing there.

'Oh thank God you're here,' she said. 'I didn't know what else to do. It's Jessie. She was due at my house this evening, to stay for Christmas, but she didn't arrive. It had started to snow, and I wondered if that was the problem, so I went down to the school-house and she wasn't there either.'

She pushed past him into the cottage as Hannah appeared at the bottom of the stairs, pulling a long shawl around her shoulders.

John closed the door against the wind.

'Miss Whelan ain't here,' said Hannah. 'I 'eard what you said. We ain't seen her, 'ave we John, not today. Did you think she might be 'ere?'

'Well,' said Agnes. 'I didn't know where else to look. I thought she might have walked up here like she does sometimes, to wish you a happy Christmas or something.' It sounded weak and she knew it, but it didn't matter. Jessie wasn't here.

'Have you driven up, in this weather?' said John.

'The car's by the road. It wasn't too bad, until I got to the end of the lane.'

'And you didn't see Miss Whelan?'

'Not a sign, but it was hard to see anything, you know. If she'd seen the car she would have waved, surely, unless …'

'Unless she was hurt or something you mean,' said John.

'She could have slipped, fallen. It's bitter out there. She could have set off somewhere before the snow started and then … well, she could be anywhere. We have to find her.'

'We will,' said John. 'You stay here, Hannah. Miss Plane and I will take the car as far as we can. Is there anywhere else she could have gone? Did she say anything to you?'

'I know she and Nellie Kitchin went up to the Hall yesterday,' said Agnes. 'It was something to do with poor Alice, I think.'

John peered out of the window at the snow as the wind moaned in the fireplace. 'Could we get to Kitchin's place, to ask Nellie?' he said, turning back into the room. 'We need a place to start looking or she could be anywhere.'

'If you go now afore it gets any thicker out there,' said Hannah. 'I'll stay 'ere with Fred. We wouldn't be much use, any road. You two take the car while you can. Won't get down t'lane to Kitchin's if snow's lying, but our John can get down there. Are you wrapped enough? Tek this shawl, plenty more o' them upstairs. You get everything on that'll fit under yer coat, our John.'

Hannah turned to the dresser and took down one of the big square tins. 'Tek this too, and a knife. Gingerbread. That'll keep you going, and 'er too if you find 'er.'

John clutched the tin of gingerbread as he and Agnes slipped and slithered over the little bridge and down to where the car stood gathering snow at the end of the lane by Hill House. They inched back down the valley. Snow swirling in the car's lights made it impossible to see more than few feet in front of them, and Agnes asked John to wipe the inside of the windscreen to stop it misting up. It took far longer than normal to drive the mile or so to the end of Kitchin's farm lane. John got out and set off alone towards the house. He banged on the door as he stood on the threshold, calling Bill Kitchin's name and his own to avoid being attacked as a stranger. Everyone, even off-comers like John, knew Bill's reputation for violence.

Nellie appeared first. She opened the door just an inch or two, squinting through the crack at the young man standing on her step in the middle of a cold black night.

'What?' she said. 'Who are you? No, I know. You're that lad they pulled out of the – '

'Yes, that's me, Mrs Kitchin. I live up at the mill with Hannah and Fred. I'm John, John Pharaoh.'

'Whitehaven Pharaohs?' said Nellie, still peering round the door.

'No,' John said, rubbing his cold hands together. Before he could think how to explain himself, she opened the door and pulled him inside, putting a finger to lips as she did so.

' 'E's asleep,' she said, gesturing into the house. 'Dinnut wake 'im.'

John blew on his numb fingers, looking in vain for the warmth of the fire that was merely a glow in the range.

'I'm with Miss Plane. She's got her car, at the end of the lane.'

'Aye,' said Nellie, still glancing behind her and gesturing for John to keep his voice down.

'We're looking for Miss Whelan,' he whispered. 'Miss Plane said that you and Miss Whelan went to the Hall. Can you think where Jessie, where Miss Whelan might have gone?'

Nellie put her hands to her mouth, and then held onto John's arm.

'She went to see 'im, to tell 'im what that girl said.'

'What girl?' John was straining to follow what Nellie was saying.

'Phyllis, that no-good Phyllis,' said Nellie. 'I knew she was lying, at th' inquest, and she was. She told us.'

'Nellie,' said John, speaking into the woman's face. 'Slow down. What did Phyllis tell you? Is it about Miss Whelan? Do you know where she might be?'

'Phyllis told us about 'im, that Leadbetter.'

'The vicar?' said John.

'No, the young 'un, Andy. And Miss Whelan went up there. We were all there, and then she walked back wi' me.'

'When was this, Nellie?' said John. 'And where were you?'

'At quarry,' Nellie answered simply, as if it was perfectly obvious. ' 'E lives there. 'E went away and we came back 'ere.'

'So is she here?'

'Nay, lad. She saw me back and then she went. It were late and the snow were bad. I wanted 'er to stay but she wouldn't. Mebbe 'e followed us. Oh, God. Where is she?'

'When did she leave here?'

'Just after we got back. She could see Bill were still asleep, so she left. Said she was walking 'ome, like. Back to Newton. It were bad out, but she wouldn't stay. Said she 'ad good shoes and a shawl and she went.'

'But she didn't get back,' said John almost to himself.

'Is that it?' said Nellie. 'What about 'im?'

'Don't worry about him,' said John. He had no idea which 'him' Nellie was talking about, but by now he didn't care, turning to leave the cottage while Nellie stood in the doorway watching, her hand still to her mouth.

He found some branches to put under the wheels of Agnes's car to give it some traction before it would start, and they carried on down the road towards Newton. The snow had eased a little, but the wind that had blown it away was bitter, making the air even colder than before. As the sky cleared, tiny points of light appeared. When John got out to push, as the little car slid almost into the unforgiving wall, he saw above his head the wide band of the Milky Way.

They were nearly back to Newton when John caught sight of what looked like a bundle of rags lying by the wall. 'Stop!' he cried, and the back of the car slewed sideways as Agnes stepped hard on the brake. He was out in an instant, bending over the heap, finding the shoes and the feet, one at an unnatural angle. As he touched them, the heap began to move.

* * *

John awoke the next morning on the big couch in Agnes's living room. The remnants of last night's warmth had faded and the room was cold. He pulled the knitted blanket up towards his face. Through a gap in the curtains a thin shaft of light seeped into the room. For a moment he forgot where he was. Then he remembered, and an instant later he knew that Jessie Whelan was his mother. During the night, the pieces of the puzzle had aligned themselves in his mind. He had his mother's name – Jessie. He had the fact that she had been to college, and that wasn't common round here, except for teachers. He had her age, roughly. And he had two images of a woman with dark hair blowing round her face: one image was in his photograph of Jessie Thompson on board the *Lady Moyra* crossing Morecambe Bay in 1914. The other image was in his memory, as Agnes Plane's car passed through Newton on the day he left hospital. He'd seen a woman standing at the door of the school, dark hair blowing around her face. He was certain. The woman they'd found close to death in the snow last night was his mother.

For a while, the thought overwhelmed him. He lay still, hardly daring to move in case something bubbled up to prove that he was wrong. He made himself go back and check what he knew, to find the questions he would need to ask. He should say something to her, but what if he was wrong? If it were true, the shock might hurt her. Then another thought struck him. Maybe she already knew. She had walked to Mill Cottage that day to find him, and when he came into the house it could have been the shock of seeing him that made her faint. Would a mother, any mother, recognise so instantly someone she had last seen when he was a few days old?

A floorboard creaked a little, beyond the door. Maybe it was her, come to find him, to tell him what they both knew. He held his breath.

'I've brought you a cup of tea, John,' said Agnes, coming into the room. She put the cup and saucer down on a table next to the couch. Through the open door the smell of bacon made him suddenly ravenous. 'She's still asleep, and the doctor's on his way. The roads are very bad, it may take him a while.'

'Is she alright?' he asked, rubbing his face and pushing a hand through his hair.

'I think so. The ankle may be sprained, or even broken, but I've given her something for the pain. We warmed her up before any serious damage was done, but you never know. She might have hit her head. Can't see any obvious wound, but best to wait for the doctor anyway, don't you think?'

'Of course, yes,' said John. His mind was snapping, sharp but shifting too quickly. For so many weeks he'd been taking one step after another without thinking about where it might take him. Now the picture was confused by fear and uncertainty. She'd given him away once. Would she want to see him now, after all this time?

'Are you alright, dear?' Agnes voice cut through the fog. 'You look so tired. Shall we ask the doctor to look at you, too? He's a good friend, I'm sure that would be fine.'

'No, no, really,' said John. 'I'm just, you know, tired. Didn't sleep much really. Last night's a bit of a blur.'

'It would have been no trouble to make up another bed, but I needed to get her warmed up.'

'Yes, yes,' said John. 'The couch was fine, I just didn't sleep much.'

Half an hour later he pushed his chair back from the table in Agnes's small morning room. It was after nine and the sun had not yet risen above the line of the fells to the east. The trees in the garden were still, and beyond them the sky, pale grey and featureless. A fire crackled in the hearth but the room was still cold. Bacon and eggs with toast and tea had warmed him, but it was only a moment before the confusion of the previous night hit him again. A sudden panic turned the taste of breakfast to ashes in his mouth. For a moment he thought he might be sick. He dare not stay, see her or speak to her. She wouldn't believe him, or acknowledge him. He couldn't bear it. He had to get out, back to Mill Cottage and Hannah, to feel safe again.

Agnes was in the kitchen.

'I have to go,' he said. 'Hannah will be worried. I don't want her risking coming down here while it's so bad, nor Fred. It's Christmas … they need me …' His voice tailed away, aware of the weakness of his excuse. He just had to get out, before she woke up, or saw him there. Agnes seemed shocked. She reached out to him, holding his arm with an urgency that surprised him.

'But we need you too, dear,' she spluttered, talking fast and too loudly, 'You have to help me clear the drive, for the doctor, and, and it's too far for you to walk back to the Mill. We can send someone up with a message for Hannah. So you can stay, you don't need to leave. You can help me look after Jessie until the doctor gets here. I was making her a drink, look, for you to take up, so you can't leave yet.' John was astonished to see tears in Agnes's eyes; he could not see the deeper distress as her dreams crumbled, dreams of the love and reconciliation that she would witness and be part of, embraced and thanked by both.

He shook his head and turned away, picked up his coat from the hall stand, and put on his boots in the porch as Agnes watched, tears now running unchecked down her anxious face. Outside the air was clear and very cold. His boots squeaked on the snow as he walked carefully up the sloping drive towards the road and then back towards his home and the woman he most wanted to talk to.

When he pushed open the door of Mill Cottage the first thing that struck him was the smell of meat and onions and spices he could not name. Hannah felt the blast of air and turned towards him, smiling and wiping her hands. 'He's 'ere,' she called out. 'He's 'ere, Fred. Our John.'

John shut the door and stood quite still as Hannah reached up to hug him. 'We were feared for you, lad, in the snow and all. Couldn't do 'owt but wait. Fred said you'd be at Applegarth, likely safe and sound. But did you find 'er – Miss Whelan? Is she alreet?'

Fred had come in from the yard, a pile of logs balanced on one arm, and joined them, smiling broadly. He dropped the logs into the basket and shook John's hand.

'We found her by the road,' said John, replying to Hannah's question, 'just this side of Newton. She must've slipped, hurt her ankle and couldn't get up. Don't know how long she was there, but she was really cold and faint, mumbling, making no sense. We got her back to Miss Plane's and now the doctor's coming. Miss Plane thinks she'll be alright. I had to leave. Couldn't stay.'

'What's wrong, lad?' Fred turned John's face towards him and looked at him. 'It's cold, reet enough, but tha looks bad.'

'Let's get that coat off you,' said Hannah, turning John back towards her, 'and them boots. Place 'as warmed up nicely. Drop of that damson gin, Fred, that's what 'e needs.'

The two of them fussed over him, and John let them do so, glad to avoid decisions and be passive. He felt safe, sure of their steady affection for him. Now he could relax a little, at a distance from the numbing fear that his real mother would soon find him and reject him for the second time. He kept quiet, pretending to doze a little while Hannah and Fred returned to their tasks, Hannah cooking her Christmas pie and Fred by the window with a half-completed hookie rug spread on his knee, sorting colours from a bag on the window-sill beside him. John did not see Fred's questioning gesture to his wife and her raised shoulders in response. It was only when Hannah sat down at the table behind his chair that John sat up and turned towards her.

'I think I know, Hannah,' he said, 'About my mother. I think I've found her. It's Miss Whelan.'

Across the room, the rug slipped from Fred's lap on to the floor.

John began to talk, quietly at first, facing Hannah but looking past her, towards the range where the Christmas pie sat in the oven.

'I found some things in Ulverston,' he said, 'to do with my mother, my real mother. Then I went to Barrow and talked to – but that doesn't matter. I found out some things. My real mother's name was Jessie, Jessie Thompson. She lived in Barrow and she went to college before she had me, and her aunt knew some people who wanted a baby, so …'

'Go on, lad,' Hannah was struggling to keep up, but she knew he needed to talk.

'It all fits,' he said, desperate to convince himself. 'Miss Whelan's called Jessie, and she went to college, and – look. Please, look at this.' He got up suddenly and retrieved a battered envelope from the pocket of his coat hanging by the door. The photograph was reluctant to emerge.

'See. At the end of the middle row. Look at the girl with the hair blowing over her face.'

'Where?'

'On the right.'

'Where's this?' said Hannah, turning the photo over.

John was frantic. 'It doesn't matter. Just look at the girl. That's my mother in 1914. Can't you see? That's her. That's Miss Whelan.'

Hannah turned her head to look with her one good eye, then got up and went to the window, still looking and drawing the photo towards her face. John stood behind her, peering once more at the photograph 'It's her, isn't it?'

Hannah turned towards him. 'It could be her, pet. But that was a long time ago. People change.'

'But the name,' said John. 'Jessie?'

Hannah looked at his desperate face. 'It's a common enough name. Could be just a coincidence.'

John took the photograph from her and stared at it.

'I know it's her. When I woke up this morning at Miss Plane's house I just knew. Everything fits. And I think she knows it, too. That day, when she came here and she fainted when she saw me. She must have known herself. Don't you see?'

Fred spoke from his seat at the window. 'But she just said she'd 'ad some dizzy turns, was going to talk to t'doctor. She would have said summat, surely to God.'

'Hold on,' said Hannah. 'Slow down, the pair of ye. Let's just think a bit. Do we know where Jessie lived before she came to Newton?'

'Down south somewhere,' said Fred, 'not Barrow. And why would she change 'er name like that? What's wrong wi' Jessie Thompson? Why Whelan? I'm not sure, lad. 'Ave you said owt to anyone else?'

'No,' said John, looking from Fred to Hannah and back. He wanted them to see it, to be sure as he was. Why weren't they?

'I know it's her. I can feel it.'

'John, lad. We're not doubting you, we just want you to be sure. You've worked so 'ard at this. But you can't just tell 'er summat like this without being sure. Think what it could do? Right or wrong, summat like this could finish 'er.'

'Why?' said John, 'How?'

'Well she'd lose 'er job, for a start,' Fred chimed in again. 'Church won't let 'er carry on teaching bairns if she's 'ad a bairn 'erself, and not wed. And the 'ouse too. That goes wi' job. What would she do then?'

John sank back into the big chair and put his head in his hands. 'I thought she'd be happy about it,' he said miserably. 'I thought she'd want to see me, to know that I'm here.'

'And she will, John, course she will,' said Hannah, gesturing to Fred to shut up. 'But she might 'ave to keep it quiet, like. So you'll 'ave to take care, that's all we're saying, right Fred?'

'Aye,' said Fred. 'Is there anyone else you think might know about it?'

'The man I spoke to in Grange, Mr Crane, was sure about the photo, and that the girl had had a baby. He was sure, but he'd kept it quiet all this time. He was glad for me.'

'And we are too, lad,' Hannah put an arm round his shoulders. 'Could you talk to someone else first, round the houses, like? Someone who knows more about Miss Whelan than we do. That Miss Plane, she's her friend, ask her about it. Tell 'er what you found out, see what she thinks. But don't just blurt it all out, John. Be careful. Folk can be very cruel.'

John thought back to how upset Agnes had been when he left. Did she know something, too? He stood up and moved towards the window.

275

'Look at me, Hannah. And you, Fred. Do I look like Miss Whelan, at all? Here in the light. Look at my face.'

They both stared at him.

'Nay, I can't be sure,' said Hannah after a moment. 'I could say you 'ad the same dark hair, the same shape around the chin even, but what if you do? You might even be related to 'er, at a distance like, a cousin or summat. Doesn't make her your mam.'

'That's reet,' said Fred. 'Mebbe you're family, but not 'er son. We don't know enough, lad, not to be sure.'

John stood by the window, where the gleam from the snow illuminated the pain and indecision in his face.

'Tell you what, pet,' said Hannah. ''Ere's what I would do. I'd go and see Miss Plane, on yer own. Tell 'er what you've told us. Ask 'er what to do, what she thinks. She'll know stuff we don't, you see. And she'll 'ave an idea what to do.'

'But not today,' said Fred. 'Christmas Day's no time to turn up at someone's door with questions like that. You've waited a long time, lad, and it'll keep a bit longer. Boxing Day tomorrow, you can get a ride down early to t'Farriers with folk going to see the hunt off. But today we stay 'ere, eat Hannah's pie, have a beer, do nowt. That's my plan.'

'And it's a good 'un, Fred,' said Hannah, loving her husband even more than usual for his good sense.

'I've waited so long,' said John.

'So you can wait a while longer,' said Hannah.

CHAPTER 32

JESSIE WAS ASLEEP when Agnes ushered Dr Dawson into the room, and it took a few moments to remember where she was and what had happened. Her head hurt, and she winced as she moved her foot. As Dr Dawson waited patiently she pulled the borrowed shawl around her shoulders and smiled.

'So sorry to call you out at such an inconvenient time, doctor,' said Jessie. 'Just a silly accident last night and I'm making such a nuisance of myself.'

'Think nothing of it, Miss Whelan. My wife and I were out and about this morning, church you know, and Joan is having a good old chat with Agnes, while I see to you. So it's no bother at all. Happy Christmas to you, by the way.'

'And to you,' said Jessie, thankful for the tone of normality after the tension of the past few days.

Dr Dawson pronounced the ankle to be sprained but not broken, bandaged it up as tightly as Jessie could bear, checked her pulse and her eyes for any signs of concussion after her fall against the wall.

'That ankle may take a while to heal,' he said, picking up his bag, ' but you've survived the hour or two in the frost very well, all in all. A few days' rest and you'll be hobbling about feeling much better. You'll be staying here I take it? Need a bit of nursing,

277

regular meals, that sort of thing. Can't think of anywhere better for a spot of convalescence. You were staying with Agnes anyway I understand.'

'For a few days, yes,' said Jessie. 'We alternate at Christmas, and this year it was my turn to come here.'

'Perfect,' said the doctor, 'so I'll leave you to enjoy the rest of the day. No more walking in the snow for a while!' And he was gone. Jessie heard the voices downstairs and the sound of the front door closing.

She lay back, wincing before she found a comfortable position. The pain in her mind was not so easy to placate. Gradually, shreds of the conversation with Andrew were returning to her. He had said that he tried to save Alice, and she wanted so much to believe him. And that night, when he had hurt her, did he really not remember? He'd been drunk, she knew that, but was that a reason, or an excuse? For a while, listening to his voice and watching his face in the glow of the fire she had wanted to forget what had happened, as he had done, and hold him again like before. She knew she should not, that it was weak and foolish, but he said he loved her and she had been so lonely for so long. But it didn't matter. Nothing mattered. He had gone, and her life was as empty as before. She was still at the heart of no one's life, except her own.

She heard the door being gently pushed open and kept as still as she could, hoping that Agnes would go away. Agnes, on the other hand, was desperate to speak and could not wait.

'Dr Dawson says you'll be fine in a few days, apart from the ankle,' she said, stepping further into the room. She coughed slightly before speaking again.

'Someone else was here too, last night. Do you remember anything? Do you know who found you out in the snow?' Agnes sounded excited but Jessie wasn't sure why. She turned her head.

'You found me, didn't you?' she said. 'You went looking for me when I didn't arrive?'

'Well, yes I did, dear, but I had someone else with me.' Agnes waited for a question, but Jessie waited too.

'John was here, John Pharaoh. I picked him up at Mill Cottage and he spotted you as we drove back from the Kitchin's.'

Jessie's heart flipped.

'Why did you go there, what did Nellie say?'

'Nothing that made much sense, according to John. He spoke to her, gathered you'd set off from there and we followed the road back here until he spotted you by the wall. Thank heaven he did, dear, or else – '

'But what did Nellie tell him?' Jessie interrupted, dreading what might have been said.

'Nothing, dear, really. Why, what was going on? What were you doing there?'

'It doesn't matter,' Jessie replied, leaning back onto the pillow in the hope that Agnes would leave her alone. She wondered about John.

'Did John say anything?'

'About you, you mean? No he didn't. Seemed very keen to get away actually, back to Mill Cottage. He's such a nice boy, very fond of the Porters and concerned for them. If he is your son, Jessie, he's a credit to you.'

Agnes knew it was the wrong thing to say as soon as the words were out. Jessie turned towards her suddenly.

'How can he be a credit to me?' she said. 'I gave him away, remember, when he was four days old, to people I didn't know. He's their son, they raised him, he's a credit to them, not to me.'

'I'm sorry, dear, I didn't mean – '

'And anyway,' Jessie went on, the anxiety of the past days leaking into the words as she spat them out, 'there's nothing magical in motherhood, Agnes. It's not a spiritual connection, just biology. He doesn't know me any more than I know him. And if he is my son, what happens then?'

Agnes sat on the little chair by the door, wilting under her friend's anger.

'I don't know, dear.'

'No you don't, Agnes. You've never had a child and you can't possibly understand.'

Agnes sobbed suddenly, but Jessie could not stop herself, the bitter words pouring out of her again.

'This is my life. Twenty years ago I made a mistake, and now I'll have to pay the price, after all I've done, the job, my house, my life here, all gone, and all you want is "Happy ever after". This is my life Agnes, for pity's sake, so just let me decide.'

She looked hard at the weeping woman. 'Oh please Agnes, you didn't, did you? You didn't say anything to him, about me?'

'No, no!' cried Agnes, knowing how close she had come to doing so. 'He just woke up and had some breakfast and then he said he had to go. I couldn't stop him. I didn't say anything to him, truly.'

'So what does he know? What did he find out in all that snooping around? I can't bear just waiting for the knock on the door. Maybe I should just ask him straight out. Maybe I should just leave.' She ran out of breath and lay, staring at the ceiling, furious at herself and what lay ahead of her.

Agnes blew her nose. 'If you lose the job, and the house, you could always stay here with me,' she whispered. 'And John, too. It's not too late, Jessie. You could start again, the two of you, as a family.'

Jessie groaned. 'For God's sake, Agnes, don't say any more. Let me think. I have to think. Did John say anything about coming back?'

'No,' Agnes sniffed. 'But it's Christmas Day. Nothing will happen today.' She got up slowly. 'I'll leave you now. You need to rest.'

As Agnes escaped from the room, Jessie turned her head to the wall, hating herself.

It was well into the afternoon and already twilight when Jessie slowly came down the stairs, using Agnes's father's walking stick to support her injured ankle. Her head ached and she felt wretched. She had been viciously unkind to Agnes, in her own home, on Christmas Day, and she was ashamed. Agnes heard her on the stairs and hurried out into the hall, smiling a little too brightly.

'Oh you're awake, that's good,' she said. 'Just in time for a proper meal. You haven't eaten much all day and I delayed the roast as long as I could.'

'Yes, I can smell it,' said Jessie, smiling. 'That's probably what woke me up.'

Agnes had laid the table in the dining room with her best china and glasses, and the cutlery she had inherited from her mother and used only on special occasions. The obvious care she had taken made Jessie feel even worse. They talked for a while of inconsequential things, of school and the village, but Jessie's heart was too full to be distracted for long. She pushed her half-empty plate to one side and placed her hands side by side on the table, composing herself.

'I must apologise for the way I spoke to you earlier, Agnes,' she said carefully, looking up only as she reached the end of the sentence. 'It's been a difficult time, but that's no excuse really for such rudeness. It must have upset you, today of all days, and I'm sorry.'

Agnes reached across the table and laid her hand on Jessie's. Her eyes were bright.

'I was upset,' she said, 'but I understand, I do. I can't imagine how you must be feeling if you believe that this boy is your son, yours and Clive's.'

Jessie put her other hand over her eyes.

'I still can't be sure. I need to talk to him but I don't have the courage to face him. Not yet.'

'Do you think he knows?' said Agnes, taking her hand away to find a handkerchief and wipe her eyes. 'He's been trying to find out, we know that. Going to Ulverston, and Barrow too, from what Hannah was saying.'

Jessie looked up sharply. 'You didn't tell me that. He's been to Barrow?'

'That's what they said.'

Jessie wondered whom he could have seen there. Both Cora and Barbara were gone and she couldn't imagine that they had confided in anyone else. Agnes got up to clear the plates, and Jessie sat alone in the warm room for a few minutes, thinking in circles, working out how to protect herself. It was left to Agnes to ask the question Jessie had not asked herself.

'How do you think John's feeling about this? He may have found things out gradually, but the thought that you are his mother, his real mother, how will he cope with that?'

The question hit Jessie hard. 'He will know that I gave him away. He could hate me for that.'

'Oh no!' cried Agnes, 'That's too harsh. It was long ago and things were different then. And you and Clive were going to marry. You told me that. If he hadn't been killed so tragically, you would have been together, as a family.'

'John could still hate me, even if he knows all that. Wouldn't you? I would. Maybe he reacts angrily to things, like I do, rather than being sad about them.'

More food was offered and refused, but still Jessie sat at the table, trying to fill the blank space in her life that loomed ahead of her, beyond the warm cocoon of Applegarth and Christmas Day. No more was said: the subject was closed for a while at least. Jessie sat by the dying fire until the throbbing of her ankle drove her upstairs again, to lie restlessly. One young man had gone, and she believed she would never see him again. The other, younger still, hovered beyond her control, weighing her future in his hands. Finally, as sleep was within reach, she thought about Clive. If John were their son, what would Clive have wanted?

Chapter 33

Boxing Day morning. The yard of the Farriers in Newton was crowded. Men in nailed boots and rough woollen jackets, caps pulled low on their heads, stood in small groups, their breath wreathed around them in the crisp air. A watery sun had only just begun to lighten the sky. Boys, muffled by their mothers against the cold, kicked a stone between them, pushing each other around. Inside the pub, women and girls sat, waiting. John Pharaoh sipped a mug of tea that Elsie Eilbeck had offered him, and listened to the voices around him.

One voice, confident and piercing, cut through the babble.

'Haven't seen him at all,' Lionel Leadbetter was saying to Elsie as they stood in the doorway watching the scene outside. 'He should have come to dinner last night, but no sign, no word. Caroline's a bit bothered.'

'Not been in 'ere either,' replied the landlady. 'Expected him Christmas Eve, when all the rest from the quarry were 'ere, but he never showed. He'll be reet, turn up at last minute you see.'

'Leaving it late, but nothing unusual there, I suppose.'

'Right enough, vicar. Can I get you anything?'

'Not just yet, Elsie, thank you. Have to do my bit shortly, before they all set off.'

Lionel buttoned up his coat and strode out into the yard. The first of the dogs were streaming down the lane towards the pub, thirty or so hounds, white, brown, grey, alert, tails held high. Stan Crudders, wearing the green jacket inherited from his father and still too big for his narrow frame, whistled them in. It would be a good day. The morning mist was clearing and a rust-brown animal would show up well against the white of the fells. One of the outlying farms towards Bootle had reported a fox gone to ground on the lower slopes of Black Combe. They were ready.

The crowd stood silent for a moment while Lionel asked for divine help with their efforts. No one had ever asked him to do it, but no one had the courage to stop him either. As he finished, Stan put the horn to his lips and blew, once, again. The dogs yelped and jumped, the smell of the doomed fox in their nostrils, carried by the wind from the south. Men and dogs streamed down the road as children waved and women picked up their baskets to head home. John finished his tea and set off towards Applegarth, his heart thumping in his chest.

Just before he reached the top of the drive, he heard the hoot of a car horn behind him. It was the big Armstrong Siddeley with the vicar at the wheel and his wife beside him. Everyone knew the vicar's car. John followed the car down the drive. Lionel Leadbetter eased his large frame out of the driver's seat.

'Good day to you, young man,' said Lionel. 'Coming to visit Miss Plane?'

'Well, I –' John began, but the vicar didn't wait for a response.

'Got something to ask her, don't you know,' Lionel continued, as if John hadn't spoken. 'Won't take a tick, if you could hang on.'

He banged sharply on the outer door. Caroline Leadbetter held out her hand to John. 'It's John isn't it? You live up at Mill Cottage? Happy Christmas to you, a little late, but never mind.'

'John Pharaoh,' said John, shaking the gloved hand as politely as he could. 'And Happy Christmas to you, too.'

The porch door opened, and Agnes stood there, a dressing gown pulled tightly around her. 'Good heavens,' she said. 'Quite a crowd. Good morning to you all. As you can see, I wasn't expecting visitors just yet.'

'Ah, Agnes,' said Lionel. 'Sorry to call so early ...'

'Come in all of you,' said Agnes, stepping back to open the inner door. 'Too cold to stand out there with the door open. Come away in, there's a fire on already and it's a bit warmer than out there. Now what can I do for you all?'

John looked around the room. No sign of Jessie. Had she gone? He would have to wait until the Leadbetters had done whatever they came to do. Caroline Leadbetter held her husband's arm. 'Nothing to worry about, Agnes,' she said. 'We were down at the Farriers, for the hunt, and thought we'd take the chance to ask if you'd seen Andrew at all?'

'Andrew? Where is he?'

'Well, that's just it, dear, we're not sure. He was due to come for dinner last night, but didn't appear. Now the hunt's away and still no sign of him or his dogs. Not like him to miss the hunt ...'

'Or his mother's Christmas dinner,' Lionel interrupted. 'Have you heard anything?'

'Me? No, nothing,' said Agnes. 'What about you, John?'

John wasn't sure what to say. He shrugged, 'I haven't seen Andy ... for ages. Been off work –'

'Yes, yes,' Lionel interrupted. 'So none of you have seen him then. Told you so, Caroline. He'll have gone off somewhere, grumbling about something no doubt, or just to avoid spending time with me. Sometimes I wonder ...'

'Now Lionel,' said his wife. 'These good people don't want to hear about all that. They haven't seen him, so we'll leave them alone. So sorry to intrude so early, Agnes. Come along, Lionel. He'll probably turn up sometime today with a perfectly reasonable explanation, and if we're not at home we'll miss him again.'

'If you're sure,' said Agnes, ushering them out of the room. John heard the front door close and then the car doors, before the powerful engine sprang to life and they were gone.

John was standing quite still, looking at the frost on the garden when Agnes came back into the room.

'I'm sorry you've had to wait,' she said. 'It's almost impossible to stop the vicar if he wants to speak. Not very good at taking turns,' she laughed.

He turned towards her, ignoring her effort to lighten the mood. 'Where is she?' he asked. 'I need to talk to her. Is she alright?'

Before Agnes could reply, the living room door was pushed open. Jessie limped slowly into the room, wearing the dressing-gown that Agnes had lent her. She caught sight of John and stopped short. They looked at each other. Jessie pulled her hair back from her face. John felt the flush on his neck. Agnes looked desperately from one to the other.

'Here she is,' she said. 'Come and sit down, Jessie, take the weight off that ankle.'

John stood back, stumbling against the couch as he did so. Agnes fussed over Jessie, who still said nothing.

'Now, John,' said Agnes, leading him to a chair like a child. 'You sit here and talk to Jessie while I get properly dressed like a Christian woman and then make us all some coffee. Put another log or two on the fire will you, dear? It feels quite cool in here all of a sudden.'

And she was gone. John chose one log, then another, with elaborate care, and put them on the fire. His mind was suddenly blank. Jessie watched him, but lowered her gaze as soon as he sat down.

'Are you alright?' he said, touching the side of his face where her bruise looked most livid. 'And the ankle? Is it …?'

'No, not broken. Just sprained. The doctor's been, said I would be fine, apart from the ankle. I have to thank you and Agnes for finding me. I couldn't move and it was very cold.'

'Mrs Kitchin told us that you'd been there, so we knew …'

'What did she say?' Jessie looked up at him, her tone sharper than before.

'Just that you'd walked back there with her and then set off to Newton. There was some other stuff but I couldn't make sense of it. Nothing that mattered. She was bothered about her husband waking up.'

Jessie nodded. 'Do you know Bill Kitchin?' she asked.

'I've heard a few things,' said John, 'some of them not very nice.'

Silence fell again, broken only by the crackling of the fire and the cawing of rooks in the bare trees outside. Jessie sat quite still. John took a deep breath. 'There is something I want to ask you,' he said. Jessie closed her eyes for a moment, before making herself look at him.

'I need to tell you something first, though. It was something that happened in May, before I came here.' He looked at Jessie: her expression gave nothing away. He would have to go on.

'My mother … Enid Pharaoh, she was very ill. We were in our house in Ulverston. She mixed me up with someone, with her husband. She thought I was her husband and started talking to me as if …' He dried, struggling to find the words, even though he'd rehearsed them the night before, lying in bed at Mill Cottage watching the gold crescent of the rising moon move slowly across his window.

Jessie waited, and John pressed on. 'Well, never mind all that,' he said. 'What matters is, I found out I was adopted when I was just a few days old. My aunt, Enid's sister, and my Uncle George, they encouraged me to search for my real mother. I went to Barrow, and then I found someone who knew.'

'Who?' said Jessie.

'It was the choirmaster from St Luke's. He lives in Grange now. I showed him this picture.' John held the battered envelope in his hand, surprised how much his fingers were shaking. Jessie watched, unmoving, as he finally pulled out the photograph.

'Look,' he said, offering the photo to Jessie, who stretched to take it from him, then turned to find more light as she looked at it. After a moment she lowered her head and her hand, leaving the photo resting on her lap.

'Mr Crane, the choirmaster, recognised the young woman in the picture who had got pregnant. He knew this woman's mother, and her aunt …'

'Barbara,' said Jessie without looking up.

'And he told me that her name was Jessie Thompson, and that she was at college.'

He stopped. Jessie turned away and covered her eyes with her hands. He saw her shoulders moving but she made no sound. After a few moments, she turned round, her eyes full of tears, and handed the picture back to him. Without a word she got up and hobbled painfully to the door. 'Wait,' she said to John, holding up her hand to stop him helping her as she opened the door and went out into the hall and up the stairs.

It was a few minutes by the clock but felt much longer before Jessie returned, carrying a small box in one hand while she used the other to steady herself. He got up, but again she waved him away. She sat down finally, put the box on the little table beside her and opened it.

'I have a picture to show you,' she said, and handed a small photo over to him. John found himself looking at someone almost identical to himself. He looked up.

'His name was Clive Whelan,' said Jessie quietly. 'He was your father.'

'And you are my mother?'

'Yes.'

'What happened?' said John, not knowing what else to say. He wanted her to talk, tell him things, anything.

'We were going to be married,' she said flatly. 'But he was killed, just after … just before he knew that I was expecting a baby. No one knew. I had to tell my mother. She wanted … she and my Aunt Barbara sent me to a home.'

'In Carnforth?'

'Yes, in Carnforth.'

'It's not there any more. They pulled it down.'

'Good. I never knew what they arranged, my mother and my aunt. All I knew was that someone came to take you. They carried you away.'

Jessie faltered. Her voice broke as a sob rose in her throat. Again she raised her hand to keep John at a distance. She swallowed.

'I never knew where you were, or what had happened to you. I lied to get back into teachers' college, then I moved up here, years ago. I had no idea, until that day –'

'At the cottage, when you fainted?'

'It was like Clive had come back. I couldn't breathe.'

John looked again at the picture of his father.

'Was he in the war?'

'No, he was at Vickers,' she said, looking past him out into the garden, 'working on one of the airships when he fell, hit his head. No one knew about us. I read about it in the paper.'

Again she stopped and lowered her head. This time John leaned across to touch her hand, but she pulled it away.

'When did you know?' she said.

'After I talked to Mr Crane I was sure, but I didn't know what to do. I'd been ill, lost my job. I wanted to come straight down here, but I talked to Hannah and she said to wait a while.'

'Hannah knows?' Jessie looked up. 'What did you tell her?'

'What I've told you,' he said, seeing the fear in her eyes. 'I had to tell someone, there was no one else.'

'Who else knows?' she asked, dreading what he might say.

'No one, I swear. They understand what this might mean, for you.'

'What?'

'About your job, at the school, what might happen if people knew.'

'There would be no job, that's what would happen,' she said bitterly. 'Lionel means well, but the church ... So no one else knows?'

'Just Hannah and Fred, and they understand, they do. If I – if we ask them to keep it a secret to their graves, they will, I know they will.'

'Yes,' she said.

Jessie leaned back in the big chair. John put a footstool at her feet and she raised her painful foot, lying back and closing her eyes. He looked at her. This was his mother. He'd been looking for her for months and here she was. It was not at all what he had expected. He'd imagined someone looking older, thinner. At the beginning, when he first started to search, he'd expected that she would cry when he announced himself, and say she was sorry and pull him towards her and hold him tightly. Talking to Hannah had helped to alter that expectation, but he was still unprepared for Jessie's fear of him; it was fear that he had seen in her eyes. To her he was a threat, an avenger, a ghost. He spoke into the silence of the room.

'Tell me about him, my father.'

Jessie opened her eyes and struggled to sit up.

'He was a wonderful man,' she said. 'Tall, like you, with the

291

same long face and dark hair. Long fingers,' John held up his hands, and she smiled. 'He was working on the airships because of his skill as a riveter. They wanted him to go down south. He had a great future. He asked me to go with him as his wife, and then … We were together for months but I lied so well to my mother that she never knew.'

'It must have been a terrible shock for you,' he said.

'And for her, too, I suppose. It took me years to forgive what she did. I'm not sure that I have forgiven her, and she's dead now, so it's too late. But it was wartime, terrible things happened. I was lucky, managed to finish my training, get a job. I survived.'

'And so did I,' said John. 'They did their best for me, but I always knew that something wasn't right. I just wish they'd said, told me earlier.'

'And now you know,' she said. 'What will you do?'

Before John could reply, the door opened a fraction and they heard Agnes's voice.

'Can I come in?' she asked.

Jessie looked across at John, who nodded.

'Yes, do. It's your house, after all.'

Agnes was wearing one of her smartest outfits and Jessie smiled at her, recognizing the trouble she had gone to. 'John and I have been talking,' said Jessie. 'Agnes, this is my son, mine and Clive's, our son.'

John got up and Agnes reached to hold him close, while Jessie watched.

'Oh my dears,' said Agnes, wiping her eyes with a tiny handkerchief. 'I'm so happy for you both.' She bent to kiss Jessie, who patted her back but didn't attempt to get up.

'I've been hiding in the kitchen, waiting and wondering. And hoping too, I admit. Two such wonderful people, and now they've found each other.' She smiled at them both.

John stood where he was, feeling numb. For weeks he had had concentrated on finding his mother and now that the goal was reached he was empty, drained. Jessie seemed distant, detached, and he didn't know what else to say to her.

'No more talking for a while,' said Agnes. 'It's time to eat and I won't accept any excuses. Come through to the dining room and we'll have a good breakfast, late, but all the more welcome for that. John, can you help Jessie, please, if I lead the way?'

He bent to help her up out of the chair and she let him. They didn't speak.

When they were settled at the table, Agnes brought through plates loaded with more food than they could ever hope to consume. They began to eat and Agnes hovered solicitously, desperate to hear what they had said to each other. In the more formal setting of the dining room, Jessie seemed to relax a little.

'I heard the vicar earlier,' she said. 'Was Caroline with him? Just coming to check why we weren't at church yesterday?'

'Actually no, dear. They came to ask if we'd seen Andrew.'

Jessie dropped a knife that clattered onto the plate in front of her.

Agnes glanced at John before she went on, 'They said he hadn't come home for Christmas dinner and then he didn't appear for the hunt either – most unlike him – and did we know where he is. I said no, and John hadn't seen him for days. They weren't too worried, more annoyed with him, I think.'

Jessie said no more, keeping her eyes down, and concentrated on her kippers.

A few moments later, when Agnes left the room to get more toast, Jessie pushed her plate away and touched her mouth with a large linen napkin. John looked up but she didn't look at him.

'I think I've had enough,' she said, pushing herself upright. 'I feel very tired all of a sudden. Will you excuse me?' And as Agnes came back into the room, Jessie limped past her, without a word. Agnes and John listened, as she stumped slowly up the stairs.

'What happened?' said Agnes at last.

'I don't know,' John replied. 'We weren't talking much, and then she said she'd had enough and she just left. She said she felt very tired.'

'Well, of course, that will be true,' said Agnes. 'Both of you must be feeling the strain of it all. I do myself! Maybe we should just let her rest a while. Do you want to rest, dear? There's that big couch that you slept on the other night. No more visitors today, I hope. No one to disturb you.'

'Actually, I don't feel tired,' said John. 'Confused, but not tired. Things aren't working out the way I expected.' He waited, buttering his toast idly as if thinking about something else, which he was.

'I wasn't sure what to say, or what would happen,' John continued. 'But I wasn't expecting her to be afraid of me.'

'Afraid?' Agnes was shocked. 'Are you sure?'

'No, of course I can't be sure, but that's how it feels. She's been asking me who else knows about me, about us. I had to persuade her that Hannah and Fred wouldn't tell anyone. We haven't talked about what we're going to do. I don't know what she wants me to do.'

'I wondered about that,' said Agnes, 'and about how you might be feeling. It must be very strange for you.'

'I've been trying to find what I should do, Agnes. She thinks if everyone knows that I'm her son that she'll lose her job.'

'That could happen, I'm afraid,' said Agnes. 'Women teachers have lost their jobs recently just because they're women. Some people think it should be the men who get first pick of the jobs when times are hard.'

'But if we're both living around here, won't people see some

294

likeness between us if they see us together? What do we do when folk ask questions, like they always do round here?'

'That may be what's bothering her,' said Agnes.

John ate his toast in silence. 'It'll have to be me,' he said finally, 'the one that moves away. We can't both stay here, not now.'

'But you've just found each other,' protested Agnes, as her vision of the happy family crumbled to nothing.

'No, Agnes,' he said. 'I found Jessie, she didn't find me. She didn't want to find me, that's what I think. She's afraid that me being here will finish her.'

'Oh John, that's a terrible thing to say. She's your mother.'

'Aye, she is,' said John, 'but maybe she doesn't want to be. She gave me away then, twenty years ago. She doesn't want me now, either.'

He leaned back in his chair and looked up at the ceiling. Agnes saw a single tear run down his face.

Upstairs in the narrow bed, Jessie shifted uncomfortably. The overwhelming tiredness she'd felt downstairs had abated. Now she listened to her heart thumping and wished that she could sleep. She'd known that this might happen some day, but it was still a shock. All these years she'd put her past behind her, lying to protect herself, staying in control. And now this boy, this ghost of Clive had tracked her down. All she saw in him was his father. She didn't know him, had not seen him since he was a few days old, and although he was pleasant and polite she could find no strong feeling for him, no surge of maternal passion, just fear that his arrival could rob her of everything she had built for herself. For a brief moment she wondered about him simply as a young man, not as her son, but it was too hard and she dismissed the thought. He wasn't a child: she wasn't responsible for him. Her life was going to change, that was unavoidable, but it was she who would decide when and how. No, she thought, she could not just wait for the axe to drop. She would hand in her notice, move north to the greater anonymity of Whitehaven, or Workington, or Carlisle even, and start afresh. She was still young, good at her job. Now that Andrew was gone she would never put herself at someone's mercy, never again. Agnes was right: she must have been mad to take such a risk. She could trust no one but herself.

Jessie Whelan, strong, independent, and deeply lonely, turned her face to the wall and fell asleep.

CHAPTER 34

'I'M GOING TO LEAVE Eskdale,' said John, turning towards his mother. Behind him the gusting westerly scratched white lines on the grey and marbled sea. 'There's no job now to hold me. No quarry soon if the rumours are true, with Andrew gone the place is a mess. I've got some money, but I need to work. Plenty of pits and quarries up and down the coast.' He hesitated, looking down at the Wellington pit chimney, unused but still rearing towards the racing clouds down by the harbour. 'Couldn't work underground, not if my life depended on it, but they all need people up top, keeping them organised, getting money in, paying money out. I'm good at that.'

Jessie listened in silence. She remembered the conversation with Clive, all those years ago, about his plans for the future, the pride in his skills. This was Clive's child, after all. She wondered what John had inherited from her.

297

They were standing together on a hill above Whitehaven, the town further up the coast that had grown rich from slavery, rum and coal. It was early in the New Year. They hadn't met since Boxing Day, and even now Jessie was too anxious about being seen with John for them to meet in Newton, or in the valley. They agreed to meet here, where she felt safer, more anonymous. They'd come north from Newton by train and walked up the hill towards the Haig pithead. John wanted to have a look at the houses that surrounded the pit, high above the smoke and smuts, closer to the sky. Inland he could see the line of the fells. He could live here: the view would keep him going. He asked her to come with him and she agreed: it felt safer to be with him if they were doing something, not just sitting looking at each other.

Christmas at Applegarth had been difficult. Agnes's dream of an unconventional family of three was too hopeless to be discussed, and the reality was too painful. The two women had colluded in keeping silent about anything that really mattered, filling the quiet of the short dark days with reading aloud to each other and playing rummy. Their only visitor had been Caroline Leadbetter with news of a telegram from Liverpool. Andrew had sent his mother his love and the news that he was going to Montreal.

The news was received quite differently by each of them. Caroline was ashamed at her relief that the unbearable tension between her son and her husband was removed. She had no doubt that Andrew would be safe and prosper. Agnes was more pleased at Andrew's disappearance than she could show: her hopes of quiet domesticity with Jessie rose again. Of the three of them, Jessie was the least surprised, but the possibility of never seeing Andrew again seeped slowly into her mind, and she cried in private when Caroline was gone.

For the quiet week after Christmas at Mill Cottage, John relished his time with Hannah and Fred, absorbing the tolerance and compassion that he so admired in them and had found so hard to emulate. His feelings about Jessie veered between confusion, acceptance and disappointment with a speed and unpredictability that upset him too much to share. While Fred was out one evening, Hannah watched John carefully, before speaking.

'She's a fine woman, your mam.'

He didn't reply, still pretending to study the map in front of him.

'It's hard for you,' she went on. 'Hard to sort out what happened all them years ago, why she did what she did.'

'That was twenty years ago,' he said, without looking up. 'I thought that now, you know, she'd be able to …'

'To love you?'

'Aye.'

'Not so easy, lad. There's something between a mother and a baby, though I've never 'ad it myself, nor likely to,' said Hannah, her knitting abandoned on her lap. 'Something in the blood, they say. But who knows really? Love grows when folk are together. You and 'er don't know each other. It'll tek time, I reckon. Don't want too much lad, not yet. Give 'er time, ye ken, to recover.'

'How long?' he said. 'She might not even like me. Don't know much about me dad. She loved him, but was he like me?'

'You dinnat need to be like 'im,' she said. 'You are who you are. She'll see that soon enough. Patience. Just think of 'er as a new friend, someone you've met, someone worthwhile. Talk to 'er like you talk to us, me and Fred. We like you. She will too, just give 'er time.'

A few days later John's mind was made up. Jessie was surprised by his announcement about leaving the valley. His words fell between them like a stone into a well, and it was a few moments before she responded.

'Will we see each other?'

'Why not?' he said. 'It took me a long time to find you, Jessie. I wanted to know who you are, and who my father was. After that I had no idea what would happen, and I still don't. I didn't think ahead, about how you might feel, about your job …'

'I never thought I would ever see you again,' she said, flatly, as if she were talking about the weather. 'Are you disappointed? Did you want me to welcome you with open arms?'

John dropped his head. He could not tell her how much he had wanted that. He was trying to think of Jessie as a new friend, as Hannah had suggested. The effort exhausted him.

Jessie broke the unbearable silence.

'It's not far, if you buy that bike you want,' she said, aware how trite she sounded. 'Not far to Mill Cottage, or to Wasdale. I know you love it there.'

'It's not far to Newton either,' he said. 'But I'm not sure you want to see me.'

Jessie felt the lie before she spoke it. 'Of course I want to see you,' she said. 'After all these years I want to find out who you are, be part of your life, as long as …' She faltered, losing the words.

'As long as nobody knows who I am?' he asked, turning towards her.

Silence returned. Jessie pulled her coat tighter around her against the wind. Rain was hiding the horizon. They would have to move soon. John raised his head as the first pricks of the shower reached them.

'Didn't you have a sister?' he said. 'One of the people I saw in Barrow mentioned a sister, and Mr Crane did, too. Younger than you. Where is she now?'

'Beatrice, her name is,' said Jessie. 'She married very young, just after the war broke out, and they went to New Zealand.'

'Do they have any children?'

Jessie shielded her face with her scarf. Suddenly she grasped what he was thinking. 'You mean, we could say that you are her child, my nephew?'

The rain was heavier now, but neither of them moved. 'That would explain a family likeness, wouldn't it?' he said, looking at her. 'What would Beatrice think about that?'

'Haven't heard from her in years,' said Jessie, 'Not since our mother died. They had two children, Rebecca and Norman. The elder one must be about your age now. My mother just seemed to cut Bea out of our lives after they went away, just like she did with my dad. It was a kind of delusion. She put all her hopes on me, and then ...'

'You haven't forgiven her, have you?'

'For throwing me out like she did? No, not really. It was a shock. I expected more from my mother.'

John said nothing. His silence struck Jessie like a blow.

'And you expected more of me,' she said, as a tear ran unchecked down her face. 'Maybe you have to learn how to be a mother, and I never did.'

Still he was silent.

The rain drove them away from the exposed hilltop. As they walked down into the noisy town, the pit wheels were turning, bringing gangs of blackened men up from the coal seams beneath the sea.

Jessie was ahead of John on the narrow track. She turned and looked up at him. 'It would be very hard for you to lie about where you came from,' she said. 'You've had a life in Ulverston, your aunt and uncle are still there.'

John stood still, thinking, and she waited. When he spoke it was clear and quick. 'We could say that it was your sister that had the baby, before she married and went away. I was adopted by Enid and Arthur, and everything since then has been the same, except that one thing. Beatrice need never know. I was looking for

301

my mother, just like I did, and I found you, my aunt. How does that sound?'

Jessie didn't reply at once. She was shocked by the ease with which she was losing a son and gaining a nephew.

'What about the people who already know?' she said. 'There's the Porters, and Agnes, and your aunt and uncle in Ulverston.'

'Uncle George and Aunty Anne know I've been looking for you but they don't know I found you,' John replied evenly. 'I didn't tell them. I don't have to, although I don't really want to deceive them about it. Leave that with me. If we ask the others, they'll respect what we want, don't you think?' He remembered something. 'Sometimes Fred talks about other peoples' lives, and how little we know about them. He believes – they both do – that people have a right to live their lives without being judged and gossiped about. I must tell George and Anne the truth, but I know they would respect it, I'm sure they would.'

'And Agnes would, too,' said Jessie. 'Agnes is a good friend.' Now that Andrew has gone, she added inwardly.

'I think so,' said John. 'She's always been very kind to me.'

In the small café by the market Jessie and John drank hot chocolate and shared a piece of cake. The grey January day moved towards darkness, bringing with it the end of a private truth and the start of a public lie.

If you've enjoyed the story, you may want to…

- Order another copy to pass to a friend.

- Read *Forgiven,* Part 2 of the trilogy, set among the coal mines and fells of the Cumberland coast in the gloom of post-war rationing and cold. Jessie Whelan's struggle continues, caught between her secret and the possibility of future happiness.

- Look forward to Part 3 *Fallout* (publication Summer 2014). The story moves forward to the 1950s, as the race for nuclear weapons at Windscale brings both fear and hope to Jessie Whelan's life.

- Follow Ruth Sutton's blog on *ruthwords. wordpress.com* and check her website *www.ruthsutton.co.uk*

- Follow Ruth Sutton also on Facebook and on *Twitter@ruthsutton*